The Junkyard Kids

The Junkyard Kids

Printed in the United States of America

First Printing, 2017

ISBN 978-0-9983329-1-8

William "Papa" Meyer (right)
December 25, 1999

Without your wisdom and constant encouragement, this book would not be a fraction as great as it turned out to be. Thank you for sticking with me these last four or so years, making sure that I grew not only as a writer but as a person, so I hope the struggles and messages presented within this story reach at least one person and make them realize that most obstacles in life are not too great to overcome.

With you, I'm glad that I not only have a grandfather but a friend and a mentor.

All illustrations done by the talented artist Matthew Ryan

For commission pricing please visit matt.org.uk or contact
illustration@mattr.org.uk

Table of Contents

Chapter One

The Place We Call Home

I rested my back against a rusty chain-link fence and lit the cigarette that sat between my lips. A few sparkling embers burning at the end of it caught my eye and made me realize that it was the only heat source for miles. The only other thing I had to keep warm was a few newspapers on an old, ragged sofa in the junkyard behind me. And besides that, I had my wife beater and jeans which didn't do a good job since they were filled with holes and tears.

With smoke drifting from my nostrils and off into the air, I looked at the full moon hovering in the night sky. Living in the middle of nowhere obviously didn't come with streetlights, so it's glow was the only thing that let me see more than two inches in front of my face. Even then the only thing I could see was the road kill that was flatter than paper against the concrete, and I'm sure them dead rats and possums smelled like rotten garbage in the middle of summer, but by then I'd been there

1

for so long the odor didn't even faze me.

While I took my final hit, the lights of the nearby city caught my eye. Just then memories flashed of the days when I wasn't a nobody flashed in front of eyes, and it made me realize that *no one* was an actual person.

And that person was me.

I wondered how I got to a point so low that all I had to offer was my breath and the lint in my pockets. The only answer I got was a smoke filled breeze.

I flicked my cigarette butt into the street and walked through the gate of the chain link fence. There was nothing to see but the towers of crushed cars that led me into my home. Shards of metal stuck out from almost every direction, so when it was dark, it was hard to leave or enter without getting sliced up.

There was no way in hell I was gonna get stabbed, so I took out my lighter and lit it, noticing the rats scurrying away from the light. As soon as I looked up, someone sitting on the trunk of a car raised his middle fingers.

"What's wrong, kid? Ya look like ya seen a god damn ghost." He jumped down to the gravel, giving me an evil grin.

"Fuck off, Leon!" I stepped by him, dodging stacks of metal and crushed vehicles, and reached two shadowy figures who were lying on my raggedy sofa, asking, "Tabitha, Sean! Either of you got another smoke?"

"Damn, dude." Sean shielded the light from his eyes. "I only got five left."

This surprised me considering we didn't have so much as spare pocket change. The only way we were able to get more was to either beg in the city or, if we were lucky, find ones that weren't completely smoked.

"Seen him lately?!" Leon kept up his cackles behind me.

"Fuck off!" I flipped Leon the bird, but I doubt he saw it. "What the hell's he talkin' 'bout?"

"Forget it, man. Ya know how Leon is." Sean slipped a cigarette in my palm while my back was still turned. "Here."

"Alright, thanks." I put it between my lips and lit it as quick as I could. "I owe ya one."

Just as I blew out a puff of smoke, I turned around to see my younger brother, Xavier. The only reason I recognized him in the dark was because of his height. For as long as I could remember, he never grew any taller. He was childish, but he was probably the kindest one of our group of unwanted misfits.

Xavier stepped toward me but frowned when he saw the cigarette in my mouth. Even though he never said anything about it, there was no doubt in my mind that he hated seeing me hacking up my lungs like some 60 year-old man instead of a 23 year-old.

"Don't even mention—" Sean spun his head over his shoulder. "You hear that?!"

"What?" I looked toward the entrance to see the headlights of a car and Leon already gone.

"Do you think they're cops?!" Tabitha ran her hands through her hair.

"I ain't got a clue, but I ain't gonna find out!" Sean grabbed her arm and dashed behind a nearby minivan.

Xavier ran to the other side of the junkyard, and he had a good reason to. Nobody and I mean *nobody,* just came in the junkyard like that. And since it was the middle of the night, it didn't seem likely that it was any folks who were interested in buying the property.

I quickly jumped behind my sofa and pulled it backward. Before the vehicle had even fully entered the junkyard, I was already convinced they'd find me.

With their headlights lighting up the junkyard, they stopped. At the sound of that roaring car engine, my heart raced. Two men stepped out and walked to the trunk. I tried to see if they were cops or not. But all I saw was a moth fluttering in the headlights.

Sean tossed a small pebble toward my direction. "You see anything?"

"Nah," I said.

One of the men walked out from the back of the vehicle. As soon as I saw his leather jacket, all the air in my lungs escaped. Thank God! They weren't cops.

The man glanced in my direction. I ducked and held my breath again. For a second, I thought he saw me, but then I peered over the couch. Neither of them seemed to notice. They were just having a conversation. Unfortunately, the noisy car engine drowned out every word they said.

The man in the leather coat pulled out a gun. He cocked it. And then he squeezed the trigger. Again and again. Shots rang off. Blood splattered across the gravel. His victim screamed in pain, his limp body plopping to the ground.

And just like that, it was over.

I cupped my mouth, shut my eyes, and ducked. The air became thick. But I didn't dare to breathe anyway. Both my lips trembled. Sweat poured, soaking my clothes. Did he see me? I had to check. When I peeked over the couch, he looked in my direction again. Then he threw the gat in the shadows near me. He hadn't noticed me. I was safe.

The killer grabbed the body by its legs. Then he dragged it across the gravel, leaving behind a thin trail of red ooze. That wasn't the worst part, the part that made me sick – it was the corpse's eyes. They stared me down like a vulture watching the final movements of its prey.

I didn't know what to do. There was no way in hell we could've had some dead body rotting away where we lived. Police didn't come around the junkyard, but on the off chance they did, they wouldn't believe any of us. I mean, homeless folks like us didn't get much respect.

The murderer was halfway across the junkyard. By that time, something I realized made my heart stop. He was planning to leave the body behind the same minivan that Sean and Tabitha were using as a hiding spot.

With my hands shaking, I looked around for something I could use as a weapon. Then I remembered the gun that the murderer threw into the shadows.

"C'mon!" He tugged and pulled at the legs of his victim.

I quickly crawled to the area where I heard it land. But when I got there, my shoulder bumped into an empty soda can. It fell to the ground and clanked against a brick.

"Who the fuck's there?!" The killer spun around. "Come on out, asshole!"

I didn't dare to move.

"I said come out, fucker!" He stared in my direction.

It felt like an eternity before he finally turned around. A long, silent breath escaped my lungs. I moved forward and felt metal brush against my hand. I picked it up. It was heavy – just heavy enough to possibly be the gun. Then I felt the trigger, and I knew for sure.

When I turned again, I noticed the murderer was at the corner of the minivan. Before I knew it, I was behind him, gun aimed at his back.

"Fuck!" He spun around and pulled out a switchblade. "What the fuck do you want, fucker?!"

I couldn't speak. He shook. I shook. Neither of us really knew what to do. I tried telling him to leave. But the words just wouldn't come out of my mouth. He looked scared – just as scared as I was in fact. All I wanted was for him to leave. Maybe if I lowered that damn gun, he would. So I did. Big mistake.

He tried to dash behind the minivan. Everything slowed down, almost to the point where time froze in place. Beads of sweat dripped off my face. A wad of spit made its way down my throat. I raised the gun and squeezed.

In the blink of an eye, the bullet entered and exited his shoulder. He stopped in place. A yelp came from his mouth. I squeezed two more times. This time he stumbled back.

With one last squeeze, a bullet pierced the back of his skull. Blood and brains sprayed in the air like a geyser. Then he fell to the ground.

The pistol slipped from my hands and hit the gravel. I took a deep breath and tried to take in the sight of the two corpses. "H-holy shit!"

A shadow coming from behind me covered the body. "What did ya just..." Sean choked on his own words. "What the fuck did ya do?!"

"I thought you was behind the..." My bones stiffened, and I fell flat on my back. Nothing but babbles came from my lips.

"Ya fuckin' idiot!" Leon stormed into the middle of the junkyard. "Why did ya get involved?!"

"I thought he was gonna kill..." I rose to my feet and caught my breath. "I thought he was gonna kill Tabitha and Sean!"

"No!" Sean put his hands over his eyes. "Me and her moved back a while ago!"

"Dammit!" I ran my hands through my cornrows. "Where's Xavier?!"

"We ain't got time for that fuckin' bullshit right now!" Leon glared at me. "We need to get those two fuckers outta here!" He pointed toward the dead bodies. "Ya god damn nutcase!"

I gripped the sides of my head. "Xavier?!"

"Where in the hell are you goin'?" Leon watched me pace around the junkyard.

"You alright, Xavier?!" I cupped my hands over my mouth. "Xavier?!"

Xavier was nowhere to be found.

Tabitha walked toward us. "M-maybe you scared..." She put her hands in the pockets of her hoodie, her soft voice matching the whispers of the wind. "I mean maybe the ruckus scared him off, ya know?"

"I don't think he—" I couldn't stop shaking long enough to say what I wanted to say.

Leon looked directly at me. "Enough with this bullshit!"

"Alright!" The sight of the blood sent shivers down my spine. "Let's just get these two outta here!"

Chapter Two

Forgotten Memories

Eleven years earlier...

I extended my arm and pulled Xavier out the muddy creek he'd fallen into, realizing his jeans were covered in all kinds of filth. Our mom wasn't gonna like that since she had just bought them the day before.

Xavier pulled himself together and then wiped off what he could. After a few attempts, he stopped and put his hands over his eyes, saying, "It was an accident!"

"Just calm down." I turned to the part of the creek bank that collapsed below his feet to see the muddy water still splashing against small trees and rows of cattails. "I don't think she'll care about ya shirt."

"Can ya check my back?" he said, turning around and spreading his arms out. Globs of mud covered his back from head to toe.

"Shit! Just try and..." I put my hand to my chin. "Just try and wipe it off."

Xavier and I walked along the dirt path that led out of the forest area. He took my advice and scooped off as much mud as he could, but there was too much of it. There was no way our mom wouldn't notice.

Besides the squawking of the crows above us and the old, dried up leaves that crumbled under our shoes, what caught my attention were the rustling sounds in the bushes beside us. Strangely enough, every time I turned my head it stopped.

I tapped Xavier on the shoulder. "Hear that?"

"What?" Xavier glanced around the forest. "The birds?"

I shook my head and looked toward the distance to see the orange sunset. This made my heart speed up a bit since it meant we were late for dinner. Just then that damn rustling sound started back up.

"Or was it the bushes movin'?" Xavier used his fingernails to scrape off more of the mud.

Whatever was making the sounds was just some animal. If not, then it was someone playing a prank. Or maybe it was my imagination. It had to be. But if it was why was my gut turning? And why did I have the urge to run? I couldn't put my finger on it, but it was like the woods itself was watching us. Or someone hiding in it.

We reached the end of that old, dirt path and reached a sidewalk. I grabbed Xavier's arm, looked both ways, and then ran across the street as fast as I could. By that age, he was probably old enough to cross himself, but it was just a habit that never died.

"What about dad?" Xavier headed for a stop sign that was covered in graffiti.

"I don't think he'll care that much." I kicked a small pebble and watched it bounce into a storm drain. "He never really does."

Xavier reached his hand out and dragged his fingers along the wooden fence next to us. Usually, he would talk nonstop no matter what went on, but he still looked like he was worrying his head off.

After crushing a soda can with the sole of my sneaker and watching an army of ants scatter from it, I told him I didn't think it was a huge deal. Then I tried changing the subject by asking him what he thought we were going to have for dinner.

Xavier put his hand to his chin and thought for a moment. "Maybe Mac n'—"

Suddenly, two large pit bulls snapped at us from behind a tall, wooden fence. They snarled at us and exposed their rotted teeth through holes in the wood. No doubt they would've torn us to shreds if they could.

"Get back in here now!" The owner's shouts did nothing to stop the growls.

"Same thing we had last three nights for dinner." I tried my best to speak over the beasts.

"Well, maybe we'll get something different tonight," Xavier said, covering his ears.

"Yeah." I looked over my shoulder and spotted a police cruiser a block behind us.

The street lights flickered on, leaving an orange tint along the sidewalk. It was way past the time we were supposed to be home. Even though our neighborhood wasn't the worst in the city, our mom hated it when we stayed out that late. By then, she was usually pulling her hair out and calling everyone she knew.

"We got an extra jacket at home?" Xavier shivered. "I'm cold!"

"What are ya talkin' about? It ain't even cold!" I remembered his clothes were still wet. "Oh yeah, I think I got one in my—"

"Y'all need a ride?" someone interrupted.

The same police cruiser I saw was parked beside us. An officer with slicked back hair and a bird-like nose stepped out. He walked around the engine, leaned against the front of it with his arms crossed, and gave us a toothy grin, saying, "I'm Officer Zeke. Need a ride?"

"Oh really?! Lemme see ya badge!" Xavier blurted out.

"Xavier..." The officer made the hairs on my neck stand up, but I didn't see any reason to be rude. Maybe it was just because he was a stranger. Still, I looked around for any folks who might be nearby, but there was no one.

"Alrighty then." While Officer Zeke walked toward us, his shiny, black boots tapped against the concrete. He stopped in front of us and pointed to the metal badge pinned to his chest.

"Zeke Jenkins?" Xavier asked.

"Yup!" Officer Zeke nodded, walking to the driver's side. "Y'all still want that ride?"

"Sure, I guess," I said.

"Alright then," Officer Zeke said, "y'all just hop right on in."

A few seconds later, I was taking the most uncomfortable ride of my life. Officer Zeke wouldn't stop talking about himself—personal things you wouldn't talk about with people you don't know. Nothing bad, just awkward topics.

Two blocks down, we came to a sudden stop outside of a familiar house.

"Y'all take care now." Officer Zeke extended his hand.

As soon as I shook it I felt sick. There was grease and sweat all over his palm. After I released my grip, I wiped my hand onto my jeans and hurried out the cruiser.

"Wait for me!" Xavier cried.

We walked through the white picket fence surrounding our house and onto the stone pathway, which was barely visible with the tall grass and overgrown weeds. As soon as we stepped onto the porch something struck me.

"You ever seen that cop before today?" I asked.

"No, never."

"So..." I stopped and looked back at Officer Zeke. "How'd he know where we live?"

Xavier's eyes grew big. "I dunno."

That creepy officer had our nerves jumping, but as soon as we walked through the door, the smell of our mom's Macaroni 'n Cheese eased our tensions. She seemed too distracted by something to care that we were home late or even that Xavier had ruined his new pair of pants. It wasn't like her at all. The funny thing was that our dad was the exact same way. His eyes just stayed glued to the television set in our living room.

"Dad!" I walked behind the couch and put my hands on his shoulders.

"Not now." He shook his head.

"But..." I looked at the television.

A woman in a red dress appeared on the tube, saying, "The serial killer in Violet Haven, known as 'The Devil's Haven' to residents, has been given the nickname Bloody, Bloody Bijou by local citizens. The name was chosen due to the killer's gruesome murder methods and the fact that he keeps a piece of jewelry as a prize from each of his victims." She shifted through the stack of papers in her hand. "So far he has claimed fourteen lives and police have yet to find a lead." The newswoman brushed away a lock of her blonde hair from her face. "The first of his suspected victims, Eli and Clyde Jenkins, have still yet to be found. Police officials refused to release the name of the victim's eleven-year-old son who also disappeared around the same time."

"Dad—" I started again.

"I said not now." He shook his head and turned up the volume.

"A few days ago," the newswoman continued, "police received a letter from Bijou which was written in what is assumed to be the blood of one of

14

his victims. The letter itself simply read 'There are demons inside me and they won't leave...because I won't let them.'." She shifted through the papers in her hands again. "And now here's Steven Max with an exclusive inside on the situation."

The broadcast changed to a man outside of a house surrounded by squad cars and ambulances. "This is Steven Max and I've arrived on the scene only moments after police discovered two bodies." He turned around just as three paramedics wheeled out two stretchers from the home. "Bloody, Bloody Bijou's killing spree began last year in 1983, and it doesn't seem like he's stopping anytime soon." He turned to a crying woman to his left. "What can you tell us about this?"

"I knew those people since I was four!" She wiped her eyes and grabbed the microphone. "Bijou is a monster! I don't understand how someone can..."

"David! Turn that off! You'll scare the boys!" My mom walked in front of the television before turning it off.

My dad stood up from the couch and crossed his arms. "Muriel, we gotta—"

"I don't care!" She grabbed my dad's shoulder and dragged him to the kitchen. "It's time for dinner!"

My dad sat down at the kitchen table and let out a sigh. "That means you too, boys!"

The second I reached the table a steaming plate of Macaroni n' Cheese met my eyes. To tell the truth, after eating the same food four days in a row, I would've rather eaten from a dumpster.

"Can't we have something else?" Xavier stirred the food around his plate.

My mom slammed her palm against the table. The water in our glasses shook. "You wanna eat nothing instead?!"

"N-no." Xavier stuffed his face.

"By the way..." My mother took her seat. "You wanna tell me what happened with all that mud?"

"Xavier fell in the creek!" I blurted out. "It was my fault! He never wanted to—"

"Enough!" My dad raised his palm. "We gotta talk about that serial—"

"No!" My mom slammed her hand down a second time. Xavier's glass tipped over. "Not in front of the kids, David!"

My dad nodded and gulped down his food. Xavier and I finished ours a few moments after him. With our parents acting so strange, neither of us wanted to stay up any later than we had to, so we took our plates to the sink and scurried to our room.

Xavier changed into his Bugs Bunny pajamas, turned on the lava lamp that sat on our windowsill, and jumped in his bed. "Goodnight."

"Yeah." I slipped in my bed with my street clothes still on. "You too."

"If you boy's goin' to bed then turn off the lights." My mom appeared outside our door and switched off the light switch. She closed the door until only a small amount of the hallway light shined into our room.

"Electricity ain't free!"

"Xavier," I whispered.

Xavier snored. He always fell asleep first, but with everything that happened, I wondered how he was able to on that night.

My mom's voice entered the room from the hallway. "Wadda we do with Xavier? I just got him—"

"Forget about that, Muriel! We should leave town!" My dad's voice shook.

"I ain't hidin' from that damn Bloody, Bloody Bijou!" My mom snapped back.

My dad and mom moved further down the hallway until their voices faded. Soon the sound of the hallway light switch clicked, and besides the dim, purple glow from Xavier's lava lamp, our room was left in darkness.

Only a little while later, I fell asleep.

Sometime later my body fell off the bed, jolting me from my sleep. Once I stood up, I called out to Xavier, but he didn't reply. It was only after I turned on the lights that I noticed he was gone.

The strange thing was that his lava lamp was still on. He *never* just left it on like that. A few months after he got it, he saw a news report about how an old lady caused a fire by leaving hers on for too long. Ever since then he made a habit of turning off the lamp whenever he left the room. My brother was so scared it didn't matter if he was going to school or going to the bathroom—he always turned it off.

And yet that purple wax was still floating to the top of the glass.

My guard was up before I even left the room. I crept through the hallway and down the stairs.

When I reached the living room, my gut spun like a hurricane. Xavier was in the kitchen sitting in a chair. He had a blindfold over his face. Small amounts blood covered his pajamas.

Suddenly, a large shadow stretched over me. I froze. Someone pressed a knife to my neck. And then his hand to my mouth. If I was able to scream, I would've brought the house down.

The intruder pulled the blade away from my neck. A moment later, he struck my temple twice. I tried to run. But then my body collapsed. Just before my eyes closed, I saw it.

I saw the predatory, blood thirsty stare behind his leather mask.

Chapter Three

Long Night

Present day...

The sight of the dead bodies shook me to my core. But I knew what had to be done. I grabbed its legs, turned to Sean, and said, "Hey, man, come help me with this!"

He made his way over. It looked like there were tears forming in his wide eyes. For a second, I thought he was gonna cry—at least until he gripped the body by its ankles.

Blood poured from the carcass as the two of us walked toward the car. The entire time Sean looked like he was about to puke. There was definitely a bit of green in his face.

When we walked by Tabitha, tears rolled down her cheeks. It didn't feel right to ask her for help. I mean, she already looked like she was about to faint. Xavier probably wasn't too happy either. I was sure he watching us somewhere in the dark. Deep in my mind, I knew that situation must've affected him more than the rest of us.

"I th-think here's good for now." Sean placed the body near the back of the car.

I dropped the corpse. It hit the gravel with a plop, leaving the head rolling back and forth.

"Shouldn't we—" Sean began.

"Hold up!" I dropped down and rolled the body onto its stomach.

Sean watched me pull out a wallet from the man's back pocket. "We can't do that!"

"We're broke, Sean!" I pulled out the driver's license and took a good look at it.

"So what?! He's dead!" said Sean.

"You wanna starve to death?!" I put the license back and checked the money fold. It's sad to say, but there was more money in there than I'd seen in years. And it couldn't have been more than 50 bucks.

Leon stepped out from behind the car and placed the second body next to us. "What the hell are we gonna do now?"

I slipped the wallet into my back pocket and pointed at the trunk. "We g-gotta put them in the there."

"M-maybe we can just—" Sean stuttered.

"There's nothing else we can do, man!" I spread my arms out. "We gotta get them outta here!"

"This is such bullshit!" Leon pounded the side of the car.

I looked to Sean and nodded. "Ready?"

"Yeah," Sean sighed.

It was like something straight out of a horror movie, and Sean didn't have a hard time making it obvious that he didn't want any part in it. I didn't either but what could we do? Who would help us even if I never stopped that man? We had no other place to hide. Not only that, but we couldn't have gone to the cops. They would've arrested us in a heartbeat. Nobody cared about a bunch of uneducated, homeless losers like us.

"Alright, go get the keys," I said to Sean.

"Straight bullshit!" Leon threw something at an old taxi cab, shattering its windshield.

After Sean did what I said, the headlights disappeared and we were left in darkness.

"God dammit, Sean!" Leon groaned.

"Shut up, Leon!" I pulled out my lighter and spun its wheel. A small fire blazed a few feet from my face. On the ground, the flame glowed in the pools of blood and the eyes of the corpse.

"Here." Sean came back and handed me the keys.

"Thanks." I popped open the trunk before tugging at one of the bodies. "Let's go."

It took the three of us less than five minutes to get both bodies in the trunk of that car. However, it left our palms and clothes drenched in blood.

"We need to get them far away from here." I stuffed the lighter back in my pocket. "Any ideas?"

"Iron River," Leon growled. "The water should wash off our fingerprints."

"Iron River?!" Sean shouted. "That's over 10 miles from here! We'd have to walk all the way back!"

"Well, we better start movin' then." I walked to driver's seat and placed the key in the ignition. "C'mon." After pushing the brake and random gears, I realized I had no idea what I was doing since I'd never driven a car.

"Lemme do it." Sean pulled me from the car and sat down. He fumbled with the key and a few seconds later the engine roared. It looked so easy when he did it.

"S-see? Just like that," Sean quivered.

"Let's get this over with." Leon hopped in the passenger's side. "We don't got all night."

"No shit." When I got inside the car, my intestines slithered inside my gut so much that I had to stop myself from running out the car.

Sean turned the car around and headed out the front gate. Just before we left, I looked through the back window and caught a glimpse of Tabitha, who uncrossed her arms and gave us a half-wave. I waved back. Then I spotted Xavier creeping out of the shadows. He just stood there watching us leave into the night.

Sean left the junkyard and drove toward the city. There was nothing to see on either side of that lonely road except endless farmland on one side and a never ending forest on the other. Well, I lied. There was the wooden city sign to our right, which read, "Welcome to the Devil's Haven." The original name was 'Violet Haven', but someone changed it with spray-paint years ago.

I tried taking my mind off the earthquake in my stomach. "Check the glove compartment."

"Good thinkin'." Leon opened it and took out a pack of smokes and a wad of cash.

"Holy shit!" Sean drove forward. "How much is that?!"

"No idea," Leon smirked, tucking the cash into his pocket. "But we ain't got time to count it."

"L-lemme get a cigarette." I pointed to the pack of Marlboros in his lap.

"Knock ya'self out." Leon tossed it over his shoulder.

My fingers jittered so much that I could barely put the cigarette in my mouth. As soon as I did, I lit it as quick as I could. Smoke immediately spiraled around the car.

"Pass it up here!" Sean held his hand up. "You ain't the only one who's twisted about this!"

"Right." I gave the cigarette to Sean who took a few hits and handed it off to Leon.

I wanted for Leon to pass the cigarette back, but he never did. He was always selfish, but I wasn't up for arguing with him that night.

"Gee, thanks a lot, Leon." I lit two more and gave one to Sean and kept one for myself. Not before long, the vehicle was filled to the brim with smoke.

We drove deeper into the city until rundown shops and buildings were all we saw. Leon's directions started making me wonder if he really knew where we were going until I spotted a river just past a group of trees.

"Drive between that clearin' right there." Leon pointed next to a dead end at the end of a cul-de-sac.

"Are ya sure?" Sean drove off the road and onto a dirt path which led into a thick forest area.

"Yeah, I'm sure. Just keep goin' and make a left at those boulders ahead," Leon said, pointing through all the dust filling the air.

The closer we got to the river, the tighter the knot in my stomach became. Then I saw the moonlight glistening in Iron Rivers pitch black waters, and it felt like the knot was so tight it'd never go away.

"I don't think," Sean whimpered, "we should do this."

"It's a little too late for cold feet." Leon grinned.

"He's right, Sean." Even though I said that I secretly sided with Sean. I didn't wanna do it. I just wanted to go home. "Stop near that oak tree," I said, smoke drifting off my breath. "I think that's far enough."

"W-we really gonna do this s-shit?" Sean wiped the sweat off his face.

"The hell else can we do?" I looked at the row of houses sitting on the other side of the river. A light flickering on and off in one of the attic windows caught my attention for a split second. "Drop them off at the police station?"

"Shit, man!" Sean shook his head. "I dunno!"

Leon exited the car and walked to the trunk. "We don't have all night to decide."

"This ain't really—" Sean mumbled.

"Hurry up!" Leon talked like it was something he'd done hundreds of times.

"L-let's just get this over with." Sean slipped out the car and made his way to Leon.

"I said hurry up!" Leon placed his hands on the trunk.

"Shut the hell up, Leon!" I stepped out the car, wiped away the sweat on my forehead, and treaded toward them. It felt like the entire world was watching us

"Just do what I do." Leon pushed the car forward.

All three of us pushed that car together. Sean began more of his mumbling, which sounded muffled for him being so close to me. Then I noticed his mouth wasn't moving. I glanced at Leon. His mouth wasn't moving either. Where was the noise coming from?

It didn't click in my head until Leon spoke.

"Oh, and by the way." His eyes glared at me with an evil grin on his face. "One of those guys was still breathin'."

"H-he…" I stopped pushing the car. It took a few seconds for my mouth to work. "He was what?!"

Leon's smirk grew. "He was breathin'. Neither of ya noticed it. I didn't care enough to tell ya."

"Oh fuck!" Sean looked like he was about to have a mental breakdown.

"Help!" Wheezes came from inside the trunk.

"Fuck!" Hearing the man's suffering made me want to crawl in a ditch and just die. I turned to Leon for an explanation.

All he did was shrug. "If I told ya this before what would you have done? Call the cops? Take him to the hospital? Ain't nothin' we coulda' or woulda' done." He pressed his hands back on the trunk. "He was as good as dead back then, and he's as good as dead now." The grin on his face kept growing. By now he looked psychotic. "So wadda ya gonna do, kid? Are ya gonna let this poor guy suffer?" His demented stare gazed right through me. "Or are ya gonna do a good deed and end his misery?"

I stood there for a few seconds and thought about what I could do. It was horrible and there was no way I would have ever admitted it, but I knew he was right. The only thing I could do was to slowly place my hands on the car and hold my breath.

"Good." Leon turned to Sean. "Comin'?"

Sean didn't say anything. He dropped to his knees and buried his face in the ground.

"Just leave him alone." Leon shook his head.

I pushed the car toward the river. The dying man's blood filled wheezes filled my ears. I tried to block them out by focusing on the sound of the river water. It didn't work. The wheezes just seemed to grow louder.

"It'll be done with soon enough." Leon didn't seem to be bothered.

The car reached the river bank. Water filled my sneakers, freezing my feet.

"Anyone there?!" More bloody wheezes came from the trunk.

"Ignore it!" Leon shouted.

We pushed until we were waist deep in the water. By then we didn't need to do anything else. The river swallowed up the car in a matter of seconds. Soon there was nothing to be seen but its roof. That hunk of metal was gone.

And so was the man inside.

I dragged myself out of the water and took a deep breath. The man's bloody wheezes replayed over and over again in my head. I clenched my stomach. With all the rumbling that went on down there, it was like someone replaced my stomach with a washing machine.

"Alright, are ya ready, you nutcase?" Leon pulled himself from the river. "I'd tell ya that you've lost it but," he said, looking me square in the eyes, "ya can't lose something ya never had."

Chapter Four

The Rabbit and the Crocodile

Eleven years earlier...

I opened my eyes. A pillowcase was over my head, and I was bound to a chair. There wasn't an inch of my body that could move. But it wasn't because of the ropes.

It was because of the fear.

I wondered where my mom and dad were. Then I heard them scream from the top of the staircase. No words from them. Just screams. Torturous screams. Blood-curling screams. Screams that pierced my ears like an arrow through flesh. And all I could do was sob and listen. Because to me, nothing existed in those moments but their screams.

Through the pillowcase, I could see their silhouettes. Then I noticed a third one. The intruder. At the top of the staircase, he was fighting my parents. He bashed my dad's head into the railing of the stairwell. Hard. And I mean really hard.

"Oh, God!" my father cried.

The madman did it again. And again.

"Please stop! What are..." my mom shrieked. "Stop it!

I'd seen horror movie's before. Xavier always got scared. Sometimes I'd tease him about it because they were so cheesy to me. But now I was living through it, through the terror, the nightmare. Hearing my mom's deafening screams, the cracking of my dad's skull. Seeing them being overpowered by a masked lunatic made my limbs feel like they were filled with concrete.

A twisted laugh filled the room. The madman shoved my father down the stairs. My mom screeched loud enough to leave the devil shaking at his throne. But it just wasn't loud enough—I could still hear my dad's bones splitting in half.

"Xavier!" I whispered. "Y-you there?"

He did nothing but sob.

My mom screeched as the intruder threw her down, too. Then everything went silent. That is, until the intruder crept down the staircase.

"Honey, do something!" screamed my mom.

"Just grab the boys and run, Muriel!" answered my dad.

"Oh God, he's comin'!" my mom cried.

The creaks of the staircase stopped. Another evil laugh boomed.

"Let go of me!" my mom continued.

With the three of them a lot closer, they were easier to see through the fabric. But I was wishing they weren't. I mean, I could've closed my eyes, but I had to see what happened. As much as the scene made my limbs clamp up, I had to make sure my family was going to be okay. But it didn't seem like they would be.

The maniac shoved my mom into a mirror. It cracked. She fell to the floor. Then, as glass rained down, she sobbed harder. And so did I.

"Muriel!" my father shouted. "No!"

A noise entered my eardrums. And melted them like it was acid. The man in the mask had my mom by her hair. After getting down on one knee, he smashed her face into the floor. Blood splattered. He did it again. More blood. A small pool of red ooze was forming at this point. The savagery continued. Even when I turned away, the sounds were still there, taunting me. It's like they were there to let me know I couldn't stop it. Any of it.

He picked her head up one last time. And just let it fall. Her skull hit the floorboards. Her body twitched in the blood pools. The soulless intruder cackled. Then he casually walked away. And headed straight for Xavier.

"Don't touch him!" my dad slurred.

As soon as the masked man reached Xavier, he swung his fist. A wail that could've put a banshee to shame exited my brother's mouth. The man in the mask unraveled a roll of a duct tape. After ripping off a piece, he covered Xavier's mouth. Then he pulled out his blade.

My heart fluttered. I wanted to shut my eyes. They wouldn't budge.

Something inside me wanted to know that he'd be okay—that he wouldn't be hurt. But then the madman raised the knife. And slashed open Xavier's back. My brother squealed through the duct tape, his tiny voice filled with pain.

My stomach turned. I tried to escape the ropes. But they wouldn't loosen. I wriggled my body. The chair I was in rocked back and forth, tapping the floor. The intruder noticed. His sights were dead set on me. Then, with his knife soaked in my brother's blood, he came for me.

Soon he was in front of me, putting duct tape over my mouth. Then whipped out a camera and lifted the pillowcase. Its flash went off, and I was left blind for a moment.

When my vision returned, his eyes were in front of mine. A bloodthirsty crocodile couldn't have had a more murderous gaze. With that, I was like a wounded rabbit staring into a row of razor sharp fangs. And no matter how hard this rabbit squirmed, the crocodile just sat there, loving every moment of the terror it caused.

He pulled the pillowcase back down. Then I felt it—the tip of his knife against my gut. He pressed harder. Just hard enough to separate my flesh. Blood dripped. Sweat poured from my face like rain from the sky. Another thrust from him. I choked on my breath. It wasn't over. He started to twist.

"No!" My mom's cries drew his attention.

The madman stomped his way over to her. She tried to escape. But her body was in no shape to do that. As soon as he reached her, he struck her with his fist. An agonizing moan filled my ears. He did it again. And

Again. And again. He wouldn't stop.

It was like he was mad at her for not being dead.

They went silent. Another flash from his camera went off. Next to my parent's bodies, he stood there and stared at the pools of blood.

Maybe they were still alive. Maybe they just needed to go to the hospital. I could call an ambulance after he left and they'd be okay, right?

Wrong. The intruder was hell bent on making sure that didn't happen. He bent down and sliced open their chests. It was like a bursting water balloon when the blood came. Tears fell from my eyes. My skin clammed up. What I was seeing was pure nightmare fuel.

Minutes went by. He finally rose to his feet. Then, soaked in blood, he turned his head toward me. This little rabbit was back in the homicidal gaze of the crocodile. And nothing but a miracle could save my furry tail.

That miracle came. Suddenly, half a dozen police sirens blared in the distance. The maniac lunged at me, stopped, and then ran through the sliding door in the kitchen.

I shook my head until the pillow case flew off. Big mistake. Without the fabric, everything was much clearer. That included my parent's motionless bodies. With my dad's twisted limbs and the pile of broken teeth next to his caved-in face, it looked like he'd been run over by a tractor. And then there were the flabs of flesh missing from his chest and his exposed ribcage and lung. I puked.

I looked to my mom and puked again. What disturbed me the most wasn't her bleeding face, her broken limbs, or even the intestines spilling from her belly. It was her cold, dead eyes.

Or at least the stillness in them.

My body stiffened like a wooden board. As hard as I tried, I couldn't take my eyes off them. The blood—it kept flowing like a river. And with so much of it, I knew they were dead. Even then I kept hoping they'd get back up. But they never did.

Before I knew it, the house was swarming with cops and we were taken to an ambulance. While a medic treated our wounds, Xavier buried his face in his shirt, crying, "I want mommy! Where's dad?!"

If my heart was made of glass, it would've shattered from just listening to him.

"It's gonna be..." Warm tears rolled down my cheek.

"Wadda we do now?!" Xavier's head fell onto my shoulder.

"D-dunno." I wiped my nose and eyes.

"We gonna make sure you boys be just fine," the medic in the driver's seat said. After the medic treating us closed the back doors, he drove down the street. "You don't got no other family to stay with?"

I shook my head and took a deep breath. "They were our only..." I tried. "I mean, we don't..." I couldn't hold it in. Tears dripped to my lap and I collapsed onto Xavier.

"I gotcha, man," he said, sinking his head.

I wiped my eyes, turned, and looked out the back window. Most of our neighbors had already gone back to their homes, and the ones that stayed were being asked to leave by cops.

Then I saw someone standing on a street corner. It was Officer Zeke, but what was odd was the creepy cop was dressed in all black, not his blue police uniform.

When we caught eyes, he darted into the shadows.

"Don't worry, boys." The medic driving the ambulance turned on the emergency lights. "We're gonna find a safe place for y'all."

Chapter Five

The Number 23

Present day...

After Iron River swallowed up the car, the three of us headed back through the forest. Sean and didn't say anything the entire way.

Leon's grin stayed spread across his mug. It just made me wanna break his teeth in half.

When we got to the city, we walked through different neighborhoods and backstreets until we met one of the main roads. Nothing in sight was pretty. I mean, the sidewalks were covered with shards of glass and garbage. Shops were rundown and boarded up. Groups of goons stood on the street corners, drinking gin and eyeing us as we walked by. It wasn't the best part of the city. But it was far from the worst.

Unfortunately for us, we usually had to go through the grittiest streets just to find a meal, since the dumpsters and trashcans in bad areas were always the ones that held the most unfinished food.

"Where we goin'?" I nudged Sean on the shoulder.

"I think there's a b-bus stop close to here." He pointed out in the distance.

Although I had been living in that city my whole life, there were parts of it even I wasn't familiar with. On the other hand, Sean pretty much had most streets mapped out in his head. That dude was like a human GPS.

"Ya sure they run this late?" Leon asked.

"Yeah." Sean put his hands over his face. "P-pretty sure."

The thought of that man drowning in the cold water created a sinking feeling in my chest. As the memory replayed in my head, my breaths got shorter. Even then, Sean seemed like he was taking it much harder than me.

And then there was Leon. He didn't bat an eye. He acted like nothing happened. I mean, he always acted screwy, but I never knew how coldhearted he was.

"Think I see it." I pointed passed a row of maple trees and to a blue sign out in the distance.

"Y-yeah, that's it." Sean wiped the snot from his nose.

"How much they chargin' these days?" I asked.

"I think a buck fifty," Sean replied.

I glanced over my shoulder to check for anybody who might've been watching us. The fact that no one was there didn't make me feel better, but it was just so hard to believe that we were actually getting away with what we did.

The streets were empty except for a man staggering out of a bar. He stumbled into the middle of the road. Just then, a speeding motorcycle came from around the corner. And headed straight for him.

The man didn't seem to notice.

"Hey!" I bolted toward him.

"What are ya doin'?!" Leon shouted.

I grabbed the man's arm and pulled him out the way just in time. The motorcycle sped off into the night.

The man stared at me with a dazed look in his eyes. "I think I would've been dead if it wasn't for you."

"Ya gotta be more careful, man," I told him.

"Hold on." The man stroked his chin. "Do I know ya from somewhere? They call me Thane."

"I don't think so." I shook my head.

Thane let out a loud laugh and zipped up his brown leather coat. "Must have had more beers than I should've had."

He stared at me for a few seconds and then looked over my shoulder. This look appeared on his face, but I couldn't identify the emotion behind it. Fear? Maybe guilt? No, it definitely wasn't guilt. It was more like surprise mixed in with curiosity.

After a few seconds, he said, "Say, do ya know that taller man over there?"

"Who? Leon?" I asked.

"Yeah, him," Thane nodded. "The one with the long, uncombed hair."

"Yeah, I do," I responded. "Do you?"

He didn't answer my question. Instead, the guy leaned closer and said, "Monsters are real, ya know." His eyes widened. "And he's one of them."

"W-what?" I stepped back into the road.

Thane didn't say anything back. He just walked toward a blue Mercedes and hoped inside. And just like that, he sped off.

"What did ya mean by—" It was too late. He was gone.

"Are ya finished screwin' around?!" Leon shouted.

I shook my head and ran back to Sean and Leon. After I reached them, I started to think about Thane's warning. What did he mean by that? And how did he know Leon?

"Who the hell was that?" Leon asked.

"Just some drunk dude," I responded. "Let's just go."

While we continued toward the bus stop, I took out the wallet I'd taken earlier. The second I flipped it open, I saw our victim on the driver's license. It made my stomach flip. I pulled out five bucks as quick as I could and put the wallet back in my pocket.

"Think I got enough for all of us." I knew that Leon would've rather walked home than dish out any of the money he found, and I was sure that I was gonna fight tooth and nail to get him to split it up with us. "When does the bus get here?"

"Comes about every half hour," Sean whispered, clutching his stomach.

"Well, what time is it now?" Leon gritted his teeth together.

"I dunno," I shrugged, wondering why he even asked. Not a damn one of us owned any watches and he knew this. Our group usually just guessed what time it was by how much light there was outside.

Leon kept up his piss ant attitude until we reached the bus stop. "Ya sure the bus runs this late?" He leaned against one a poor maple tree.

Sean didn't answer. He just stared at the concrete, rubbing his own arm.

"Sean?" I placed my hand on his shoulder.

"Hmm?" Sean glanced at me.

"Leon want to know if—" All of a sudden, I was blinded by the headlights of a large vehicle. A few moments later, the bus came into view and stopped in front of us.

Its doors opened. I walked toward the old, dirty bus. The second I entered, the driver scowled at me, keeping his eyes on my clothes. I glanced down to see what he was staring at. It was blood. Small specs of it. The river water didn't wash it all off, so there were plenty of tiny, red dots that could be seen.

"F-for three." I forced a smile and held up the money.

The overweight driver sat there. He looked at me while running his fingers through his long, grey beard. Somehow, it's like he just knew. I darted my eyes and spotted a camera perched above my head. It was aimed right at me. It wasn't good. Something inside me told me that camera was gonna be a problem sooner or later.

The driver finally broke the silence. "We charge two dollars a person these days." He pointed to a sign that said something about a recent fare raise. "You ain't got enough."

"Right." I pulled out the wallet again and grabbed a dollar.

The driver took the money and hesitated. After staring at us for what felt like forever, he gave us our tickets.

Leon rushed for a front seat. I walked to the second farthest seat from the back and sat down. Sean took the seat directly across from me and lied down on his side in the fetal position.

I rested the side of my head against the glass window and read the graffiti on the seat in front of me which read, 'Never give up though the odds are more than the heart and soul can bear. You never know when the darkest sky may become surprising clear'.

I repeated the words over and over in my head to try and somehow erase the nightmare we all just went through.

"Hey, driver, ya wanna hear a joke?" Leon taunted.

The driver stayed silent.

"Why is six afraid of seven?" Leon asked.

The driver slowly shook his head.

"Because seven is a serial killer." Leon cackled.

"Very funny, smartass! You done?!" The bus driver asked.

"Yeah, sure." Leon snickered a bit before going silent.

Half an hour went by. Sean was twirling his hair and looked like he'd just run a marathon. Leon calmed himself down by peeling the paint off a nearby metal railing with his fingernail. We stopped. Outside, a hooded man, who was smoking, leaned against the bus stop pole and had his hand in his coat pocket.

The bus driver opened the doors. The man tossed his cigarette to the ground and blew out a trail of smoke in the air. He entered with a smirk on his face, asking, "What's poppin', blood? Two-hundred cents, ain't that right?"

"My name isn't 'blood' it's Marty." The driver said before taking two bucks from the hooligan's hands.

"Chill, man!" The shady man turned to Leon.

"Find somewhere else to sit," Leon seethed, using his legs to block off the seat.

"Well, ain't everybody happy and cheery tonight." The man continued down the aisle.

"Punk ass." Leon rose his middle finger to the man.

I didn't know why Leon was acting like that. It was hard to tell if he had a personal grudge against the man or if he just didn't like something about the guy. Knowing Leon, though, he probably just saw something he didn't like.

The man walked up to a young girl reading a novel and bit his lip. "Hey, Sarah, when you gonna let me get up in that? You know you want some of this!"

"As if!" The girl named Sarah never even looked up.

"Tell ya what..." Jerome pulled out a notepad and pen. After ripping out a page, he wrote something down.

The driver started the bus before Jerome took his seat. He swayed back and forth before grabbing one of the metal bars above his head.

"You still there?" Sarah brushed her braids away from her face.

"Yeah, I'm still here. I ain't goin' nowhere." Jerome handed the young girl the scrap of paper. "How 'bout you hit me up when you ready?"

"Okay, yeah, sure, whatever." When Jerome turned his back, Sarah crumbled the paper and tossed it to the ground.

"Sup, blood?" Jerome reached my seat and sat down before I had a chance to tell him to get lost. "You doin' good?"

"Yup." I looked out the window.

"Ya lookin' for some crystal?" A grin formed on his face.

I folded my arms and put my head down. "I dunno anybody named Crystal."

"Nah, nah." He pulled out a tiny, plastic bag from his pocket and scooted closer to me, whispering, "I'm talkin' 'bout this kinda crystal, blood."

The bag was filled with crystal meth. The only thing I'd ever smoked was weed a few times here and there. "I don't do that shit."

"Really? Well, it's just that…" Jerome put his hand back in his pocket. "I got some money problems."

"Oh, yeah?" I rolled my eyes. "That's real nice. So does everybody else."

He pulled out a pocket knife.

"I got nothin'," I said, shrugging. "Sorry."

"Don't you fuckin' lie to me." Jerome pressed the knife against my side.

"Alright, alright, shit." I pulled out the wallet.

"Thanks, blood!" The thuggish robber snatched it from my hand and stuffed it inside his pocket. A black pager fell out when he removed his hand. "Gotta help each other every now and then, right?"

The bus made two more stops before Jerome finally pulled the knife away and stood up. He snickered at me and then dashed off the bus and into a nearby alleyway. When he was gone, I picked up the pager he dropped.

Just as I tucked it into my pocket, the bus continued down the street and then stopped at a burger joint further down. Leon stood up and made his exit without waiting for either of us.

"Sean." I kicked his leg lightly. "Let's go home."

"Right." He jumped from his seat and trailed a few feet behind me.

Just before we got off the bus, I turned around and walked back to the girl named Sarah. "Hold up, Sean."

"Watchoo want, nigga?" Sarah closed her book and flipped me off.

"Nothin' from you, hoodrat." I picked up the scrap of paper she tossed on the ground earlier.

"You gonna call him?" she giggled.

I unfolded the paper to see Jerome's name and the number to the pager I found. Then I walked back toward Sean. As I exited the bus, the driver took one last glance at me. Something told me that he wouldn't forget about the blood stains on my clothes.

"Leon's ass didn't even wait for us." Sean's voice was muffled by the roar of the bus's engine.

"Fuck Leon." I coughed when I breathed in the trail of exhaust left behind by the bus.

"Hey, we need to talk about something soon."

"What is it?"

"Not now."

"Yeah, but what it is?"

"Xavier."

"What about him?" I tightened my fists.

"Trust me on this." Sean turned his head and looked me in the eye. "You need to get rid of him."

Chapter Six

Death's Cologne

Sixty-Seven days later...

A policeman by the name of Officer Mercer put his hand over his eyes to shield them from the sun. "I think that's far 'nuff!"

After the roar of the nearby tow-truck engine stopped, water escaped from every crevice of the vehicle that had just been fished out of the river.

"Jesus, it's hot as hell." Officer Mercer lifted his police cap and used the back of his hand to wipe away the sweat on his brow.

"What do ya think happened, boss?" Officer Mercer's partner, Officer Tanner, took a closer look.

"No idea, rookie, but run the license plate number and see what turns up." Officer Mercer took a step forward and covered his nose. "Hold it! You smell that?!"

A putrid odor entered the nostrils of Officer Tanner. "Yeah." He buried his face in his arm. "What is it?"

"I got a pretty damn good idea." Officer Mercer walked to the tow-truck and waved to the driver. "Hey, John, got a crowbar?"

John tossed an old, rusty crowbar out the window. "Just bring it back when you're done!"

"No problem." After picking it up, Officer Mercer then treaded to the vehicle in front of him, trying not to lose his lunch. However, with the nauseating aroma growing stronger with each step he took, it was hard not to. "Jesus H. Christ!"

"Boss, ya need some help?" Officer Tanner neared Mercer.

"Not just yet." Once Officer Mercer pried the trunk of the car open, the rotten stench exploded into the atmosphere, encasing both officers.

"Oh, my sweet Jesus!" Officer Tanner covered his mouth and nose.

"My fuckin' God!" Officer Mercer's eyes watered. "See that?!"

"What the hell are those things?" Tanner inched closer.

"Give it a minute." Officer Mercer took a quick swig of the plastic bottle of orange juice in his hand–which was half filled with hard liquor–then put a cigarette in his mouth.

Officer Tanner stared in the trunk. It didn't register in his brain at first, but when it finally did his heart stopped. The objects he was staring at were two severely bloated corpses, and with their bulging eye sockets and the gunshot wounds covering their bodies, they barely resembled human beings.

"Holy f-fuckin' shit! Are those—" Officer Tanner took a step back, staring with his mouth wide open at the pools of coagulated blood surrounding their bluish skin. "Are those b-bodies?!"

"They sure are! Go ahead and call HQ." Officer Mercer lit his cigarette. "We got a double homicide on our hands.

Chapter Seven

Bonfire

Present day...

I jolted myself from my sleep. A usual night of tossing and turning had left my sweat soaking into my blanket of newspapers.

"Are you okay?" Tabitha waved from the other side of the junkyard.

"I'm fine." I closed my eyes and replayed the same dream I'd been having for the past couple of years. It was always the same. Everything would be fine and then this evil monster would come from nowhere, swinging an axe until there was nothing but blood, bone, and flesh left.

She cupped her hands over her mouth. "Are you sure?!"

"Yeah, thanks." I looked down to see dozens of bedbugs biting my ankles, crawling into and then under my skin. "Shit! Shit! Oh shit!" Their bites caused blood to drip onto the couch.

"What is it?!" Tabitha bolted across the junkyard.

"Look!" I brushed away the bugs.

Tabitha stopped a few feet from the couch, looking around frantically. "What?! What happened?!"

"You don't see them?!" I flicked away more of the nasty bugs. "The bedbugs on my legs?!"

Tabitha took a long look at my ankles. "Are y-you alright? There aren't any bedbugs."

I stared at her. When I looked back to my ankles, I noticed she was right; the bedbugs and blood had disappeared.

"I've known you for a while now, but—" Her head spun around the junkyard. "You're starting to scare me."

"Nah! I wasn't—" I looked around the couch, flipping the cushions. "I swear to God they're here! There was blood!"

Tabitha shook my body. "There aren't any bedbugs around here."

I let out a nervous laugh. "Yeah," I said, nodding. Sweat flew off my face. "I guess I j-just need more sleep."

Tabitha raised her eyebrows. "M-maybe that's it, you know?" She walked back to the other side of the junkyard.

Xavier walked toward me, raising his eyebrows just like Tabitha did. "What happened?"

"Nothing, man." I gave him a thumbs up. "You alright?"

An empty look filled his eyes. "Yeah."

"That's a lie, and you know it." I crossed my arms.

"Why did ya..." A frown formed on his face.

"Why did I what?" I asked. "Kill that guy? I had to save Sean, man. I didn't know—"

"No," he said, trembling. It looked like he was trying hard to fight back tears. He wiped his nose and then looked at me with heartbroken eyes. "I mean why did—"

"There's something else I have to tell you!" Tabitha yelled, walking back toward us. "Before I forget!"

"And what is that?" I responded to Tabitha while eyeing Xavier. "And where did Sean and Leon go?"

"Leon said something about picking up supplies." She sounded even more concerned than before. Her voice quivered. "And well—"

"What supplies?" I wiped away more sweat from my face. "And how come nobody told me?"

"I dunno anything about it, really. They didn't say why or where they were going." She took a seat right next to me. "They both just up and left."

"Alright." I believed her. She wasn't known for telling lies. "Xavier, did they say anything ?"

Xavier shook his head and took off. He made it feel like he was upset, but I couldn't think about any times where I did him wrong.

"M-maybe Xavier could..." Tabitha mumbled, her lips becoming all quivery and whatnot. It was starting to look like she was afraid of him.

"Xavier is a good kid and all..." She crossed her arms and put her head down. "But, you know, I think maybe he just—"

"You think he maybe just what?" I curled my lips and clenched my fists.

"Look," Tabitha started, "I don't think you realize this but Sean thinks of you like a brother." She placed her hand on my shoulder again. "We just don't want anything bad to happen to you, you know."

"What do ya mean by that?" I slowly turned my head.

"Imagine you told a lie so big, deep, and complex that it became the truth..." Her sad eyes met mine. "But only for you."

"I don't understand." I said, shaking my head.

She sighed. "Forget about it. You've really done a lot for us, but..." While she stood up off the couch, the golden locket around her neck spun. "There's just something happening, and you don't realize it."

"And just what would that be?" I asked.

"I can't say. If I told you the truth, it would..." She trailed off to the other side of the junkyard, avoiding eye contact with me. "It would just break you." With the breeze flowing through her long, brown locks, she turned her head over her shoulder. "I *promise* you'll get better one day."

About an hour later, I was still trying to make sense of what Tabitha had said. Her words made me wonder if the rest of the group didn't like Xavier or if he was getting into some trouble. Everyone was acting strange, and I just couldn't figure out what was going on.

The pager I'd found on the bus beeped. I pulled it from my pocket and looked at the phone number on the screen. A phone number popped up in the greenish glow of the backlight.

`After the beeps stopped, I pressed the side button to check the time. "October 27th, 1995, 7:28 pm." I read the words out loud and turned the damn thing off.

"Knock fuckin' knock." Leon walked through the junkyard with Sean, carrying several garbage bags.

"I thought ya would be more cautious." I looked at Leon and Sean. "Ya know, not goin' out in the city in broad daylight."

"Had to take care of business." Leon grabbed a brown, paper sack from one of the garbage bags and then tossed it a few inches from my foot. "Bon appétit, asshole."

When I opened it, I saw two half eaten cheese burgers and a bunch of stale fries inside. "What the—"

"It's food, man." Sean pulled out two more paper bags and gave one to Tabitha.

I had no clue where they found those nasty ass burgers, and to be honest, I didn't wanna know. However, we'd eaten worse before so there was no way in God's great, green earth that I was gonna complain. Eat or die; that was it.

Along with the burgers, Sean and Leon had somehow gotten ahold of some kerosene and a big, plastic bottle of cheap vodka. Our group gathered wood, cardboard, and other stuff to make a fire inside an old, rusty industrial drum. Then we drank.

As the hard liquor slithered down my throat, my vision became blurred, and my thoughts became cloudy. Even after I could barely speak, I kept downing as much as I could. There's no way I could speak for the rest of them, but I never drank for fun. I drank to forget who I was. I drank to thin the line between reality and fantasy. I drank to numb my mind until I forgot that I existed.

Most folks would've said I was another lazy bum, and they probably would've said they would've done things different if they'd lived my life, but if they'd lived my life then they would've had my memories, my thoughts, my world view, and my personality. Simple and plain, those folks would've been me. And if they lived my life and did everything I did, saw everything I saw then they wouldn't have done a god damn thing different from me.

And then they would be sitting on that couch in front of that fire, wishing they were somebody else.

"W-we gotta g—" Leon let out a belch and leaned back into the detached car seat he'd found. "Get outta here 'for they find us."

"How could we? We barely have enough money to make it out of this city." Tabitha—she was the only one of us who never drank—shook her head.

"Yeah, that's why I g-gotta plan to get us some money." Leon stared into the fire.

"And just what w-would that be?" I asked.

"Ever hear of Robin Hood?" Leon put his hands behind his head.

"Yeah..." Sean replied.

"W-we just gotta find s-somebody with a lot of m-money," said Leon.

Tabitha, Sean, and I all looked at each other and shook our heads.

"We're c-criminals, not Robin Hood, Leon! We're the bad guys!" I leaned forward, nearly falling off the couch. "And you ain't serious are you?"

"Y-yeah, I am." Leon dropped his head. "Look, we even..." He stumbled over his words. "I mean, we either s-stay here and get c-caught or we leave."

"Where would we even go?" Tabitha grabbed Sean's hand.

"Anywhere'd be b-better than here," Sean said.

"I suppose." Tabitha put her hand to her lip.

"So what h-happens if we get c-caught, L-leon?" I had to fight to stop myself from passing out.

"We ain't gonna get c-caught if we don't screw shit up," Leon said.

I didn't wanna agree with him, but he was right. Again. After all, we needed to leave, and it had to be soon. I mean, we couldn't hide in that junkyard forever, but robbing someone wasn't something I liked. Even so, we didn't have many options since the small amount of money we had wasn't even gonna get us out of the city.

"So what's the p-plan?" I rubbed my eyes.

"I'mma start lookin' for a-anyone who g-got a lotta money." Leon spit to the side of the car seat. "I'll let y'all know."

"Alright, sounds g-good." When I lifted my head, I spotted Xavier standing on the far side of the junkyard. "Xavier, ya h-hungry?"

"No, thanks." He stood there, shaking his head.

"That's b-bullshit and you know it." I lifted myself off the couch but fell back. When I finally got on my feet, I stumbled toward the plastic trash bags and picked them up. "We got cheeseburgers and..." They were empty. "What the f-fuck, Leon?! Ya only got four of them!"

A smirk inched across Leon's face. "He don't need that shit."

"Fuck y-you, Leon!" I tossed the bag into the fire and staggered toward Xavier.

"Burn in h-hell, asshole!" Leon let out his high-pitched cackle.

"Ya sure you ain't hungry, Xavier?" I asked, ready to walk all the way to the city if I needed to.

"I'm fine," he said, yawning.

I leaned my body against a washing machine when I reached him. "When's the last t-time you a-ate?"

"I think yesterday."

"What'd y-ya eat?"

"I got a piece of fruit."

"Where the h-hell you'd get f-fruit from? The city?"

Xavier nodded.

"Someone g-gave it to ya?"

"Not really. I took it from—"

"Alright, alright, I g-got it. You gonna go back to sleep?"

"Yeah." Xavier yawned again before disappearing behind a stack of cars.

I turned back around and stomped toward our bonfire. "Leon, what w-was that?"

"What was what?" He closed his eyes and slumped back into the car seat.

"Just forget it! We'll talk about this p-plan later." After collapsing over the arm of the couch, I stared into the dying fire until it and my mind faded.

Chapter Eight

A Not So Safe Place

Ten years earlier...

Soon after our parents had been murdered, the cops started an investigation. Many months later, it was a failure—the case had gone cold. All they were able to tell us was that our parents were the victims of Bloody, Bloody Bijou. But even then no one was any closer to finding out who he was. I kept mouth shut about Officer Zeke because my young mind was convinced he'd never be convicted since we were used to bad cops getting away with their crimes.

The authorities looked for foster homes for Xavier and me to live in, and Officer Zeke of all people, was the first to recommend one that his aunt Agatha ran. The other officers all agreed that it would be best for us, but only days after we got there we found out that Agatha was a cruel old woman and the other kids in the home were ruthless savages.

One day Agatha had caught Xavier eating food before dinner, telling him, "Don't you go starting trouble again, ya hear?"

"I won't."

"You won't what?"

"I won't, ma'am."

"You look me in the eyes when you speak to me!"

Xavier lifted his head to make eye contact with the old hag. "I won't, ma'am."

"Good to hear." She shook her head and then walked to the other end of the house.

"Let's go outside." I turned around and swung open the front door.

Xavier stepped onto the front porch. "Are they ever gonna find the guy that killed mom and dad?" he sighed, shifting his eyes away from me.

"No idea." I gritted my teeth and took a seat on the top step of the porch. After that horrible night, I never thought about my mom and dad. To me, they never existed. It might sound coldhearted, but it was easier for me that way.

Xavier sighed again and looked at the other kids in the yard. "Look!" He pointed over to a fight that was about to start.

"Why don't ya ever fight back, ya fat sack of shit?" A kid, who I knew as Brandon, pushed a bigger child to the ground and kicked him in the side. "You pussy!"

The kid that Brandon was messing with was found living just outside the city a few months back. He was bigger than any of us and could've beaten Brandon down if he wanted to. But he never did. In fact, he never spoke a single word, and to be honest, I didn't even know what his name was.

"They're so mean to him." Xavier shook his head. "Why?"

"I dunno, but I'm tired of seeing it." I clenched my fists and stomped toward the group of bullies.

Brandon turned toward me with a devilish smile on his face. "What's up, bitch?" He picked up a pile of dirt and then threw it in my eyes.

"Dammit!" I wiped it away, trying to regain my vision.

"The hell you gonna do, bitch?" Carl, Brandon's buddy, shoved me a few times.

I let a left hook crack against the side of Carl's jaw. "Fuck off!"

Carl took a step back. He glared at me. A second later, he was throwing punches like there was no tomorrow. A blow to my nose sent me crashing to the dirt.

"Lookie here, boys, we got ourselves a cat fight!" Brandon folded his arms and grinned.

Carl grabbed my skull and kneed me in the face. When I got the chance, I pulled him down with me. The two of us wrestled on the ground, striking each other's faces until I got him in a choke hold.

"Alright, that's enough!" Agatha stormed into the yard.

"Get off of him!" Brandon kicked me in the face, making me release my grip.

Fists flying, elbows swinging, lips splitting and faces swelling. A bloody nose here and a black eye there—it was everyday stuff. Always over something petty. Xavier and I wanted nothing to do with it, but Brandon and his friends always found a reason to start something with us.

"C'mon, let's go!" Brandon led Carl and the rest of the kids back to the house.

I pinched my nose to stop the bleeding then turned to the bully victim. "You alright?"

He nodded and rose to his feet.

"Hey, how come ya never talk?" Xavier walked behind me.

The towering giant shook his head, placed his hands in his pockets, and then darted his eyes.

"Why don't you ever fight back?" I asked coldly.

His eyes stayed pointed at the ground.

"You could stick with us, ya know." Xavier extended his arm. "My names Xavier."

The silent kid shook my brother's hand. Then he dropped to his knees and wrote 'My name's Mike' in the dirt.

"So that's ya name?" Xavier asked. "Wanna be friends, Mike?!"

Mike did nothing but stare at us and nod. The way he raised his eyebrows made it look like he never heard the word 'friend' before.

"We should go back." I turned to see Agatha staring at us through one of the front windows.

"Right." Xavier followed close behind. He looked back at Mike. "You comin'?"

Mike nodded and trailed behind us.

Agatha kept up her staring. Before we even reached the porch, I could tell she was gonna let all three of us have it.

Chapter Nine

Where the Killers Hang

Present day...

A few days after we had our bonfire, Xavier, Tabitha, Sean, and I got ready to meet Leon in the city. Leon had left the junkyard a few hours earlier, running his big mouth about how he found a house that had a lot of money inside. He told us to meet us near a barber shop on some street called Palm Street. Unfortunately, the directions he gave us were trash. All he told us was that it was near an overpass and a burger joint on Union Road. It left us wandering around the city—we got lost a few times because even Sean had trouble finding it—for hours before we finally came across one of the shadiest streets I'd ever seen.

"Talk about the slums." I looked at a group of fiends smoking crack in plain sight.

"Police don't even come here." Sean pointed to an overpass sitting just beyond a telephone. Dozens of old, blue sneakers hanging by their laces. "Alright, there's the overpass so now where's the barbershop?"

"Dunno. I don't see it either." As I walked forward, I had to step over a small pool of blood dripping into a gutter. "Might be up ahead."

"Hope so," Sean said.

As we walked beneath the overpass, I noticed several teens dressed in rags; all huddled around a small fire. "It's like they're dead. They look like they already gave up on life."

Seeing young, abandoned kids wasn't new. Teenagers always roamed the streets, trying to find a way to escape from hell. Unfortunately, it was hard when the flames of poverty burned everyone's exit plan to smoke and ash. It was the same reason our city was filled with homeless folk. Well, people like us, I mean. People like us were the ghosts living in society's blind spot. And we'd never have our struggles acknowledged because our struggles would never be known. People like us were noticed about as much as bubblegum under park benches. All we wanted was to be treated like human beings.

But we never would be.

Unfortunately, that meant the only thing that would be there for us was the misery that wrapped itself around us like a cozy blanket on a snowy Christmas Eve. Except instead of keeping us warm, it kept a permanent frown on our faces and made sure we always had an ache in our chests. And then when we eventually died alone in the cold, it would keep us company while thieves emptied our pockets.

"Just leave it. You know how it goes here." Sean pointed to a couple of missing posters on a telephone pole. "Nobody can do or say anything to make this shit any better."

"Yeah, but shit…" I glanced back at the group and wished I could do something to help them. Unfortunately, it's pointless to make a wish when you're too poor to spare a nickel to toss in the wishing well.

Palm Street was filled with abandoned houses and buildings which all were in the worst conditions I ever saw. An entire wall was missing from one of the structures, one house was collapsed in on itself, and another had been burnt to a crisp. That street was a paradise for criminals and any folks who wanted to do some dirty work.

Suddenly, out of nowhere, someone threw a bottle of whiskey at us from a nearby porch. It crashed into a truck's headlight, sending liquor spilling onto the pavement.

I looked up. On a porch a few meters away, half a dozen men dressed in all blue were all pointing guns at us. By the angry snarls on their faces, I could tell they didn't want to play around.

"What set y'all claim?" one yelled.

Tabitha's lip trembled. "We aren't in a gang. We're just—"

"Shut the fuck up, bitch!" The gangbanger tossed an unopened can of beer at us. "Keep ya heads down and keep walkin'!"

And so we did. However, when we were further down the road, I turned my head over my shoulder to see them still eyeing us. Even after reaching the end of the road, they still kept their gaze on our group.

We were sheep in the lion's den. And my heart must've known it because it was exploding like a nuclear bomb.

Sean pointed to a barber shop on the other side of the street. "There it is!"

"Yeah, I see it." I looked around. "Where the hell is Leon?"

"I don't see him either." Sean glanced around the street.

With Leon nowhere around, we walked a few paces toward the barber shop. Just then Xavier darted between the trunk of a Jeep Wrangler and the engine of a Toyota Camry.

"Xavier what are—" I began.

"Wanna good time, honey?" A hooker wearing fishnets and a black low-cut top walked toward me and put her hand on her hip. "Twenty-five bucks fo' an hour."

"Nah, I'm good." I shook my head.

She turned around toward Xavier.

"And he's too young for that shit!" I said.

"Watchoo talkin' 'bout, baby?" She looked around.

"Talkin' about my kid brother right there." I pointed to the shadows. "Right there between them cars."

"Ain't see nobody up in here." The floozy woman turned around and shook her head. "Yo' cuckoo for coco leaves, honey!"

"Xavier! Get up outta there, man."

He climbed outta his hiding spot and walked toward me.

"What are you doing?"

He reached me just as Sean and Tabitha continued toward the barber shop. "I don't belong here."

"Yeah, neither do I, but you're makin' people think I've lost it."

A black dude near us who had his back pressed against a brick wall caught my eye. He brushed his dreadlocks away from his face, lowered his sunglasses, and then took a long hit from his blunt. Then, while smoke flowed from his nose, he gave me a wide smile, not a happy one either. It was a smile that meant trouble.

"We'll go home soon after this, alright, Xavier?" With my body shaking so much, it was hard to hide how nervous I was. "We won't even be in this city in a few days so just chill."

Soon our group reached the barbershop. All four of us just stood there like clueless cattle in a slaughterhouse.

"Think he's already inside?" Sean pressed his face against the glass window.

"Don't think he would be. I mean—" I began.

"Took y'all long enough!" Leon exited a nearby alleyway.

"So you give us almost no details about how to find this place, and then you get all mad when we have trouble findin' it?" I clenched my fists.

"This is the only god damn barber shop on Palm Street, you dumbshit." He spread out his arms.

"No fucking shit!" I raised my middle finger three inches from his face. "The problem was findin' this street!"

Leon grabbed my wrist and snarled. "Do that shit again, and I'll cut it off!" After pulling out a knife, he pointed it at me. "Fuck with me!"

"Leon, come on!" Sean rushed in between the two of us.

"Don't push start if you don't wanna play, bitch!" I pulled away and put my fists up. "This game ain't fun," I yelled, snarling, "and there's no fuckin' reset button!"

"There's no time for this bullshit!" Leon put the knife away and faced the other direction. "Just shut up and follow me." He spun around and looked me in the eyes. "Just don't make me solder up that mouth!"

Just as the street lights flickered on, Leon walked back into the alley he came from. Even with my blood boiling, all I cared about was getting out of that city. So I followed him. After all, the sooner we got that money, the sooner I never had to see him again—well, if he was telling the truth at least. And I had my doubts.

"Why the hell ya choose this place?" Sean walked by a drug addict sitting behind a dumpster.

While we passed, the man looked up at us with wretched eyes and a face covered with filth.

"'Cause nobody's gonna miss what nobody's supposed to know about." Leon stopped at a basement window before picking up a brick and breaking the glass. "Nobody's gonna be running their mouths here." He slid his body through.

Sean shrugged and jumped through. Tabitha followed but let out a yelp when she sliced her arm on a shard of glass.

"Xavier, I'mma go first, got it?" I slipped my body through.

After my shoes slapped against the concrete, I grabbed my lighter and flicked it on. The room lit up. Sean, Leon, and Tabitha's eyes all met mine.

"I'm comin'!" Xavier slithered through the window and landed on a fish tank. Oddly enough, the glass didn't break.

I followed Leon to a wooden staircase on the far side of the basement. Two metal drums in the corner caught my attention. All hell broke loose when I walked toward them.

"Don't fuckin' touch either of those!" Leon picked up an old toaster and threw it across the room.

I dodged it by a hair. "What the fuck is wrong with you?!"

"Leave them the hell alone!" Leon turned around and struck his fist through the wall.

"Alright, damn!" I had no idea what set Leon off, but there was no time to figure it out.

After we made it up the basement stairs, we opened a door to find a dark, dusty hallway on the other side.

"Alright, search this place from top to bottom." Leon took out two lighters and handed one to Sean and the other to Tabitha.

"What are we looking for?" Tabitha asked.

Leon walked down the hallway and into a living room. "Anything that looks valuable."

Chapter Ten

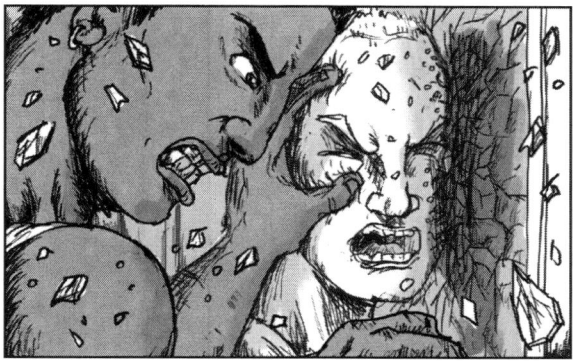

Mirror, Mirror on the Wall

Ten years earlier...

Brandon pointed to the slice of cornbread on my plate. "You gonna eat that?" He snatched it away and then took a bite. "Of course not, bitch."

That guy couldn't leave me alone even when I was eating, and I was tired of it. I stood up from my seat so fast my seat flew backward. That punk turned around with a smirk on his face. Then he just walked back to his chair like we were peasants he allowed in his kingdom.

"Just let it go," Xavier begged, urging me to sit down.

He was right, but I was tired of Brandon's crap. Before I left the table, someone put their hand on my shoulder. It was Mike. He towered above me, looking like he just wanted everyone to get along. The humble giant took a seat next to me, broke his cornbread in two, and put half on my plate.

"Well, damn. Thanks, man." I stuffed the entire slice of cornbread into my mouth.

He nodded and quickly finished off his food.

Not too much later, the doorbell rang. Agatha rushed down the stairs and opened the door. The person at the door spoke. A chill slithered down my spine. It was Zeke—the murdering lunatic was back. And I sure as hell knew he wasn't dropping by to say hello.

"Y'all boys remember me?" Officer Zeke walked into the living room. "Why don't ya both step outside and we can talk."

"F-for what?!" I gripped the sides of my pants.

"Don't be disrespectful!" Agatha stomped toward Xavier and me and then pulled us away from the table. The mean, old woman dragged us through the kitchen and threw us into the backyard.

"Oh, you don't need to do all that." Zeke followed us outside.

"These boys don't know anything about respect!" Agatha returned inside and slammed the door behind her.

"W-what do you want?!" Xavier shivered.

Officer Zeke pulled out a pen and pad. "I just wanted to get a few bits of info from y'all about that horrible, horrible night."

"We already told the other officers everything we know!" I wanted to run away.

"I know, but I wanted to make sure y'all didn't see who..." Zeke stopped and cleared his throat. "I mean, I wanted to make sure there wasn't anything we missed."

"Of course that's why." I folded my arms.

"So the only things he took were—" Officer Zeke began.

"Our parent's wedding rings!" Xavier said.

"And y'all don't suspect anyone?" Sweat dripped down Officer Zeke's forehead.

"No." I darted my eyes.

"Well, I think that's all I needed." Officer Zeke abruptly ended the conversation, ran back into the house, and shut the door behind him.

Xavier and I rushed over to the window and looked inside to see Officer Zeke talking with Agatha.

"Can ya hear him?" I asked Xavier.

"No. How about you?" he asked back.

I shook my head and watched Officer Zeke point toward us. Agatha nodded and gave him a smile.

"Wadda ya think they're talkin' about?"

"It's about us, Xavier! We gotta leave from here!"

"Where?! And why?"

"Because I think it was him! I think Zeke is Bloody, Bloody Bijou!"

When I turned back to the window, I saw Zeke heading toward us again.

"Shit! He's comin'!"

The shady officer opened the sliding glass door and waved to us. "Y'all be good now. I'll be back real soon." He closed the door and made his way through the living room.

I turned back to Xavier. "I saw him that night!"

"What?! Where?!"

"He was on the street—"

"There were a lot of cops outside. Maybe he was just—"

"No! He wasn't near the house! He was dressed in all black far away from the other cops, and he ran when he saw me!"

"Really?! What do we do?!"

"We gotta leave before he comes back again! Before he kills us! I think he knows I know! Let's talk about it later!"

We both stepped into the kitchen. Everyone was gone.

"You hear that?" Xavier said. "Sounds like there's a fight upstairs!"

"Mike!" I dashed through the kitchen and living room. After I reached the staircase, I tripped over the first step, which caused the wood to come loose.

"C'mon!" Xavier rushed in front of me, pulling me up.

We reached the top. A crowd was standing outside the upstairs bathroom. Xavier and I shoved through the group of kids. As soon as I stepped foot into the bathroom, I saw Mike curled up on the floor.

"Bitch!" Brandon kicked Mike in the ribs.

"Get off him!" I pushed Brandon into the shower curtain as hard as I could.

He grabbed the shower curtain. But it ripped and he hit his head against the wall. Soap bars and shampoo bottles rained down on top of him. It was wrong, but it put a smile on my face to see that.

Carl ran up and put me in a headlock. "Don't feel good does it, monkey lips?"

"Asshole!" I struggled to free myself but slipped on the tile. Even after we crashed to the floor, he still had a tight grip around my neck.

"I'mma kill you, mother fucker!" Brandon jumped to his feet and stomped me in the face.

The beating continued. Kicks to the ribs. Blows to the face. I suffered through all of it. And there wasn't a thing I could do to stop them.

"Mike, help!" Stars filled my vision.

Mike rose to his feet and pulled Brandon off me.

"Oh, hell no!" Brandon spun around and punched Mike's gut. "Don't touch me, lard ass!" He pushed Mike against the wall and then pulled Xavier into the bathroom.

"Oh, Brandon, you play too much!" Agatha chuckled before turning her back to the brawl.

"Get your ass in here, brat!" Brandon shoved Xavier's head in the toilet bowl.

Xavier trashed his limbs. But Brandon only shoved his head in further. The sound of bubbles rising to the surface filled my ears. As much as I struggled, I couldn't get to him. Carl had me pinned good. That powerless feeling sent shivers down my spine.

"Get off him, you punk!" I yelled.

Mike suddenly pulled Brandon off Xavier.

"Let go you fat sack of—" Brandon started.

It was too late. Something changed in Mike's eyes. The peaceful look on his face had turned into a vicious snarl. And with his powerful hand gripping against Brandon's head, he did something no one expected. He let out a roar. Then slammed Brandon's face into the bathroom mirror. It was gruesome. It was brutal. And, God forgive me, it was fucking glorious.

Glass shards rained down. Mike pulled Brandon away from the mirror. Brandon gasped for breath. Blood and saliva dripped from his mouth. I thought it was over. But it happened again. Mike forced Brandon through the shattered mirror. By then dozens of mirror shards had slid into Brandon's flesh.

"Stop it!" Carl yelled.

Nothing Carl said stopped Mike's rampage. A cracking sound exploded in my ears. It was the sound of Mike bashing Brandon's forehead into the sink counter. Mike released his grip. Brandon's body fell to the floor like a lifeless ragdoll. But Mike wasn't finished. Brandon took knee after knee to the face. It was like watching a chimpanzee getting beat down by a full grown silverback gorilla. Eventually, Mike finished. And by then Brandon's swollen face was covered in cuts and bruises.

Carl let go of my neck. Wrong move. The second I was free Mike turned around. Carl took a step back. His back hit the wall. His eyes darted around the room, and he raised his fists. Too late. Mike's nostrils flaring, he unleashed an entire arsenal of blows to Carl's face. Hook after hook. Swing after swing. Carl's skull slammed back, breaking through the drywall. But Mike didn't stop there. He wrapped his hands around Carl's face. Then, while slobber dripped off his lip, he smashed his forehead into Carl's nose.

It was my turn. When I got the chance, I grabbed a mirror shard off the sink counter. Then drove it into the back of Carl's calf. Carl fell to the ground, blood dripping from his wound.

"You fucking psychopaths!" Carl cried, crawling outta the bathroom on his stomach. "Agatha, help!"

I looked at Mike and Xavier. "You both alright?"

They both nodded.

The old hag made her way up the stairs. "What the hell is going…" Her jaw dropped as soon as she saw the trail of blood left by Carl. "Who did this?!"

Carl clutched the back of his leg and struggled to his feet. Then he pointed to me. "He did!"

Agatha rushed toward me and slapped me in the face. "All three of you will clean this mess up and then go straight to bed!" She grabbed Carl and Brandon's hands and helped them both downstairs.

After the rest of the kids left, I turned to Mike. "We're gonna run away from here."

His eyes widened.

Looking him dead in the eyes, I whispered, "Do ya wanna come with us?"

He nodded.

"Okay, we leave next week," I said.

Chapter Eleven

Find the Stash Spot

Present day...

I pointed to a door on our left. "Alright, Sean and Tabitha, check in that room right there. Me and Xavier are gonna go check the one at the end of the hall."

"Got it." Sean led Tabitha toward the room before disappearing behind it.

When I raised my lighter, pictures of hellish demons hanging on the wall made me quiver. I walked passed them and into the room. It was empty besides a desk and two cardboard boxes in the corner.

"Xavier, wanna go check in that desk over there?" I walked toward it and looked at its dusty wood.

"N-not really." Xavier walked to the corner of the room and sat down near the boxes.

"Oh, c'mon." When I opened the desk drawer, the hairs on the back of my neck stood up. Inside was this old axe. But that wasn't the part that made shivers shoot through my limbs—it was all the maggots covering the axe.

And the blood, guts, and rotting chunks of human flesh they crawled through.

I jumped in the air. My lighter went out.

"Don't leave me here," a voice whispered. "Please don't let me die."

Sweat poured down my face. "Xavier, did ya say that?! W-was that you, man?!"

"Did I say what?" he asked.

"Oh, f-fuck..." After spinning the lighter wheel, I glanced around. No one else was inside the room except Xavier. Then I looked back to the bloody mess. It was gone. The drawer was empty.

I dropped to my knees and closed my eyes, trying to stop the thoughts of gore and violence from spreading through my head. Truthfully, I would've liked it better if some damn ghost or maybe even a demon was the one haunting me. But, no. It was my own mind.

A few minutes went by before I was able to pull myself together. I rose to my feet and walked to the closet, asking, "Xavier, y-ya find anything?"

"N-no." Xavier walked toward me. "A-are you alright?"

"I really don't know, man." I swung open the door and spotted a police uniform hanging in the corner. "What the hell is that doin' here?"

"Dunno," he replied.

"This ain't from some party store." I stepped forward and ran my hand down the fabric. "This shit's real! Let's find what we need and get the hell outta here!"

Both of us walked to the two cardboard boxes. In the first box, there was a tobacco pipe, a few notebooks, two bottles of cologne, a bottle of whiskey, and a candle stick. So in other words: nothing important. However, I couldn't say the same thing about the second box. I pulled out a handmade turtle made of clay and a photo album.

"Hey, Xavier, check this out." I spun the turtle over and saw 'Zeke Jenkins' was carved into its belly. "Zeke?!"

"What?!" Xavier jumped back.

"Zeke's names on this thing. I don't think it's a coincidence we're here." I dropped the turtle then flipped through the photo album.

The first few pages were filled with photos of happy looking groups of people, but further down all there was were newspaper clippings.

"What is it?" Xavier peered into the book.

"Old newspapers." I held the lighter up to it. "'Bloody, Bloody Bijou strikes again.'" I flipped back to the family photos and stopped at a young boy smiling.

"Can I see?" Xavier asked.

I showed him the picture. "You know who that is?"

He shrugged.

"I think this is Leon as a kid." I took another look. "Dude actually looked like he was happy."

At that point, it was more than obvious to me Leon was hiding something. There was no way in hell he was gonna tell me himself, so I stuffed the book down the front of my pants and then walked toward the exit of the room. Leon never talked about himself or his past. I'd always known he was missing a few screws, but learning he had some type of connection to the serial killer who killed my parents made my knees so rubbery I could barely stand.

"Where are we? And just what the hell happened to him?" I asked myself.

."Happened to who?" Tabitha asked as I opened the door.

"Oh, nobody." I turned back toward Xavier. "I'm just talking to myself."

"Oh, right." She turned to Sean who shrugged. "Well, we didn't see anything, so we're gonna go find Leon."

After finding out the living room was empty, I looked to the staircase on our right. "I don't think anything is in this damn house."

Sean held his lighter up and headed up a staircase. The rest of us followed. I thought about telling them about the voice I heard and the bloody axe I saw in the room. But I just couldn't bring myself to do it. They were already worried about me, so I didn't see any need to put more stress on them, especially with all the other problems we had. Besides, I wasn't about to risk Leon finding out. I mean, that dude would've taunted me until his heart stopped.

Plus, my thoughts wouldn't stop going back to the hallucinations. To tell the truth, the axe didn't scare me as much as that voice did. There was something about it that just sent shards of ice slicing through my skin. It was like I heard someone say the same thing before.

Sean reached the second floor. "Leon?"

Leon poked his head out of a door on the right. "Y'all find anything?"

"Nah, we ain't found jackshit." Sean replied.

Leon opened the door wider. "Alright, help me search this room. I already searched the one across from this one."

After Sean, Tabitha, Xavier, and I walked into the room, we realized there was nothing inside its dark, dusty, four walls but countless cardboard boxes and a mattress in the corner.

"We gotta dig through all this?" Sean asked.

"No." Leon snatched a box and emptied it out. "Just dump everything on the ground. Don't worry about putting anything back."

"Leon..." I did what he'd just done. A wrench, a screw driver, and other tools fell to the floor. "Where are we?"

"Just followed some guy here." Leon dumped out another box. "I know he's loaded."

"How? And who is this guy?" I asked. "And this is the ghetto. If this fool is loaded then why doesn't he live in the suburbs?"

Leon's lips curled. "Don't know. Don't care."

"And..." I made eye contact with him. "Why the hell is there a cop uniform in the closet downstairs?"

"What?!" Sean gasped.

"What do you mean a—" Tabitha began.

Leon picked up a wrench and threw it at a picture on the wall, cracking its glass. "Shut up!"

I stared at Leon. "What are we really doin' here?"

"I told you," he seethed, "tryna find money."

"None of this makes any sense." I shook my head and continued emptying the boxes.

"Just trust me, you dumbfuck." Leon kicked a box.

Besides Xavier, who stood near the doorway, our group emptied out every box we could find. 15 minutes later, the room was a mess of cardboard and old junk.

"There's nothing here!" I shouted.

"Keep ya voice down, dickwad!" Leon whispered angrily.

"You said this place was abandoned!" I stomped toward him.

"It is at this particular moment." Leon turned toward the mattress and then pulled out his knife.

"What are you doin'?" I stepped back.

"Just watch." Leon walked toward the mattress and dropped to his knees. "Bring that damn lighter over here."

"Why?" I walked over to him, held my lighter above his head, and watched closely.

Leon pointed to a seam on the mattress. Then he cut a hole in the fabric and pulled a paper bag out. "Hold the lighter."

"There..." Just when I was about tell him we should head out, I watched him pull out a brown paper bag—a brown paper bag filled with rolls of 100 dollar bills.

"Didn't I tell ya, nutcase?" Leon grinned.

"Sean, Tabitha, come check this out!" I yelled.

"What is it?" Tabitha walked over and gasped as soon as she looked inside the bag.

"Holy shit!" Sean pulled out a roll. "There's gotta be at least 15,000 bucks in here! Probably more!"

"This still seems odd." I eyed the money. "This city is too big to—"

"Got it!" Leon pulled out a small wooden box from the mattress. "I knew this shit was here!"

"What is that?" I leaned forward.

Leon spun around and dropped the box. Ziploc bags filled with jewelry spilled out onto the floor.

"Shit! Look what ya made me do!" He scrambled to pick everything up.

"That was you!" I spat.

"Just shut up!" Leon finished putting everything back inside the box. "There should be one more thing."

"What?" Tabitha asked.

"It's a small book." Leon put the wood box inside an old knapsack he found.

"Wadda ya mean a book?" Sean tucked the bag of cash down his pants.

"A photo album actually." Leon tossed two boxes across the room. "It's gotta be—"

There were footsteps. Leon glanced over his shoulder and froze. I turned around. The man with dreadlocks was standing at the door. And he had a knife in his hand. He stepped forward. Another man stepped out from behind him.

"Ain't never seen none of y'all niggas 'round here," said the man with the knife. "See, I'm Tony, and this here is Kiki. We know everybody 'round here." He pointed the blade at Sean. "Y'all lost?"

"They ain't lost," Kiki said.

Tony darted toward Sean, Tabitha, and Xavier. Kiki rushed at me and sent a punch straight into my mouth. When I got a hold of myself, I jumped to my feet. Then threw a left hook to his face. Before I could throw another one, Leon tackled Kiki to the floor.

I ran behind Tony and slammed his skull into the wall. He spun around and sliced the skin below my eye. Blood dripped down my cheek. It didn't stop me from letting my knuckles make contact with his mouth. Feeling my blood rush, I swung again. Another direct hit. Before I knew it, I was sending blow after blow to his head. His body swayed. One final, hard swing later and he dropped to his knees. All outta breath, I wrapped his own dreadlocks around his neck. Then I pulled until he fell flat on his stomach.

I tightened my grip. "Sean! The knife!"

Sean rushed over and grabbed it from Tony's hand. After he placed it against Tony's neck, I let go.

"Stop!" Kiki flailed his limbs.

"Leon, that's enough!" I watched Leon strangle the life out of Kiki. "Ya hear me? You're gonna kill him!"

The moonlight coming through the window behind me shined in Leon's face, creating an evil, glowing glare in his eyes. "I know!"

"Stop!" I shouted.

"Hey, dreadlocks." Leon chuckled and brought his knee down on Kiki's elbow. "Tony right?"

"Watchoo want, bitch ass cracka'?" Tony spat.

"Watch this." Leon pulled on Kiki's forearm until the bone snapped.

"Fuck!" Kiki screamed in pain. "Fuck man!"

"Oh shit!" Tony tried to break loose.

"I don't think so." Leon walked over to Tony and kicked him in the head until the punk was out cold. "Let's get outta here. We're gonna have to search this place later."

"But—" Sean began.

"What'd I just say?!" Leon stormed out the room.

"He's right!" I looked to Sean. "We gotta go!"

Tabitha pointed to the gangbangers. "But what about—"

"Forget 'em!" Sean and I bolted out of the room.

"Xavier, come!" I yelled.

The five of us dashed out that house as quick as we could. But what we saw made us stop short—three more gangbangers were waiting for us outside.

"Yeah..." Leon stepped back.

One of them pointed a broken bottle at me. "Y'all niggas supposed to be dead!"

"Fuck this! Let's get outta here!" Leon bolted off to the left.

We followed him into a nearby alleyway. Death threats echoed between its brick walls. My chest rattled. I glanced behind us—all I saw were angry scowls.

Leon made it to the end of the alley. He bolted across the empty street. As the rest of us neared the end, a thug grabbed Tabitha's hair. Sean pushed him into a group of trashcans. Then, as cars started to fill the road, we ran toward Leon. I made it. Tabitha made it. Then came Sean.

But Xavier didn't. He was still in the middle of the road. And a car was headed straight for him.

I didn't even give it a second thought. Before I realized what I was doing, I pushed him out of the way. He fell on the concrete, and his body rolled to safety. But then the headlights shined in my eyes. And for a second, my heart stopped.

The driver hit the brakes. But by then it was too late. He had already slammed into me, and I was already halfway in the air. Tires screeched. Everything turned upside down. Then it all stopped. And I fell. Straight into the windshield, shattering its glass. Soon I found myself rolling off the hood and flying across the street.

"Shit dude!" Sean shouted.

"Oh my God!" Tabitha put her hands over her face.

I rose to my feet and shuddered, trying to shake off what just happened. While I clutched the gash on my shoulder, Xavier and I limped to the sidewalk.

"What's wrong with ya?! You're gonna get us all killed!" Leon took a good, long look at the gangbangers waiting for the road to clear. "Get your god damn head straight!"

Leon sprinted down the sidewalk. Tabitha and Sean ran after him, both of them looking back at me with frowns on their faces.

Leon had already disappeared. However, Sean and Tabitha were nice enough to wait for me.

One of the gangbangers dashed across the street, yelling, "Where y'all think y'all's goin'?!"

"Where'd Leon go to?!" I panted, my legs shaking like someone injected acid into them.

Sean led us through the yards of the houses on that street. At the very last one, he turned and sprinted through the side yard toward a gate. By the time we reached it, Leon was already on the other side.

Sean and Tabitha hopped over. Then I started to do the same. But as I was halfway up the fence, the upstairs house light above me turned on. An old woman stuck her head out the window. When she saw me, she howled for her husband like some god damn coyote. Then he appeared. And so did the 12 gauge shotgun in his hands.

Right after I made it to the other side, Xavier jumped over. And as we ran, I was sure we'd be shot dead. But that old man never squeezed the trigger. In fact, when I glanced back he was aiming his gun at the gangbangers. I guess he figured our group was in trouble and wanted to help.

Sean poked his head over the fence. He reached out his hand and pulled me over. Xavier found a hole in the bottom of the fence just big enough for his tiny body to slip through. As soon as my feet hit the ground, we dashed after Leon through another side gate.

"Does he even know where he's goin'?" I looked up to see the edge of a large forest area.

"No idea!" Sean trailed Leon through a group of moss covered trees. "Just keep runnin'!"

About five minutes later, we jumped over a small stream of water, stopped near a large boulder, and then caught our breath.

Seconds later Leon came out from behind a fallen tree and walked straight toward me. Then he grabbed me by my shirt, yelling, "This god damn bullshit with Xavier needs to stop!"

I pushed him off and stepped back. "What's the problem now?!"

"This kid is gonna get himself killed." Leon turned around and walked away. "I ain't dealin' with this forever!"

"The hell is he talkin' about?" I asked.

Tabitha turned to Sean before looking back to me. "I think he just means you shouldn't be so rash, ya know?"

Sean grabbed her arm and stepped over a fallen tree.

"I swear Leon's nuts!" I turned to Xavier. "Let's just go back home."

Xavier ignored me and walked in the wrong direction. There was a blank stare in his teary eyes. "I ain't goin' back there."

"Xavier, that ain't the right way, buddy!" I trailed after him.

"I don't belong here!" He bolted off into the forest, his voice cracking.

I ran after him. "Xavier!"

"The hell?! Stop him!" Leon ran after me.

I ran after Xavier. Every part of me was exhausted, but I couldn't let him escape. If he got away, I was sure he wouldn't find his way back home.

"Stop you idiot!" Leon began to catch up with me.

"Come back!" After jumping over a small boulder, a small bush got tangled between my legs and sent me tumbling over my own feet. As soon as I caught my balance, I tripped over an old tire and slammed my face into the base of a tree.

"Just leave Xavier!" Sean shouted.

"Xavier!?" I ran through a sea of dead leaves, watching Xavier disappear into the forest.

"Gotcha, jackass!" Leon tackled me to the ground.

Sean rushed up and held down both my arms.

"Let me go!" I thrashed my body.

Leon picked up a large tree branch. "Just hold him down!"

"I can't. He's too—" Sean began.

I pushed away Sean and rose to my feet. But then Leon swung. That branch hit me so hard I lost control over my body and fell straight to the dirt.

Leon—who was fading from my vision—walked over and lifted my legs up. "We need to get him home before he wakes up."

Chapter Twelve

People of Interest

Present day...

Officer Tanner strutted down the police station corridors, but came to an abrupt halt when he noticed Mercer peeking through an office window. "Boss what are—"

"Hush, Rook." Officer Mercer pressed his ear to the office door of Officer Zeke. "I know Zeke's up to no good."

"Who's Zeke?" Officer Tanner scratched his head.

Officer Mercer turned his head. "Who's Zeke? Zeke is—"

Officer Zeke swung the door open and stuck his head out. "C-can I help y'all?"

Mercer's nostrils flared. "You sure as hell can't, ya sneaky little rat."

There was silence. The two locked eyes. There was nothing more that

Mercer wanted to do than to rip Zeke's head off.

Suddenly, an old, bearded officer poked his head around the corner. "Everyone doing okay here?"

"You…" Zeke looked at the scar on the whiskery officer's right hand, sweat dripping down his face like a pig in summer. "I…" He turned back to Officer Mercer and trembled.

"What's the problem?" The bearded officer let out a heartfelt chuckle.

Zeke swallowed a wad of spit and then ran off down the hall, nearly tripping over himself.

"Did I say something?" The elder officer scratched his head.

"No, that's Zeke. He's always like this," Mercer seethed, shaking his head. "Looks like its gettin' worse." He turned to the senior officer and extended his hand. "Say, don't think I've ever gotcha name."

"It's Officer Walker." Officer Walker shook Mercer's hand.

"Crazy. I've seen ya 'round here plenty of times. Just never had a conversation with ya." Officer Mercer said.

After Mercer, Officer Tanner shook Officer Walker's hand, giving a wimp grip. "Tanner."

"Nice to meetcha," Officer Walker said. "Anyway, I'm off the clock." He strutted back to the lobby. "And tell that Zeke kid to take a chill pill."

"Oh yeah, that reminds me," Mercer said, "there's a domestic disturbance over on Antelope Boulevard."

"Should we check it out?" Tanner asked.

"Not today. We got other things to do." Officer Mercer marched toward a muscular officer who had a scar near his eye. "Hey, big guy, there's a situation on Antelope Boulevard. Think ya can handle it?"

"Yeah, I...got it," the brawny officer said.

Because the brawny officer took a lot of pauses when he talked, Officer Mercer thought he was a little off. "Good. Sharon'll give ya the details."

"Right then." The muscular officer walked back toward the lobby.

"Jesus, what is that guy made of?!" Officer Tanner compared his own arm to the bulging biceps he had just seen.

"Yup. Seen 'em around a few times." Officer Mercer took a sip of his coffee. "He don't talk much though."

"It's Tanner, Boss," the rookie officer responded.

Mercer's eyes glazed with superiority. "What's that?" The veteran officer tossed his disposable coffee cup in the trash and then marched toward the lobby's exit, his boots slapping against the tile.

"M-my names Tanner, Boss." Tanner avoided eye contact with the much more experienced officer.

"Alright, Tanner, looks like we need to teach you some respect," Mercer started. "Here in VHPD, we have a little something called..." A surge of disgust spread through his chest when something outside the police station caught his eye.

"Boss, everything alright?" Officer Tanner asked

"Yeah, everything's just fine," Mercer gritted.

Zeke made his reentrance into the station and put his head down.

Officer Mercer exited the department with a scowl on his face.

Officer Tanner followed. "What's the deal with that guy, Boss?"

A chilly breeze brushed against Mercer while he walked down the concrete steps. "Just follow me, and we'll talk."

Tanner scratched his head. "Alright, whatever you say."

After Mercer reached his squad car, he swung open the driver's side door. "That guy is a filthy rat."

Officer Tanner entered from the other side.

"Zeke," Mercer said, shaking his head. "Officer Zeke."

"What'd he do?"

"He was at a murder scene one night."

"What's so strange 'bout that, Boss? He's an officer ain't he?"

"Yeah, but this was different." Mercer looked out the window toward the police station. "There's no reason he should have been there. He was there before any of us, and he wasn't even dressed in uniform." Mercer turned back and looked Tanner in the eyes. "I think he did it."

"How does that prove—"

"It doesn't but listen." Officer Mercer started the car and switched on the windshield wipers when he noticed the rain that was starting to pour down. "Bloody, Bloody Bijou."

"Bloody Bijou, the serial killer?! You're telling me you think—"

"I don't think; I know. Zeke thinks we suspect he did it and that we're all out to get him. Which we do..." For a moment, the grimace on Mercer's face turned to a smirk. "And which we are."

"Are ya serious?! How come nobody's caught him yet?!"

"Because there ain't 'nuff evidence and he's a sneaky 'lil fuck. His damn aunt defended him until the day she died."

"Do you think he killed—"

"His aunt? No, no, the autopsy reported she croaked from a heart attack. Interestingly enough, she ran a foster home, and three of her boys disappeared. Nobody's ever found any trace of 'em."

"What's that got to do with this, Boss?"

"Two of them three boys almost got killed by Bijou. And wanna hear the icing on the cake?"

"What's that?"

"We sent down a couple of officers to check things out." Officer Mercer stroked his chin. "Not only would nobody say a word about them boy's disappearing, but we couldn't find a single scrap of evidence they were ever there, even though I have two officers who swear they were." He crossed his arms. "No documents, no clothes, not even a god damn toothbrush. It's like them boys just vanished off the face of the planet." While the rain poured down harder, he turned up the speed of the windshield wipers. "The strangest part about it was the fact that our records of them boys also disappeared. It's like they never even existed."

"God damn." Officer Tanner tilted his cap. "That's actually kinda scary, Boss. It's like an episode of Unsolved Mysteries!"

"Yeah, and there's more." Mercer shook his head. "Zeke's parents were never found either. Both of 'em was presumed to be dead right after they—"

An officer outside tapped on the window. "Sir, we got a lead on that case you've been workin' on."

As soon as Officer Mercer rolled down the window, rain bounced off the edge of the glass and into the ride. "Which one? Oh yeah, by the way, Lucas, this here is Rook..." Rolling his eyes, he removed the key from the ignition. "I mean, Officer Tanner."

"Nice to meetcha," said Officer Lucas.

"Now about that case?" Officer Mercer asked.

"I was talking about those two bodies found in the trunk of that car," Officer Lucas said.

"The one dumped in the river, Boss?" Officer Tanner asked.

"Yeah, that's the one!" Officer Lucas put his umbrella over his head and then leaned against the side of the cruiser.

"Well, watcha got for me?" Officer Mercer pulled out a pack of cigarettes.

"You know chief's gonna have your head if he catches you smoking in the cruiser again," Officer Lucas smirked. "You already got caught with those bottles of vodka in your office yesterday."

"What he don't know won't hurt him." Officer Mercer lit the cigarette and then blew out a trail of smoke. "Or me."

"Anyway, we got a guy who was stopped a few days ago. Was a known meth dealer." Officer Lucas said.

"So how does this help me?" Officer Mercer slumped down in his seat.

"His car was searched. Officers found a few meth pipes and *this* in the trunk." Officer Lucas pulled out a plastic evidence bag containing a brown leather wallet. "It's a wallet belonging to one of the victims."

Officer Mercer stepped outside. A huge rain drop immediately put out his cigarette. "Where is he?"

"In the interrogation room," Officer Lucas responded.

Officer Mercer stopped. "Alright, Tanner, let's go."

The three officers headed back to the police station. Along the way, Officer Lucas gave Officer Mercer and Officer Tanner details of the suspect's criminal history. After Officer Lucas had gone to retrieve the case files, Officer Mercer filled Officer Tanner in on why there were so many meth dealers around the city.

"Keep forgettin' you just transferred," he said. "Started poppin' up a few years ago, but it all went to hell so damn fast that I had to personally arrest a good friend of mine." With the ache in his chest, he just managed to fight off the sadness that was trying to take over his usual stone face. "And then my brother overdosed a few years back. Walked in his apartment and saw his body in the corner. Eyes rolled in the back of his head. Had the needle still stickin' out his arm."

"Jesus!" Officer Tanner gasped.

"Yup," Officer Mercer replied, grabbing a box of donuts off the front desk. "Put my hand on his shoulder, and he just fell over."

Just then Officer Lucas returned, flipping a manila envelope in the air. The three of them continued down the hall until they stopped outside a large double sided mirror. On the other side, a young black male in a red, baseball jersey sat across from an interrogating officer.

"The guy's names Jerome." Officer Lucas pointed through the window.

All three officers peered through the glass and into the room, watching their co-worker try to get information.

"So what happened? Drug deal gone bad? Owed you some money?" the interrogating officer asked.

"You dumbass pigs got the wrong guy! I ain't do shit! Ain't never killed nobody, blood!"

"Oh come on! We found one of the victim's wallets in the trunk of your car!"

"I jacked that shit, you stupid mother fucker! I jacked that shit off a nigga on the bus!"

"Which bus?"

"I don't remember! That shit was weeks ago!" Jerome rubbed his chin. "I think it was the Number 23!

"What'd he look like?"

"He looked like a god damn nigga!"

"And I suppose Santa Claus put that meth pipe in your trunk too as an early Christmas gift?"

"I ain't playin' with ya!" Jerome spat furiously. Blood rushed to his face, making it look like an oversized cherry. The angered thug pounded his fist on the table several times.

On the other side of the mirror, Officer Mercer rubbed his chin, closely examining the interrogation. He turned to Lucas. "Ya check that wallet for fingerprints yet?"

"Not yet, but I'll get that to forensics." Lucas trailed off down the hall and then disappeared around the corner.

After Officer Mercer tapped on the mirror, the interrogating officer rose from his seat and exited the room.

"Why don't cha take a 'lil break, buddy," Officer Mercer said. "I'll take this one for ya."

"You sure about that? He ain't cracking." The officer lifted his cap and scratched his head. "He knows we found the wallet in his car. And I told him we found his finger prints in the victim's car but he ain't buyin' it."

"Alright, I'mma see what I can get out of him." Officer Mercer moved the box of donuts toward the officer. "Here take one."

"Thanks, but no thanks. Wife says I'm startin' to get fat." The officer rubbed his gut and headed down the hall.

"Ain't we all," Officer Tanner shouted.

Mercer entered the interrogation room, meeting eyes with Jerome.

"I am Officer Mercer." Mercer took a seat at the metal table.

"The hell does this mean for me?" Jerome leaned forward.

"That's gonna depend on you." Officer Mercer slid the box of donuts to the center of the table.

"Lemme get one! I ain't ate since way before y'all brang me here!"

"Take as many as ya like."

Jerome snatched the box and stuffed his mouth with donut after donut. One after another, he just wouldn't stop consuming the pastries as if his stomach was a black hole in deep space. Soon his face was covered in sprinkles and different colors of frosting.

"So ya like donuts do ya?"

"Hell yeah. I mean, who don't?" Bits of food sprayed from Jerome's mouth.

"You ever been to that donut shop near the high school?"

"Ya mean Reid High?"

"Yup, that's the one."

"God damn! I went to Reid! Used to hit up that donut joint every day befo' class!"

"You went to Reid? Got a sister who went there back in the day."

"No shit!? She ever tell ya 'bout this mean ol', stanky history teacher named Mrs. Cookson?"

"Think she mentioned her once or twice back when she was a sophomore."

"Aww shit! I remember this one time my nigga snuck into class 'fo she got there. Nigga put a whole box of laxatives up inside her coffee. Bitch was up in the bathroom 'til school ended!"

"Small world," Officer Mercer chuckled, flipping through the envelope. "Now let's get started."

"Already told y'all—"

"I'm thinkin' you were tryin' to sell those two guys some meth and they didn't pay up what they owed."

"That shit ain't—"

"No? So what happened? You couldn't take their money so you took their lives?"

"I'm tellin' ya I didn't—"

"You panicked and put 'em both in the trunk of their own car, right?

Drove 'em into the river and just left 'em there?" Mercer cleared his throat. "Look, we're all human, and we all make mistakes, but when we do, we have to pay for them." His eyes met with Jerome's. "Shit, I'd be scared too, but *you* don't need to be. You got me here to help ya."

"That ain't what happened!" Jerome slammed both of his fists down on the table, rattling the empty box of donuts.

"So what *did* happen?" Mercer opened the envelope and slid a photograph of one of the decayed bodies to the other side of the table.

Jerome cupped his hands over his face. "Aww shit! The fuck is this?!"

"Why don't *you* tell me?"

"I told y'all I jacked that wallet off a nigga on the bus!"

"The number 33, right?"

"Nah, number 23!"

"Then tell me 'bout this bus," Officer Mercer said. "And you better make it quick. It's almost my lunch."

"Alright, blood." Jerome exhaled. "I was headin' back from the strip club, and I got on the bus. I sat in the back next to this nigga, and I jacked the wallet from him. Didn't think he was a murderer, just thought he was a sucker."

"What'd he look like?" Officer Mercer pulled out a pen and pad.

"Had cornrows. Nigga's skin was a 'lil darker than mine and looked like he ain't shaved in 'bout two weeks. Clothes was all dirty." Jerome paused. "And I remember he had on a wife beater. I don't remember nothin' else."

Mercer wrote down everything on the notepad. "So cornrows, skin a 'lil darker than yours, beard, dirty clothes, wife beater? Anything else?"

"Blood, that was over two months ago! You expect me to remember everything?"

"Anybody who can verify this?"

"Nah, I was..." Jerome's eye's widened. "Sarah!"

"Just who the hell is Sarah?"

"She was..." Jerome stomped his foot on the floor. "Damn! That bitch done went off to college down in Texas!"

Officer Mercer started to rise from his seat. "Right, then I guess we're—"

"Marty!"

"Who's Marty?" Officer Mercer sat back down.

"That fat ass bus driver! I know he saw that nigga! Saw him on the bus a few days ago, so I know he's still workin' there! Go ask him ya'self!"

"Marty, the bus driver." Officer Mercer wrote the name down on his pad. "Think I got everything I need."

"C'mon, blood! You ain't gonna let me go?!"

"Not just yet." Officer Mercer rose from his seat and exited the room, slamming the door behind him.

"Didn't tell me you had a sister, Boss," Officer Tanner said, looking through the window.

"What's that?" Officer Mercer asked.

"You was talking about how ya sister went to that Reid High School," Officer Tanner responded.

"Oh yeah," Officer Mercer chuckled. "I don't got a sister."

"Really? So what about him?" Officer Tanner pointed toward Jerome.

"Ya know, I don't think he done it." Officer Mercer looked his partner in the eye.

"Wadda ya talking about, Boss? This guy—"

"When's the last time you was feelin' guilty and felt like eatin'?" Officer Mercer asked. "That guy finished off that entire box of donuts in under 15 minutes."

"But—"

"On top of that, I showed him the pictures of the victim's body. Didn't look guilty. Just reacted like how you'd expect anyone else to react," Mercer grinned.

Officer Tanner scratched his head. "Yeah, but—"

"Let's get down to the bus station." Officer Mercer walked back to the lobby. "I'm gonna test this Marty guy's memory."

Chapter Thirteen

Something Wrong With Me

Present day...

When I opened my eyes, I found myself on the gravel of the junkyard. There was so much damn sweat soaking into my clothes it looked like I'd jumped into a pool. Dried blood had caked onto my shoulder, and the gash under my eye still stung. For a few seconds, my mind was actually at peace. Then everything came back at once. "Where's Xavier?!"

"I'm not sure," Tabitha began. "But I'm sure he'll come back soon, ya know?"

"Sean did ya see him come back?!" I stepped toward him.

'Nah, man I ain't seen him." Sean turned to Tabitha who gave him a stern look. "Yeah, but he's gonna come back soon."

"Where's Leon?!" I looked around the junkyard. "Maybe he—"

"Leon's over there." Tabitha pointed to an old Toyota.

"Been in there all god damn day," Sean said.

Gravel crunched below our shoes while we walked toward the beat up car. Once we got close, I tapped on the window, asking, "Leon the hell you doin'?!"

"Chillin'." He wrapped a pearl necklace around his finger. "Wadda y'all want?"

I pointed to the junkyard exit. "We need to go back to—"

"We ain't goin' nowhere!" Leon jumped outta the car. "We're leavin this shithole in three days."

I pounded my fist on the roof of the car. "I ain't leavin' Xavier here!"

Sean, Tabitha, and Leon did nothing but look at each other.

I stormed off to my side of the junkyard.

As soon as I got near the couch, I pulled out the photo album—it was still tucked in my pants—and placed it under a cushion. After that, I sat down and thought about what to do.

They all hated Xavier. They were glad he was gone. I could tell. I wasn't stupid like they thought I was. They were planning to leave without the two of us. But even if they did leave there was no way I'd leave until I found my brother. What would I do after I found him though?

"I don't really know what to say to him," Sean whispered to Tabitha as they approached me.

"I'm sure he's fine," Tabitha whispered. "Maybe we should focus on leaving for now."

"I know ya want him gone." I looked them. "But I'm not gonna leave this place without him."

"All we want is for you to come back to us." Sean looked me dead in the eyes. "You ain't like ya used to be. You've been actin' strange."

"Wadda ya mean I've been actin' strange?!" I slapped the arm of the sofa.

"I don't mean it like that it's just..." Sean turned to Tabitha.

"Don't worry about it." I gritted my teeth. "I got it."

"Nah, we just..." Sean sighed, putting his head down.

"We still got some of this left." Leon tossed the bottle of vodka to our feet. "Maybe it's just what he needs."

Sean and Tabitha eventually calmed me down. And soon after that, we drank until the sun went down. But Xavier was still missing. I couldn't understand how Sean, Tabitha, and Leon stayed so calm about it. It made me wonder if they did something to him.

"How 'bout Montana?" Sean took a swig of vodka.

"Wadda we..." Leon belched. "Wadda we gonna do in Montana?"

"We haven't even talked about how we're gonna get out of here," Tabitha said. "We don't even have a car."

"So what if someone else's just disappeared?" Leon responded.

"Don't think w-we should be cealin' stars…" Sean covered his mouth and let out a puff of air from his nostrils. "I mean, stealin' c-cars and shit."

"Got any better ideas?" Leon killed the last of the vodka.

"There's a train…" Sean started.

"So stealin' a whole tamn drain…" Leon cackled at his own mistake. "I mean, a whole damn train is better?!"

"We ain't gonna steal it." Sean looked like he was gonna puke. "We can h-hide in one of them b-boxcars."

"Well, shit," Leon said. "I don't even know where those things go."

"I think they go to Southern California," Tabitha said.

"Southern California?" Leon rubbed his chin. "Well, why not?" A glaze took over his eyes when he turned to Tabitha. "Sean, think ya can g-get more kerosene? Fires dyin' down."

"Yeah, sure." Sean headed toward it.

Leon walked toward us, taking a seat next to Tabitha. "What's up sexy?" The smell of hard liquor trailed off his breath. "Ya look kinda nice right now."

"Yeah," Tabitha said softly. She turned her head away.

"Leon! Knock that shit off!" I shouted.

"Shut ya god damn mouth!" Leon turned back to Tabitha and kissed her neck.

"Leon, please stop," Tabitha cried.

"Oh p-please. Ya know ya like that shit." Leon pressed his hand against her breast.

"Fuck off!" I stood up and threw Leon to the gravel.

"What's goin' on?" Sean ran over with the can of kerosene in his hand.

"This asshole's 'bout to end up dead!" Leon rushed at me and hit me square in the mouth.

"The fuck?!" I tackled Leon to the ground and let one fly right in his face.

"Stop it!" Tabitha shouted.

Leon clawed at my shoulder wound. His nasty trick left me howling in pain until I broke free. And then all my anger came out at once. It's like I wasn't even me. Before I knew it, I was unloading on Leon like a World War 1 machine gun. I picked up a nearby brick. And then smashed it into his face. Repeatedly.

"Oh my God! You're gonna kill him! Stop it! Stop it! Stop it!" Tabitha screeched. "Sean, stop him!"

"Holy shit! Stop it!" Sean ran up and pulled me off of Leon. "What the f-fuck's wrong with you?!" He gripped the sides of his head. "What's wrong with you?!"

"I just..." I looked over to Leon to see his face was a bloody pulp. "Dunno what happened."

Sean walked toward my direction. He put his hands on my shoulder and looked me in the eyes. "There's somethin' wrong with ya."

"No!" I pulled away from him. "I'm fine! I just—"

"No, you ain't!" Sean eyes locked with mine. "You don't even see it!"

"Oh fuck!" Leon lifted his bloody, swollen face and sprung to his feet.

"You alright?" Sean walked toward him.

"Get the fuck away from me!" Leon pulled out his knife. "No one fuckin' come near me!"

Sean took another step forward. "I just wanna—"

"I'll stab you!" Leon pointed the blade toward Sean. "Don't touch me!" He ran to the other side of the junkyard and then came back with his knapsack. "I swear to God..." The knife stayed pointed toward Sean, Tabitha, and me. "I'm gonna kill all of ya."

And with that, he dashed out the junkyard and into the night.

"What did ya do?!" Sean shouted. "Wasn't the money in that backpack?! How are we gonna get outta this city now?!"

"He touched Tabitha!" I wiped the blood off my face.

"I know, but," Tabitha cried, "I can't live like this forever!"

"We gotta g-get that cash back." My body still shakin', I looked at Tabitha and then Sean. "I think I know where he's gonna go."

"No!" Sean headed for the junkyard exit. "We're gonna get that shit now!"

"Did you see that knife?!" I shouted.

Tabitha wiped her eyes and then crossed her arms. "He's right Sean."

I walked toward the couch, pulled out Leon's photo book, and then walked back to them. "I wanna show you guys something I don't think Leon wanted us to see."

Chapter Fourteen

Want to get Away

Ten years earlier...

A trip to the hospital for Carl and Brandon and they were good as new. Well, almost. Brandon's so many bandages on his face he looked like he'd been mummified, and Carl was left walking with a limp. However, they were still up to their usual crap. In fact, they were a helluva lot more hostile than before. Agatha, on the other hand, went about her business like nothing happened.

Of course, the cops were called and we were all given a stern talking to about how young boys should behave, but that was it. In some other city, Agatha probably would've had to have pulled strings so that the home wouldn't get shut down. But no. The police didn't care.

They never did.

"Alright, we're leavin' tomorrow night after everyone's asleep." I sat down on the front porch and stretched out my legs.

"Yeah, but where are we gonna go?" Xavier asked.

"Dunno," I said. "I was thinking about hidin' somewhere for a little while."

"But where? We'll just be homeless?" Xavier cried.

"We won't be homeless." I looked at him and Mike. "We just gotta find our way."

"What about—" Xavier stopped short.

 Brandon stormed out the house with his middle finger raised. "Watcha punks lookin' at?!"

Carl came out a few seconds later. "That's right ya better keep ya asses there, ya pussies!"

"I swear this guy..." I said.

Suddenly, Xavier pointed at a police cruiser that had just parked in front of the house. "It's Zeke! He's back!" He rushed back into the house.

I tugged on Mike's shirt and then followed Xavier to the backyard. If Officer Zeke found us, I was sure we would be killed.

"What does he want?!" Xavier ran onto the grass.

"I think he knows we know he did it!" I shouted.

Mike, Xavier, and I sprinted by a row of wilted rose bushes and to the wooden fence that separated the front and the backyard.

"Is he gonna kill us, too?" Xavier's voice shook.

I looked through a hole in the fence. Zeke got outta his cruiser and strolled to Brandon and Carl.

"Dunno," I said, "but that's another reason we gotta leave."

"Wadda they doin'?" Xavier tried climbin' the fence.

"Don't!" I pulled him back down. "He'll see ya!"

"So how am I gonna see?"

"I'll tell you." When I looked through the hole again, they had all disappeared. "Shit! They went in the house!"

"Where do we go?!" Xavier trembled, looking around the yard. "What about in the forest behind that fence?"

It was a good hiding spot. But as soon as I started to run toward it, the sliding glass door swung open.

"Hey, y'all! I just wanted to have another word with both of ya." Officer Zeke walked down the concrete steps with Brandon and Carl smirking behind him.

"Wha—" I choked on my own spit. "Wh-what do ya want with us?"

"Just wanna talk with y'all." Zeke pulled out a pen and pad.

"Ya already did!" Xavier yelled.

Zeke approached the three of us slowly. "I know, but I just—"

"Arrest all of 'em!" Brandon yelled out. "They're causin' nothin' but trouble!"

"No, no, I'm not here to arrest anyone." A grin formed on Zeke's face. "Brandon and Carl, right? Why don't y'all go play in the front?"

Brandon and Carl frowned and then disappeared into the house.

Zeke stared at Mike. "You too, big guy."

Xavier stomped his foot to the dirt. "He can stay!"

"Well, I just thought y'all'd want some privacy," Officer Zeke said.

"He's fine." I crossed my arms.

"Okay, then." Zeke flipped one of the pages of his pad. "Well, we've decided we're gonna take y'all to the next city over." He wiped a couple of drops of sweat from his brow. "Over in Stonemoor, so you boys will be safer."

"W-when?" Xavier asked.

"Well, I was just 'bout to make arrangements with Agatha and get y'all outta here by tonight," Officer Zeke responded.

"Who's gonna be takin' us?" Xavier asked.

"I'll be takin' y'all as soon as I talk to Agatha 'bout this," he said.

"What 'bout tomorrow?" I was convinced that he was gonna try and kill us.

"Actually, I was hopin' to get y'all outta this city as soon as possible," he responded, "since we dunno when or if the killer's gonna strike again."

"We..." I stopped and looked at Mike. "Just wanna say goodbye to our friends."

117

"Well, if that's the case then it would have to be first thing in the morning." Zeke turned around and walked back to the house. "Why don't y'all stay here while I go find Agatha?"

After Zeke was gone, we stood there in silence trying to figure what to do. If we didn't leave that night, then I was sure we were gonna end up dead somewhere.

"We gotta get outta here tonight!" I whispered.

"He'll be lookin' for us though!" Xavier peered through the house window.

"We'll hide in there." I pointed at the forest. "We'll come back out after a few days."

"In the woods?!" Xavier asked. "How are we even gonna get food?"

"We can take some from the house before we leave," I responded. "Either that or we just gotta go without it for a while."

"Shouldn't we tell Mike..." Xavier put his thumb to his lip. "'Bout..."

I turned to Mike and told him about the situation, about how our parents were murdered, about how we thought it was Officer Zeke, about everything. He seemed like he was more concerned about getting us to safety than he was surprised about the whole thing.

The three of us walked back to the sliding glass door just to see Brandon and Carl on the other side. Just by the smirks on their bratty faces, I could tell the two troublemakers were cooking up something awful.

Brandon aimed an imaginary gun at my forehead. Then he mouthed the word 'bang' and squeezed the trigger.

Xavier opened the door and stepped inside. "Just leave us alone."

"You're gonna die," Carl whispered.

"Get outta his face." I shoved Carl, making him trip over a stool and fall over backward.

Carl jumped back up and raised his fists, ready to fight. But to my surprise, Brandon put his hand on Carl's shoulder and shook his head, saying, "Not just yet."

Carl glared at me. "But he—"

"What did I just tell you?" Brandon's eyes locked with Carl's.

Xavier stepped forward. "Why don't—"

"Shut your fuckin' mouth before I wire it shut!" Brandon hissed.

"Fuck off!" I grabbed Xavier's wrist and led him across the living room.

"We gotta find Officer Zeke's address." I lowered my voice and headed for the stairs. "Maybe we can go there when he's gone and find something to give to the police."

"Where are we gonna find his address at?" Xavier whispered back.

"Agatha's room." I directed Mike and Xavier's attention to the top of the stairs. "He said he was related to her, so she's gotta have something in her room we can use to find him."

When we got to the top, Agatha's croaky voice could be heard from the room we all slept in.

"There once lived an old woman who lived in a shoe; she had so many children she didn't know what to do. She gave them some broth without any bread, then whipped them all soundly and put them to bed," she read.

There was a sick twist in her laugh while she read that little nursery rhyme to the younger kids. Luckily, it was loud enough to where I could slip into her room without her hearing me. Even then there was a constant pounding in my chest that just wouldn't stop—it got worse when I saw her collection of creepy dolls resting on the furniture in the room. With their emotionless faces, they just made me shudder, but what was funny was the fact there was something even more disturbing in that room of hers. Over on her dresser, a framed portrait of a happy couple and two young boys sat in between two stuffed clowns. As I got closer, I realized that one of the boys in the picture was a younger version of Officer Zeke.

That happy smile on his face just made me sick.

A gentle breeze from the ceiling fan brushed against my neck while I searched the dresser drawers. But soon I realized there was nothing but clothes in each of them.

"What are the two of you doing?" Agatha's voice trailed from the hallway. "Get out of here!"

A moment later, Xavier and Mike's shoes stomped against the staircase. Then the old woman's footsteps came toward the room. For a second, my body froze. But then without thinking, I darted into her closet and closed the door behind me.

Agatha burst into the room and walked to her dresser. She looked through each of the drawers and then spun her head around the room. "Who's been in here?!" The old woman walked back to the door and swung it open. "What have you two been doing?!"

"N-nothin'," Xavier yelled from downstairs.

"Stay out of there and wait for dinner!" Agatha slammed the door shut and walked back to the dresser. "Horrid brats."

I leaned closer and looked through the gap between the closet door and the wall. To my surprise, tears were rolling down her cheeks. It was the first time I'd ever seen anything other than anger from her. The old crone took the portrait off the dresser and sat down on her bed.

"Oh, Clyde and Ely! You both went too soon!" She wiped away the mascara running down her face. "I know that you didn't do it, Zeke. I won't believe any of that nonsense." More tears streamed down her face. "But I really wish your brother would return home. He used to be just the sweetest boy." She buried her face into the portrait. "Our family's fallen apart." The broken hearted woman pulled out a handkerchief and wiped her eyes.

She walked back to the dresser and placed the portrait back where she'd found it. Then she stared at my direction. My veins pumped ice. I held my breath, backed up, and covered myself with a nearby coat.

Her heels tapped against the floor as she walked toward me. The closet door swung open. She moved closer. And closer. And closer. Finally, she placed her hand on the coat I was under. And started to lift the fabric.

"Agatha!" Carl burst into the room. "Xavier tried stealin' ya strawberries!"

"What'd I tell you about coming in here without knocking?" Agatha slammed the closet door shut.

Carl stomped his foot. "But he—"

"Get out!" Agatha screeched.

The door slammed. Both of their footsteps trailed off.

I let out a long stream of air from my lungs. While my legs shook, I pulled the coat off my body and dashed outta the closet. The thought of leaving the room empty handed crossed my mind until I saw a nightstand next to her bed. A small, black, leather address book rested on the top. I walked over and picked it up.

"Let's see now..." I flipped through the pages until I got to the Z section and found Zeke's information.

As soon as I saw his number and address were, I ripped the page out, stuffed it and the book down my pants, and then darted downstairs. Everyone was already settled at the dinner table. I had to hide the address book. There was no telling how much trouble I'd be in if Agatha found out I stole it.

The bottom step I'd broken earlier caught my attention. I bent down, pried the board off, and then slid the address book inside the hollow step. Not too long afterward, I was using my shoe sole to stomp in the wooden board and loose nails back into place.

"What the fuck are you doin', asshole?" Brandon yelled from the kitchen table.

I rose my middle finger up and stuck it around the corner of the stairwell.

"Yeah, fuck you too, jackass!" he shouted.

After I stomped in the last nail, I walked toward the kitchen and returned the glare that Brandon was giving me.

Chapter Fifteen

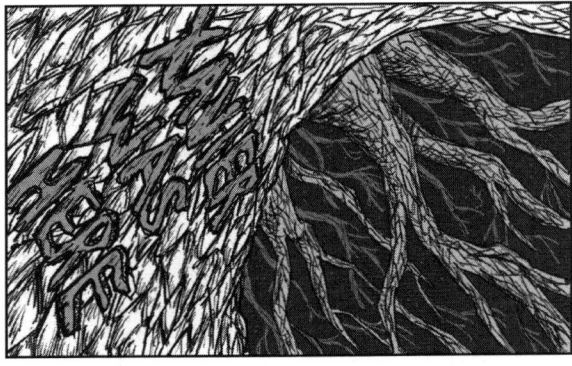

Where's Xavier?

Present day...

I handed the photo album to Sean. "Alright, check this shit out."

"What the hell is this?" he asked.

"You remember that book Leon was looking for?" I said.

"This is it?" Sean handed it back to me.

"Yeah, he's gonna be lookin' for this." I flipped it open to a photograph of Leon and another man. The face of the other man made my stomach flip.

"'A brother is a friend given by nature.'" Tabitha read from the top of the picture. "I didn't even know Leon had a brother."

"Yeah, I didn't either." I had to take a second look because I just thought my eyes were playing tricks on me. They weren't. There, standing next to a very young version of Leon, was Officer Zeke in his police uniform, grinning wide.

It was hard to keep vomit from spewing outta my mouth but I managed.

"What's up with all these newspaper clippings?" Sean flipped toward the back of the album. "'Bloody, Bloody Bijou takes another victim.'" He slouched back into the couch and read one of the articles to himself.

"Bloody Bijou the serial killer?!" Tabitha gasped. "Whatever happened to him?"

"They never caught him." Visions of my mom and dad soaking in pools of blood flashed in front of me. I grabbed the sides of my head and tightened my jaw.

Sean flipped the page and continued. "'More bodies found.'"

"Are you alright? You're sweating, ya know?" Tabitha turned to me. "You look kinda sick."

I nodded my head. "I think I'm just too close to that damn fire."

Sean pointed to a picture on the news article. "Hey, ain't that the same guy?! Leon's brother?! It says here he was a suspect in the murders."

"It is!" Tabitha took the photo album and flipped the page. "This is bizarre! Here's another one: 'Last two surviving Bijou victims disappear.'"

Questions about where Xavier went off to spun in my head until I couldn't focus on Tabitha or Sean's words.

I staggered off the couch. "I gotta…"

"You sure you're alright?" Tabitha asked.

"Yeah, I just..." Stars appeared before my eyes. "I just gotta go clear my head."

Tabitha put her hand to her lip. "Alright."

I treaded outta the junkyard until I reached the lonely road and was able to see the forest. While I stared at the crescent moon hovering above its swaying trees, I wondered if I'd ever see my brother again. What if he was injured? What if he was already dead? After swallowing a wad of spit, I ran across the road, slipped my body through a fence of rusty barbed wire, and headed toward the forest. It didn't matter if Sean and Tabitha left with me. I wasn't leaving until I found my brother.

After passing a few tractors and farm houses, the edge of the forest finally stood in front of me. Birds squawked in the trees above me. Mosquitos buzzed in my ears. Besides those two noises, everything was silent.

"Xavier! We gotta go home, buddy!" Twigs and dead leaves crunched under my shoes while I walked through the trees.

Not long later, all the twists and turns left me walking around in hopeless circles. But all the bushes and fallen trees in that forest couldn't stop me from finding the place where I'd last seen Xavier.

Around two hours later, I came across the same spot I'd seen the night Xavier disappeared. Something told me to turn around and go back home. The feeling that something was wrong was as thick as the trees that surrounded me.

But I didn't listen.

Bushes rustled. When I turned, I saw Xavier crawling out from under them. As soon as he made eye contact with me, he dashed off into the forest again.

"Xavier, stop!" Boulders and fallen trees blocked my path. But they couldn't stop me. At that point, I don't think anything could. "Where the hell are you going?!"

"You said you wouldn't leave!" He dashed around a tree and ran up a hill.

"Are ya..." Suddenly, I stopped dead in my tracks when I saw something resting against the trunk of a tree. It was the same bloody axe that I'd seen on Palm Street, bits of flesh and blood sliding off its handle. A second later, my eyes lost focus of it, and it vanished just like before.

"Just go!" Xavier shouted.

The sight of the axe left me shaking. Along with that, the fact that my brother was acting like I was some kind of monster created a sinking feeling in my chest. We were always together; never letting anything split us apart. I'd have rather spent the rest of my life living like rats with my brother than living like a king without him.

I shook my head, trying to forget the axe, and continued running after Xavier. But by the time we reached the top of the hill, my lungs felt like they'd been filled with boiling water and the injuries on my shoulder and head ached. On the other hand, Xavier was still running at full speed. He turned and ran through a pair of pine trees and left me gasping for breath.

We must've run more than a mile before the two us stopped. Xavier reached an old tree stump and acted bizarre. He laid flat on his back in front of it and then just folded his hands on top of his stomach.

"Stop playin' around!" When I made it to the stump, I leaned against a nearby tree, panting. "There's no time for this!"

"Ya just left me here." A frown appeared on his face. "Ya told me you wasn't gonna do that." He pointed to a nearby tree that had three words carved in its bark. "Ya don't remember?"

I walked to the tree. The words 'Xavier was here' carved into its bark. When I read that, my entire world came crumbling down.

Chapter Sixteen

Becoming a Monster

Ten years earlier...

At midnight the three of us snuck out of the house and into the forest. As we walked uphill through the trees, I imagined the three of us living a long, happy life when I saw that the house was nothing but a pinpoint behind us.

About an hour later, we reached an upside-down wheelbarrow. At that point, Xavier complained about how tired he was. I couldn't really blame him with how late it was, so I told him we'd stop after going on for a little bit longer. But Xavier wasn't having it. He pointed his finger at a small tool shack up ahead and suggested we just sleep there for the night. As much as I wanted to go on, I couldn't argue with the fact that I was as exhausted as he was. Eventually, I gave in and headed toward it.

When I was close enough to grip the shacks metal handle, I pulled the door open. Its hinges creaked while old cobwebs drifted off its wood and into the wind. Two counters sat inside on either side of me. To the left, power tools and electrical equipment sat neatly on the top. To the right, there were a few shovels, a rake, and an old axe.

I picked up the axe and ran my fingers along its rusty blade. "Guess we can stay here for the night."

"So you punks wanna run away?!" Brandon shouted.

I spun around to see him and Carl stepping out from behind a tree. They both pulled out knives.

"Just leave us alone!" Xavier cried.

"I don't think so!" Carl shouted back. "Shut ya mouth!"

"What the hell do ya want?!" I squeezed the axe handle and then walked down the steps of the shed.

Brandon rushed up and pressed the switchblade against Xavier's neck. Mike swung his fist, causing Brandon to fall to the forest floor. Xavier escaped.

While I ran toward them, Carl tackled me to the ground. The axe fell into the leaves. The punk got on top of me. And pointed the knife at my neck. My heart skipped a beat. I gripped the blade, slicing open my palm. Blood spilled into my hair, making him smile. I screamed in pain. And glanced at the reflection of the blade. There was a look of pure fear on my face.

He thrust the knife. It slid deeper into my palm and touched my throat. That wasn't the worst of it—it was his damn laugh banging in my ears. The madman sat there and laughed at the sight of me fighting for my life.

Just then I sent a jab to his nose. Two more jabs to his jaw and he stumbled back and dropped the knife. That loser wasn't gonna finish me off. However, when I saw the hatred in his eyes, it was obvious he wanted to.

I rose to my feet and put my hands up. Before I knew it, both of us were bludgeoning each other's faces in. Flesh ripped. Blood splattered. Knuckles cracked against skin. Both of us sent and received blow after blow, trying to be the last one standing.

Eventually, one of my blows was hard enough to send him down. But it just wasn't hard enough to knock the bloodthirsty stare off his face. He scrambled to the blade. But I swung one final time. His eyes rolled before he even hit the ground.

Behind me, Brandon swung his knife. Mike took the slash straight below the eye. Blood dripped from his face and he fell to the ground. Before Brandon was able to slash Mike again, Xavier grabbed him from behind.

I picked up the axe and sprinted full speed at Brandon. "Xavier hold him!"

"I can't!" he yelled back.

When I reached Brandon, I swung as hard as I could. He ducked. But the axe kept going. And it was headed straight for Xavier.

It sliced right through his neck.

Everything—time, my breath, the bugs crawling in the dirt, the leaves falling, even the particles floating in the air—seemed to stop. Everything but the blood gushing from my brother.

Xavier shook. For a few moments, I thought he'd be okay. But then he plopped to the ground.

And then his eyes rolled back.

"Xavier!" I plucked out the axe. "Xavier! C'mon, buddy!"

The life in his eyes started to fade.

Carl rose from the ground, stumbling over a tree root. "You just killed ya own—"

"Brandon, Carl, Mike! Ya gotta fuckin' help!" I placed my hand over Xavier's wound, trying to stop the blood. "Don't leave him to die!"

Xavier tried to speak. But all that came outta his mouth was a large, oily, red bubble. It popped, sending specs of blood spraying onto my face.

"Fuck this shit!" Brandon bolted through the forest back toward the house.

Carl trailed after him.

"Ya can't leave us like—" I covered my mouth, letting the tears fall from my eyes.

"Oh fuck!" I ripped off my shirt and used it to cover his injury. "Mike!"

Mike dashed toward me and placed his hand on Xavier's forehead.

"Don't leave me here," Xavier whispered softly, tears escaping his eyes. "Please don't let me die."

"I'm not, buddy," I whimpered. "I promise I..."

An eerie stillness filled my brother's pupils. His body became motionless.

"Xavier." I fell back into the tree behind me. "Stop playin' with me, Xavier!" My voice quivered. "Come on, man!"

Mike bent down and put his ear against Xavier's chest. I reached for my brother's arm. But then Mike grabbed my wrist. There was a deep sadness in his eyes.

"What the fuck are ya doing?!" I pulled away from him. "He's gonna be fine!"

After a few more seconds, he shook his head.

"He's my god damn brother!" My voice cracked. "He can't be..."

My little brother had fallen into a permanent sleep, and no matter how many times I shook him, no matter how many times I called his name he wouldn't wake up. Every time I looked at him a part of me withered away.

A few hours later, the sun rose. Mike walked over to the shed, came back with two shovels, and then looked me in the eyes. I collapsed to the ground once I realized what we had to do.

As the sunlight shined in my eyes, I picked myself up, keeping my head down. Mike walked toward me and tried to hand me one of the shovels. I shook my head and grabbed my little brother by the hand, letting my tears hit the leaves below.

About two hours later, we reached the top of the hill. I rested Xavier's bloody body against a tree and then took a good, long look over the edge and at the sun rising above the thousands of trees. Then I just stood there and thought about Xavier; about all the good times, the bad times, and all the times in between.

It didn't help the aching in my chest one bit.

After I grabbed a shovel from Mike, the two of us sank them into the ground, tossing the leaves and dirt behind us. I could barely keep the handle steady.

Before I knew it, the hole was finally deep enough. It was time. I dropped my shovel and walked over to Xavier, his head tilted to the side. The young, lifeless eyes of his seemed like they were staring right through me.

I grabbed his arms and hauled him toward his grave. Piles of leaves gathered under his feet, scrapping against the ground. When I reached Mike, he clutched Xavier's arms and helped me lower the body into the dirt.

A few moments later, we were shoveling dirt over his body until there was nothing left of him to be seen. As Mike patted down the dirt, I looked to the sky and wished it was me being buried instead of him.

I picked up a rusty pocket knife off the ground and used it to carve the words 'Xavier was here' into a nearby tree.

"I only had...one other friend in my life other than you and him."

Mike's low tone caught me off guard. When he turned to Xavier's grave, the stone face he always had melted away. "But I think..." He turned and walked deep into the forest. "Ya gotta find ya own way from here."

Then just like that, he was gone. And I was left all alone. For some reason, I expected Xavier to crawl out and tell me it was all a sick joke. When I finally realized it wasn't, I pressed my back against a nearby tree and just stared at his grave.

Little did I know, my mind would wrap itself in lies to itself just to keep Xavier alive.

Chapter Seventeen

Love and Loss

Present day...

Memories of that night hit me like a speeding Amtrak. I looked back at the tree stump to see he had vanished into the shadows.

My world shattered like a broken wine glass, and I was forced to face reality. At that point, all the women, money, and drugs in the world wouldn't make me feel better.

Even though I knew he was gone, I still looked around for any trace of him. But there was nothing besides the insanity creeping over my shoulder. It was like waking up from an unpleasant dream just to walk through a nightmarish reality. And there was no way to go back to sleep. So in a last ditch effort to keep my mind together, I looked at the words again and hoped they'd disappear.

They didn't.

I collapsed. As soon as I hit the ground, my body slid on the dead leaves that covered the forest floor. While they carried me downhill, any feelings of peace I had were put on lockdown inside a mental prison. The entire world around me seemed to crumble.

Eventually, I stopped near a large boulder. But I didn't get up. I just laid there on my side and sobbed. There wasn't a part of me that didn't wish I would've stayed in my little fantasy land. If I had a choice, I would've rather just kept living the lie that my brain created. But there was no way to, and with Xavier gone life just wasn't worth it. He was one of the only things that kept me going.

After what seemed like forever, I finally rose to my feet. Even though tears blurred my vision, I walked through the trees. I didn't know where I was or where I was going. But there was so much guilt in my chest I didn't even care if I made it back to the junkyard or not.

Sometime later, the city lights came into focus. Then I heard the sound of traffic. Through the trees, I could see the headlights of the cars speeding on the nearby highway. More lights came into view, and I eventually stepped out the forest and onto a sidewalk and tried to figure out where I was.

I continued down the street, treading passed a strip club and an adult book store. Besides the image of Xavier and the bloody axe, my mind was as empty as the very roads I was walking on. That memory wouldn't leave no matter how fast I breathed or how hard I pounded my head.

After I turned around the corner, I caught a glimpse of my reflection in the window of a convenient store. There was no emotion. Nothing that could be recognized as a human expression. In fact, the pure deadness in my eyes made me jump back. When I took a second glance, I saw nothing more than another street rat running through a maze, looking for food that wasn't there.

After a few hours, I was at the junkyard entrance. Dawn broke almost as soon as I saw that Tabitha and Sean were passed out on my couch. There was so much I wanted to say to them both, but I couldn't find the words. I thought they were my friends. How could they hide that from me? Did they think it was funny? Were they screwing with me the whole time?

"Where you been to?" Sean lifted his head and yawned. "Is it mornin' already?"

"You don't look so—" Tabitha stopped short.

"Why the fuck didn't anyone tell me?!" I yelled. "Everyone just thought it was fuckin' funny?!"

Tabitha trembled. "No, w-we—"

"Shut the hell up!" I rushed at the two of them and stopped right in front of Tabitha.

"Shit!" Sean held his hands out, trying to calm me down. "Take it easy, man. We just couldn't—"

I walked over, grabbed him by his collar, and lifted him off the couch. "You knew!" All the tears in my eyes came out at once. "You knew the whole time!"

Chapter Eighteen

Rival Influences

Five years earlier...

Sean entered a gated basketball court and headed toward a tall, black man named Jamal, asking, "What the hell you doin' here?"

"Let's see them hands white boy!" Jamal put his fists up.

"You ready to get whooped again, Jamal?!" Sean threw a cross to Jamal's mouth.

Jamal dodged and hit Sean in the jaw. "Ain't beat me yesterday and ya ain't gon' beat me today, white boy."

"God damn!" Sean slipped on the ice below him and fell into a pile of snow.

"Givin' up already, fool?" Jamal dropped his hands.

"Hell no!" Sean rose back to his feet and charged at Jamal, throwing blow after blow.

Jamal dodged every punch Sean threw. "Yo' ass really ain't cut out for this." He threw a jab to Sean's forehead, knocking him down again. "Alright, take them gloves off. That's enough for today."

"Oh come on!" Sean pounded his boxing gloves together. "We're just gettin' started!"

"Nah, I gotta stop. Hurt my shoulder the other day at the gym," Jamal said.

"Fine," Sean responded.

"Besides ya need to practice yo' damn foot work," Jamal said. "If someone wanna jump, they won't play fair like I do."

"Gotcha." Sean brushed the snow off his jeans. "By the way, how much are you benchin' now?"

"Just hit 225," Jamal boasted.

"Stop lyin'!" Sean lightly hit Jamal in the chest.

"Ain't lyin', fool." Jamal removed his gloves then shook his head. "Oh yeah, you hear 'bout that fight with Tyson and Douglas up in February?"

"Hell yeah! Who do ya thinks gonna win that?" Sean asked.

"Tyson for sure. Douglas ain't got no chance." Jamal unfastened the Velcro strap of Sean's gloves and then removed them.

"I'll bet ya on that." Sean walked with Jamal. "Let's just get the hell out this basketball court. It's too cold to be out here anyway. I can see my own damn breath."

"How much ya wanna bet?" Jamal exited the basketball court through a chain linked fence and then sat on a row of benches. "Oh yeah, and hand me that right there." He pointed to a green backpack on the ground.

"How's twenty-five bucks sound?" Sean handed the bag to Jamal.

"That's pocket change!" Jamal laughed, reaching into his backpack and removing a cold can of Budweiser.

"So ya ain't gonna take the bet?" Sean eyed the beer.

"Yeah, I'mma take you up on it," Jamal responded.

"You ain't gonna back out when ya lose are ya?" Sean sat down beside Jamal.

"Hell nah! I rarely lose, but I always pay up when I do." Jamal dusted off some of the snow that had collected onto his backpack.

Sean reached for the beer. "Lemme get some of that."

"You's only 14, white boy!" Jamal pulled it away.

"So what? You drink all the time!" Sean responded.

"Yeah, and I'm nine years older than you, fool." Jamal popped the tab and took a drink. "Focus on them studies, for now, ya dig?"

"Fine." Sean crossed his arms.

"Don't wanna be in this city forever do ya?" Jamal asked.

"Hell nah! I'mma be an airplane pilot!" Sean pounded his fists together. "Been gettin' all C's and B's lately."

"That's right!" Jamal patted Sean on the shoulder. "That's what I'm talkin' 'bout, white boy! Don't wanna see another F on that report card, ya hear?"

"Yeah, I hear ya," Sean smiled.

"Oh yeah, you been watchin' them new episodes of Fresh Prince of Bel-Air?" Jamal took another sip of his beer.

"Nah, my brother," Sean said, shivering, "doesn't really like it."

"'That's all cool. Just got one of them new VCR's, so I been recordin' some of the episodes. I'll bring 'em next time."

"Thanks, but I don't think—" Sean began.

A car horn sounded across the street.

"The fuck you doin' Sean?" Sean's older brother, Chase, yelled from his black truck.

"Damn! I gotta go!" Sean grabbed his backpack and darted away as fast as he could.

"Same time next week, white boy?" Jamal yelled.

"Maybe," Sean hollered.

"Watchoo mean maybe, fool?" Jamal shouted back, spilling some of his beer onto the wooden bench below.

"I dunno. We'll see." Sean jumped over a mound of snow and

sprinted across the road to his brother.

"Get your god damn ass in here!" Chase hollered.

"You ain't gotta yell!" Sean opened the door.

Chase snatched Sean's collar and pulled him into the truck. "Shut the fuck up! I thought I told ya not to hang out with that filthy fuckin' nigger?!" While he sped off, ice and show crushed beneath the trucks rubber tires.

"So just who made you God?" Sean asked.

"Keep that shit up if ya wanna broken jaw!" Hatred scorched inside Chase's dilated pupils. "Them god damn coons ain't no good and that one ain't no different."

"I look up to that guy more than I look up to you, you racist fuck!" Sean bashed his fist into the dashboard.

"I told ya to keep that fuckin' shit up, boy!" Chase backhanded Sean in the face. "Think if mom and dad was still alive they'd be proud of you disrespecting me like this?!"

Sean's cheeks turned bright red. "Think they'd be proud of you and your fake ass Neo-Nazi friends sellin' crystal meth?"

Chase slammed on the pedal. As soon as he did, the truck slid on the ice and rear-ended the red Honda in front of them. Sean was thrown from his seat, his face smashing into the windshield.

"What the fuck did you just say?!" Chase slammed Sean's head against the passenger's side window until the glass cracked.

"What the fuck are ya doin'?! Are ya on that shit?!" Sean tried to push Chase away, but he was no match for his older brother's strength.

"That's right, you little shit!" Chase grinned, revealing his extremely rotted teeth. Then he sent three powerful punches to Sean's jaw.

"Stop Chase!" Sean sobbed and put his hands over his face.

"Why?!" Chase laughed, continuing with the firm blows. "I thought you liked to box?!"

"Stop!" Sean couldn't dodge the blows no matter how hard he tried.

"This is for your own—" Chase began.

The owner of the red Honda knocked on the window. "Mind watching the damn road, idiot?"

"Fuck off!" Chase grabbed a metal baseball bat from the back seat and kicked open the door. With one hard swing, he hit the man in the face, sending him to the ground.

"Stop! What are you doing?!" The man retreated to his car.

Chase rushed after him, hitting the Honda's taillights until plastic shards flew in the air. Just before the man sped off, he swung the bat one last time, shattering the back window.

"That's right! Get lost, asshole!" Chase tossed the bat into the back of the truck and returned to the driver's seat.

"What the hell happened to you?! What did that shit do to ya?!" Sean sobbed.

"Just shut up!" Chase snapped back, recklessly peeling out.

"You're gonna kill us both!" Sean squeezed his temples.

"Think I give a fuck!" Chase passed a slow-moving minivan by driving over the concrete barrier and into oncoming traffic.

Sean grabbed the wheel and guided the truck back into their lane. "I told ya get off that shit!"

"Don't ever tell me what to do, boy!" Chase pulled back the sleeve of his shirt, showing Sean his track marks and white supremacy tattoos. "Who the fuck do you think runs this city?! What the fuck do you think pays the bills?!"

"So ya get everyone addicted to this stupid shit just to pay our bills?!" Sean spat.

"I don't give a rat's ass if the whole planet dies off as long as I got a fat knot in my pocket!" After Chase slammed on the brakes, the truck slid on the ice and stopped in the middle of an intersection.

"Shit!" Sean panted, looking at all the angry drivers honking their horns. "You're holdin' everybody up!"

"Wipe that sappy look off ya face, you slimy cunt!" Chase pressed the pedal and took off down the street.

They continued driving until they stopped outside a house which had rotted wood, a few broken windows, and an unkempt lawn. Chase exited the vehicle and walked toward Sean's side, pulling him out and throwing him into a pile of snow.

"What the hell was that for?!" Sean jumped to his feet and followed Chase, watching the nearby neighbors retreat to their houses.

"'Cause I don't raise bitches!" Chase shouted while he walked through their front yard.

All of a sudden, growls came from an apple tree growing in the yard. Becoming startled, Sean slipped on the concrete path and slammed his face into a lawn mower. Soon the growling sounds had changed into vicious barks. With drool dripping from their yellow fangs, two monstrous pit bulls chained to the tree charged at him. One reached him. It bit his pant leg and tore apart the fabric.

"Cerberus, Dip! Shut your god damn faces!" Chase picked up a crowbar covered in dry blood and fur. "You don't want none!"

"The hell we gonna eat for dinner?" Sean reached the front door, shivered, and brushed the snow off his jacket.

"Eat whatever ya want, boy." Chase entered the house and walked to two men named Taz and Spike who were sitting on a plastic covered sofa.

"What's good, Chase?" Taz asked.

"When'd y'all put that up?" Chase admired the large swastika flag that they had pinned to the wall.

"While you was picking up Sean." Spike fumbled around with paraphilia in a small, metal box.

"Looks damn good!" Chase smiled. "Hand me that shoelace on the coffee table."

146

"Ya really gonna shoot up in mom and dad's living room?!" Sean cried, watching Taz toss the string to Chase.

"Mom and dad have been dead for years!" Chase wrapped the shoelace around his bicep. "Ya got that shit ready, Spike?"

"Gimme a minute." Taz removed a small bag of crystal methamphetamine from the same box.

"Alright, gimme that Smirnoff," Chase seethed, grabbing a bottle of vodka from the coffee table.

"Ya seen my English book anywhere?" Sean looked around, worrying he would get behind on his studies.

"That school stuff's a scam, Sean." Taz grabbed a copy of Mein Kampf off the arm of the sofa and handed it to Sean. "That's the only shit you need to read. Study it, breathe it, and live it."

"Yeah, how 'bout no." Sean handed it back.

"I swear this kid don't know what's good for him." Chase chugged down mouthfuls of vodka.

"Of course not." Sean shook his head and walked toward his room.

"Where in the hell are you goin'?!" Chase yelled.

"Gotta study." Sean entered his room and slammed the door.

"We just told ya that garbage is useless!" Chase hollered.

Once Sean was sure that his older brother and his friends wouldn't hear him, he headed toward his phone and dialed Jamal's number. He stood there, listening to the other line ring until someone finally answered.

"Hello?"

"Hey, Jamal, it's Sean!"

"What's good in the hood, white boy?"

"Nothin's good, man! Listen I need to get the hell outta here!"

"Alright, I got ya fool. I guess ya can take the couch for a few nights. My sister's stayin' with me right now, so—"

"Nah, I mean for good! Shit's gettin' bad here!"

"Alright, alright, if it's really that bad just meet me up in my crib."

"Where do ya live at?"

"7543 Ocean Drive. It's that red brick apartment complex across from that old ass barber shop."

"Yeah, that sounds familiar, but I dunno how to get there." Sean scratched his head.

"So what if we just meet up in the b-ball court?"

"Nah, I can't have 'em seein' me walkin' down the street with my suitcase."

"Alright, how 'bout I just pick ya up from ya house?"

"I don't think that's such a good idea."

"Why not?"

"Well, because…" Sean hesitated. "Alright, I guess that'd be fine as long they don't see ya."

"Okay, cool. What's ya address, fool?"

"661 Lonely Hills Boulevard." Sean's heart pounded like a bongo drum when those words escaped his breath.

"Alright, got it."

"Thanks!"

"Damn! What's up with ya, white boy? Breathin' all heavy and whatnot? You alright?"

"I thought that was you."

"It must be this old ass phone. I really gotta get this thing looked at."

Chapter Nineteen

Trail of Breadcrumbs

Present day...

Officer Mercer and Officer Tanner had set off to the city bus station. When they pulled outside of it, they eagerly waited to see if Marty, the bus driver Jerome mentioned, actually existed or not.

"Alright, Rookie, here it is." Officer Mercer exited his cruiser to see homeless people loitering against the brick wall of the building.

"Man, oh man! This place sure does need renovation!" Officer Tanner followed Mercer into the station, passing a few trashcans that were overflowing with garbage.

"You got that right." Officer Mercer reached the front desk and tapped on the glass.

"How can I help you boys today?" An elderly woman in a red wig asked from behind the counter.

"We're here lookin' for one of your drivers that goes by the name of Marty." Mercer glanced around the room.

"Marty Robins or Marty Moore?" The old woman chewed on the tip of her pen.

Tanner shrugged his shoulders, saying, "well, we—"

"Alright," the woman sighed. "What does he look like?"

Mercer pulled out his pad and looked through his notes. "Overweight. Beard. White guy. Drives the number 23. And looks like he's got an attitude."

"Yeah, that's Moore." The woman lifted a clipboard from her desk and ran her finger down the paper on it. "Looks like the bus he's on should be back in about 15 minutes. Just wait outside and look for it."

Tanner tipped his cap. "Thanks, ma'am!"

"Alright, so looks like there might be somethin' to Jerome's story," Mercer said.

Mercer and Tanner exited the building. Mercer lit a cigarette and used his boot to kick away flocks of seagulls begging for food. Tanner chatted with a homeless man wrapped up in newspapers, discussing Violet Haven's increasing crime rates.

A few minutes later, the number 23 bus arrived precisely on schedule with the rest of the city buses. After it stopped, a large group of passengers exited, spreading out throughout the terminal.

"I think I see him in there, boss." Tanner walked to the bus and stuck his head inside, seeing a large, grumpy man behind the wheel. "Are you Marty Moore?"

"Sure am." Marty removed a triple cheeseburger from his lunch box and took a bite.

"We got a couple of questions for ya." Mercer stepped inside.

"'Bout what?" Marty took another bite before even swallowing what was in his mouth.

"'Bout one of your riders a few months back." Mercer watched Marty lift the cheeseburger bun and throw away the pickles. "You may or may not remember."

Marty let out a long sigh through his nostrils. "I'll try."

"We're lookin' for a black male with cornrows. He was reported to be wearing a wife beater at the time," said Mercer.

Marty let out another sigh. "Doesn't sound familiar."

"Are ya sure 'bout—" Mercer started.

"I said it doesn't sound familiar!" Bits of food sprayed from Marty's mouth.

"That's a shame." Mercer turned. "Well, thanks for—"

"Wait!" Tanner jumped inside the bus. "A man named Jerome was on the bus that same night. Calls everyone 'blood' and causes trouble."

Marty dropped his cheeseburger. "Jerome? Yeah, I know that punk." He stroked his beard. "Wife beater? Cornrows?"

"Yeah, that's it!" Tanner smiled.

"I think I remember that night." Marty placed the burger back in the bag. "There was this one black guy that was wearing a wife beater and had cornrows like you said. There was blood on his clothes, and he was kinda scruffy. Looked like he hadn't had a good shower in a while. His jeans were dirty and filled with tears and holes. I'm pretty sure he was just another worthless street rat."

"Was he with anyone else?" Tanner took out a pen and pad and wrote down everything.

Marty put his finger to his chin. "Don't think so, but then again I see a hellavu lot of people."

"Do you remember where you picked him up at?" Mercer gave Tanner a pat on the shoulder.

"Yeah, I do." Marty tucked the fast food bag in under his seat. "It was over by that Mongolian restaurant that just opened up a few months ago."

"That ain't too far from Iron River!" Tanner's eyes grew wide with excitement.

"Settle down, Rookie." Mercer looked at Marty and pointed at the camera above the windshield. "What about that?"

"That?" Marty slumped back in his seat. "Yeah, that thing records 24/7."

"How long do they keep the tapes?" asked Mercer.

"Lemme think," Marty said. "I think for about six months or so. Just go ask the workers in the station."

"Oh yeah, ya wouldn't happen to know the exact date of that night would ya?" Tanner asked.

"Actually, I do now that I think about it," Marty responded. "By coincidence, my nephew's birthday was two days before, so that night had to have been August 21, I'm guessin'."

"Alright, got it." Mercer turned around. "And thanks for the help."

"Yup." Marty shook his head.

Mercer led Tanner back to the old woman behind the glass window in the station. "S'cuse me again," he said, "but Marty said ya had some security footage from the buses that we need to look at."

"Well, we do, but they aren't actually videos. Our cameras only take stills," she said. "They take a picture every five or so seconds, but you're welcome to look if you like."

"Yeah, that'd be great," Officer Tanner said.

"Just follow me." After grabbing a ring of keys, the old woman rose from her seat and walked through a wooden door, meeting Mercer and Tanner on the other side. "This way."

Mercer and Tanner followed her through a dirty hallway filled with garbage until she stopped outside of a door marked 'Employees Only.'

"Alright, boys." The pleasant old woman unlocked the door and led them inside. "What date and which bus are you looking for?"

"We're lookin' for August 21, 1995, from the number 23 bus."

Officer Mercer looked around at the cold, clammy room which was filled with large cabinets that held what looked like thousands of VHS's.

The old woman headed near the back of the room to a cabinet that had the number 23 marked on the side. After a few minutes, she returned with an empty VHS sleeve.

"That's odd," she said. "All the tapes are there except for this one."

"That *is* odd," Officer Mercer said, stroking his chin. "Way too odd."

"Well, there are actually two cameras on the buses." She handed Tanner the sleeve. "One in the front of the bus and another in the back. The ones in the back are kept in a separate room since we don't have enough space in this room."

"Do ya have any recordin's of this here station?" asked Officer Tanner. "And can ya take us to the other room please?"

"Yes, we sure do, but I don't know what day they broke in..." she said.

"Just get us the tapes from the past two weeks for now," Officer Mercer responded.

She walked back to the far side of the room and returned with several VHS tapes.

Officer Mercer took the tape from her and inspected it closely. "Looks like they didn't take this one."

"And if you'll just follow me down the hall." She led them out of the room, closing the door behind her. "I'll get you that other tape.

After they reached the room, the old woman unlocked the door and let the two officers in first. Then she walked to cabinet a few feet away from the room, returning with the August 21, 1995 security tape from bus number 23.

"There's a VCR and TV that you can use back behind the front counter if you like," she said.

"Yeah, that'd be great," replied Officer Tanner.

The three of them made their way back to the front of the station. When they arrived, the woman led Mercer and Tanner behind the counter and into a small janitorial closet to the right. Mercer then popped in the security tape from the number 23 bus and pressed play. Almost immediately after, stills from the bus played on the medium sized television, grabbing Mercer and Tanner's attention.

"I'm gonna go to about 11:00 pm." Officer Tanner picked up the remote and pressed fast forward until the timer in the corner of the screen hit 11:00 pm.

"Just pay close attention from here on out," Officer Mercer said, keeping his eyes glued to the screen. He didn't dare to blink.

The three of them watched while passengers got on and off the bus until Mercer spotted an African-American male wearing a tank top.

"Right there!" he hollered. "Pause it!"

Tanner pressed pause.

Mercer moved closer until all he saw were pixels of the man on the bus. "Cornrows. Dirty. Unshaven. Little darker than Jerome. Blood stains on his clothes." He snatched the remote from Tanner and pressed play.

A little longer into the tape and Jerome got on. The two officers and the old woman watched as he walked to the back of the bus and sat down next to the suspect. Jerome then robbed the man of a wallet.

"Son of a bitch." Mercer smirked, continuing to watch until his suspect got off the bus with two others. "He wasn't lyin'."

"Looks like he's got accomplices," Tanner said.

"Sure does." Officer Mercer ejected the tape and tucked it into his belt. "Now let's see 'bout those other tapes." After putting in the VHS tape of the bus station from the previous day, he saw footage from outside the station.

Soon he fast forwarded through the footage and switched the tape with another. Then another. Tape after tape was played until no more remained.

"Can we get more of these tapes?" he asked.

"Yes, just let me return these to the security room," answered the old woman who then collected the VHS tapes and before leaving.

A few minutes went by, and she returned with more just as promised. The cycle repeated. But Officer Mercer found nothing.

"Hmm, do ya think we can get every tape of the station from August 22 from August 29?" he asked.

Once again, the old woman left the room and returned with more tapes. Mercer viewed them until he popped in the security tape from August 27. Just as the tape was nearing 10:30 pm, a masked man appeared on the screen, walking through the parking lot with a crowbar. The man then stopped at a window and pried it open. At 11:02 pm, he exited the building, carrying what looked like one of the security tapes.

"Well, I'll be damned." The old woman put her hand to her chin. "We were robbed, and we didn't even know it."

"Looks like it." Mercer ejected the tape and handed it off to Tanner. "We're gonna send another officer down here later to check out that window and collect some evidence."

"Okay," she said. "Well, I'll see what I can do to help them."

"Thanks, ma'am, but you've been enough help," Officer Tanner turned to leave the room. "Our officers will take it from here."

Mercer and Tanner walked through the terminal until they exited the building. From there, they headed back to their squad car, eyeing everything around to see if they could gather more evidence.

"That break-in was less than a week from the first tape," said Officer Mercer. "And those kids on the bus don't look like the types to go this far just to get that footage."

"Think they had someone else do it?" asked Tanner.

"I don't see why," Mercer frowned. "If ya ask me I'd say we ain't the only ones lookin' for those kids."

A few hours later, both officers had setup a meeting about their suspects at the police station. Officer Mercer and Officer Tanner soon found themselves standing in a room in front of about two dozen officers, each one seated in a desk and equipped with a pen and pad.

"Well, Tanner, tell everyone what we know about the suspect," Officer Mercer grinned.

"Well, I..." Officer Tanner gulped. The beads of sweat forming on his face and the incessant shaking proved the officer was no good at public speaking. "He—"

The group of police officers roared with laughter.

"Enough!" After Mercer stomped his boot on the ground, the group fell silent. "My partner here has somethin' to tell us all, and we're all gonna listen." He turned to Tanner. "Go ahead, buddy."

"Th-thanks, Boss," Officer Tanner said, shaking off his nervousness. "On the day of October 27, 1995, two bodies were found dumped in the trunk of a car in the waters of Iron River. Through thorough investigation, we've found a possible suspect."

Mercer pulled out a sketch drawing. "This is a sketch of the suspect. He wears—"

Just then the door swung open, and an officer walked inside carrying a large, blown up photograph of the stills from the bus station. "Just got this finished up, Mercer."

"Perfect timin'!" Officer Mercer walked over and took the large photograph before returning to his partner. "This is the suspect," he said, noticing the wave of fear that rushed over Officer Zeke's face.

The large, muscular officer who Mercer had run into before raised his hand. "Do you know where he..." He stopped for a few seconds, putting his hand to his chin. "Might be?"

"Currently, we do not," Officer Tanner responded. "But we are on the lookout."

"Anyways, as everyone can see, he's black, has cornrows, and is most likely homeless," Officer Mercer continued. "He also has accomplices. Two of them. However, we were unable to get clear images of their faces in the stills we acquired."

"These men are extremely dangerous. Please use caution if you see them. As of right now, that's all the information we have." Officer Tanner turned to Mercer. "Anything you'd like to add?"

"Just one more..." Officer Mercer stopped when he saw how much Zeke was sweating. "You okay there, Zeke?"

"What?! I mean, I'm fine!" Officer Zeke let out a loud, nervous laugh. "Why?"

"You just look a 'lil pale..." Officer Mercer responded.

"Yeah, I think I'm just c-comin' down with the flu..." Officer Zeke dashed out of the room. "Gotta go!"

Officer Walker laughed, slamming his palm down on his desk. "He really is an oddball isn't he?"

"Why is he still here?" an officer in the group asked. "We all know he did it. We all know he's the serial killer."

"He's disgraced himself," another officer said, shaking his head. "He should've left years ago! I don't know why he never resigned! There's not a single officer in this entire department that'll even work with him!"

"There's got to be some piece of evidence somewhere that'll prove he did it!" Officer Lucas piped in. "There's got to be!"

Soon enough, the entire room was engulfed in one massive discussion regarding Officer Zeke. Some offices hurled insults about him. Other's talked about conspiracy theories about why he was never caught. And a few just sat there in silence, not knowing what to make of it all. Either way, the chatter was so loud that Officer Mercer swore he was in a high school classroom.

"That's enough! As much as I hate that worm, this isn't about him!" Officer Mercer boomed. When the chatter died down, he held up the photograph once again. "This is what this is about!"

"Anyway, anybody got any questions or information they'd like to share?" Officer Tanner asked.

"Yeah, I got one." Officer Walker stroked his beard. "This case looks interestin'. Would I be able to get updates on this?"

"Updates will be available as they come along," responded Officer Mercer. "Just come see me at my office. We'd love to get any help we can get."

Chapter Twenty

Confrontation

Present day...

I tightened my grip on Sean's collar. "Y'all knew the whole time! Why the fuck didn't anyone tell me?!"

"K-knew what?!" Sean asked. "What are ya talkin' about?!"

I pulled him closer. "Xavier!"

"Oh shit!" Sean's eyes grew wide.

"We just didn't think—" Tabitha mumbled.

"What's that?!" I let Sean go, causin' him to stumble backward. "I don't hear ya!"

"We just couldn't do it." Sean kept his eyes focused on his feet. "I never thought it was funny."

"Liar!" I yelled. "Y'all knew I was a lunatic the whole—"

"Sean's telling the truth," Tabitha said softly, looking like she was fighting to hold in her tears. "What could we have said or done? You loved Xavier so much. All of us knew you would have done anything for him..." She looked at Sean and then back to me. "But he just wasn't there."

"So what the fuck are we gonna do now?!" My voice cracked.

"I don't really know." Sean shoved his hands in his pockets.

"We..." Tabitha walked over to the couch and picked up Leon's photo album. "We could still try to get outta here. I mean, get outta the city, ya know? We could still find Leon and—"

I snatched the album from her and flung it to the far side of the junkyard. "Do ya think I give a fuck about any of that stupid shit right now?!"

"Look, man, I didn't know what to say to ya." Sean stepped forward and placed his hand on my shoulder.

I brushed his hand off. "Don't touch me!"

"Okay, just listen. We always knew you were..." Sean trembled. "We always knew you were sick."

"You've helped all of us. You did a lot of great things for us, but it's just..." Tabitha turned to Sean.

"We could just kinda sense it. Somethin' just was never really right. I remember back when you first started talkin' to ya'self." He looked me square in the eye and stepped toward me. "I kept hoping you'd get better, but you just kept getting worse and worse."

"It was so heartbreaking to watch. I hated seeing you like that." Tabitha put her hand to her chest. "There was nothing we could do." She used her thumb to dry my eyes.

"So Leon wasn't playin' around." I dropped to my knees. "I really am a nutcase."

"You aren't a nutcase. You're our friend." Tabitha grabbed my arm and lifted me to my feet. She pressed her hands against the sides of my face. "Didn't I promise that you'd get better one day?"

"This shits never gonna get better." I sat on the couch and used my sleeve to wipe my eyes and nose.

"It will be one day," Sean said. "We just gotta keep our heads up."

As I slumped back into the sofa, the only thing I imagined was blowing my brains out.

"You gonna be alright?" asked Sean.

"Nah, I ain't," I responded. "Just leave me alone."

"Well, we gotta run to the city to find some food anyway. We haven't had food since the other night." Sean wrapped his arm around Tabitha.

"You sure you don't want one of us to stay?" Tabitha asked. "It's not a problem at all, ya know."

I sighed and rolled over. "Just go."

"Alright," Tabitha replied. "We'll be back soon."

I listened to their footsteps crunch against the gravel until they faded away. Soon the only sound that gave me comfort was the flock of crows cawing in the distance. Falling asleep only made everything worse. All I saw was blood and madness.

By the time I opened my eyes, it was already dusk. Tabitha and Sean were still gone, but the only thing I cared about was having a drink. The first thing that came to mind was the bottle of vodka Leon had brought back. I peeked over the arm of the couch but saw nothing except a pile of scrap metal.

I lifted my head up and searched the junkyard until I spotted the bottle a few feet away. When I stood up I fell straight to the gravel, and couldn't even keep my eyes focused. Just to get to it, I had to crawl on all fours like some filthy animal.

Eventually, I reached it. After I unscrewed the cap, I drained what was left, laid on my back, and felt the fire. It didn't help. My mind was still making it feel like I was living in a nightmare. Because I was. The only solution I could think of was lying in a pile of twisted metal. So I crawled over to it and found the sharpest shard I could find.

Then put it to my neck.

My heart fluttered. While I held it tightly against my flesh, the tip just barely slid through my skin. A small drop of blood fell to the gravel. Just when I was about to thrust it in further, I heard Sean's voice.

"What the hell are ya doin' man?!" He dropped the paper bag in his hands and dashed toward me.

"I ain't doin' shit!" I stepped back and pressed the shard deeper.

Tabitha walked toward us. "Sean what's going—"

"He's tryna kill himself!" Sean waved his arms. There was a look in his eyes that made it seem like he was about to lose a family member.

"Wh-what do you mean?" Tabitha quivered.

"The hell do ya mean 'what do you mean'?! Just look at him!" Sean pointed at me.

"Please just put it down..." Tabitha whispered, tears forming in her eyes.

"Why the hell do you even give a shit?!" I slid the shard further in my neck.

"Stop it!" she cried.

"I asked you why do you even give a shit?!" I shouted.

"Because you can't leave us here alone!" Tabitha shouted. "Are you really just gonna leave us alone in this shithole to rot by ourselves?!"

"I just..." The shard dropped from my hand. "I ain't tryin' to—"

"Just come and eat with us." Tabitha walked up to me and led me to the couch. "We'll talk, alright?"

A few minutes later, we were sitting on the couch and talking about what we were gonna do now that Leon left. Tabitha wrapped an old cloth around my neck while Sean ate some of the fast food they'd found. Both of them offered me slices of pizza, but just the smell of it made me sick even though I hadn't eaten in days.

"So what the hell are we gonna do now?" I watched Tabitha scarf down an old slice of pizza.

"Dunno." Sean stuck his hand into a greased stained paper bag and pulled out a handful of curly fries. Then he stuffed them into his mouth all at once. "What do ya wanna do? We still gotta get up outta here somehow."

"I don't really know, man." I unfolded my arms and stuffed my hands in my pockets.

"Well, the only thing I got in mind was to go after Leon," Sean said, bits of fries spewing from his mouth. "I got no clue how we're even gonna find 'em."

Tabitha started. "What about—"

"There is one thing I gotta show ya," I sighed.

"What is it?" Tabitha twirled her gold necklace around her finger.

"Over there." I pointed behind her toward the middle of the junkyard. "Leon's photo album." I began lifting myself off the couch, but then she stopped me.

"I'll get it, alright?" She walked to the album, came back, and then handed it to me.

"Thanks." I opened it to Officer Zeke's picture. Heat spread throughout my body while I ripped it from the album and crumpled it with my fist.

"What's up with that?" Sean asked.

"We need to find this guy." I tossed him the crumbled picture.

Sean uncrumpled it and held it in front of his face. "What?! This guy?!" he gasped. "Why?!"

"What's going on?" Tabitha asked.

"He wants to go after the serial killer!" Sean responded.

"Why?!" Tabitha's stood straight up and looked me dead in the eyes.

"Because he," I said, "killed my parents."

"What?!" Sean said.

"Yeah," I responded. "They were the last ones before he stopped."

"How the hell would we even find this guy?" Sean asked. "This guy's a god damn cop!"

"Wait. He's Leon's brother isn't he?" Tabitha asked. "If we find Leon then we'll find..." She turned Sean and then me.

"Bloody, Bloody Bijou," Sean said.

"His real name is Zeke." I could feel blood rush to my face.

"So how are we going to find Leon?" Tabitha asked. "He could all the way in another state by now."

"He's gonna go back for the photo album," I responded.

"Don't tell me ya wanna go back to Palm Street," Sean said. "We almost got killed last time."

"We don't really have any other options," Tabitha replied. "He took all the money."

"When should we go?" Sean asked.

"As soon as we can." As raspy and miserable as my voice was, I wasn't sure if either of them could hear me. "He ain't gonna hang around here forever."

"Gotcha," Sean responded. "We gotta find a way to get back in that house unnoticed though. Half that street will recognize us if they see us."

Chapter Twenty-One

Family Secret Revealed

Five years earlier...

Sean whispered into his telephone, "Yo, Jamal, they're about to leave right now.

"Alright, I'll be waiting across the street from ya house," Jamal responded.

"Thanks, man!" Sean hung up the phone, walked over to his closet, then pulled out a large suitcase filled with clothes and schoolbooks.

"Sean get the fuck out here now!" Chase's bellows were loud enough to bring the house down.

"Wadda ya want?" Sean walked out of his room and poked his head around the corner of the hall.

"I got business to take care of," Chase said. "If Sally stops by make sure she gets that plastic bag on the coffee table." He exited the house, slamming the door behind him.

With the thought of a new life in his head, Sean headed back to his room and then tossed more of his possessions into the suitcase. Every few minutes he pulled back the window curtains and checked outside. The very thought of Jamal arriving at the same time that his tyrant brother returned was making his stomach flip.

Half an hour later, he looked outside and noticed a white Acura parked across the street. Then he saw Jamal exit the vehicle. It was time. All the emotional, physical, and psychological abuse he'd suffered, all the turmoil, all the belittling would be no more. He'd finally be able to put all his focus into following his father's footsteps and become a successful airplane pilot. But most of all, he'd finally have a positive role model that he'd be able to look up to.

With a wide grin on his face, he used his skinny arms to drag his suitcase to the front of the house. After opening the door, he cupped his hands over his mouth and yelled, "Hey, man, this thing's heavy!"

"We need to get ya scrawny ass in the damn gym, fool." Jamal ran across the street but stopped after he noticed the growling dogs in Sean's yard. "God damn them some mean ass mutts!"

"Just help me with this! I dunno how long they'll be gone!" Sean fidgeted, looking up and down the street.

"Just chill, white boy! We got this!" Jamal entered the yard, walking as far away from the pit bulls as he possibly could. Once he reached Sean, he lifted the suitcase with no problem like it was filled with feathers. "This all ya got?"

"Yeah, everything's in there." Sean took another look down the street.

"Alright, cool." Jamal lifted the suitcase in the air. "Now let's—"

Sean fell backward into a pile of firewood. The sight of Chase's black truck driving toward them was more than enough to send him into cardiac arrest. "Oh shit! It's him!"

"W-what?!" Jamal dropped the suitcase.

Sean turned his head around, looking for a place to run. "Get in the house!" With nowhere else to go, he hauled the suitcase back inside.

"Hold up, white boy!" Jamal stepped toward the front door." He ain't *that* bad is..." The swastika flag on the wall caught his eye. "What the hell is—"

"C'mon! He's gonna kill you!" Sean frantically pulled Jamal into the house and then closed the door. "This way!" He heaved his suitcase behind him until the two of them reached his room.

"Oh damn! This ain't good, man!" Sean paced around the room, listening to the music booming from Chase's truck. "You gotta hide somewhere!"

"What 'bout in there?!" Jamal headed toward Sean's closet.

"That's the first place he'll look if he suspects anything!" Sean took another look out the window to see Chase exiting his truck. "He's comin'!"

An idea popped in his head that was just crazy enough to work. Grabbing his suitcase from Jamal and then laying it on the floor, he yelled,

"I think that things big enough to fit ya!"

"Are ya sure 'bout that?" Jamal shivered, unzipping it.

"I hope so!" Sean helped him dump out the clothes and schoolbooks before shoving everything under the bed. "Alright, get inside!"

"I don't think this is a very—" Jamal started.

"The fuck I tell both of ya?!" Chase screamed. "You filthy mutts!"

Sean's very bones shook. In a panic, he had Jamal lie curled up inside the suitcase. His heart pounding, he used his weak arms to drag it toward his closet. Suddenly, the front door swung open. Sean froze in place. He struggled to breathe. The door slammed shut, shaking the house. Letting out the air in his lungs, Sean pushed on. Chase's stomps were coming toward his room. This was it. The next few moments meant life or death. With every ounce of strength he had, Sean hurled the suitcase into the closet. Not a second later, Chase burst into the room.

"Sean! Where's my..." He looked at Sean. "It's the middle of fuckin' winter, boy. Why in the hell are ya sweating? Why do ya look so nervous?!"

"N-nothin'." Sean's legs felt like they were made of melting butter.

"You hidin' somethin' ain't ya?" Chase smirked, looking around the room.

"N-nah." Sean looked to the ground.

"You're shaking, boy," Chase growled, grabbing Sean by the throat and shoving him against the wall. "Don't you lie to me!"

"I ain't lyin'!" Sean pushed off Chase's hand and then rubbed the back of his head.

"Oh yeah? We'll see 'bout that." Chase headed toward the closet and rummaged through Sean's belongings.

Sean grabbed a knife off a nearby dresser and hid it behind his back. His hands shook. He walked forward. The young boy was more than ready to take a life if it meant saving his friend.

Chase slammed the closet door and checked under the bed. "What the hell is all this crap?!" After pulling out a large pile of clothes, he then threw it all at Sean. "The fuck I tell ya 'bout leavin' ya god damn dirty laundry under your fuckin' bed?!" He bashed his fist through the wall and exited the room.

Sean stood in place. The front door slammed. A few minutes later, when Chase's loud music finally faded, he let out the air in his lungs. The scrawny teenage boy collapsed to the floor. There he stayed, sweating from every pore in his body. Visions of what would've happened had Chase discovered his secret flashed before his eyes. It would've been a bloodbath. He knew this. Only when he heard Jamal's voice did he get up and open the suitcase.

"Damn! You wasn't lyin', white boy!" Jamal stood up and wiped away the sweat from his brow. "Get ya stuff and let's get outta here!"

Sean jammed his stuff into his suitcase and then hauled it out of the room. "Yeah, let's go."

After ensuring their escape from death, they drove across the city and eventually stopped outside a red brick apartment complex.

Jamal stepped out of the car and removed the suitcase. "Anyway, this is it." He then led Sean to a tall, metal gate and entered a number on a dial pad.

"Yeah? Who is it?" Clemecia, Jamal's younger sister, asked through a speaker.

"Yo', Clemecia, it's me!" Jamal said. "Open the gate!"

"Alright," she said.

After an annoying buzzing sound emitted from the speaker, the lock clicked. Jamal swung open the gate and directed Sean toward a flight of concrete stairs. After they reached the second flight, they walked down the hallway, stopping at the last apartment.

"We're outside." Jamal tapped on the door. "Clemecia!"

Clemecia swung open the door. "What the hell ya knockin' like..." She smiled when she saw Sean. "Oh, hi, I'm Clemecia!"

"Name's Sean. Nice to meet ya." Sean shook her hand.

"Alright, 'nuff of that, Clemecia. Sean you can put ya that suitcase in the corner over there for now." Jamal pointed next to a television while he wiped his feet on the doormat. "What's Tonya cookin' up?"

"Dunno. She ain't start dinner before she left," Clemecia responded.

"Well, we still got that lasagna from last night, don't we?" Jamal entered the apartment.

"Yeah, we got plenty left." Clemecia stared at Sean, twirling her hair.

"Alright, I'mma heat that up." Jamal headed to the kitchen.

"So how long ya stayin' here?" Clemecia took Sean's hand and led him to the couch.

"Probably awhile," Sean responded.

"Really?" Clemecia used her forefinger to poke his arm.

"Clemecia, leave that poor boy alone!" Jamal yelled.

"Ignore 'em," Clemecia giggled. "So what's ya girlfriend's name?"

"I don't have—" Sean began.

Just then the door swung open. A tall woman walked in the house and placed her jacket on a nearby coatrack. "Damn! It's cold as hell outside!" She turned around, looking at Sean. "Who's this?"

"That's Sean!" Jamal yelled, taking a large bowl filled with lasagna out of the microwave.

"Oh, hi, my name's Tonya. I'm Jamal's fiancé," she said, smiling. "I heard so much about you." She walked to the kitchen and kissed Jamal on the cheek. "This guy never shuts up 'bout ya. Sean this, Sean that. Acts like you're his damn son."

"He really do." Clemecia nodded.

"So I guess you two don't want dinner?" Jamal asked.

"Made by you? Hell nah! Think I wanna go to the hospital?" Clemecia cackled.

"Alright, alright, 'nuff of that!" Jamal brought the lasagna to the table, scooping it out onto four plates. "Dinner's ready."

The four of them enjoyed the leftover lasagna. During dinner, Jamal and Clemecia's constant bickering reminded Sean of how he and his brother used to fight before everything went to hell. Sean sat there silently, thinking back to the good times. Unfortunately, he soon realized he would never be able to relive those days. Gang violence and drugs had taken over his brother, and it didn't look like anything would ever be the same.

Not wanting to ruin everyone else's good time, he stuffed his face to hide his sadness.

"Ya eat fast as hell, white boy!" Jamal said.

"Don't call 'em that!" Tonya said, slapping Jamal in the shoulder.

"Nah, it's all good," Sean responded, twiddling his thumbs.

"Ya sure?" Tonya asked.

"Yeah, it's no big deal," Sean replied.

Tonya shot Jamal a dirty look. "I still don't like it."

"He just said he don't mind!" Jamal shrugged his shoulders.

"Ya don't like them white folks callin' you 'nigga' but ya wanna call Sean 'white boy'?" Tonya put her hands on her hips.

"Alright, alright, I'mma stop." Jamal took a bite of his food.

About 20 minutes later, Jamal finished his last bite and stood up from his chair. "Alright, just leave the dishes on the table. I'mma clean 'em later."

"Oh, yeah right!" Tonya crossed her arms.

"Nah, I'm for real." Jamal picked up his plate walked to the kitchen, and dropped it in the sink. "See?"

"Alright, fine." Tonya placed another slice of lasagna on her plate. "Anyway, can you go out and pick up some milk? I forgot to get some while I was out."

"Can't it wait until tomorrow?" Jamal moaned, looking at the clock above the sofa.

"No, I got my bake sale tomorrow afternoon!" Tonya said. "I've gotta start on my banana bread first thing in the morning!"

"Fine, fine, fine." Jamal walked to the front door. "'You gonna be cool here, Sean?"

"Yeah, I'll be good," Sean said, giving Jamal a thumbs up.

"Alright, white..." Jamal twisted the door knob and slipped outside. "I mean, Sean." Just as he was about to close the door, he popped his head back in. "Oh yeah! I almost forgot 'bout this!"

"What'd you forget?" Clemecia asked. "Ya brain?"

Jamal let out a fake laugh. "Very funny." After grabbing a plastic shopping bag off a nearby chair, he reached his hand inside and pulled out a beanie.

"A snowman beanie?" Clemecia taunted. "I don't want that mess!"

"Good 'cause it ain't for you!" Jamal tossed it to Sean. "Your ears always lookin' cold! Thought you could use that."

Sean ran his finger over the snowmen on the beanie and then pulled it over his head. "Gee, thanks, man. For real."

"Ya could've bought him a better one, Jamal." Clemecia said.

"Nah, it's all good," Sean smiled. "I like it."

"Yeah, no prob." Jamal exited the apartment.

Tonya lifted herself from her seat, walked down the hall, and returned with a soft, blue blanket. "The couch gonna be good for you, Sean?"

"Yeah, that's fine." Sean took the blanket. He then walked to the couch, settling himself in.

"Let me know if ya need anything." Tonya turned off the lights and walked down the hall to her room.

Clemecia walked toward the sofa. "I'm gonna watch some—"

"Go to bed Clemecia!" Tonya snapped.

"Oh my God! Fine!" Clemecia crossed her arms, storming to her room.

"Hey, Tonya, will Jamal be back soon?" Sean rested his head on the arm of the couch.

"Yeah, he'll be back in a 'bout an hour," Tonya responded. "Night, Sean."

"Night." Sean stared into the darkness and questioned what his life could've been if his parents never died. Everything seemed unreal. He wondered if it was somehow his fault.

A few minutes later, Clemecia poked her head around the corner of the hall. "Hey, Sean, you still up?"

"Yeah," Sean lifted his head. "You alright?"

"I'm fine. I just..." Clemecia crossed her arms and walked to Sean. "It's freezin' cold, and I can't sleep."

"You can't turn on the heater?" Sean asked.

"That don't work," Clemecia said. "I'd be comfortable if someone was with me."

"Okay." Sean followed Clemecia down the hall and entered the room.

Clemecia pressed her lips against his. "Just close ya eyes and follow me."

Chapter Twenty-Two

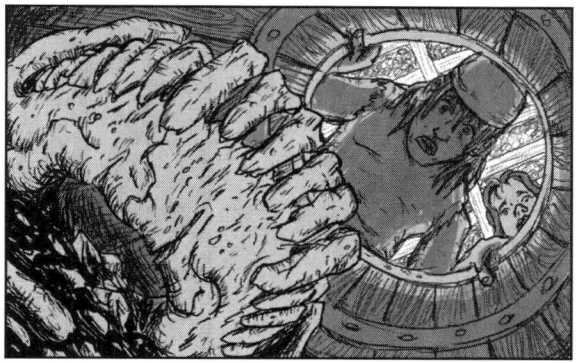

Bones of the Unknown

Present day...

The powerful beam of the sun met my eyes, waking me up from the nightmares that haunted me worse than ever before. After wiping the sweat off my forehead, I grabbed the pager from my pocket and then turned it on.

"4:37 PM," I read out loud.

"You finally up?" Sean jumped off the hood of a red Toyota a few yards away. "You been sleeping like a bear in the middle of winter."

"Yeah, I'm up." I pinched the skin between my eyebrows. "Where's Tabitha?"

"Right over there, man." Sean turned his head toward the front of the junkyard. "Tabitha!"

"Yeah?" Tabitha turned around and headed toward our direction.

"What's up?"

"We still gotta go after Leon," Sean responded.

"I don't think now is the best time for—" she began.

"Nah, he's right," I shook, trying to stop the gruesome visions from flashing in my head. "We gotta get him before he just up and leaves." I pressed my hand against my eyes when I realized I couldn't do it. "I mean if he hasn't already."

"Really?" Tabitha put one hand on her hip. "You're in no shape to—"

"Didn't ya say you don't wanna be stuck in this place forever?" Even though I couldn't admit it to her, I knew she was right. In a thousand years, I was never gonna be able to fully recover, and right then my mind and body wasn't in any shape to go after Leon. In all honesty, it didn't even feel like I was alive, but it just wasn't in me to ruin Tabitha and Sean's chance to start a new life even if mine was in shambles.

"Yes, but, I—" Tabitha put her hand over her face.

"Then we gotta go." I stood up from the couch and picked up Leon's photo album, tucking it down the back of my pants.

Together we traveled back to Palm Street. Unfortunately, we spotted one of the punks that had chased us down along the way, so we cut through an alleyway. The three of us climbed a ladder to the top of the roof filled with a few dozen ravens. As soon as I pulled myself over, they scattered into the sky and landed on a nearby telephone wire.

Sean turned his head and looked off the edge of the roof and toward Palm Street. "What the hell? That ain't right."

"What is it?" I asked

Sean pulled Tabitha up from the ladder. "Just forget it."

On the other side of the rooftop, there wasn't much to see besides generators and air conditioners. That is until I poked my head over the ledge and saw a white van parked in an alleyway. But that wasn't what struck me as odd. It was the two men dressed in black who were jumping out of it. With a wad of cash in their hands, they approached a gangbanger at the end of the alley and traded it for a small package wrapped in plastic.

"We're all good here." One of the men in black placed the package in the front seat of the van.

"Thanks for business." The gangbanger nodded and exited the alley.

Sean nudged me on my shoulder. "Looks like a drug deal."

As soon as the gangbanger left, the two men went to their van and pulled out a two-way radio. It sounded like they were giving off police codes.

Sean looked me square in the eyes. "Or somethin' a lot bigger."

"C'mon! I think I see another ladder over behind those air-conditioners." Tabitha walked to our right and pressed her hands on the barrier of the roof. "Yeah, there's definitely one over here."

Sean and I followed her and stuck our heads over the ledge. With all the pants, shirts, sheets, and other laundry that were hanging from clothes lines below, I couldn't get a good view of the grill in the yard below. But I could definitely smell the beef that was cooking on it. Just the scent alone made me sick. Even with how empty my stomach was, I still couldn't picture myself taking the smallest bite of food.

A few minutes later, all three of us were on the ground. As soon as Sean laid his eyes on that nice, juicy steak, he rubbed his stomach. After eating nothing but garbage for God knows how long, it was hard not to blame him.

"Ya sure you don't wanna take that steak?" he asked. "Nobody's around."

It was odd. Even though I felt like I was gonna collapse from starvation, my stomach flipped when I even glanced at those sizzling pieces of meat. "Nah, I don't really feel hungry. Let's just keep movin'."

Going over a chain-linked fence and through the backyards of several abandoned houses, we ended up at the end of Palm Street. To avoid being seen, our group crouched down and darted behind cars and telephone poles.

"I think that's a cop cruiser right there." Sean's eyes stayed glued to a white car parked by a fire hydrant.

Tabitha put her hand over her brow. "I don't think it is."

"I'm pretty sure it's undercover," he responded.

"How can ya tell?" I asked.

"Look at it closely," Sean said. "Tinted windows. No markings. Plus it's a Ford." He turned and looked me in the eyes. "Undercover cop cars always drive in Fords."

"It could just be a regular car, ya know?" Tabitha took another look.

"Nah, I saw two more near the overpass back when we was on the roof," said Sean.

"I thought you said cops don't come around here?" Tabitha asked.

"They don't," he responded. "Looks like somethin's gonna go down here real soon."

"We should probably forget about it and go." Tabitha continued down the sidewalk.

"Alright, fine." Sean said.

When we were sure that nobody would see us, we scurried across the road toward the alleyway behind the house. Just before we disappeared into it, I glanced back to see the same gangbanger walking down the steps of a porch. And with another package in his hands, my gut told me to scram. But once again I didn't listen.

"God damn." Sean waddled through the alley, darting his eyes at piles of garbage and cracks in the brick walls. "This place looks even worse in the daylight."

After having to climb over another fence, we met the same basement window we'd gone through with Leon, its glass still broken. While I slid through, police sirens blared in the middle of Palm Street.

Sean panicked, forcing Tabitha into the basement. "What'd I tell ya?"

"Do ya think they saw us?" I asked.

Sean slid through the window. "I don't think so."

"Well, let's…" The two barrels in the corner caught my eye, making me wonder why Leon flipped out so bad. "Hold on a sec."

Tabitha put her hand on my shoulder. "Don't tell me you're going to—"

I brushed it off and headed for the barrels. "I know that dude's hidin' something."

"Just be careful!" Tabitha cried.

After I reached one of the barrels, I tapped my knuckle on the side of it. It sounded empty, so I couldn't figure out why Leon threw such a fit. Still, if curiosity was the one that killed the cat, then I must've been next on its list.

I dug my fingers under the barrel lid, slowly prying it off inch by inch. It took a few minutes, but when I finally got it off, all I saw was this weird, brown sludge at the bottom. Then I noticed the old rings of blood caked onto the inside of the metal. That wasn't the worst of it. It was the two objects soaking in the sludge. But they were both so broken down that I wasn't sure what I was seeing until a few moments later.

Then it hit me. I backed away from the barrels. "Holy shit!"

Sean rushed over and then looked inside the drum. He froze in place. "Is that what I think it is?!"

"Y-yeah, I think it is!" A cold shiver slid along my spinal cord.

Two human body parts sat soaking in the slime, rotting away for God knows how long. One was a discolored hip bone, half of it gone. The other was some poor, tortured soul's jaw bone—I could still see the cavity fillings.

My core shook. Even worse was the fact that Leon knew about it. Did he murder those people? Or did someone else do it? Was it Bloody, Bloody Bijou? The more we dug into Leon's past, the odder things got.

Sean looked inside the barrel again with Tabitha. "There's somethin' else down there!" he said.

"I don't really wanna..." I watched Sean take a crowbar off a nearby shelf and then dig a necklace outta the drum.

"Looks old as hell." He held it up in the air.

"Let me see." Still shaky, I took the pendant and ran my finger over the words inscribed on its metal. "It says 'Together forever – Ely and Clyde Jenkins.'"

"Ely and Clyde? Those news articles you showed us said they went missing over a decade ago." Tabitha took the pendant and wiped the sludge off the metal. "I think Ely and Clyde are..." She put her hand to her chin. "I mean, I think Ely and Clyde *were* Leon's parents."

Did I say things were getting odd? I meant bizarre.

"This is them?! Somebody left his parents in some dirty ass basement?!" Sean gasped. "What kinda fucked up life did this dude live?!"

"Looks like it. And only God knows." My chest heaving, I picked up a metal pipe off the ground and then slowly crept toward the stairs leading out the basement. "Just keep ya voices down. We don't know what else Leon's hidin' from us."

Chapter Twenty-Three

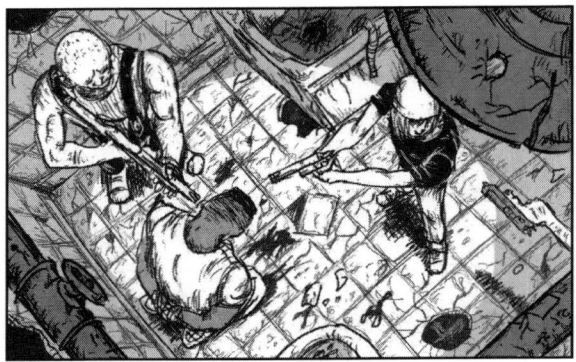

In Too Deep

Five years earlier...

Clemecia smiled while she got dressed, asking, "You up yet, Sean?"

"Yeah." Sean put on his clothes, observing the Salt-N-Pepa posters plastered on the walls.

"Go act like you been asleep in the livin' room. I'll get Tonya and we'll cook some breakfast." Clemecia responded.

"Sounds good." Sean exited the room.

"So what did y'all do last night?" Tonya's voice came from the end of the hall.

"N-nothin'." Sean put his head down.

"Yeah, right!" Tonya laughed, heading back to the kitchen.

Sean rubbed the back of his neck. "Jamal ain't up yet?"

"Jamal's ass never even came home last night! Gone to a god damn strip club, no doubt!" Tonya spun her head at the sound of a buzzer. She then walked over to the front door, pressing a button sitting next to an intercom. "Watch! Betcha it's him!"

"Yo' it's me!" Jamal's voice trailed through the speaker. "Think y-ya can send Sean down? I got some stuff to carry back up."

"Where the hell you been?" Tonya asked.

"Just been out..." Jamal's voice shook. "W-with some friends."

"Ya sure 'bout that?" Tonya put her hands on her hips.

"Yeah, everything's good," Jamal said. "Just send Sean down."

"Alright, I'mma let him know." Tonya released the button. "Please go down there and see what he wants, Sean."

Sean nodded and then exited the apartment. While he walked down the hallway, familiar, angry voices filled his ear, making him shake. He crept to the balcony. What he saw made his body twitch. It was Chase, Taz, Spike, and other members of his brother's gang holding guns to Jamal's head.

"Come out and play, Sean!" Taz laughed.

"Let 'em go!" Sean yelled.

"Just run, Sean!" With the barrel of a gun in his mouth, Jamal's words didn't travel far.

"No! If you run..." Chase cocked back his pistol and then aimed it at Sean. "Then you both die!"

Sean trembled as he made his way down to them. When he neared the gate, Chase's gang lifted their pistols at him. Shaking in place, he stared Jamal in the eyes. The young boy wondered why he didn't see this coming. After all, his brother wasn't the one to play games. Yesterday a life filled with abuse and neglect seemed to be over. Yet, less than 24 hours later, it was coming back in full force worse than ever. And he'd managed to get his closest friend caught in the middle of it.

While he slowly twisted the handle, Sean's heart sunk. Before he could even step out the gate, Spike pulled him through by his wrist. A pillow case was placed over his head, ropes around his limbs. However, Chase and his gang weren't satisfied. The nefarious group tied a cord around Sean's neck, cutting off his air. Soon after, Taz slammed the misguided boys face into the concrete. Before he knew it, Sean found himself inside a trunk.

Jamal's cries for help echoed in Sean's ear while one of the goons shut the trunk door. Before long, the car's engine had drowned out the cries. A Metallica song boomed in his eardrums. He fought to breathe. Stars appeared before his eyes. When he tried loosening the cord, it tightened, increasing the amount of stars.

While the gang sped over curbs and speed bumps, he hit his head against the trunks metal. His body squirmed, eyes bulging. By then, the stars had become rapid flashes of light. Sean gasped for one last breath. But the cord wouldn't allow it. And he lost consciousness.

A few minutes later, Spike opened the trunk, asking, "Hey, is this kid dead?" He pulled the pillow case off of Sean's head and then untied the cord.

Sean wheezed. When he opened his eyes, he saw Chase and Spike staring him in the face. He looked around to see meth lab equipment in the living room of an empty house. "Where the hell are we?!"

"Keep ya fuckin' mouth shut!" Chase unbound Sean's hands and feet.

Sean was led to the back of the house and up a badly damaged, wooden staircase. Chase kept his pistol pointed at Sean's head until they arrived outside a door on the second floor. After Spike kicked it in, Sean's spine stiffened. In the middle of the ancient, mold-consumed bathroom before him, was Jamal on his knees, Mossberg shotgun aimed at his temple. Behind Jamal, Taz cackled psychotically.

"The fuck is this?!" Sean covered his mouth. His lip trembled.

Chase pulled out a .44 Magnum. "Thought I said to keep ya fuckin' mouth shut?!"

"Let's just get this over with!" Another gang member walked up the stairs with three snapping pit bulls.

"Someone's gonna die!" Chase handed the Magnum to Sean. "Now who's it gonna be?"

"I ain't..." Sean took a deep breath. "Killin' nobody."

"It's you or him!" Chase shook his head. "I told ya not to hang 'round this fuckin' nigger."

"Fuck!" Jamal cried. "We friends remember?! Don't ya remember, Sean?!"

"Who's it gonna be, Sean?!" Chase slapped Sean in the back of the head. "You got 30 seconds before we kill you *and* him! 30, 29, 28..."

"You think we're playin' with you, bitch?!" Taz grinned, brushing away the ring of crystal methamphetamine lining his nostril. "Mother fucker, we'll rip the spine right outcha asshole faster than you can change a tampon!"

"Don't make me do this shit, Chase!" Sean pointed the gun at the side of Jamal's head.

"Come on, buddy!" Jamal struggled to get away, his eyes overflowing with tears. "Don't do this! They don't care 'bout ya, Sean!"

"19, 18, 17..." Chase tapped his foot on the ground.

"What else am I supposed to do?!" Sean took a step forward, aiming the Magnum at Jamal's forehead.

"13, 12, 11," Chase continued.

"No!" Sean let off two shots.

Both bullets ripped through Taz's throat, causing him to drop his shotgun. Not even a second later, blood poured out like water from a running faucet. He wrapped his hands around his wounds. His face hit the floor. The deranged gangster choked violently on the bullet clogging his windpipe. Then he took his final breath. Blood filled his lungs, and his body went limp.

"Jamal, get up!" Sean's body slammed Chase into the dogs and the other gang member, sending them all tumbling down the stairs. "Grab the shotgun and let's go!"

"Y-yeah, man!" Jamal picked up the shotgun and then bolted down the stairs with Sean.

Once they reached the bottom, they jumped over the recuperating thugs. Sean took the lead, running like a starving wolf after an injured elk.

Soon they had exited the house. But more gang members were waiting outside. Immediately, the two dashed through the snow, shots popping off behind them.

Jamal sped up to avoid the powerful jaws of the pit bulls hunting him down. "Where the hell do we go, kid?!"

"Dunno, just run!" Sean dashed down the street, passing old, abandoned houses.

Soon Jamal and Sean's path was blocked by a chain-linked fence. Before they could even begin to climb it, one of the bloodthirsty dogs clamped its fangs onto Sean's ankle like a vice grip. Jamal spun around and then squeezed the trigger of his shotgun. Blood and brains of the beast flew through the air. Only seconds later, the sharp teeth of the other two dogs dug into Jamal's leg.

"They're comin'! Just shoot 'em both!" Sean tugged at his hair.

Jamal blew off the leg of one dog and sent a second shot bursting through the chest of the other. He threw the empty shotgun to the side and scurried up the fence with Sean. At the top, razor wire cut deep through their flesh.

Sean jumped down to the frost covered ground. "There's another fence up ahead!"

"Through there!" Jamal dropped to the ground and then dashed toward an alley on their left.

Chase's black truck recklessly drove over the chain-linked fence. Bullets from their guns flew through the air like birds in the sky.

Sean fired two shots behind him, hitting a thug in the forearm. "Ya even know where that goes?! Could be a dead end!"

"Too late to turn back! Just keep goin'!" Jamal howled, knocking over metal trashcans.

The truck stopped. Chase's crew jumped out. After they reloaded their guns, they continued chasing Jamal and Sean. As they ran, they squeezed their triggers. Bullets bounced off the walls, crumbling the bricks it was made of.

"We can't run forever ya know!" Jamal yelled.

"I know! We just gotta—" Sean began.

"Hey, Sean watch this!" Spike aimed his shotty at Jamal and then squeezed the trigger.

Jamal's lower back caught the shot. Pellets shattered his spinal cord, sending bone fragments exploding into his esophagus. He hit the snow. His body spun into violent tics, his limbs flailing and eyes spiraling.

"Jamal!" Sean cried, stopping dead his tracks.

Blood and saliva dripped off Jamal's bottom lip. He became still.

Tears filled Sean's eyes. He stood there hoping Jamal would get up to tell him everything would be alright. "Fuck man! Get the fuck up! We gotta go!"

"You're next, Sean!" Spike popped three shots from a 625 Smith and Wesson.

A bullet clipped Sean in the arm. Wrath blazed in his eyes like heat from a furnace. He aimed the Magnum at Chase. Then squeezed the trigger. A hollow-point thrashed through Chase's eye socket, sending him to the ground.

After seeing his older brother fall to the ground, Sean darted out of the alley and toward another row of abandoned houses. "Jamal!"

"You little shit!" Spike had caught up. He grabbed the back of Sean's shirt. "That was ya fuckin' brother! And Taz was mine!"

"Ain't got no fuckin' brother!" Sean's heartbroken voice cracked. He spun around, pistol-whipping Spike in the face.

Spike collided with the ground, snow covering his leather jacket.

Sean sprinted to one of the empty houses. After running up its snow covered steps, he swung open the door. He then slammed it shut and locked it tight.

"Get the fuck out here, you pussy!" Spike yelled while he body-slammed the front door.

Sean ran through a trash covered living room and to the kitchen. He pressed his back against the wall, sliding to the ground. He couldn't help putting his hands over his face and sobbing.

After a few moments, the young, terrorized adolescent squeezed his wound to try and stop the blood from seeping out.

"I'mma shove this pump up ya ass, boy!" One of the gang members named Cole, let off a shot through the door.

Sean scattered through a hallway and to the back of the house. As soon as he entered the room at the end, a window above a radiator caught his sight. He jumped over trash bags and empty beer cans. Before he knew it, he was using the Magnum to break through the glass.

Suddenly, an enraged, overweight man stormed into the room. He pulled out a knife. "Who the hell are you?!"

Chapter Twenty-Four

Framed

Present day...

As sweat dripped from my face, I tiptoed to the top of basement staircase with Tabitha and Sean. When I reached the top, I stepped into the hallway, whispering, "Nobody's here."

Sean snuck to the window and then peered through the blinds. "Damn. They got 'bout ten squad cars outside."

"We don't got time to check that out." I poked my head into the room where I'd found the photo album. "Just start searchin' the house."

Tabitha and Sean walked down the hallway and disappeared into one of the rooms. I walked through the doorway and checked the closet. The police uniform I'd seen earlier was gone.

Tabitha poked her head through the door. "I don't see anyone."

"He's been here." I walked toward her and then left the room.

"How do you know?" she asked.

"That police officer's uniform I saw's gone." I walked with her down the hall.

"Maybe someone else came and took it?" she suggested.

"I doubt it," I replied. "You guys check all the rooms?"

"Sean's checking the last one on this floor." She led me down the hall.

Sean exited one of the rooms. "Let's check upstairs."

After we reached the second floor, we walked into a dark room filled with trash. Tabitha immediately screamed. A man in a black jumpsuit and ski mask stood in front of us. Even with the mask, I could tell it was Leon. His long, uncombed hair still flowed behind his back.

He let a punch fly to my mouth, making me drop the pipe. When I tried to grab it, he snatched it up and struck my back. Then he bashed the side of Sean's head.

"Oh my God!" Tabitha ran down the stairs.

Leon pulled out his knife. A hard kick to his shin and the bastard dropped the pipe. Another kick. He stumbled back and fell down the stairs.

I grabbed the pipe and darted after him with Sean. When we reached the hallway downstairs, we saw Leon standing next to Tabitha at the end of it.

There was blood on his knife.

"Tabitha!" Sean's eyes grew wide. "Don't, Leon!"

"Leon, stop!" My heart slowed down. "Stop!"

Leon slid his blade into Tabitha's stomach. She screamed in agony. My gut sunk. I ran toward Leon and bashed the pipe against his head. The coward ran into the basement. Blood oozed from Tabitha. She collapsed. Sean ran to her. I followed Leon. But by the time I entered the basement, he was gone.

"Get back up here!" Sean poked his head into the basement. "Get the fuck back up here!"

I rushed back to Tabitha. She didn't look good. She didn't look good at all. Outta all of us, I couldn't understand why he stabbed Tabitha. She never did anything to him. In fact, she probably cared more about him than he did. Tabitha was just that kind of person.

Sean covered his mouth. "Oh fuck, man!"

"Oh, God! It hurts!" Tabitha cried.

"We gotta stop the blood, Sean!" I crouched down and pulled out the knife. Blood rushed out the wound and filled the creases in the floorboards. "You'll be fine, Tabitha!"

"Okay." She nodded and kept her eyes on me.

"Stay with us, Tabitha!" I placed my hand over her wounds.

"I'm here," she whispered. "I think I'm gonna make it."

"Ya sure 'bout that?!" Sean quivered.

"Yeah, I'm sure," she whispered. "I never thanked either of you, ya know."

"For what?!" Sean used his shirt to wipe his eyes.

"Just being alive," Tabitha smiled. Her eyes shifted between me and Sean. "Just being here with me on this earth, ya know? I dunno where I would be right now if you guys never found me."

Sean grabbed her hand. "No problem."

"Sean, go after Leon!" I looked him in the eyes.

"But she—" he started.

"Just fuckin' go!" I handed him my pager and Leon's photo album. "I'mma make sure she gets help!"

He trembled. "But—"

"Now!" I pressed my hand back on Tabitha's injury.

"Fine!" He bolted into the basement.

I turned back to Tabitha, holding back tears. "You ain't gonna leave us, right?!"

She coughed up blood. Then her body convulsed.

I dashed through the front door toward the cops. For some reason, I thought they could help us. But I was so caught up in saving Tabitha I didn't realize I was still holding the knife.

Or that there was blood all over my clothes.

"Hey! We need some fuckin' help!" I screamed.

One of the cops aimed his gun at my forehead. "Freeze! Drop the weapon and put your hands in the air!"

The other officers pulled out their pistols.

"You stupid idiots!" I did as they said. "My friend needs help!"

"Get down on your knees and lay flat on your stomach!" The officer carefully approached me.

A few minutes later, I was handcuffed and in the back of a police cruiser. I shook off my nerves when I realized Tabitha would be fine. Now the only problem was finding Leon. Well, that and explaining the situation to the cops.

An ambulance arrived on the scene a short time later. A few moments later, two medics were hauling a stretcher and a box of medical equipment into the house.

"Thank God." I leaned back into my seat.

Once I saw the first medic pulling the stretcher outta the house, I pressed my head against the driver's seat, wondering how long she'd be in the hospital. But then I took another glance out the window. My heart sunk so low it put the Titanic to shame.

Tabitha was dead.

Chapter Twenty-Five

Behind Closed Doors

Five years earlier...

The man pointed the knife at Sean. "What the hell are you doing in here?!"

"Leavin'!" Sean shouted.

"You ain't goin' nowhere!" The man ran toward Sean, waving the blade through the air.

Sean lifted the Magnum to the man's face. But the overweight man slapped the gun away and sliced Sean's cheek. With nowhere to go, Sean backed into a corner. The man charged forward. Sean's body trembled, his chest heaved.

Sean didn't know what else to do. He closed his eyes and squeezed the trigger. A shard of metal flew through the air and into the aggravated man's stomach. The man dropped to the floor, squealing in pain.

At the front of the house, Chase's gang cracked the front door off its hinges. Sean darted toward the window. But then he heard the faint voice of a young girl.

"Anyone out there?!" she yelled. "Please help me! I'm down in the basement!"

Sean hesitated for a moment, trying to fight the urge to flee. With his heart racing, he jetted to the hallway. He stopped. There was an open door to his right. Inside, a wooden staircase led down to a semi-lit basement. From down below, the girl's cries grew louder.

"Guess who it is, bitch?!" Spike blew a hole through the front door.

Sean didn't wait for Spike to reload. He bolted into the basement and locked the door behind him. The frightened, heartbroken boy then sprinted to the bottom.

What he saw was pure horror.

"Over here! My name's Tabitha!" The girl named Tabitha was bound to a heavily blood-stained mattress. Her face had been masked with a cloth. "Is anyone there?!"

"Yeah, I'm here," Sean shook, examining the bruises covering her body from head to toe. Once he heard Spike bang on the basement door, he scampered to the bed and removed the cloth.

"Who are you?! Where are the police?!" Tabitha thrashed around, her lip quivering like the string on a harp. "Why do you have a gun?! Who are those people yelling?!"

"We don't got time for this!" Sean shouted, untying her legs. He eyed the bloody chains hanging from the basement rafters.

"Open the damn door, Sean!" Spike pounded on the door.

Sean continued to untie Tabitha. He eyed the gruesome Polaroid photographs pinned to the clothes lines above him. Each one depicted an atrocity that made his stomach flip like a gymnastics team.

"Got it!" Sean trembled, throwing the rope into a box of VHS tapes which were only marked by date.

"My arms!" she yelled. "Please!"

Shots flew through the basement door. Sean's muscles stiffened. He ran toward a window on the other side of the room.

"No, no!" Tabitha squirmed. "Please don't leave me!"

Sean stopped, realizing what Spike and the others would do to her. It took him less than five seconds to spin back around and dart to her arms. It didn't matter if she was a stranger—he couldn't leave her to die. Jamal would have done the same, and he knew it.

"I said open the god damn door, Sean!" Spike let off another shot.

Sean tugged on the rope until it came loose. After helping her off the mattress, he took her hand and raced to the window. Once they reached it, Tabitha attempted to jump up and grab the windowsill.

"I can't reach it by myself!" Tabitha cried. "You have to help me!"

"Yeah, I got it!" Sean gave her a boost.

Spike kicked the basement door off its hinges. "We're here, punk!"

Tabitha had climbed to the other side. She stuck her arm back through. "Grab my hand!"

"You ain't goin' nowhere!" Spike stomped down the stairs with the others.

Sean grabbed Tabitha's hand, lifting himself up. She grabbed his collar and pulled it until he was outside the basement. Less than a second later, they were sprinting to the street.

"Cole, E.J.! They're comin' 'round the side!" Spike yelled out from the window.

Two men emerged from the backyard and emptied their clips. Sean pulled on Tabitha's arm, leading her to the end of the cul-de-sac. Shots flew through the air. Tabitha jumped. Sean shook.

"Where the fuck do we go?!" Sean yelled.

"Through there!" Tabitha pointed beyond the houses at the end of the road. "I think there's a factory on the other side!" She spun her head around. "Who are those people?! Why don't you shoot them?!"

"No ammo!" Sean tossed the gun to the side then ran to the backyard of one of the houses. "And don't worry 'bout who they are! Just run!"

They climbed over a wooden fence and dashed through a field of frost covered tumbleweeds.

Sean's head filled with visions of being brutally beaten and murdered. Spots appeared before his eyes. His lungs burned. Despite all of this he grabbed Tabitha's sleeve. Together, they ran through the field and under a gigantic, steel transmission tower.

Soon they came upon a rusty chain link fence. Sean grabbed its bottom and pulled it up. Tabitha slid under. Then while Sean was about to do the same, his brother's gang closed in. His pulse raced. He lost his grip and slipped.

"We just wanna play Sean!" E.J. laughed.

The hairs on the back of Sean's neck stood up. He scampered to the top of the fence. "Tabitha, run!"

"Ain't gonna tell that slut what you just did, Sean?!" Cole ran up and rattled the fence.

Sean lost his balance and fell flat on his face next to Tabitha. "Run!"

Tabitha helped Sean up and darted toward an Oldsmobile lying on its side. "Shouldn't we take cover behind that car?!"

"For what?!" Sean panted. Every breath was like a painful inhalation of 1,000 needles. "We'll just corner ourselves!"

"Yeah, but they still have guns, ya know!" she replied.

"I don't think they got any more bullets!" Sean tried to ignore the cramp in his chest. "They haven't let off any shots in a while!"

Tabitha tripped over a metal pipe and fell. Cole caught up to her and immediately shoved her face in the snow. Her weak body was no match for the massive muscles buldging from his arms. It was up to Sean to save her.

And he did. He kneed Cole in the face. With that blow, the steroid-abusing thug fell to the ground.

"You're fuckin' dead!" Cole screamed, clutching his eye.

Sean and Tabitha bolted to a nearby lumber factory filled with large logs and massive piles of sawdust.

"Through there!" Tabitha pointed at a tan painted building.

Sean sprinted to it. But then he saw the 'Closed until further notice' sign on the door. He pounded his fists on the door. But it was no use. The door was locked tight.

Tabitha picked up a metal pipe off the ground, hitting a window with all her might. "I can't break—"

"Got 'em cornered right here, boys!" Spike yelled.

"Don't think I can run much more!" Sean clutched his wound and trailed up a stairwell to their left.

"I know!" Tabitha cried, looking at the blood oozing down Sean's arm. "We have to stop soon! You'll bleed to death!"

At the top of the stairwell, they reached another door. Sean clutched its handle only to discover that it, too, was locked. Their only escape route was a railing that led to the roof. They'd have to jump. But there was a six-foot gap in between. Missing the ledge would mean a straight drop to the concrete below. However, Sean and Tabitha didn't have a choice. The other option was to face a brutal beating and a certain death.

Sean mounted the railing. He looked down. The sight of the 60-foot drop made him shut his eyes. For a moment, he hesitated. But he couldn't for long. His hunters were already halfway up the staircase. He made the jump and flew through the air. His fingertips grasped the edge of the roof. With all the icicles, he started to slip.

"Sean, help! They're coming!" Tabitha screamed.

The thought of her being raped and murdered crossed his mind. He used all his might to pull himself up. When he was on his own two feet, he turned to Tabitha.

They were coming for her.

She climbed on the railing. A breeze flowing through her blouse, she shook. Her fear of heights left her trembling. "I don't think—"

"Just jump! Don't look down!" Sean yelled.

"I can't do it!" she cried.

"Just jump!" Sean stomped his foot.

Tabitha jumped. But her legs weren't strong enough. She began to fall.

Sean grabbed her wrist and pulled her up. "Gotcha!"

"Yeah, you better run, you little shits!" Spike raised his middle finger.

Sean and Tabitha scurried down a ladder on the other side of the roof. The two of them sprinted out of the factory and into the city, eventually finding refuge behind a dumpster in an alley. By then, their muscles were so weak they were unable to stand. They pressed their backs against the brick wall behind them and then slid down to the snowy, trash covered ground.

An hour passed. Sean still shook at the thought of being found by Spike and the others. He knew they were ruthless enough to murder him and Tabitha in the middle of public. Unfortunately, what he didn't realize was he had nowhere else to go. The tattered boy couldn't go back to Clemecia and Tonya. He'd have to tell them what happened to Jamal. And that was something he didn't have the heart for. In his mind, Jamal's death was his fault, and he had it set that he would and should have been blamed for it.

Eventually, the sun went down. Shoppers from the nearby mall headed to their cars, satisfied with their purchases of clothes, shoes, and other accessories. Along with that, most business owners had shut down their stores and were heading home to watch their favorite TV shows, to see their children, or just relax for the night. With the roads empty, groups of joyful teenagers took the chance to ice skate in the streets. Every one of them was oblivious to the two street rats that had just been released in the cold, lonely, dark maze that was their city.

"I think we should go now." Just as the street lights flickered on, Tabitha rose to her feet. "Oh, that's right! Your arm!" She inspected Sean's injury. "I don't think the bullets inside. Looks like it just scrapped against the flesh."

"Still hurts like hell." Sean ripped off a piece of his sleeve and wrapped it around the wound.

"We gotta go to the hospital!" she cried.

"They'll arrest me." Sean exited the alley and braced himself against the icy breeze. "Just forget about it."

"Well, you have to go home and get some help!" Tabitha pleaded.

"Ain't got no home no more," Sean said. "Ain't got nowhere to go."

Sorrow filled Tabitha's eyes. "That's no good," she said, sighing. "That's no good at all."

"I know, but, well, I mean, where's yours at?" He put his hand on her shoulder.

She brushed it away and folded her arms. Her eyes watered as she whispered, "I dunno…"

Sean regretted asking the question. He watched the tears fall and imagined himself bashing in the head of the man who he stumbled upon.

Tabitha looked to the ground, shivering while snowflakes gently brushed against her face. "I came here from Mexico with my mother and father when I was young." Her lip shook. "A man came…" The distraught, young girl stopped walking and wiped her nose. "And he took me away about three years ago when I was 13." Her eyes met Sean's. "Took me right from my driveway, ya know?" She looked up at the crescent moon and toward the flock of ravens flying in the sky.

"You gonna be—" Sean started.

"I used to imagine I was a bird!" Her ear-splitting tone made a few bystanders spin their heads. "Down in that basement! Just lying on that fucking bed all day and night!" She pressed her hands against her face and sobbed. "I'd lay there imagining I was flying away! Flying far, far, far away! No one could catch me!" She took in a deep breath. "But then he'd come! He'd come to rape me!"

Her voice reaching the heavens, she shrieked, "And I'd come crashing down from the sky!"

"I'm..." Sean tried to fight his tears. "I'm s-sorry 'bout that."

"It's not your fault." Tabitha wiped her eyes while they entered a park consumed by leaves and knocked over garbage cans. "Your names Sean, right? I h-heard them yelling it."

"Yeah, that's right." Sean headed for a wooden bridge that sat above a litter-filled pond. "What was yours?"

She walked under the structure with him. "Mine's Tabitha."

"Alright, well, I guess we can stay here tonight." Sean collapsed to the ground and pulled a few newspapers over his body. He fell asleep almost instantly. While he slept, nothing filled his dreams except guilt and violence.

Little did they know, they had just become invisible to the eyes of everyone who would never be looked down upon just for existing.

Chapter Twenty-Six

Number 1 Suspects

Present day...

Officer Mercer paraded through the lobby of the police station, asking, "So what's left on the agender for today?"

Officer Tanner chuckled. "The agender?"

"Alright, smartass." Officer Mercer grabbed a donut from the front desk. "What's on the agend-UH?" He spun his head around, looking back at Zeke's office.

"Ain't too much left," Officer Tanner said. "Besides ya shift's over ain't it?"

"Is that so?" Officer Mercer took a bite of the donut. Jelly instantly exploded from the other end and dripped onto his uniform. "Dammit!" He clenched his teeth, slamming the pastry into a trashcan. "I hate jelly donuts."

"They ain't so bad." Tanner removed a white handkerchief from his rear pocket before handing it to Mercer.

"Those things are disgusting!" Officer Mercer wiped the jelly from his uniform and then handed the handkerchief back to Tanner. "Don't see how anybody could like that crap."

"My kid seems to like 'em." Tanner folded the handkerchief and then tucked it back into his pocket.

"So does mine, but I don't see how." Mercer looked up to see Officer Walker heading toward him.

"Mercer, right?" said Walker. "Are you still working on that Iron River case?"

Mercer nodded. "Yeah, why?"

"I've got a case I think might be related to yours." Officer Walker stroked his beard. "Mind if I take a look through those files?"

"Yeah, go right ahead," Officer Mercer grinned. "Everything's in my office down the hall. Just put everything back where you found it."

"Thanks." Officer Walker walked passed Mercer and Tanner, heading to Mercer's office.

"Anyway, I'm outta here." Officer Mercer glanced at his wrist watch.

"Takin' the squad car home again, Boss?" Tanner turned, walking with Mercer to the front of the station.

"Yup." Mercer used his thumb to wipe off the remaining pieces of food from the corner of this mouth. "Wife won my car in that god damn divorce court."

Officer Tanner stopped at the exit and opened the glass door, letting Mercer out. "How'd that happen?!"

"Dunno." Officer Mercer removed a ring of keys from his utility belt and turned back to Tanner. "Ask the judge."

He strutted down the steps toward his squad car, his boots tapping against the pavement. After reaching and entering the vehicle, he slammed his fists on the steering wheel. "Fuck that Mercedes!"

"Backup requested, backup requested!" A voice boomed from the police scanner. "We got a 966 over on Palm Street."

Officer Mercer shook his head and lit a cigarette, letting the smoke fly out of his nostrils. The stressed officer left the parking lot. While he drove through the city, a frown appeared on his mug, a sigh left his mouth, and the prideful look in his eyes turned grim.

"Two suspects in custody!" The same voice said. "Repeat! We got two suspects in custody!"

Mercer blew a puff of smoke into the radio. After taking another hit, he dug his hand into the glove compartment and then pulled out an old photograph of a newlywed couple. Looking at the face of the young, blonde woman only made the sadness in his eyes grow. He turned his attention to the younger version of himself holding her hand, wishing he could go back in time.

"A third suspect has been apprehended!" The voice jolted Mercer out of his trance. "A third suspect has been apprehended!"

He slammed his fist down on the steering wheel again and tucked the photograph back where he found it. The usual look of seriousness returned to his eyes, but a frown remained.

"A stabbing victim has been found in a vacant house!" The voice jolted Mercer a second time. "Medics are on their way!"

Growing annoyed with the constant police updates, he switched off the scanner. Then after pulling into the driveway of a two-story, light blue house, he stepped out of his vehicle.

Soon enough, Officer Mercer had entered his house, took off his police gear, and downed a glass of Hennessy. The tonic wasn't enough. It never was. He poured another four glasses and drank them like he'd just come out of a desert. Then he downed a 6-pack of beer. It took less than 10 minutes from the time when he walked through the door for him to pass out on the couch.

Three hours later, he awoke to the annoying sound of his phone's ringer. He stumbled to the kitchen and picked it up, saying, "Wadda ya want—"

"Boss, we got somethin'!" Officer Tanner blurted.

"Rookie, this better be important," Mercer groaned. "I thought I made it clear not to call me after hours."

"You did, Boss, but—"

"But?" Officer Mercer tapped his fingers on the counter. The bottle of Hennessy in front of him was calling his name, eagerly waiting to slither down his throat.

"I think we got 'em!"

"And just who the h-hell is *him*?"

"That guy from the case you been workin' on!"

"The bodies found in the river?! You shittin' me?!"

"Yeah! How fast can ya get to the station?!"

"Give me 'bout half an hour." Mercer hung up the phone and dashed to the front door.

A short time later, after a drunken drive through the city, Mercer parked his cruiser in the parking lot of the police station.

"Boss!" Tanner's faint voice shouted.

Mercer grabbed a roll of breath mints from the glove compartment. He popped one between his teeth, hoping the smell of cinnamon would disguise the alcoholic odor on his breath. The tipsy officer then exited the squad car and walked across the parking to his partner.

"Whoa, you alright, Boss?!" Tanner plugged his nose and took a step back.

"Yeah, yeah, yeah, I'm good." Officer Mercer exhaled while walking up the stairs. "Just gimme the rundown."

"We picked 'em up from a house on Palm Street." Tanner pulled the door open for Mercer after reaching the top of the stairs. "Don't got too much info on 'em right now."

"Oh really?" With the room spinning, it was hard for Mercer to shake off his intoxication.

"This guy's a god damn ghost!" Tanner followed Mercer across the lobby. "Nobody knows who the hell he is."

"Don't worry 'bout that." Mercer nodded at a nearby officer and continued with his excited partner down a corridor. "I'm gonna take care of that."

Officer Mercer strutted down the police station corridors with Officer Tanner, eagerly waiting to see the face of the murder suspect. His body swayed left and right while he walked down the hallways, making other officers swing their heads.

"Alright, he's in here." Tanner stopped outside a two-way mirror and gestured to an African-American man sitting behind it.

"Yup." Officer Mercer adjusted his police cap. "Scruffy. Cornrows. Wife beater. Scar near his eye. Dirty clothes." He folded his arms and grinned. "That's definitely the guy from the security tape."

Officer Tanner handed Mercer a manila folder. "By the way, here's all the case files, Boss."

"Thanks." Officer Mercer flipped through it then took a second look at the suspect. "Say, this guy got a name?"

"Apparently not," said Tanner. "We couldn't get one outta 'em. We couldn't even find any I.D. on 'em." He scratched his head and pressed his forehead against the glass. "Don't look like he got no home neither. It's like this guy just popped outta nowhere."

"Odd." Mercer leaned closer to get a better look, fogging up the glass with his liquor stained breath. "He's gotta have some kinda record somewhere."

"We've been lookin', Boss." Tanner removed his cap and looked Mercer in the eyes. "Thing is nobody 'round here even recognizes him. Like I said this guy's a ghost."

"Alright, just hang tight." Officer Mercer twisted the doorknob to the interrogation room. "I'm gonna find out just exactly who the hell this guy is."

Upon entering the room, Officer Mercer met eyes with a very upset African-American male who looked like he was in his early 20's. All sorts of filth covered the man's skin and clothes, making it appear like he just crawled out of a dumpster. Mercer turned his attention to the suspect's jeans, thinking that they must have been ran through a paper shredder to gain all the holes they contained.

"So how's it goin'?" Officer Mercer eyed the suspect.

"Where the fuck is Tabitha?!" The distraught man pounded his fists against the interrogation table. He then used his arm to wipe away the snot dripping from his nostril. There was so much pain in his eyes that it looked like they would burst if they absorbed anymore.

"We're gonna get to that, but first we're gonna have a little talk." Officer Mercer removed the crime scene photos from the manila folder and flipped them toward the suspect. "Oh, and you can call me Officer Mercer."

The man shook violently. "Oh shit!"

Chapter Twenty-Seven

Face to Face

Present day...

Tabitha was wrapped inside a body bag. While the medics rolled her to the back of the ambulance, a stream of vomit spewed from my mouth. Hot tears rolled down my cheeks. First Xavier. Then her. There wasn't much more I could take.

The medics entered the front of the ambulance, turned on the emergency lights, and then sped off.

"Tabitha!" I bashed my head against the window. "Fuck!"

Sometime later I found myself in a holding cell at the police station. My fingerprints and mug shot had been taken, and I'd been given two quarters to make a phone call. But there was no one to call. Even if I called the pager, I gave Sean there was nothing he could do.

Eventually, I heard a familiar voice yelling, "God damn killa's right there!"

It was Jerome. He stopped outside my cell and spat at me.

"Settle down." One of the cops next to him said. "Keep it moving."

"Y'all 'bout to pass right by 'em!" Jerome thrashed his body around. "That busta ass nigga's right there!"

"Shut the hell up, Jerome!" The cop pushed Jerome's down the corridor. "Nobody gives a shit!"

Even after the cops put Jerome in his own holding cell, he kept up his shouting until two officers appeared outside my cell sometime later.

One removed a ring of keys, unlocked the cell, rushed inside and put me in a chokehold. The second officer handcuffed me. Then they dragged me from my cell and to the end of the corridor.

"Take me to Tabitha!" I wriggled my body.

"Shut the hell up!" one snapped.

"I gotta go fill out some paperwork for Sharon." One of the officers headed back down the hallway. "You got this?"

"Yeah, no problem." The remaining officer pushed me into the room and then handcuffed me to a chair facing a mirror. "Mercer's gonna be here soon."

"What did they do with Tabitha?!" I shouted.

The door slammed. However, there was no doubt in my mind the officer behind it was still watching me. After spending my whole life hidden in the dirt, it was strange being in that kinda spotlight.

A few minutes later, a tall officer walked into the room. "So how's it goin'?"

I pounded my fists against the table in front of me. "Where the fuck is Tabitha?!"

"We're gonna get to that, but first we're gonna have a little talk." He walked over to me then pulled out pictures from a manila envelope. They were pictures of the bodies we'd dumped in Iron River. "Oh, and you can call me Officer Mercer."

The room spun so fast I thought I was gonna puke up every organ in my body. "Oh shit!"

Chapter Twenty-Eight

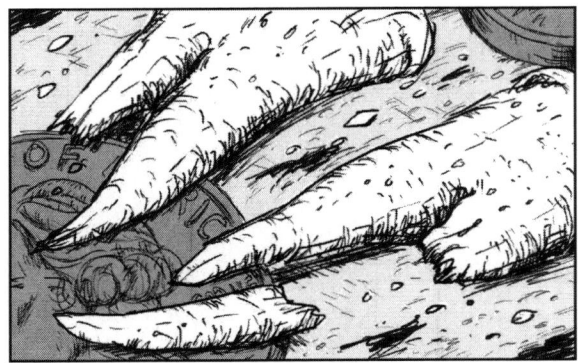

Pearly White Razors

Present day...

If I had a heart attack in that room then that heart attack would've had a heart attack of its very own. Mercer's gaze stayed glued on me.

"Lookin' awfully nervous right now." He slid one of the pictures toward me. "What with all that sweat drippin' on ya face."

I swallowed a large wad of spit and stared at the photo. "J-just feelin' kinda hot."

"When I get hot I usually enjoy eatin' somethin' cold to cool me down." He took a seat across from me and flipped through his folder. "Want me to go get ya some ice cream or a popsicle? The other officers told me they hadn't fed ya."

"I ain't r-really hungry right now." My stomach roared at the worst possible time.

"Sure sounds like ya are." Officer Mercer slid another picture across the table.

The photo of one of the discolored corpses sat inches from me. My face fell flat on the table.

"Need a minute?" He stroked his chin.

"No, I just..." I said, shakin'. I lifted my head and stared at the gory photo.

"Take ya time." He tossed me a third photo. "Take as long as you need."

That was the moment I knew I was done. "I don't..." I swallowed another wad of spit.

"Looks like them boys was in that trunk for a long ass time. Ain't seen bodies as bad as this in a while." He tilted his cap and pulled out a picture of me, Sean, and Leon on the bus. "Say, what an odd coincidence! This picture of you was taken the night of the murder!" he said, chuckling. "And it was even near the scene of the crime!"

I didn't know what to say or do. He had me cornered. And by the looks of it, he knew that I knew. Even if I admitted to it, they'd never believe my story.

"W-what did they do with Tabitha?" I sniveled.

"Is that the name of that girl you just killed?" He removed a slip of paper from the envelope, studying it carefully.

"Nah, man, she was my..." While I used my dirty wife beater to dry my eyes, I suddenly remembered the bones I'd seen. "Wait!"

"Wait for what?" Mercer smirked.

"There's bones! Human bones! In that house!" I slammed my fist on the table. "I swear!"

"Oh really?" Mercer put his hands behind his head and slumped down in his seat.

"Look in my eyes and tell me I'm lyin'!" I gestured to my pupils. "Tell me I'm lyin'!"

"Alright, I'll play along," Officer Mercer said. "So tell me 'bout these *bones.*"

"They..." I tried remembering the names we saw. "Ely! One of their names was Ely!"

"So it's Ely?" Mercer sighed. "And what's the other name?"

I put my hand to my chin, bouncing my leg. "Clyde! It was Clyde! I swear to God!"

"That's the biggest load of..." With his eyebrows raised, he leaned forward. "Wait a second. Did ya just say Clyde and Ely?"

"Yeah! I swear, man! In the basement of that house, there's these two barrels! Blood all inside! That's where they are!" I slammed my fist down again.

Officer Mercer leaned forward with his fingers interlocked. "What's the last name?"

"I can't..." I put my hand over my face. "Jenkins! It's Jenkins!

"Jenkins?" Mercer stared at me, his hand rubbing his chin. "Stay put."

"I still wanna see—" I started.

He left the room.

A few minutes later, when he returned, I locked eyes with him. "I wanna know where they took Tabitha now!"

He sat back down, folding his arms. "We're sending a few officers back over to see if your little story checks out."

"I said I wanna know where Tabitha is!" My muscles tensed.

Officer Mercer stayed quiet. After I mentioned Ely and Clyde, he just stared at me with this 1,000-yard gaze. He didn't seem like cared about Tabitha or even the corpses they found in the trunk. In fact, for a moment, it seemed like he'd forgotten about me as well.

The clock on the wall ticked. And ticked. And ticked. 20 minutes later, he still hadn't moved a muscle.

Suddenly, an officer with a lazy eye poked his head through the door. "Mercer."

Officer Mercer exited the room. He came back seconds later with a scowl on his face. "Our officers checked out the house," he seethed, returning to his seat. "There were no bones." Veins popped up from his forehead and neck. Blood rushed to his face. "There were no barrels, no blood." His nostrils flared. "There was nothing but dust and fucking garbage."

For a second, I wondered if I was seeing things again. Then I remembered Sean saw them, too. "No! They were down—"

Officer Mercer bashed his fists on the table. "Enough of this bullshit!" He rolled up his sleeves. "Let's get back on topic." He tightened his jaw. "Looks like you were ridin' the number 23 bus one night a few months back." His eyes shifted up and down the picture in front of him "Pretty strange hours for a midnight stroll."

"I was just c-comin' back from—"

"Why was there blood on ya shirt? Was it hunting season?"

"I think I injured m-myself that night."

"Tell me how."

"Well, I was..." My mind was as blank as the wall behind me. "I got jumped, man."

"What did they look like?"

"I dunno, man! It was dark!"

"They look like this?" He pulled out a picture of one of the victims standing near a trampoline. "Or how 'bout this?" He showed me a second one of the other one pushing a lawn mower.

"I don't—"

"Looks like they seem familiar to ya."

"Think I r-ran into 'em a few times."

"Hmm, so you *have* met them."

"Well, I—"

"So what happened? Did them boys owe you money?"

My breaths became quick and short. "I—"

"They say the wrong thing?" It seemed like a hammer and chisel wouldn't have been able to break his stone face.

"There wasn't—"

"Why don't we talk 'bout that young girl named Tadra?"

"Her name's Tabitha!" Tears fell from my face and onto the photos.

"Right, right, Tabitha." Officer Mercer put his elbows on the table and leaned closer. "Let's talk 'bout *Tabitha*."

"She was my friend!" The tears wouldn't stop coming.

"Well, let's see 'bout that." Mercer pulled out another slip of paper. "Says here that her body was found in an abandoned house." He lifted his eyes. "You were found soaked in her blood with a knife in ya hand."

I slapped my palm against the table. "It was—"

"That don't sound like somethin' a friend would do." Mercer looked back to the paper. "Medics tried to treat multiple stab wounds. Nobody else was inside the house." He slipped the document back into the folder. "How ya gonna explain that one?"

"They..." I bit my thumb. "I mean, he was—"

"So was it they or was it he?" he asked.

"It was…" I put my hands over my face. "It was Leon!"

"So everybody wants to say it was somebody else, huh?" He took another glance at the clock on the wall. "When we find Leon who's he gonna say it was? The milkman?"

"I don't…" Mentioning Leon made me remember he was still after Sean and me. Even though there was the risk of going to prison, I was still safe in that room. But Sean wasn't. He was roaming around the city, waiting for me to find him and tell him Tabitha would be just fine.

I realized I had to find a way out. My eyes shifted to the door and then to the gun on the table.

"Try and take it." Officer Mercer inched it toward me. "I fuckin' dare you."

I slipped my tongue between my front teeth.

"This still ain't lookin' too good for ya," he said. "Like I said before prisons a pretty scary place."

There was nothing he could do or say that would've scared me at that point. The plan I had was already frightening enough.

It would either buy me time or kill me.

"Ready to fess up?" Mercer asked. "This can be a lot easier than you make it."

I drove my teeth into my tongue. The flesh broke. Blood flooded throughout my mouth and down my throat.

"Are you…" he squinted.

I gripped the sides of my seat and sunk my fangs deeper.

"Hey!" Officer Mercer bolted from his chair.

I fell forward, banging my head on the table. A waterfall of slobber and blood poured out my mouth and down my chin, spilling onto the photos.

"Call a fuckin' ambulance!" Mercer shook my shoulder just before I blacked out. "He just bit through his tongue!"

Chapter Twenty-Nine

Flight Risk

Seventeen hours later...

Athin, blonde nurse pricked my arm with a needle, jolting me out of my sleep. She scowled and turned to the heart rate monitor next to my hospital bed. Then she jotted down a note on her clipboard and watched me tug at the handcuffs binding me to the bed.

"There's an officer right outside that door, sir." She pointed to a muscular cop standing just outside the doorway.

I looked around the room at the visitor chairs, portraits of geese on the walls, and the beam of sun shining through the window. Then I gazed into the mirror on the wall in front of me, looking at the bandages on my shoulder and around my head. It took me a second to remember how I got there, but when I felt the sharp pain in my jaw, it all came back to me.

I tugged at the handcuffs again.

"There's no way you're getting outta here." She crossed her arms and left the room.

As soon as she was gone, the officer outside walked into the room. When he was near me, he dropped a brown, paper bag onto my bed and then looked me in the eyes. "Do you...remember me?"

I sat there with my mouth wide open, staring at a ghost of the past. After so many years, Mike was in front of me like he never disappeared in the first place. He stood at least 6'5 with so many bulging muscles it looked like Hercules had slipped into a cop's uniform.

"I never told a single soul...'bout what happened that night." He put his hands in his pockets and darted his gaze to the ground. "I been lookin' for ya..." A depressing sigh left through his nostrils. "For a couple years now."

My eyes darted to the pistol on his hip. I inched my arm toward it.

He didn't seem to notice.

The blonde nurse poked her head through the door. "We're gonna have to move him upstairs for security reasons, so I'll be back in a few minutes." She shut the door and strutted off into the hallway.

I inched my arm closer. But as soon as my fingertips brushed against it, the heart rate monitor exploded. Mike grabbed my wrist. He had the same look in his eyes he had years ago when he trailed off into the forest.

"I'm gonna..." He paused. "I'm gonna get ya outta here."

"W-why?" With my tongue swollen, I could barely talk.

"Because you did the same..." He unlocked my handcuffs and then handed me the bag. "For me. Ya set me free."

I opened it. Inside was a pair of jeans, a plain, white T-shirt, and a pair of green Converse Nikes. Without questioning him, I tore off my hospital gown and slipped on the clothes. He nodded and then led me out the room and down the corridor.

A few minutes into our escape, a pair of guards strutted around a corner toward us. Mike shoved me into a nearby storage closet and slammed the door shut. Through the small glass window, I could see the guards.

One with sunglasses folded his arms, saying, "We just got word from a nurse the criminal sent here escaped. You were supposed to be watching him weren't you?"

"I just went to..." Mike looked down. "The bathroom and he was gone."

The guard stared at him, curling his lips. "What do you mean he was just gone?!"

Mike stood there for a few seconds. "He must have escaped."

"Oh great! I knew we should have had our guards watch him!" The guard stomped his foot. "He couldn't have gotten far! Go check the rooms!"

"Right." The second guard scampered down the corridor.

The first guard lowered his sunglasses. "You better find him before he gets away!" He took off after his partner.

After they left, Mike opened the door. "We have to go now."

I nodded and followed him through a door that led to a concrete staircase. We crept down about six or seven flights of stairs and ended up in the hospital lobby.

We went down a corridor on the right. But there was a guard waiting at the end of the hall. Just as he spotted us, we darted into the room of a sleeping old man.

"Hey!" The guard's stomps echoed in the hall behind us.

"There's n-nowhere to go." I glanced around the room, my face sweating.

"Through there." Mike pointed to a window near the man's bed.

The stomps grew closer. I ran toward the window and flung it open. After glancing back at Mike one last time, I slipped into the bushes outside the building. Mike hurried over and shut the window just as the guard stormed into the room.

He glared at Mike. They eventually returned to the hallway, but only after Mike gave me a quick nod.

When I was sure no one was watching, I crept behind the row of bushes that ran along the hospital wall. It took me a few minutes to reach the end, where I rose to my feet and walked toward a fence. A guard stuck his head out a window on the upper level of the hospital.

"There he is! Call the cops!" he shouted. "He's getting away!"

I jumped over the fence and bolted down an alleyway on the other side. But halfway to the exit I tripped over a three-legged dog and fell to the ground. It yelped and ran back to its makeshift cardboard box of a home.

Police sirens sounded in the distance. They were coming for me. As I rose to my feet, the dog exited the cardboard box. It snarled at me. Suddenly, its pups walked out the tattered home, blindly barking at everything they could. That full grown mutt was riddled with defects, but its children still looked up to it for protection.

If that flawed mongrel could protect its pack, why couldn't I? It was still able to feed its young, so with my battered mind, why wasn't I able to save Tabitha? With its blind eye, it could still stand its ground against me, so with all my pain and exhaustion, what was stopping me from saving Sean? And most of all, what was stopping me from saving myself?

Soon I'd exited the alley and was running full speed down the side walk. A cop speeding down the street spotted me. He stopped and made a U-turn. I continued running. However, by the time I was at the end of the block, three cops were hot on my trail.

"Freeze! Put your hands in the air!" one shouted.

I ran passed bystanders and shops. They stayed right behind me with every twist and turn. Not only that but every time I looked over my shoulder it there were more and more of them. Soon the sound of sirens blared in the dark streets, emergency lights flashing all around me.

An officer ahead of me pulled out his gun, and yelled, "Freeze!"

I darted into a nearby alley. He popped off a few shots. I flinched. Left and right, trashcans fell over while I scrambled to get away.

"I told you to freeze!" The cop and the rest of his squad chased after me.

I dashed down a connecting alley and toward a concrete staircase. There was a basement door at the bottom. If I could reach it without the cops seeing me, I'd be safe. For a while at least.

I ran to the bottom of the steps, swung open the door, and slammed it shut behind me. Washing machines, dryers, dust and a few water heaters sat in front of me—not very good hiding spots.

Then I spotted the door on my right.

"Check over there! Me and Todd are gonna check down these stairs!" A cop yelled outside.

A professional racing horse couldn't have dashed through that door faster than I did. After shutting and locking it, I turned around to see cleaning supplies on my right and another staircase on my left. With that room being so small, I couldn't help but feel like I was in the closet of a house.

"You check in them dryers." The voices of the cop traveled through the doorway. "I'm gonna check behind them water heaters."

I tiptoed passed the rotted, cobweb covered walls and toward the staircase, but stopped when two women appeared at the top.

"Did ya hear what that bitch said 'bout me last night?" One of yelled.

While they bickered, I hid behind the corner and prayed they would leave. One of them walked down the stairwell. My breaths became short and quick, making a nearby cobweb flutter back and forth.

"Renea, I gotta go wash Sofia and Steve's clothes real fast!" The woman continued down the steps.

"What the hell, Renona?!" The second woman screeched. "You said you'd watch Malik and Zyren while I go to the store!"

"Oh! I almost forgot about that!" The first woman walked away from the staircase.

Once they were gone, I carefully walked up the stairwell.

The officers pounded on the door behind me. "Open up!"

I scampered up the stairs, bolting around the corner and down the hall, passing several apartments until I saw one that read, 'Eviction Notice: All Tenants Must Evacuate the Premises!' I looked through the window. There was nothing but darkness. Whoever lived there must've abandoned it.

Sirens blared. Emergency lights flashed. Over the balcony behind me, I could see the cops speeding up and down the streets. There was no choice but to break in.

I turned the doorknob and found it was unlocked. When I turned on the lights, I realized why the eviction notice was served—the only thing that wasn't broken was a small television on a lawn chair. Everything else was either a mess or in shambles. Sadly, even with all the rats and garbage, the junkyard was in better shape than that hellhole.

I waded through a sea of empty beer cans, sat down on the sheet-less, stained mattress in the corner, and picked up a phone that sat next to my foot. My plan was to contact Sean through the pager I'd given him, but the problem was I didn't know how to use it for anything other than checking the time.

Suddenly, a paper pad grabbed my attention. Before I'd realized it, I was flipping through it, seeing different names and phone numbers from front to back.

As I got to the last page, an idea popped into my head. It was a long shot, but one of them folks in the pad had to know how to use a pager, so if I called one of them, I was sure I could get the info. The only thing was they could've found my call suspicious. What else could I do though? Stay in that apartment until I starved or the police found me?

I picked up the phone and dialed one of the numbers from the pad. It ringed twice before someone answered it, shouting, "What the hell you callin' at this time for?!

"I'm lookin' for..." I grabbed a piece of mail off the TV and looked for the apartment owner's name. "I'm lookin' for Francis Wilson."

"Francis?! That punk never gave me my damn money!" he yelled.

"Yeah, that's why I'm..." I stopped for a moment. "That's why I'm lookin' for him."

"What the hell are you saying?!" he asked.

With my tongue all swollen, I could barely pronounce half the words coming out of my mouth.

"I'm going to get ya damn money!" I said slowly.

"Gonna get my money?" His voice softened. "When?"

Helicopter spotlights flashed through the front window, making my voice shake. "Tonight."

"For real?! How?!" he bellowed. "That Francis guy's shady as hell."

"He got a new pager." I could feel my tongue swelling up even worse. "I just dunno how to call that damn thing."

"Don't know how to call a pager?! You gotta be kiddin' me! Just call his pager number and then dial the number you want him to call you back at," he said.

"Alright, I'll talk to him and then hit you back up." I hated lying to the poor guy like that. It made me feel no different from Leon.

I hung up the phone, ripped open the same of piece of mail, and jotted down the owner's number in my head. It took a few seconds for me to remember the pager number, but as soon as it came to me, I did exactly what the dude on the phone told me to do.

A few minutes later, I was looking for something to eat in the kitchen. To my surprise, it was filthier than the living room. The sink was filled with used needles, moldy scraps of food covered the floor, and a horrid smell came from the overflowing garbage can. The only thing I could actually eat was the canned food in the cupboards. It wasn't until after I searched that entire God forsaken apartment that I realized there wasn't a single can opener.

An hour of trying to find some way to open the canned foods went by. The only reason I stopped was because the phone rang. Maybe it was a friend of the old apartment owner. Or maybe it was the dude I called earlier. Either way, I walked to the phone and answered it.

"Hello?" Sean said.

"Sean!" I wiped the sweat from my palms onto the back of my jeans. "It's me!"

Chapter Thirty

Bad News and Worse News

Present day...

Sean yelled into the phone, "Where are ya?! Everybody in the entire city's lookin' for you! There's cops on every block!"

"In some trashy apartment!" The injury on my tongue made it almost impossible to say anything clearly.

"Which apartment?" Sean paused. "You don't sound so good."

"There was an accident. And I got some..." I stopped for a few seconds, feelin' an ache in my chest. "I got some really bad news."

"What is it?" he asked.

"I just..." I didn't have the heart to tell him over the phone. "Just, where are you?"

"In the subway," he said. "You know how to get to Pepper Park?"

My mind drifted, making me wonder what Sean's reaction would be once I told him.

"Hello?" he asked.

"Yeah, I do," I said.

"Alright, I'll be there," he responded. "Under the bridge."

"Yeah, man." I tried to stop my voice from quivering. "Give me some time."

"Alright, peace." He hung up the phone.

Different conversations about Tabitha between Sean and I played in my head, and each one was even more devastating than the last. So many images of his sorrow flashed in my mind I had to dig my fingers into the sides of my head just to stop them.

45 minutes later, I was at Pepper Park. Sean was right. The cops were everywhere—every street corner. And they were all looking for me. It wasn't easy getting passed them. I had to go through back alleys, on rooftops, and through a few backyards just so I wouldn't be seen.

"Over here! I'm over here!" Sean's voice echoed.

I looked around to see Sean creeping out from under a bridge. His face lit up, and he let out a loud laugh. "Made it here alive, did ya?!"

"Yeah, man..." That smile of his made my heart sink so deep in my chest a submarine wouldn't have been able to fish it out.

"What's up with ya voice?!" He stopped and gave me a funny look.

I opened my mouth and pointed at my tongue.

"God damn!" Sean stepped back. "What happened?!"

"Long ass story." I headed toward a parking lot on the far side of the park. "Look, I gotta tell you—"

He spun around. "Where's Tabitha? Still in the hospital?"

"Sean…" The words were on the tip of my tongue. And they burned like acid. "Tabitha didn't…"

"Tabitha didn't what?" His head dropped. It was like he already knew.

Tears ran down my face. "Listen, man, when Leon—"

"Tabitha didn't what?!" he shouted, clenching his fists.

"They couldn't save her, Sean!"

"W-what…"

"Tabitha's gone…"

"Shut up! Shut the fuck up!" His heart broken cries boomed throughout the park. "I don't believe you! That's bullshit! Fuck you!"

"Look, I know how you feel." I put my hand on his shoulder. "Xavier was—"

"No, you fuckin' don't! Xavier was already dead!" He pointed his finger at my face. "You ran from the truth! You couldn't handle your own guilt!" His watery eyes flared. "You was scared! I ain't never gonna be like you! I ain't never gonna be a scared lil' fuckin' bitch like you!"

"C'mon, man..." My lip dribbled, and my head tilted back. "Tabitha was important to..."

"She was important to you, mother fucker?! She was important to you?!" Sean pounded his fists together. "I fuckin' loved her!" His shattered cries could have pierced the gates of Heaven. "We never should've left the junkyard! We never should've..."

"Sean..." I shook his shoulder.

"We were street rats, but we were all alive! We were all together! You had to fuck everything..." He dropped to his knees and pressed his face in the grass.

"C'mon, man..." I quivered.

"Fuck this shit, man!" He rose to his feet. Snot dripped from his nose. "I can't keep goin' through this! I never asked to be born!" He raised his head toward the sky. "Let's kill Leon and," he heaved, "get outta this fuckin' shithole!"

There wasn't anything I could've said that would've made him feel better. All I could do was watch my closest friend break down and spiral into depression like I did with Xavier.

"Sean, we gotta..." After wiping my tears away, I grabbed his wrist. "We gotta go, man."

"I know..." He struggled to stand. "I know we do."

"Look." I gritted my teeth, fighting back tears as I dragged him toward the parking lot. "Tabitha once promised me I'd get better one day. And when I do I'm gonna make things better for you, too."

"Nothin's ever gonna get better." He pulled away. "It never does."

The two of us staggered across the grassy park to a parking lot. Sean suggested we steal one of the parked cars to get across the city faster, but before I could even tell him it was a bad idea, he'd already smashed in a window with a brick. He entered the car and popped open the trunk.

"This ain't ours!" No matter how many times I told him that he just wouldn't listen.

"I don't give a shit." His body sunk into the driver's seat. Check if..." He sighed and pressed his face against the steering wheel. "Check for any tools in the trunk."

I walked to the trunk, pushed aside a stuffed bear, a stereo, and a can of oil, and pulled out a hammer. "They got a hammer back in here."

"Anything else?" Sean asked.

I moved a blanket and a stack of newspapers. "Nope."

"Alright..." His shaking voice made it seem like he'd break down again any second. "Just bring it here."

"Where are we goin'?" I walked back to Sean and then handed him the hammer.

"A friend I knew years ago." He smashed the plastic behind the steering wheel to bits and then fumbled with the exposed wires until the engine roared. Then he punched the car stereo before turning to me, shouting, "This is bullshit!"

"It's gonna be alright." I looked through the window. "It's gonna be fine one day."

"Whatever, man." He shook his head. "Let's just go

Sean told me the easiest way for us not to be spotted would be for me to ride in the trunk. So I got in. A few seconds later, he drove out of the parking lot, leaving me rocking back and forth.

Not too much longer, we stopped. The trunk popped open, and I jumped out to see an unfamiliar street. Sean was still so distraught when he stepped out the ride he could barely stand on his own two feet.

"You gonna be alright?" I asked.

"This shit sucks, man!" Sean sobbed, slamming the door. "What did she ever do?! What the fuck did Tabitha ever do?!"

"Nothing, man." I tried holding in my own tears.

"She..." He dropped to his knees.

My shoulders drooped down. I couldn't help it either. "This is so fucked!"

"I'm gonna," Sean shouted, "kill Leon!"

I dried my eyes. "Where do we go?"

He pointed to a red, brick apartment complex. "Inside there."

"Who," I sniveled, "the hell's in there?"

"Two women I knew a long ass time ago." He picked himself up. "A dude named Jamal that lived with 'em helped me out when I was a kid."

Chapter Thirty-One

Old Faces

Present day...

Soon I was hiding behind a corner while Sean knocked on one of the apartment doors. A few seconds later, a black woman in a pink bathrobe stepped outside and stared at him for what seemed like ever.

"Hi, Tonya," Sean said.

"Sean?!" she sobbed, wrapping her arms around him. "Honey, we thought you was dead!"

Sean entered the house. Over 15 minutes must've gone by before he finally stuck his head out and told me to come in.

I wondered what the woman I saw would do when she met me. With the entire city looking for me, there was almost no way she didn't know who I was. "You sure it's alright?"

"Yeah, just hurry." Sean glanced over the railing.

I dashed to the door and met the eyes of the woman in the pink bathrobe. "How's it goin', ma'am?"

"Good." She crossed her arms and glimpsed down the hallway. "What 'bout ya'self?"

"Not too good, ma'am." I looked at Sean.

"So I heard." She tensed her muscles. "Well, come on in."

I walked through the door and looked at the family portraits on the walls. Scented candles were stacked in neat rows all over the entertainment system across from me, filling the home with a blueberry aroma.

"The madman…" On her television, a news lady in a green dress shifted through papers in her hand. "Escaped from the hospital a few hours ago. Residents of Violet Haven are advised to stay inside until further notice." The broadcast shifted to a poorly drawn sketch of me. "In another news—"

"By the way, my name's Tonya." She switched of the television with a remote.

"Where's Clemecia?" Sean looked around.

Tonya sat down in a recliner next to a fireplace filled with burning logs. "She'll be back soon. There's something ya gotta know, but I'mma let her tell ya."

"Sean was sayin' you can help us?" I looked to Tonya.

"We'll see 'bout that." Tonya adjusted her robe. "I heard you been killin' folks off." She put her hand to her chin. "Sean trusts you, but I dunno if I—"

"He's—" Sean started.

"He's a murderer, Sean!" Tonya jumped up from her chair. "Give me one good reason why I shouldn't call them boys in blue!"

"Because," Sean said, "he's helped me out more than I ever expected from anyone." He put his hands in his pockets. "And because he's the only damn person I got left on this earth."

Tonya looked at me. "Sean he's—"

"I lost my parents!" Tears formed in Sean's eyes. "I lost my brother!" He stood up, walked toward Tonya, and put his hands on her shoulders. "I lost Jamal! And now I just lost the only girl I ever loved!" His eyes met hers. "I lost everyone but him!"

"Sean, I..." Tonya glanced at me again.

"There's nobody left, Tonya!" Sean cried. "Them streets out there are home, but they get pretty damn cold, and I wouldn't be standing right here if it wasn't for him!"

"Okay, Sean." Tonya headed over to me. "Okay."

"He's tellin' the truth," I said.

She sighed. "I believe ya."

"I know I look like..." I started.

"Like ya need God." She pointed her finger at my chest. "And someone to be loved by."

Her words sliced through me with the sharpness a surgeon's blade. She actually looked like she cared about me the way one human should care about another.

The room fell silent. She just stood there and stared at me for the longest time. Then she walked over to the kitchen before coming back to me with a bible.

"What's—" I began.

"You boy's reminded me of a few verses I was readin' from Corinthians." She opened the bible and put her finger on the page. "Love is patient; love is kind. It does not envy; it does not boast, it is not proud. It does not dishonor others; it is not self-seeking, it is not easily angered, it keeps no record of wrongs. Love does not delight in evil but rejoices with the truth. It always protects, always perseveres." She glanced at me for a split second. "Love never fails. But where there are prophecies, they will cease; where there are tongues, they will be stilled; where there is knowledge, it will pass away."

"I..." I darted my eyes to the ground. Attention like that from someone who didn't wear rags or have dirt on their face was odd to me. "I don't—"

"What's that?" Tonya put her bible down. Then she put her hand on my chin and pulled down my jaw.

"What's what?" I responded.

"On ya tongue?" She squinted, raising her eyebrows.

"This?" I stuck my tongue out.

She cupped her mouth. "Who did that?!"

"I did." I looked to the side.

"B-but why?" she asked.

"They caught me." I looked her in the eyes once again. "The cops caught me so I had to get away." I pointed to Sean. "I had to save him. He could've ended up dead if I didn't."

"But..." Tonya turned her head toward Sean. "That's crazy!"

"I had to," I said.

"I noticed you was talkin' strange, but I didn't..." Tonya sighed through her nostrils. "Not many folks who'd do somethin' like that for a friend." She walked to the refrigerator, returned with an ice cube, and put it inside my palm. "This should bring down the swellin'."

"Thanks." I tucked it inside my mouth.

"Alright, so where's ya parents at? You ever tried talkin' to—" she started.

"They died years ago," I said.

She placed her hand on my shoulder. "I'm sorry to hear that. What 'bout any other family?"

"Yeah, I got..." I made eye contact with her again. "I got my brother."

"Not again," Sean whispered.

"Where is he?" Tonya asked.

"Right there." I pointed to Sean.

"Sean?" Tonya's eyebrows rose. "He can't be ya brother though."

"He might as well be." I gave Sean a nod.

"But he's white and—" Tonya began.

"I'm black?" I shook my head. "Family ain't always blood and blood ain't always family."

"I guess..." Tonya stared at me.

Just then a black woman in a purple dress walked through the door. "Tonya they ain't have that low-fat milk..." She stopped in place. "Is that S-sean?!"

"Yeah," Sean said. "Didn't think you'd recognize me."

"Oh my God!" Clemecia shrieked, running to Sean and then hugging him tightly. "I thought you was dead! I thought you died with Jamal!"

"I ain't dead," Sean said. "I'm right here."

"This is so crazy!" Clemecia continued. "I thought I'd never see you again!" She poked at Sean's beanie. "And you still have the beanie Jamal got ya!"

"Yeah, I kept—" Sean began.

A young boy in Looney Tunes pajama's walked into the living room. "Mama, I'm tryna sleep."

"Shamal come here, baby!" Clemecia said.

"Hey…" Sean looked at Clemecia's son. "He's got blue eyes. I ain't never seen a black person with blue eyes before."

I thought Sean was seeing things, but when looked closer, I saw it was true. Clemecia's son's eyes were as blue as the daytime sky.

"Yeah, we ain't seen this before neither. Turns out its just genetics," Clemecia said, smiling.

"Doctors said it was like a one in a five million chance or somethin' like that," Tonya said.

"Hold up! I've got…" Sean stepped back. "I've got blue eyes!"

"I know." As soon as Clemecia handed Shamal over to Sean, her face lit up. "That's where he got 'em from! We named him after his uncle…" She pinched Shamal's cheek. "And his daddy!"

Sean's jaw dropped. After handing Shamal back to Clemecia, he fell to the ground, his entire body quaking.

"Remember how we…" Clemecia blushed. "Ya know?"

"Of course." Sean looked at Shamal. "I just…" he babbled, his eyes switching between Clemecia, Tonya, and me. "I can't think right now."

"You okay?" Clemecia asked.

"Yeah, I…" Sean rose to his feet. "Just didn't know all this time." His head sunk. "I just wish I could've been there."

Tonya walked over to him. "There's no way ya could've known."

"I know, but I just…" Sean's knees trembled.

"Hi," Shamal yawned.

"So I guess..." Sean looked at Shamal. "I mean, do y-ya know who I am?"

Shamal shook his head. "No."

"I'm ya father," Sean said.

"You was hidin'?" Shamal yawned again.

Sean took back his son. "Nah, I been lost."

"Lost?" Shamal's eyes drooped. "Like hide and seek?"

Sean shook his head. "Not like hide and seek."

"Then what?" Shamal asked.

"I'mma tell ya some other time," Sean responded. "Ya look tired."

"I think he likes ya," Tonya said. "He look just like ya."

"He really do." Clemecia's smile turned to a frown when she noticed me. "Ain't he the murderer?!"

"Clemecia, it's—" Tonya started.

"Call the cops! He killed that girl!" Clemecia's screams startled Shamal, making him cover his ears.

"Clemecia, it's alright!" Tonya rushed across the room and covered Clemecia mouth. "He's with Sean."

"I never killed that girl." I looked to Sean. "She was a close friend of ours."

"He ain't lyin', Clemecia." Sean sighed. "I saw everything. It wasn't him."

"So what 'bout them two men?" Clemecia crossed her arms. "Don't go off on me 'bout how it was some accident."

"He had to," Sean said. "They was gonna kill us."

"Sean's only got good things to say 'bout him." Tonya said. "And from the looks of it they really need our help." She turned to Sean. "I just got one question though."

"What's that?" Sean asked.

"Why you ain't never came to us before?" Tonya asked. "Helps been here all this time, Sean."

"I was afraid that..." Sean put his head down.

"Afraid of what?" Tonya walked toward Sean.

"My brother and his friends are the ones who..." Sean put his hand over his face. "Killed Jamal."

"W-what?!" Tonya put her hands over her mouth.

Sean's cheeks turned bright red. "They killed him 'cause he was black. They took him out 'cause he was hangin' with me."

"Sean..." Tonya eyes watered up. "I never..."

"I was scared they'd kill you and Clemecia." Sean turned his head to the side. "And I was scared you was gonna blame me for what they did to—"

"Sean, it ain't ya fault!" Clemecia said. "He was actually goin' through really hard times back in them days." She led Sean to a futon next to the door and sat down with him. "It always made his day to spar with ya over in that basketball court."

"He was talkin' 'bout savin' money so you could go to college." A wide grin formed on Tonya's face.

"He ain't never told me that," Sean chuckled.

"Tell ya what, Sean," Tonya started. "Tell me what ya need and I'll see what I can do."

"Tabitha!" I spouted out, wiping the sweat off my face. "We gotta find the man who killed her!"

"Who's Tabitha?" Clemecia asked.

"It's the girl…" Sean put his head down again and sighed. "They think he killed."

"We dunno how to find him though," I said.

"That's tough," Tonya responded. "What do ya know?"

"Well, we…" Sean bit his thumb. "Not much I guess."

"Hold up!" I said. "You still got that album?!"

"Yeah," Sean pulled it out from his pants. "Got it right here." He handed it over to Tonya.

"Interesting." Tonya flipped through it. "Who are these folks?"

"Family members of that filthy murderer." I walked over to her, took the album, and then showed her a picture of Officer Zeke. "That's his brother. That's Bloody, Bloody Bijou."

"Bloody, Bloody Bijou?!" Tonya gasped.

"The serial killer?!" Clemecia walked to Tonya and grabbed the photo album.

"Yeah, that's him!" I crunched on the ice cube between my teeth. Even though my tongue still hurt like hell, the swelling went down to a point where I could speak without slurring my words so much.

"How do ya know this?" Tonya looked over to the picture.

"He..." I took in a deep breath while staring down Tonya. "He killed my parents. They put me in the back of one of them cop cars and..." I took in another breath. "I saw him in the street afterward."

"He's a cop ain't he?" Tonya asked. "Maybe he was just—"

"Look through them pictures," Sean said. "It's got a bunch of news clippin's from them killin's."

Tonya flipped through the book. "Yeah, I see 'em."

"It definitely raises some questions," said Clemecia.

"So what's the plan?" Tonya asked.

"I dunno." Sean scratched his head. "We talked about findin' Zeke and then goin' after Leon."

"Alright." Tonya crossed her arms. "Which one's Zeke and which one's Leon?"

"Zeke is the serial killer and Leon was the one who killed our friend Tabitha," I said.

"How did ya even meet?" she asked. "And I mean all of ya."

"We..." I didn't even know where to start.

"After they took out Jamal..." Sean put his head down. "I found Tabitha and me and her went and lived under that old bridge in Pepper Park."

"Oh..." Tonya sighed, putting her hands on her cheeks. "I must've driven by that park hundreds of times."

"We only lived there for 'bout a year until my brother and his gang found us," Sean said. "I didn't think my brother was still alive."

"Why not?" Clemecia asked.

"I shot h-him in the eye." Sean rubbed his forearm. "Turned out he was paralyzed from the waist down. He's in a wheelchair now, but his gang grew, and he's much, much more powerful now. He's still out there looking for me." He looked back to Tonya. "Anyway, they found us and took us to this empty house and tied us up."

"So how *did* you get away?" Tonya asked.

Sean looked at me. "Him."

"You saved him?" Tonya smiled. "How'd ya get in that house?"

"Well, I..." The memory of waking up drunk in that house's attic after trying to hang myself entered my head. "I was asleep in the attic and I..." I rubbed my throat. "I heard people screamin' so I snuck down after Sean's brother and them left and then—"

"He found me and Tabitha tied up in the basement and helped us escape," Sean interrupted.

"So what happened then?" asked Tonya.

"The three of us jumped from place to place. Alleyways. Hotel rooms. Abandoned buildings and houses. The woods. Sheds in random backyards. We lived anywhere we could." Sean responded. "One day we tried to leave this city and—"

"We stopped at that junkyard right outside the city," I said. "And then we just never left."

"That abandoned junkyard?" Clemecia asked.

"Yup," I responded.

"So what's with that Leo guy?" Tonya jiggled one of her hoop earrings.

"Ya mean Leon?" Sean corrected her. "He was already in the junkyard when we got there. He said he'd been there since he was a 'lil kid with some other dude, but by the time we got there, it was just Leon. He never told us what happened to the other guy. He just said they was really close friends." He pulled back his beanie and scratched his scalp. "Oh yeah, and it wasn't easy to convince him to let us stay."

"Wait! So you lived with this guy?!" Tonya crossed her arms.

"Yeah," A bead of sweat dripped off my nose.

"We got in a fight and then he went crazy and now Tabitha's..." Sean put his hands on his knees. "And now Tabitha's gone."

"Ya both would've liked her. She was a sweet girl," I said.

"Well, it looks like ya both been through a lot," Clemecia frowned.

"Okay, so what's the plan again?" Tonya asked.

"Like we said, we talked 'bout goin' after Zeke then Leon." I put my hands in my pockets.

Tonya put her hand to her chin. "I don't think that's the best plan."

"Why not?" Sean asked.

"Just think about it." Tonya sat back down in her recliner. "Zeke's a police officer, and ya got no idea where Leon's gone and went."

"She's right." Clemecia returned to her seat.

"Hold on." Tonya walked over to me and showed me a picture of young Leon and his family at a picnic. "Know who any of these folks are?"

"Nah, I..." I took a good look at all the faces. "Wait! I think I saw this guy a few months back!" I pointed to a man eating a sandwich. "He warned me about Leon!"

"Sounds like they don't get along then." Clemecia looked at the picture. "Says at the bottom his name's Thane Jenkins."

"When was this?" Sean asked.

"That night we took that *trip* to the river," I responded.

"I don't remember him." Sean shook his head.

"He was there." I nodded. "Trust me."

Tonya flipped through the pages. "How ya gonna find him?"

"Looks like another dead end," Clemecia said.

"Dammit! Why's this gotta be so—" Sean began.

"I think I might know." I put my hand to my chin. "It's a long shot, and I dunno if it's even there anymore..."

"If what's there?" Sean asked.

"When I was young I lived inside this orphanage. The woman who owned it was Zeke's aunt," I said.

"So you just *happened* to live with Zeke's aunt?" Tonya asked.

"No, I'm pretty sure Zeke pulled some strings so that I'd stay there," I replied. "So he could keep an eye on me."

"That makes sense," said Clemecia.

I took the album from Tonya and flipped through the pages until I saw a picture of an old lady on a park bench. "That was her!"

Tonya looked at the picture. "She'll help you?"

"I don't think so," I responded. "She hated me."

"So why her?" Clemecia asked.

"I stole a phone book from her." After wiping off the beads of sweat from my cheeks, I crossed my arms. "I hid it in the house we lived in."

"Ya really think it'll be there after all this time?" Tonya eyed me carefully.

"We got no another way to find them fools," Sean said.

"And that Thane dude looked like he didn't like Leon at all." I wiped more beads of sweat off my face.

"Sorry, I didn't even notice I still had the heater on." Tonya walked over to the other side of the room and fumbled with a dial on the wall. "And you been standin' under the vent this whole time," she said. "Anyway, what was you sayin'?"

"That dude might be able to help us find Leon," I said.

"This sounds dangerous to me." Tonya twirled her hair.

"We got no choice." Sean handed Shamal to Clemecia. "It's that or starve in these streets."

"You could..." Clemecia grabbed Sean's hand. "Just say with us. I mean, you got Shamal now."

"I know I do." Sean looked over at his son. "But we can't just let Leon and Zeke kill off more people."

Clemecia pulled her hand away. "Oh, I see..."

"It ain't even like that." Sean turned toward me. "I mean, what 'bout him? He's a fugitive. We can't just hide him here."

"And besides," I said, "he killed Tabitha."

"The cops in this town ain't gonna do nothin' about that," Sean added. "Y'all know that."

Both Clemecia and Tonya grew silent, looking each other and then to the ground. Clemecia twirled one of her dreadlocks. Tonya rubbed her chin.

"Alright." Tonya walked to the kitchen, dug out a wad of cash from a cookie jar, came back to the living room, and then gave the money to Sean. "It's not much, but I think y'all need it more."

Sean tried to hand it back. "We can't take—"

"Just take it, Sean." Clemecia put her hand on Sean's wrist.

"Jamal would've wanted this." Tonya walked back to her recliner. "Just promise me one thing, Sean."

"What's that?" Sean lifted his head.

"Come back to us, ya hear?" Tonya pointed to Shamal. "That boy needs a father, and that's you."

"Gotcha." Sean stood up and stuffed the cash in his pocket. He turned to Shamal. "I'll be back. Don't worry."

"Okay," Shamal said as he fell asleep.

Sean turned toward me. "You ready?"

"Yeah." I tucked the photo album in my pants and then headed for the door. "Let's go."

Chapter Thirty-Two

Back to the Beginning

Present day...

As soon as we left Clemecia and Tonya's house, Sean and I headed straight to the orphanage, dodging helicopter spotlights and police cars. It would've been safer for me to ride in the trunk again, but Sean needed my directions, so I rode slouched down in the backseat.

20 minutes later, we reached the street. Xavier's blood soaked face flashed in front of me. The closer we got to the house, the more it happened. Those memories brought me more pain than any physical wound ever could.

"Tell me which house." Sean drove down the deserted street through the pitch blackness. "So we can get outta here."

"I th-think it's on the right." My jaw was clenched up tight enough to make my teeth shatter. "Next street on the r-right."

Sean turned on the interior lights. His watery, bloodshot eyes met mine in the rearview mirror. "Ya look like ya losin' it. You sure ya alright?"

I dug my fingernails into my forehead. "I'm all good."

"Don't look like it." Sean eyed me carefully.

"Yeah, just d-drive." The memories wouldn't stop. I wanted to scream until I coughed up a lung.

"Alright." He turned off the light and pulled into a cul-de-sac.

Sean looked at the houses. "Recognize any of these?"

"Y-yeah, that one," I said. "At the very end. With the chain-link fence."

Sean reached the end of the cul-de-sac and stopped outside a house that was all too familiar to me. "This one?"

"Yeah, th-that's it." I rushed out the car and puked. "Just stay here."

"Are ya sure?" Sean asked. "We can try and find him some other way."

"There ain't no other way." I wiped the sweat off my face and then shook my head. "I gotta..." I trembled. "I gotta go inside."

"Alright, man," Sean nodded.

"I'm gonna be fine," I said, treading toward the orphanage.

As soon as I reached the front porch, Xavier's voice rang in my head. It wouldn't stop no matter how hard I slapped the sides of my head. I dropped to my knees. But his voice just grew louder—so loud I couldn't think. Every gruesome detail of that night flashed before my eyes.

"Hey, you alright?" Sean's voice seemed to be a million miles away. It was like a small beam of sunshine in the middle of a raging hurricane.

I slapped the sides of my head and rose to my feet. "Y-yeah, I'm fine."

Xavier's voice and the visions disappeared. After I pulled myself together, I walked to the graffiti-covered front door and turned the handle. Locked. Next, I tried the boarded up windows. No luck.

Eventually, I made my way to the back of the house. The same forest I'd entered so many years ago stood before me. With a ghastly wind blowing through its trees, just the sight of the swaying branches made me sick.

"*We don't got nowhere else to go!*" Xavier's voice echoed in my head.

I became so dizzy it felt like I was on a roller coaster. Vomit sprayed out my mouth and onto a plastic flamingo near me.

When I coughed up the last chunks of vomit, I staggered through the shattered sliding glass door. All the furniture I'd remembered was gone. The place was empty besides piles of garbage and muddy footprints on the floor.

There it was again—Xavier's voice. It just grew louder. And this time it came with a ringing sound that was so deafening it seemed to pierce my ears.

I dropped to my knees and pounded my forehead against the floor. It didn't help. It was then I realized I'd have rather have been in a haunted house than sit there with the memories between those walls. Staying there forever would've been my definition of hell.

After Xavier and the ringing stopped, I pulled myself together and continued to the staircase. With my mind still racing, I dropped to my knees and pried off the wood of the first step which revealed the dusty, cobweb-covered address book. As soon as I picked it up, dust fluttered off it and gently floated to the ground.

Even with the address book in my hands, Thane wasn't even on my map. That house had so many disturbing memories, but for whatever reason, I just couldn't bring myself to leave.

I gripped the address book, crept upstairs to the bathroom, and peeked inside. The moonlight shined through the window. Cracks and mold covered the walls and ceiling. But what surprised me was the fact the mirror was still broken.

Xavier's voice rang in my ears again. This time it came from our old bedroom.

I ran to the room, swung open the door, and then flicked on the lights. Xavier stood right by the window. He turned his head with this huge grin on his face that made it look like he just won the lottery. Then he scampered toward me.

And I smiled back at him.

"*Ya found me!*" His grin spread from ear to ear.

"Xavier!" I was happier than I'd been in years. There were so many things I wanted to say to him. "I was—"

The lights flickered off. When they came back on there was nothing in the room except for me and the cockroaches on the ground. I looked to the window. And then towards the closet. It took a few minutes for me to realize what happened. When I did, I fell to the ground and sobbed into the floorboards. I felt so god damn stupid. How I could let my mind fool me like that? How could I let my guilt drive me crazy again? It was like there was a spider remaking its web in my head, and there was no way to stop it without getting bit.

After pulling myself together, I headed back to the stairs and stuffed the address book down my pants. But then something near Agatha's old door caught my eye.

Someone was standing there.

"God damn thief!" The maniac body slammed me into the wall and snatched the book.

I swung at his jaw and grabbed it back. "Give it back!"

"No!" The psychotic madman ripped out some of the pages.

"I said let go!" I bolted down the stairs but tripped over the last step.

He charged after me. "I'll kill you!"

I sprinted out the house and to the chain-link fence. "Sean, start the car!"

"Get back here!" The raving maniac stopped at the porch, waving his arms in the air.

"Who the hell is that?!" Sean shouted.

"No one! Just go!" I yelled.

The second I entered the ride, he peeled out like Speed Racer. As fast as he was going, he couldn't compare to how fast my thoughts were racing. I trembled and thought about telling him about seeing Xavier again. He would've wanted to know but putting him under even more stress just seemed cruel to me.

"Anyway, I got it, but we gotta stop and take a look," I said.

"Gas first." Sean drove like he was being chased by a ghost. "Tanks almost empty. We can look through it while we're fillin' it back up."

A few minutes later, Sean pulled into a gas station. Puddles of car fluids on the concrete reflecting the powerful, bright lights above us had me shielding my eyes.

"Look through that address book." He pulled out the money Tonya gave us and then exited the car.

I opened it up and looked for the 'T' section, but saw that it and the 'S,' 'U,' and 'V' sections had all been torn out. Stars flashed before my eyes. I tightened my fist and crumbled the books spine. "Dammit!"

After Sean filled up the gas tank, I broke the news to him. He came up with the idea of stealing back the pages, but just the thought of going back to that house made my stomach turn. However, if we couldn't find Leon's cousin, then there was nowhere for us to go.

"What if we call some of these folks?" Sean flipped through the address book. "Someone's gotta know that guy."

"You got any idea what time it is?" I pointed to the dark streets.

"We gotta try." Sean pulled out the cash again. "There's a payphone outside the station, and we still got 'round forty bucks left. I need some quarters though."

"Alright, go right ahead and try." I passed the address book to Sean and watched him head for the tiny brick building.

"Is that crazy guy still on the loose?" A white guy walked by the car and lit a cigarette. Then he pulled up his white baseball cap which showed his dirty blonde hair. "The one that escaped from the hospital?"

"Yeah, they ain't caught that nigga yet." A young, light-skinned woman grabbed the cigarette from him and took a hit. "That nigga got them cops buzzin' like wasps."

"Did they say anything about a reward?" The man scratched the top of his head.

"Yeah." The lady glanced over her shoulder. "Them folks on the news said somethin' 'bout $5,000."

Seconds later, Sean exited the building with a brown, paper bag in his hand. He headed over to a payphone that sat between a trashcan and an air pump, dug out a few quarters from the bag, and then put them into the coin slot. After a few dial presses, he was talking with someone on the other line.

They talked for less than a minute before he hung up the phone and dialed another number. Another minute passed, and the same thing happened. This went on for what seemed like an hour, and by that time, he must've called dozens of people.

Just then two gangbangers walked toward Sean, looking at him like he was a walking goldmine.

Sean glanced at the men and then turned back to the payphone.

"Watchoo got in the bag?!" One of the thugs snatched the paper bag away from Sean and looked inside. "Quarters?! I know ya got more money than this!"

"C'mon, cracka'!" The second one slapped Sean in the back of the head.

"What's wrong?!" The other gangster hollered. "Scared of a couple niggas?!"

"Get the hell outta here!" Sean seemed like he was trying his hardest to stay focused on the phone. "Can you say that again?!"

Both gangsters began beating Sean.

I bolted toward the brawl. One gangbanger tried to reach for his partner when he saw me. But before he could, my knuckles hit his nose. He fell back. Another punch and blood poured from his nostrils.

"Die!" His buddy charged at me.

I dodged each blow, grabbed Sean by the shirt, and dashed to the car. The gangbangers weren't having none of that. As Sean got in and fumbled with the car wires, they ran after me. Each one was ready to rip the head of my shoulders.

"Hold 'em off for me!" Sean tossed me a hammer.

The gangsters ran at full speed. When they got close, I swung. One took the hit right to his eye and fell to the ground. The second thug charged forward but stumbled over his friend. I swung again. He was out cold before he even hit the concrete.

"Got it!" Sean yelled over the roaring engine. "Get in!"

I jumped in the back just as Sean peeled out the gas station.

"It's the killa'!" A shirtless man outside bellowed. "Call them cops!"

"What are we gonna do now?!" I struck the window. "Folks in this god damn city always be—"

"793 Sayonara Avenue." Sean sped over a speed bump, making hit my head on the ceiling of the car.

"What'd ya say?!" I seethed, rubbing my scalp.

"I said '793 Sayonara Avenue'." Sean slammed on the brakes. The tires screeched, leaving smoke and the smell of burned rubber in the air. "Apartment number 13."

"Are ya sure it's Thane?!" I leaned forward.

"I think so." Sean looked both ways and then sped off again. "Thane Jenkins, right?"

"Yeah, that's the name Tonya said." I slumped into my seat. "Where the hell is Sayonara Avenue?"

"It's next to..." Sean mumbled beneath his breath. He took a turn down an eerie, lone road between a long patch of trees.

"What was that?" I could feel my eyebrows rise.

"It's a lil' ways from here." Sean slammed his palm against the steering wheel. "And it's right next to the god damn police station!"

"Well, that's just great!" I elbowed the side of the car. "Nothing's ever easy is it?"

Sean sunk back into the driver's seat. "Don't look like it."

As Sean drove, I stared into the trees and wondered how two people could be in that big of a mess. Unfortunately, those questions were replaced by the memories of Xavier's death—and his voice. This time it was so loud I almost passed out.

"Doin' alright back there?" Sean peeked into the rearview mirror.

"Yeah, why?" I twirled my thumbs.

"You been muttering crap for the last few minutes." He kept his eyes focused on me.

"Oh, I was just..." I didn't even realize I was doing it. "Thinkin' 'bout h-how we gonna get Leon."

"Sure 'bout that?" Sean looked back to the road.

"Yeah, I am." I gripped the sides of the seat like I was about to be thrown out the ride.

"Alright, buddy." Sean gave me a thumbs up. "Anyway, it shouldn't be too much longer."

I turned to my reflection in the window. All I saw was the face of a broken man and the eyes of a monster.

A few minutes later, my heart almost exploded when I set eyes on the police station. With so many squad cars coming in and out of it, it looked like some sort of beehive. The cops stared us down while we passed, making me sink so slow I felt like I was gonna disappear into the creases of the car seat.

"And here it is. Sayonara Avenue," Sean trembled, driving around a corner.

"Alright, drive slower." I looked at the numbers on the houses until we were outside an apartment complex. "There it is! 793!"

"I hope he can give us somethin' we can go off of." Sean parked right outside the complex near a dumpster.

We hopped out the ride and climbed a fence surrounding a pool and hot tub filled with beer cans and a few drunken teenagers. After climbing another fence, we headed straight for apartment 11.

Once we reached it, we had to step over dozens of potted plants before we were able to ring the doorbell. All we could do was hope whoever was inside didn't call the cops when they saw me.

After a few more rings, a frightened-looking man in his early 30's answered the door, asking, "Who's there?"

Chapter Thirty-Three

Thane

Present day...

Even from outside I could see the overturned tables and chairs that'd been scattered around his living room. "Thane?"

"Y-y-yes, that's right," Thane scoped the parking lot. "A f-f-friend of mine told m-me s-someone was looking for me. Is that you?"

"Yeah, that's us," I said. "We were wondering if you knew anything about Leon and Zeke."

Thane's eyes widened. "You didn't bring them here did you?!"

"No." Sean turned to me with a puzzled look on his face. "We came alone."

"Thank God!" Thane sighed. "W-what do you want with them?"

"Leon killed a really good friend of—" I started.

274

"You're..." Thane looked at me closely. "You're the man from the news!"

"Yes, but—" I tried again.

"Please don't hurt me!" Thane tried to slam the door shut.

"Stop! It wasn't him!" Sean jammed his fingers into the crevice. "I swear it was Leon! You gotta help us!"

"You said..." Thane slowly reopened the door. "It was Leon?"

"Yeah!" Sean said. "Think you could help us out?!"

"Are you..." Thane shook while he scoped the parking lot again. "Okay, p-please come on in."

"Thank you." When I walked inside, I saw much more of the damage I'd seen before. With portraits torn off the walls and all the spilled soil on the Persian rug in the middle of the room, it looked like there'd been a hurricane inside the guy's home.

Sean stepped over a broken television set. "Did someone rob—"

"No!" Thane slowly turned to look Sean in the eye. "It was Leon!"

"Leon did this?!" I looked around. "Ain't you his cousin?!"

"Y-yes I am." The man collapsed and sobbed into his hands.

Sean rushed over and helped Thane to his feet. "You gonna be alright?!"

"N-no!" Thane bawled. "He wasn't always like this."

"What do ya mean?" I led Thane to his couch and sat him down.

"Leon used to be a really good kid." The distraught man grabbed a tissue from the wooden table in front of him. "Then his brother—"

"Zeke?" I took a seat next to him.

"Y-yeah." Thane reached for the table again and grabbed a picture of a happy family sitting around a campfire. "He was always an oddball, but one night he just lost it."

"What 'cha mean?" When I looked at the picture, my eyes locked on Zeke and Leon like a heat seeking missile.

"Zeke had this knife collection and one day he got this black leather mask..." Thane pointed at the photograph and to a man holding some firewood. "That was Clyde. That was his father—my uncle." Then he pointed to a gorgeous woman in hiking gear. "That was my aunt. That was Ely."

Sean leaned in. "And he—"

"H-he..." Thane wiped his eyes with the tissue. "Killed them both."

Sean nodded at me.

"Zeke was always kinda off." Thane put his hand to his forehead. "I didn't even realize it until many years later." He picked up a glass of Scotch near his foot. "Like I said, one night he just lost it. He m-murdered them r-r-ight in front of..." The devastated man broke down again.

"Oh damn," Sean said.

Thane eyes locked with mine. "Zeke's Bloody, Bloody Bijou! He's the one who put the 'devil' in 'Devils Haven'!"

"I knew it!" I turned to Sean.

"Wait!" Thane gripped my shoulder. "He's got Leon with him! They told me if I try to run they'll kill me!" He tightened his grip. "They told me they're looking for you! They want to kill you! Both of you!"

"We ain't gonna let that happen!" Sean clapped his hands together. "We gotta get 'em both before they get us!"

"P-please listen!" Thane held his palm up to Sean. "They're both monsters! Something changed inside Leon when he saw what Zeke did! It's like Zeke brainwashed Leon!"

"R-really?!" I asked.

"Yeah! Like I said before, Leon used to be a good kid until Zeke..." Thane seemed like he had trouble digging into his dark memories. "I remember watching Zeke take the knife and just..." His eyes watered up again when he looked at me. "He just ruined everything..."

"I'm sorry!" I placed my hand on his shoulder.

"No, it's okay." Thane blew his nose again. "They need to b-be stopped. The police in this city won't do anything," he said, frowning. "And you can't be blamed for what Leon did to your friend."

"Still can't believe Leon did all this." Sean spun his head around the room.

"Him and Zeke have c-come here b-before..." The pitiable man grabbed a nearby pillow and pressed it against his face, shuttering into it.

"They j-just won't leave me alone!"

"Well, we came here for help!" Sean's nostrils flared. "But I think you need it more!"

"Are ya one hundred percent sure Zeke is Bijou?" I pulled my hand away.

"No." Thane shook his head. "I'm one hundred and *ten* percent sure. I saw everything he did."

"How come you ain't never say nothin'?" Sean asked.

Thane shivered. "I was so s-scared that they'd k-kill me that I just kept my mouth shut."

"Damn." I stood off the couch. "I can't believe nobody's caught him after all this time."

"It's because he's a monster," Thane said. "And he's pretty damn good at playing pretend."

"Where can we find him?" I asked.

"Z-zeke and Leon have been hiding in an old building I own by the docks." Thane sipped his Scotch. "I d-don't think they're g-getting along. L-leon was bruised up pretty bad l-last time they came."

"Where exactly?" Sean asked.

"893 Seguro Road," Thane responded. "Zeke f-forced me to give him the keys."

"Damn," Sean muttered.

"I haven't been there in a few years, but I've h-heard that area isn't the best place to hang around anymore." Thane shook his head. "I'm t-terrified of both of them, so I d-don't think I'm up for driving you there. And Leon took the only s-set of k-keys, so you'll have to find some way inside."

"Don't worry." I rose off the couch.

"Yeah," Sean added. "We'd be stuck if ya hadn't helped us."

"Well, is there anything else I can help you with?" Thane really looked like he'd been left with nothing but a broken heart from his own family.

"Nah, I think that's it," I said.

Sean and I walked to the front door. But as I twisted the handle the hairs on the back of my neck stood on end. Blue and red lights were flashing outside.

Sean pulled back the curtain. "There's cops everywhere! They're surroundin' the car!"

I backed away from the door. "How the hell we gonna get outta here?!"

"You c-can go ahead and take my car." Thane picked a pair of keys off the table and then jingled them in the air. "Just please try and r-return it."

"Really?!" I said.

"But they'll see us leavin'!" Sean glanced out the window again.

"I think," Thane said, pointing to me, "he will have to leave through the kitchen w-window over there. Go through there, and you'll see a

279

wooden fence, and if you climb over that, you'll be out of the apartment complex and in small parking lot." He tossed his car keys to Sean. "I guess your f-friend can take my car and meet you there."

"Sounds good," Sean said.

"It's the only blue Mercedes in the parking lot." Thane's used his finger to gesture outside. "Sean, when y-you go outside take a left down the hallway and go all the way around. They shouldn't be able to see you."

"Alright, thanks!" I sped toward the kitchen. "Sean, go!"

"Yeah, man." Sean crouched down and dashed out the house.

When I reached the window, I flung it open and slid through. "Thanks again!"

"Just be careful!" Thane hollered.

After dropping to the stone pathway behind the apartment, I spotted the wooden fence and climbed to the top as fast as I could. However, while I dropped down to the other side, I knocked over an old BBQ grill. The noise scared a group of stray cats, making them scatter from a collection of cardboard boxes.

A few minutes after I picked myself off the asphalt, Sean pulled up next to me in the blue Mercedes. He poked his head out the window and signaled for me to get in.

I ran to the passenger's side and hopped inside. "Go!"

Sean sped off down the street. "The docks ain't too far from here, but we gotta take the back roads to dodge them cops."

We continued through the city. However, almost every twist and turn had a roadblock, almost every back street had a squad car waiting for us.

About ten minutes later, we got to a part of the city that looked like it'd been hit by Armageddon. Those streets were so gritty I honestly wouldn't have been surprised if I saw a dead body or two in the middle of the road.

"We might as well be drivin' straight into hell." Sean drove by a group of hookers standing in the parking lot of a carwash. "Sodom and Gomorrah ain't got shit on this place."

"Ya got that right," I responded.

"Alright, see all them boats?" Sean pointed in between the spaces of two buildings on our left.

"Nah, drive slower." After he slowed down, I looked to where he had pointed and caught a glimpse of a large collection of boats sitting on the water a few ways a way. "Yeah, I see them."

"That's right near where we gotta go." Sean stopped at a stop sign and then started to turn.

"Hold up!" I pointed toward the emergency lights flashing around the corner. "Stop the ride!"

"Dammit!" Sean slammed on the brakes. "There's a few cops 'bout a block away!" He glanced in the rearview mirror. "I'd take forever if we went back around!"

"What the hell do we do now?!" I spun my head around and tried to find a way around the cops.

"I hate doin' this since that Thane guy was so damn nice." Sean parked outside of a convenience store. "But we gotta ditch the ride and find another way around."

I slipped outta the car and waited for Sean. "Is this thing gonna be alright here?"

"A nice ride like this?" Sean slammed the car door and then walked over to my side. "I guarantee it'll gonna be gone an hour from now."

"Well, damn." When I stepped onto the sidewalk and looked around the street, all I saw was a few drug dealers and more hookers standing on the corner about a block away. "Where to now?"

"I guess through there." Sean pointed to a small alleyway between the convenience store and a motorcycle repair shop. "We gotta climb over the barrier on the other side of them buildings."

As soon as I stepped into the alley, I smelled trash and the rotten, fly-infested carcass of a dead raccoon. Then as we got to the exit, a third smell—the ocean's salty, fish-stained air—blew up into my nostrils. With all three odors overloading my senses, I had to pull my shirt over my nose until we met the concrete barrier.

Sean jumped up and grabbed the top of it, but lost his grip and fell back down. "Hey, help me get over this thing."

"Yeah, just hold up." I grabbed his legs and pushed up until he could stand on top of the structure.

"Alright, I'm good." Sean grabbed my wrist and then pulled me up.

"Just don't slip up here," he warned, "or you'll die."

"How far down is…" I climbed to the top, looked over the edge, and saw Sean was right. The slanted seawall led down to an endless, raging ocean. At the bottom, huge waves crashed against a long wall of boulders every few seconds, sending massive amounts of water spraying in the air. "Holy shit! That's gotta be at least a 200-foot drop!"

Sean pointed to the bottom of it. "Like I said, you'll die."

I carefully slid my body off the barrier until my feet touched the seawalls slippery surface. "With our luck, I ain't gonna be surprised if a god damn tsunami shows up."

"I hate to say it." Sean dropped down and followed close behind. "But neither would I."

During that uneasy walk, I couldn't keep my eyes off the ocean waves. Not being able to swim didn't help with the fear of death being only one, small slip away.

And to make things even worse…

"*I want mommy!*" Xavier's voice drowned out the sound of the ocean waves. His figure flashed in front of me, flickering under a street light. "*Where's dad?!*"

I jerked back, slipped, and began toppling off the edge of the seawall. "Oh shit!"

"Gotcha!" Sean grabbed the back of my shirt and pulled me back, stopping me from falling to a certain death. "Told ya to be careful, man!"

"Oh damn!" I was more spooked by the hallucination than I was about staring death in the face.

"That was close." He looked toward the waters. "Do ya see any dolphins?"

"Dolphins?" I turned back and saw his head sink.

"Tabitha told me she wanted to see some dolphins before she..." He pressed his palms against his eyes and shook his head. "Just forget it. It don't matter no more."

With the ocean water still spraying in the air, we crept down the seawall and passed the squad cars. By the time the two of us got to a point where we wouldn't be seen, our clothes were almost completely soaked.

"Think I see a ladder over there," he said, pointing up ahead.

"Yeah, it is." I walked until I was close enough to climb it, but I couldn't help shiver the entire way up from the ocean water hitting the back of my neck.

He followed. "Just don't fall again or we both die."

"Don't worry 'bout that." I clutched the top of the barrier and pulled myself over. "Just worry about what we're gonna do when we get to Leon."

"Skin his ass and wear it as a suit!" He climbed over.

"That ain't enough for that sack of crap." I turned to see newspapers floating in the wind over an empty street. "He should be burned at a stake."

He gestured to the same boats I'd seen earlier. "Anyway, Seguro Road should be that way. No idea exactly where though."

"So how the hell are we gonna find it?" I asked.

He shrugged.

"Oh good." I shook my head.

"Just gotta look around these streets until we find it," he said.

We crept through those dark, shady streets, but the area just seemed to get grittier with every corner we turned. Every breath was like breathing in pure gloom.

"You sure this is the right way?" I pointed my thumb over my shoulder. "We walked by them boats a while back ago."

"To be honest..." Sean looked around the area. "I don't."

"Then we gotta ask someone." I looked at a hooded man on a corner of the street and watched him blow out a trail of marijuana smoke. "And hope we don't end up dead."

"Wadda ya mean 'we'?" Sean looked down the sidewalk to a hooker in a pink miniskirt. "*You* gotta go and hide. This entire city knows who ya are by now."

"And ain't that a bitch." I ducked in between the space of a minivan and a Honda Accord and watched him walk toward her.

He tapped her on the shoulder. "S'cuse me."

"Hey, baby!" She smiled, revealing her missing teeth. "Do you want a—"

"I don't need nothin' but directions," said Sean.

Her smile disappeared. "Don't waste my time with that shit."

"Alright, alright." Sean pulled out some cash and then waved it in front of her face. "Still a waste of time?"

Her bogus beam returned. "Oh, I guess I can spare a few minutes. Where do you wanna go, baby?"

"893 Seguro Road." Sean handed her the money.

"Oh, that's easy." She pointed to the end of the road. "Just walk all the way down and take a left and then you'll be on Seguro."

"Thanks." Sean headed back to me.

She followed him. "Wait! Are you sure you don't want a—"

I backed into the minivan behind me. Its alarm went off. The hooker pulled out a knife and sprinted toward me. But then she saw my face. A shriek that easily beat the alarm came out her mouth. The knife fell into a storage drain.

She flinched, screaming, "It's him! It's the murderer! Call the cops!"

"No! Shut up!" Sean grabbed her arm. "Shut the hell up!"

"Let go of me! Help!" She slapped Sean in the face with her purse and ran off into the night. "Call the cops! Call the cops!"

"We gotta go now!" Sean took off toward Seguro Road.

I dashed after him. "Wait up!"

"It's the murderer!" The hooker hollered. "Call the cops!"

"We gotta find that place quick!" Sean's wheezes filled the air.

We ran down the street and onto Seguro Road. As we passed rundown homes, folks ran when they saw my face. Even with all the death threats, our only concern was Leon.

You see it?!" I said, panting.

"Nah, but it's..." Sean grabbed his chest and let out a wheeze. "It's close! I see 879 right there, man!"

"Just keep runnin'!" I shouted. "It's gotta be here somewhere!"

At the end of the street, I spotted an old, two-story, brick building on the corner. "Is that it?!"

"It says 893 right there!" Sean ran up the concrete steps. After twisting the door knob, he stomped his foot on the ground. "Locked!"

I thought about breaking through one of the windows, but that idea was shot when I saw the steel bars over them. "We can't break through the glass neither!"

Suddenly, Sean dashed through an alleyway on the side of the building. I chased after him, jumping over a group of muddy puddles. When I reached him, I found him staring at an escape ladder that led to a steel balcony.

"Leon could already know we're here!" I said.

"It don't matter! I'm gonna kill him either way!" Sean hurried up the ladder.

It was pointless to argue, so I climbed after him as fast as I could, but I was barely able to match his Tarzan-like pace. When I was halfway up the ladder, Sean smashed through a window, causing glass shards to rain down on me.

Eventually, I pulled myself onto the balcony to see he'd already slipped into the building. The second I followed him inside, the smell of gasoline flowed into my nostrils.

Sean flicked on a switch next to me. Rows of powerful, bright lights on the ceiling turned on. When I looked down, I saw the fresh puddles of gas on the floorboards.

"Somethin' don't seem right." I plugged my nose.

"I don't care!" Sean stomped over to a twisted, metal staircase. "I know he's here!"

"Sean, we can't..." I followed him, but then I stopped short. My jaw dropped. There was a row of pipe bombs strapped to the wall above his head. "This really don't look right."

"I just gotta check." Sean marched down the steps.

"Just hold up a minute." After I dashed to the bottom of the staircase, I saw more gasoline. "Sean, we gotta get outta here!"

"No!" Sean swung his head wildly around the room, looking at each corner and crevice he could find. Then he picked up a screwdriver on the ground. "We ain't goin'!"

I sighed and then picked a crowbar. "Fine. Check behind those cardboard boxes in the corner."

"Yeah, just make sure—"

Something rattled in a nearby closet.

It had to be Leon. I held my breath as I crouched to the closet, cautiously holding that crowbar in front of my face. That bastard wasn't gonna go down without a fight. He always had a dirty trick up his sleeve.

As soon as I had my hand on the handle, I turned back to Sean, whispering, "If he ain't in here then we're gone."

"Yeah." He tightened his grip on his makeshift weapon.

After shaking off my nerves, I flung open the door. The crowbar slipped from my hand and fell to the floor.

"Holy shit!" Sean stepped back and covered his mouth. "Leon!"

"What's up, punks?" Leon smirked.

What I saw was the last thing I ever expected to see.

Chapter Thirty-Four

Once Upon a Time

Fourteen years ago...

Mrs. Lounger, a young, blonde, teacher at Violet Haven Junior High stood up from her chair at the front of her classroom. "Okay, everyone, that's it for today so have a good weekend!" she hollered. "And remember to study for the history quiz on Monday!"

Before she could get in another word, her students rushed out the door. Among the class was Leon, a shy child who sat in the front row. However, unlike the other children, he stayed. With his eyes focused on the comic book clutched in his hands, he was in no hurry to leave.

"Leon! Oh, Leon!" Mrs. Lounger smiled.

"Huh?" Leon dropped the comic book and then adjusted his glasses.

"Class is over, honey." She pointed her finger to the clock above her head.

"Oh right!" Leon smiled back, stuffing the book into his backpack. "I just got—"

"Caught up in your comic book again? I'll never understand how you get straight A's and B's when all you do is read those things all through class every day." Mrs. Lounger pulled out his test from a stack of papers on her desk. "Anyway, you got a C on your last spelling test, but I'm gonna let you retake it over the weekend."

"Well, I don't..." Leon mumbled while he rose from his seat.

"What's wrong? Don't you want a good grade?" she asked.

"Yeah, but it ain't gonna be fair to everyone else." Leon headed for the door. "Thanks anyway."

"Leon, you're too honest for your own good," she smirked.

Leon swung the door open and soared through the hallways until he was outside. Most of the other children were already exiting the campus, but the only thing Leon cared about was finishing his comic book.

"Wait for me!" He caught his school bus just as it started to leave.

The driver opened the door and scowled at Leon. "Late again?"

Leon stepped onto the bus. "Yeah, but I was—"

"Yeah, yeah." The bus driver closed the door and drove forward. "Next time I'm not stopping."

"Okay, it won't happen again." Leon made his way to the last seat on the bus, and after sitting down, he pulled out his comic book and sunk his nose into it.

Not before long, two of his classmates, named Jason and Devin, slipped to the back of the bus near Leon. Jason and Devin were both notorious for harassing other students in the school, and unfortunately, Leon usually found himself at the butt of their cruel antics.

Devin leaned over the seat in front of Leon. "What the hell is that crap, nerd? Still reading those gay ass comic books?"

"I like this stuff. Ya just gotta get into—"

"Shut up, pussy!" Jason snatched the comic away.

Leon stomped his foot. "Give it back!"

"Hey, everyone! Leon's gonna cry again!" Jason's taunts caused the rest of the children to erupt in laughter.

"Hey, Leon!" Devin pulled out a grotesque Halloween mask of a decayed human face. "Check it out!"

"Get that away!" Leon stumbled back, hitting his head against the back window

"I told ya! He's scared of everything!" Devin cackled, nudging Jason in the arm.

"Leon, you're such a loser!" A red-haired girl shouted out.

"I ain't scared!" Leon jumped up and stared at the mask. "See?!"

"Whatever, pussy!" Jason ripped the comic book to pieces before throwing it out the window.

"That was a new issue!" Leon cried, watching the remnants of his book flutter away in the breeze. "I just bought that this mornin'!"

Jason and Devin laughed while they made their way back to their original seats, glancing back with their lips curled.

"Gosh darn it!" Leon pressed his hands and face against the window, thinking about how many days he spent doing yard work just so he could add it to his collection. He then sat back down in his seat and tried not to cry, pondering on why he was picked on so frequently. Was it the clothes he wore? Was it because everyone else knew he hated resorting to violence? Maybe it really was all the comic books he always read. Leon continued pondering on what exactly was wrong with him long after the bus arrived at his stop.

"Bye nerd!" Devin shot a rubber band at Leon's face.

"That hurt!" Leon rubbed his mouth while hurrying through the bus aisle, dodging spitballs and wads of paper. He then nodded his head at the driver before escaping the chaotic middle schoolers.

"Hey, loser!" One of the kids stuck her head out of the window. "Don't wet the bed tonight!"

After the bus disappeared down the street, Leon turned around and stomped toward his home. The old, light blue house he faced wasn't much, but it would at least provide him with protection from his bullies until the following Monday.

Once he reached the front door, he swung it open to see his older brother standing on the other side. "Hey, Zeke."

"How's it goin' buddy?" Zeke asked.

"I'm alright." Leon sunk his head.

"Are ya sure?" Zeke asked.

"Yeah." Leon put his hands in his pockets.

"Well, ya don't seem like it," Zeke said. "Anyway, Agatha's upstairs packin' and mom and dad are out shoppin'. Oh yeah, and Thane should be here soon."

"Thane?" Leon smiled. "We ain't seen him in a while."

"Yeah, he said he wanted to drop by before Agatha left," Zeke said.

"Oh, my!" Agatha ran down the stairs before wrapping her arms around Leon. "How's my favorite superhero?!"

"I'm fine." With a wide grin on his face, Leon held his hand out, eagerly awaiting the piece of chocolate he always received.

"Oh, that's right!" Agatha dug through her pockets before removing a small piece of caramel. "All I got today, kiddo!"

Zeke pulled off his police cap and then placed it on a hat rack. "Agatha, where were ya goin' again?"

"Over in Florida to visit Grandma Cecilia. I haven't seen her in almost a year, and I just can't seem to get a phone number from her." Agatha plucked a loose thread from her floral patterned dress. "I just have that address from those postcards she sends us."

Just then Clyde made his way through the front door, both hands gripping plastic grocery bags. "What's that about Florida?"

"We were talkin' 'bout Grandma Cecilia." Zeke let out a chuckle. "How'd ya even hear us?"

"Well, since you boys never shut the windows..." Ely shook her head after entering the house.

"Oh..." Zeke shrugged.

"It's not a big deal." Ely plucked a dried leaf off her green blouse. "Just lets the heat out is all."

"Let me take these." Agatha grabbed as many grocery bags as she could carry and made her way to the kitchen. "I'll go ahead and put these away."

"Have y'all seen my knife collection?" Zeke looked around the room.

"I think I saw them upstairs in the guest room." Agatha pointed to the ceiling. "On the dresser."

"Alright, I'm gonna—" Zeke started.

"Hold on, Zeke," Clyde said. "I almost forgot about this."

"Yeah?" Zeke spun his head around.

"This came in the mail earlier today." Clyde picked up a cardboard package off the couch.

"Leon!" Zeke grabbed the parcel before showing it to his younger brother. "Remember that Halloween contest I entered? I think this is it!"

"That was months ago though," Leon said. "And, besides, Halloween is over."

"There's still next Halloween!" Zeke zoomed up the stairs. "Let's check it out!"

"Wait for me!" Leon followed his older brother, arriving outside the guest room after Zeke had already torn open the package.

"Look at this!" While Zeke pulled out a black leather mask, bits of Styrofoam packaging fell to the carpet. "Scary ain't it?"

"I don't really…" Leon shivered.

After pulling Leon into the room, Zeke slipped on the mask and turned to the knife collection which sat exactly where Agatha had said they were. The instant he removed one of the razor-sharp, steel blades, he turned to the mirrored closet door and admired himself.

"What are you…" Leon watched Zeke wave the knife around. "What are you doing?"

Zeke's bloodshot eyes stared down Leon. "I'm Jason," he whispered, creeping toward his terrified brother. "Or maybe even Leather Face!"

"S-stop," Leon pleaded. "It's scarin' me."

"Scary?!" Zeke waved the knife in front of Leon's face. "Ya better run! I'm comin' for everybody 'round here!"

"Stop it!" Leon shrieked.

"Come on!" Zeke dropped the blade and pulled of the mask. "It's just for fun."

"I don't care!" Leon retreated into a nearby corner. "I don't like that thing!"

"Ya gotta stop bein' so scared of everything!" Zeke tossed the mask back onto the bed. "That's why all the other kids make fun of ya! That's why ya always get bullied!"

"Oh yeah?!" Leon pouted, crossing his arms. "I'm gonna be just like Thane when I grow up!"

"Like Thane?" Zeke laughed. "Working at a stupid pet shop?"

"That's right!" Leon smiled. "He's cool!"

"How 'bout the police force like ya big brother?" Zeke dug out a police badge from his pocket. "How 'bout just like me!"

"No way!" Leon's smile grew wider. "I wanna be just like Thane!"

"Nah." Zeke used his thumb to point to himself. "Be just like me."

"Alright, maybe." Leon exited the room. "Let's get some food."

"What's going on up there, Leon?" Clyde's voice echoed up the stairs.

"We wasn't..." Leon stopped halfway down the staircase.

Thane crept through the front door before locking eyes with Leon. "Hey, how's it goin', buddy?"

"Thane!" After dashing down the rest of the staircase, Leon gave Thane a hug.

Thane laughed. "How old are ya now, Leon? 70 right?"

"Very funny." Leon took a step back and then wiped his nose. "And I'm still 11."

"Oh, and your brother didn't let you play with his knives again did he, Leon?" Ely put her hands on her hips, eyeing Zeke while he came down the stairs.

"No." Leon shook his head and ran to the front door. "Hey, Thane, wanna go to the park? I ain't been there in forever."

"Nah, buddy, I—" Thane started.

"I think Thane's more scared of the dark than Leon," Zeke snickered. "He even still wets the bed."

Ely shot Zeke a dirty look. "Don't be rude!"

"What?!" Zeke's snickering switched to full blown laughter. "He does!"

"He does not!" Ely placed her hands on her hips.

"Stop bein' so mean to Thane every time ya see him!" Leon stuck his tongue out at Zeke.

Ely shook her head. "So, Thane, what have you been up to lately?"

Thane removed his leather jacket before placing it on a rocking chair. "Just house sittin' for Grandma Cecelia while she's away."

"Oh yeah? How's that going?" Ely asked while walking to the fireplace to put in a new log.

"Well, Grandma's been gone so long it's like I pretty much own the place by now," Thane said, chuckling. "She does live in a nice neighborhood though."

"She really does," Ely said. "How long has she been gone anyway? Grandma Cecilia I mean."

"Feels like years, but I think it's been around six months." Thane took a seat on the rocking chair on top of his jacket.

"You sure do miss her don't you?" Ely took a seat on the couch.

"Yup, she's just the sweetest old woman," said Thane. "Oh, and that reminds me..." He reached into his pocket and pulled out a postcard. "She sent another card. I think it's for Leon this time."

Leon grabbed the postcard, gripping it excitedly with both hands while admiring the picture of a turtle in the sand on the front of it. When he flipped it over, he was delighted to read about his grandmother's adventures in the southern state. "Whoa! She says she saw an alligator!"

"An alligator?" said Clyde. "That's crazy!"

"I know!" Leon grinned.

"Say, Thane, didn't you get a new job at that pet store that just opened up a few months back?" Clyde sat down next to Ely, putting his arm around her.

"Yeah, but the thing is..." Thane nodded. "Some of the animals got out, and now we can't find them. I guess one of the workers forgot to secure their cages and they escaped through the backdoor after closing hours."

"Well, that's sad." Ely picked up a cup of tea off the table in front of her. "I'm sure they'll come back sooner or later."

Leon set his postcard down on the table. "Can we go to the park now?"

Thane looked to the acorn shaped clock above the blazing fireplace. "I think I'm gonna stay here and hang out with Agatha, but why don't ya go on and head over there? I'll be here for awhile."

"Well, we haven't eaten..." Ely began.

"Oh please." Clyde clapped his hands together. "Let the boy have some fun!"

"I guess it would be alright." Ely turned to Agatha. "Agatha, do you think you could drop him off?"

"I could drop him off." Agatha grabbed a napkin and wiped her hands. "But I wouldn't be able to pick him up because of my flight. I'm leaving in half an hour."

"Oh, that's right!" Ely smiled.

Leon headed to the door. "Can I walk back myself?"

"You think you can find your way back?" Clyde asked.

"One of us can pick you back up, Leon," Ely said. "You're scared of the dark remember?"

"I am not!" Leon crossed his arms. "I ain't scared!"

"He's growing up, Ely." Agatha fished out her car keys from her purse. "I think he'll be just fine."

"Well, alright then." Ely grabbed an orange off the kitchen table and peeled it. "Just remember not to go with anyone you don't know."

"Cool!" Leon bolted out of the house, passing Thanes raggedy, old pickup truck and jumped in the front seat of Agatha's Toyota Corolla. "Let's go, Auntie Agatha!"

"Oh my! Slow down!" Agatha wobbled after him, carefully trying to avoid slipping on the lawns muddy grass. "My legs aren't what they used to be!"

"You can't run?" Leon shouted.

"No, honey." Once Agatha reached her car, she walked to the driver's side. "My legs aren't like yours. They're old and tired."

Leon slammed his door shut. "That ain't good!"

"You're telling me?!" Agatha laughed. "I'm the one who has to deal with it!" After slipping inside the car, she took off down the road. "Alright, hold on tight! Don't want you falling out!"

"Okay!" Leon leaned his head back, his gaze glued to the leaves drifting in the autumn wind.

While the two of them drove down the street, Leon couldn't help but wonder why Zeke was so obsessed with his knife collection. Just the thought of his older brother wearing that eerie leather mask and waving his blade in the air made his spine shiver. When he thought about it, his heart pounded faster, making the blood drain from his face. He shook off his nerves by wiping the sweat from his forehead, convincing himself that he just needed to stop being so scared just like Zeke said. Maybe if he was braver the other children wouldn't tease him so much.

A few minutes later, Agatha came to an abrupt stop near a park that sat near a river. In the center of its freshly cut grass stood a sign that was labeled 'Iron River.'

"Thanks, Auntie Agatha!" Leon hopped out of the car.

"You sure you can find your way back from here?" Agatha asked. "Are you sure you won't be scared?"

"Maybe you..." Second thoughts filled Leon's head, making him wonder if he should go back with Agatha. However, he suddenly remembered what Zeke had said earlier. "I'll be just fine, Auntie Agatha." He ran toward the park. "Thanks!"

"Anytime, honey!" Agatha hollered.

Leon ran across the road, spinning his head both ways to check for cars. When he neared the park, he jumped over the sidewalk and planted his feet into the firmly cut grass. Then he looked up and spotted Devin and Jordan. They both noticed him before he was able to find a hiding spot.

"Well, well, well, look who it is!" Jordan adjusted his basketball cap. "It's the pussy!"

Chapter Thirty-Five

Group of Shadows

Present day...

Officer Tanner dashed down the corridors of the police station toward Mercer's office. "Boss! Boss!"

"What is it, Rookie?" Officer Mercer stepped out of his office before pulling off his police cap.

"We got a sighting on that fugitive over by the docks!" Officer Tanner panted. "Over near Seguro Road!"

"So that makes four so far." Officer Mercer scratched his head and then placed his cap back on his head.

"Four?" Officer Tanner raised his eyebrows.

"Yup." Officer Mercer walked with Tanner to the lobby toward Officer Paul. "We've been gettin' multiple calls all over the city. Most have just been false flags, but our closest lead was at a gas station."

"You think that was him, Boss?" Tanner grabbed a maple donut off the front desk. "The one on Seguro?"

"I ain't too sure." Officer Mercer folded his arms, thinking about his options. "That car he was supposedly in was found down the street from here. He'd have to be a god damn idiot to come this way."

"I guess you's right, Boss," Officer Tanner shrugged, taking a bite of his baked good.

"Alright!" Officer Mercer turned his attention to Officer Paul. "We got another sighting on our hands over near the docks! Who do we got left?"

"We just got Zeke," said Officer Paul. "That slimy snake."

"Dammit!" Officer Mercer slammed his palm on the front desk. "Who else?! There's gotta be someone else!"

"There's no one left," Officer Paul exclaimed. "We got a few recruits around the station, but most of them just got here from the academy. I don't think they're ready for this. In fact, I'm off the clock right now, but if you really need help, I'll tag along."

"God dammit!" Officer Mercer gritted his teeth. "Alright, I guess we ain't got no choice. Go get that rat and meet us in the parking lot!"

Mike exited a corridor and approached Mercer. "Sir, I overheard and I wanna...come along."

"Oh no! I don't think so! After lettin' him get away like that?! Not on my god damn life!" Officer Mercer shook his head. "You stay here and do paperwork or somethin'!"

"But—" Mike started.

"No 'buts'!" Officer Mercer slammed his fist against the front desk, making a pen filled mug tumble off the edge and crash to the floor. "He escaped because of you!"

"I…" Mike's head sunk. He then returned down the same corridor he appeared from.

"Alright, let's go!" Officer Mercer marched toward the station's exit. "Absolutely ridiculous!"

After Tanner reached the entrance, he held the door open for Mercer. "Are ya sure we got enough officers, Boss?"

"Well, actually…" Mercer stopped where he stood and pointed toward Officer Walker who was smoking a cigarette at the bottom of the stairs. "You there! You're comin' with us! I don't care what ya doin'!"

Officer Walker strutted to a squad car parked behind him. "Sir, yes sir!"

"Officer Walker? He looks…uh… like he's 'bout to retire, Boss." Tanner walked with Mercer across the parking lot.

"Don't care!" Officer Mercer flung open the door of his squad car and slid inside. "We need as many people as we can get." After lighting a cigarette, he started the vehicle and looked in the rearview mirror, scowling. "There he is. That sneaky little rat."

"Who?" Tanner looked in the rearview mirror to see the devious Officer Zeke walking to his squad car. "Oh, it's him."

"I should run his ass over with this damn car." Officer Mercer actually considered the deed while backing up his vehicle. "One less snake in the world that's for sure."

"Not tonight, Boss." Tanner kept his eyes glued on Zeke. "Just stay focused."

"Guess you're right." Officer Mercer blew a fresh puff of smoke into the mirror. "Let's just go."

Officer Mercer and the rest of his group left the police station, speeding through the night toward the grittiest part of Violet Haven. The sirens of their squad cars blared in Mercer's ear, keeping him high and alert during the time he was usually dozing off. Oddly enough, even if he was tucked in his cozy bed, he wouldn't have gotten an ounce of sleep while knowing the criminal was running rampant throughout the city. However, unbeknownst to his partner, he was actually glad that the perpetrator had escaped from their clutches—he loved a good rundown.

Less than 15 minutes went by and Officer Mercer was already pressing the petal to the floor. "Looks like we're almost there. Are ya ready for this?"

"Hell yeah, Boss!" Officer Tanner clapped his hands together. "Let's get 'em!"

"After this, we'll finish off the night with a trip to the bar." Mercer turned to Tanner and gave him a quick smirk. "On you."

"Come on!" Officer Tanner sunk his head.

"I'm just kiddin'!" Officer Mercer padded Tanner on the shoulder.

"We'll split the tab."

"Ya had me there for a minute," Tanner laughed.

Officer Mercer swerved around a corner, admiring a view of the vast ocean waters. "Should have seen the look on ya face."

"So we got a jokester tonight?" Officer Tanner chuckled.

"Seems like it." After passing a pet shop, Officer Mercer drove around another corner. "Feel pretty damn good."

With rows of dark alleyways resembling grottos in the pits of hell, even the bones of Officer Mercer and Officer Tanner were rattled by the grittiness of those streets. Before they even reached their destination, every hair on their bodies stood on end.

"Looks like a hurricane ran through here, Boss." Tanner eyed a group of bums huddled around a fire blazing inside a metal drum.

"This here is the slums, Rookie." Officer Mercer sped down the street, listening to the foghorn blaring in the distance. "Ain't nothin' left of this place."

A second foghorn blared while Officer Tanner said, "Well, shit, Boss. I ain't never even been down here."

"I don't blame ya. I've only been over in these parts once or twice." A third and final foghorn sounded just as Officer Mercer turned down Seguro Road. "Anyway, get ready."

Officer Mercer stopped outside an old, brick building and exited the squad car. Only seconds later, the rest of his crew pulled up to the curb and quickly jumped out their vehicles. After hiding behind the vehicles, they pulled out their pistols and aimed the weapons at the building.

"This is the VHPD!" Officer Paul yelled through a loud speaker. "Come out with your hands up!"

Chapter Thirty-Six

Trapped

Present day...

I covered my mouth when I caught a glimpse of Leon's mutilated body. If I hadn't known him for so long, I wouldn't have recognized him.

"How the hell..." Leon tried to break free from the barbed wire wrapped tight around his neck. "Did y'all even find me?"

"We just..." Sean's lip dribbled up and down.

"Where's Tabitha?" Leon's hoarse voice traveled in whispers. When he opened his black and blue eyes, all I saw were these large, red spots. "Ya just left her at the fuckin' junkyard by herself?"

"Tabitha's..." Sean looked to the floor. "Tabitha's gone."

"What the hell do..." Leon's jaw dropped which let me see all the blood in his mouth and a few missing teeth. "What do ya mean she's gone?!"

"She was m-murdered. We thought..." Sean glanced at me. "We thought y-you was the one who did it."

Blood dripped from Leon's mouth. "I ain't killed no one!"

"D-dammit!" Sean tugged at the barbed wire on Leon's neck. "The hell is goin' on?!"

After Sean finally freed Leon, we dragged him out the closet and rested his body in front of a large, metal cabinet on the other side of the room. Leon was struggling to hold onto life, but with so much blood oozing out the slashes on his flesh, it didn't seem like he had a very good grip.

"Who the fuck did this?!" Sean shouted.

More blood poured from Leon's mouth. "My own fuckin' flesh and blood. I tracked him down here." His eyes rolled to the back of his head.

"Who was it?!" I dropped down and put my ear close to his split lip.

"I..." Leon turned his head to the side. "Can't even say his name," he said, trembling. "That lunatic ruined my whole fuckin' family." Tears poured into the cut on his temple. He turned his face toward mine until our eyes met. "And yours."

"Who?!" I grabbed his shirt collar. "Zeke?!"

Leon hacked up so much blood that this time it looked like he was gonna puke up an organ or two. Over the next few minutes, he kept coughing up small amounts of blood until I shook his shoulder and he wouldn't respond.

"Leon!" I shook his shoulder again.

"He's gone!" Sean grabbed my arm. "We gotta go!"

"I ain't gonna leave him like this!" I grabbed Leon's wrist. "Help me get him outta here! Grab his—"

When Sean backed into the red cabinet, a duffle bag fell off the top of it. He picked it up and emptied it out. And there they were—Ely and Clyde's hip and jaw bones.

I almost vomited. "What the hell?"

Sean jumped back. But then he slowly inched toward the bag when he spotted a long, greasy wig, a ski mask, and a black jump suit.

I picked up a photo album near his feet which was a bit thicker than the one we'd found on Palm Street. In fact, the cover even had a picture of the house. After I opened it, I almost pissed my pants. On the first page was a photo of Ely and Clyde...

But on the second there was one of their bloody, chopped up bodies.

"Jesus H. Christ!" I jumped.

"What is it?" Sean shivered and kept his eyes on the decade old bones sitting on the ground.

I turned the page to see a happy, Asian family at a backyard BBQ. And then their butchered corpses. The next two photos were even more gruesome. The first showed a man and his girlfriend, and the second showed their carcasses sprawled inside a bathtub. "Oh, Jesus!"

"What?!" Sean asked.

As I flipped through those pages, I had no idea I was witnessing the artwork of a serial killer. Every picture was worse than the last—most made my stomach turn. It looked like the murderer always tried to outdo his last kill by making the next victim suffer much more than the last.

When I got to the back, vomit spewed from my mouth. A second look and I considered scratching my own eyes out.

It was my mother and father.

Sean pulled at his beanie. "What the hell's goin' on?! We gotta go!"

I knew he was right, but seeing those last pictures was something I had to do. With shivers rocketing through my body, I turned the page. A young version of myself tied to a kitchen chair sat in the picture in front of me. Memories of that night flooded my head. And even though I knew what was next, I had to see him. For some reason, I had to torture myself.

When I turned the page, my entire body clamped up. One glimpse of Xavier's face and I was on my knees, peeling the flesh off my forehead with my fingernails. Then just as a foghorn sounded, the eerie ringing sound came back to my ears.

Sean snatched the album from my hand. Two more foghorns blared while he flipped through it. "Holy shit!"

"*I thought ya loved me!*" Xavier's voice caused the room to spin before my eyes.

"I did! I mean I fuckin' do!" I dug my fingernails deeper. "It was an accident!"

Sean tugged at his hair when the sound of police sirens blared outside.

"What the hell are ya talkin' about?! Do ya hear that?!"

I shook my head and crawled to a boarded window near the front door. Red and blue lights flashed through the cracks and crevices in the wood.

"We gotta run!" Sean ran toward me, snatched the back of my collar, and tried dragging me to the staircase. "We can get out through—"

"Ain't nowhere to go, Sean!" I shook my head again and pulled away from him, letting the ringing sound die down. "Ain't no way outta here!"

"What 'bout the way we came out?!" Sean pointed toward the staircase. "We can take a—"

"They'll gun us down the second they see us!" When I looked at Leon, the only thing I could think 'bout was that night I left Xavier in the forest. "And besides we can't just leave Leon like this!"

"What the hell are we supposed to do then?!" Sean shouted. "Ain't no way—"

"This is the VHPD!" An officer outside shouted from a loud speaker. "Come out with your hands up!"

I ignored Xavier's whispers and looked through one of the holes in the wooden board. "Just chill, and we'll think of something."

Chapter Thirty-Seven

Starting the Body Count

Fourteen years earlier...

L eon put his hands in his pockets. "I ain't no pussy!"

"Hey, I think he's scared again," Jordan said, chuckling.

Devin cocked his head back, laughing. "What are you gonna expect from a coward?"

"I said stop!" Leon stomped his foot on the ground.

"Uh-oh." Devin pulled a cigarette from behind his ear and put it in his mouth. "I think the cowards gettin' angry."

"I think you're right." Jason removed a lighter and handed it to Devin.

"Whatever." Leon eyed the cigarette in Devin's mouth. "Ain't ya too young to smoke?"

"Oh, so now you're a snitch, too?!" Jason snapped.

"Snitches get stitches." Devin lit the cigarette and took a long inhale before handing it to Jason. Then with a smirk, he exhaled the smoke into Leon's face.

"I ain't no snitch!" Leon snapped back.

Jason took a hit and then handed the cigarette to Leon. "Prove it."

"I ain't never…" Leon started, eyeing the deadly cancer stick between his fingertips.

"You ain't never what?" Devin pulled out a switch blade and waved it in front of Leon.

"I…" Leon stuttered, wishing he had just stayed home. "Fine." After placing it between his lips and inhaling, a burning sensation filled his throat, making him violently cough the smoke back up.

"Baby's first cigarette." Devin let out another laugh and took back the cigarette.

"I ain't never gonna smoke again!" Leon shouted. "That stuffs nasty!"

"Scared of cigarettes now?" Devin handed it off to Jason. "Leon really is a coward!"

"I told you I ain't no coward!" Leon pouted.

"Alright." Jason took off his backpack and dug out a black, plastic box. "You know what's inside here?"

"No." Leon used his shirt to wipe the fog off his glasses.

"You know what an M-80 is?" Devin smiled, revealing his braces and crooked teeth. "The firework?"

"Y-yeah," Leon shivered, knowing they were about to pull something devious. "W-why?"

"Good." Jason opened the box and handed the M-80 on to Leon. "You see that fat kid by the river feeding the ducks?" He turned around and gestured to an overweight boy sitting on a bench a few yards away. "Take this and put it in the hoodie of his jacket."

"Just make sure not to blow your damn hands off!" Devin spat.

"W-what?" Leon stuttered.

"You heard us." Devin handed Leon the lighter. "If you do this we'll make sure nobody ever messes with you again." He took another hit of the cigarette. "You'll be cool after that. After that, you can be our friend."

"Yeah." Jason gave Leon a thumbs up. "You'll be one of us."

"I d-don't know about that," Leon whimpered.

"Just do it!" Devin waved his switch blade in front of Leon again.

Leon hesitated for a moment, looking at the M-80 and lighter inside his palms. He wanted to run away more than anything.

But then again, he *did* want people to accept him.

"Well?" Devin tapped his foot.

Leon looked over to the lonely, young boy. "It won't hurt him will it?"

"Nah, nah." Devin playfully elbowed Jason. "It'll just scare him."

"Well..." Leon clutched the lighter and firework and then walked toward the boy. "If you say so."

"Hurry the hell up!" Devin whispered from behind.

Leon scurried across the grass. Once he got close enough, he lit the firework, placing it near the lonely boy's head. Sparks and smoke filled the air. At the last second, he stopped and threw the M-80 toward a stone path. It exploded. Bits of concrete flew in every direction.

Once he was sure there was no more danger, he rose to his feet and turned to the overweight child, asking, "Are you okay?"

"Yeah..." The boy spoke in a lone tone, pausing frequently in between his sentences. "I am."

"I'm sorry." After noticing that Devin and Jason had fled, Leon walked around the bench and took a seat. "You wasn't scared?"

"No..." The boy shook his head. "I wasn't."

"Really?" Leon admired the boy's courage. "What's ya name?"

"It's..." The boy lifted his head toward the fading sunset. "Mike."

"Mine's Leon..." Leon said.

"Well..." Mike started. "What do ya like...to do for fun?"

"I like readin' comic books. Ya know, 'bout superheroes and whatnot," Leon smiled. "Why do ya stop when ya talkin' like that?"

"Doctor said..." Mike froze in place. "I got brain damage...from my father" He threw a piece of bread into the water toward a swarm of ducks. "He got drunk and just...kept hittin' me one night."

"Really?!" Leon rethought about how easy his life was. "You don't look like you like talkin' to people."

"Not really, but..." Mike threw another piece of bread to the ducks. "You look confused."

"Why you ain't like talkin'?" Leon kicked a stone to the water.

"'Cause people ain't so...nice," Mike said. "That's why I like animals. They..." He stared at the ducks. "Don't hate me..." When he looked at Leon, a grimace appeared on his face. "Like people do. Hate me...for no reason like ya friends."

"I don't think they hate—" Leon began.

"They do. I could hear...what they said." Mike grabbed a handful of chips and threw them into the river. "They sounded like they hate...you, too."

"They always say I'm a coward," Leon pouted.

"You ain't the one who is..." Mike put his hand in his pocket and removed a small bag of trail mix. "A coward. They are. Only cowards do what they been told..." He opened it and handed a few pieces to Leon. "When they know it ain't right."

"I just didn't wanna hurt ya." Leon tossed the trail mix in the river.

"Exactly." Mike looked Leon in the eyes again. "Only cowards hurt people for no reason."

Leon compared what Zeke had said with what Mike was telling him. "You live 'round here?"

"No," Mike said. "I don't."

"Where you live then?" Leon asked.

"Anywhere nobody…" Mike sighed. "Can find me."

"You don't got no home?!" Leon gasped. "You look the same age as me though!"

"I ain't had no home…" Mike sighed again. "For two years."

"That ain't no good," said Leon.

Leon sat there with Mike, staring into the horizon and wondering how someone their age could be homeless like that. It just wasn't right to him when he considered the fact that Mike seemed like such a good person. He wanted to help, but he just didn't know how.

Realizing it was getting late, Leon stood up from the bench. "You gonna be here tomorrow?"

"Yeah, I…" Mike turned around and pointed to a forest behind them. "Will. I'm gonna be sleepin' over there until…someone chases me off."

"Ya want me to bring some food?" Leon said with a smile.

"That would be…nice." Mike extended his hand.

"Alright," Leon gripped Mike's hand, shaking it. "I'mma come back."

"I'll be…" Mike let go of Leon's hand and smirked. "Waitin'."

"Cool." With a toothy grin and a new friend, Leon strolled through the park and back to the street. "See ya then!"

The street lights flickered on, giving the evening an eerie glow. While he made his way back to his house, he wondered if Devin and Jason would start more rumors at school.

"Okay, I just gotta go straight down this road...." He looked at the leaves drifting in the wind. "And I'm home." While walking down the sidewalk, he couldn't help but check over his shoulder every so often to see if his devious classmates had followed him.

Leon eventually reached the end of the street, but something struck him as odd when his house finally stood before him. Thane's car was missing. He was sure that his cousin had mentioned that they would hang out together later on in the day.

"Hey, I'm back!" When he ran to the front door and pulled on the handle, he discovered that he had been locked out. "Mom, let me in!" He pounded on the door. "Anyone there?! It's Leon!"

Several minutes went by, and still no one answered. Leon was left outside his home, leaving him to pace up and down the porch. When he looked through the living room window, he noticed it was dark inside besides the dying embers in the fireplace.

He eventually decided to check the back of the house for the sliding glass door on the other side. To his delight, he found it was unlocked, and so he happily slipped inside. Afterward, he called for his family a few more times, and after receiving no answer, he headed to the garage, thinking everyone had planned some sort of surprise.

"Leon!" Clyde's voice rang from upstairs.

"Dad?!" Leon charged across the house and up the stairs.

"Don't come in…" Clyde shuttered.

"Dad, what are ya doin'?" As soon as Leon reached the guest room, he let out a heartbreaking cry. "D-dad?"

Clyde's face collapsed into a pool of blood, sending the thick, red liquid splattering onto the wall. His body had been brutally tortured beyond what Leon's young mind thought was possible. Ely wasn't much different. With a deep slash in her throat, she looked like a horrific version of a human Pez dispenser.

"Dad?!" Leon looked at the stab wounds on his mother and father's bodies, slowly taking in what was going on.

"Leon…" Blood poured from of Clyde's mouth.

"W-what happened…" Leon cupped his hands over his mouth and dropped to his knees, his eyes watering. "Mom? Mom?!"

"Leon, just…" Clyde's head dropped to the ground. His eyelids began to shut.

"Mom's gonna be okay isn't she?!" Leon could barely breathe. "Where's everyone else?!"

"J-just run, Leon!" More blood gargled from Clyde's mouth, staining the beautiful white carpet fibers below. "Just run!"

"I can't just…" Leon suddenly noticed Zeke's blood soaked leather mask in the middle of the floor. "Zeke did this?!"

"I said..." Clyde's eyes became still.

Leon shivered. A river of tears dripped down his face, hitting a puddle of blood on the floor. Sticking to the idea that the whole situation was some kind of prank, he truly believed that the two of them would begin laughing manically any second. "Wake up, Dad!"

Just then a vehicle pulled into the driveway. Leon shook away his tears and ran down the stairs, bolting across the living room and through the hallway. He nearly tripped on the corner of the couch on his way to the garage, but once he entered it, he looked for a place to hide. A second later, a long dining table sitting next to a stack of car tires caught his eye.

Someone entered the house and slammed the door shut. Portraits on the wall shook. Leon panicked. With his heart pounding, he gasped for breath and flew toward the table.

Just as Leon hid himself, Zeke stormed into the room carrying a cardboard box. He dug into it, pulled out a plastic tarp, and then spread it across the garage floor. While whimpering to himself, he retreated into the house.

Leon crawled deeper into his hiding spot, wiping away his tears. He wondered if he could run fast enough to escape, but Zeke returned. And when he did, Leon froze like he'd been buried by an avalanche. With his mouth wide open, he watched his older brother drag their father's corpse into the dusty garage.

Chapter Thirty-Eight

Friendly Fire

Present day...

Officer Tanner kept his pistol aimed at the door of the old, brick building. "Do ya think we're gonna need to call back up, Boss?"

"I ain't got a clue, Rookie." Officer Mercer eyeballed Zeke. "Just stay focused. It don't look like nothin's happenin' yet."

"Do ya think he's really in there?" Tanner asked.

"Huh?" Officer Mercer was much too focused on Zeke to hear what the younger officer was saying. "What was that, Rook? I didn't catch that."

"I said do ya think anyone's really in there?" Tanner asked.

"We'll find out soon enough." Officer Mercer switched his eyes back to Zeke, noticing there was something off about the shady officer.

Zeke's hands were shaking so much that he could barely keep his pistol steady.

"We have the area surrounded!" Officer Paul shouted through a loud speaker. "If anyone is inside come out!"

"Alright." Mercer snapped himself out of his trance. "If we don't receive a response in 15 minutes we go in."

"Right, Boss," Tanner said.

Over the course of the next few minutes, the squad kept their positions, each member carefully watching the building for any signs someone could be within its ancient brick walls. Mercer kept one eye on the building and the other on Zeke's odd behavior. Mercer's suspicions eventually grew so great he became convinced Zeke had something to do with the situation. Unfortunately, the fact Zeke was becoming more and more anxious didn't help ease Mercer's belief.

"I don't think anyone's—" Tanner began.

Just then a wooden board covering one of the windows fell down, leaving a scrawny, black male scrambling to put it back.

"There!" Officer Mercer pointed toward the suspect. "That's him for sure!"

"We have the area surrounded!" Officer Paul's voice traveled through the loud speaker in echoes. "Give up and come out peacefully!"

Officer Tanner's hands jittered with excitement. "Don't look like he wants to listen to us, Boss!"

"Don't look like it. I'm gonna call a chopper." Officer Mercer removed his radio from his vest and put it up to his mouth. "This is Officer Mercer can we get—"

"He's gonna kill me," Zeke muttered.

"What was that?" Officer Paul asked.

Zeke didn't respond. Instead, he stood there whimpering, and even with the cool, salty, ocean breeze brushing against his body, sweat completely soaked his uniform. Then he suddenly began muttering to himself, startling the rest of his group.

"What's he sayin'?" Mercer lowered his radio.

"10-9, Mercer, 10-9." A woman's voice boomed from Mercer's radio.

"10-6, 10-6," Mercer responded, keeping his attention on Zeke.

Over the course of the next few minutes, Zeke's anxiety grew worse and worse. In fact, the jittering in his body became so intense it looked like he was suffering from some type of illness. With drops of sweat dripping from his nose, his bizarre behavior continued to startle his partners.

"Chill out!" Mercer was having trouble staying focused on both Zeke and the fugitive.

"Calm down, son!" Officer Walker walked up and placed his hand on Zeke's shoulder. "Nobody here is going to hurt you!"

Zeke flinched. His breaths became short and fast.

"Tell us what's wrong!" Officer Paul shouted.

"I just told ya. He's gonna kill me," Zeke whispered.

"No one's gonna kill ya, Zeke. Calm—" Officer Mercer started.

"Yeah, he will!" Zeke pressed his hands against the sides of his head.

"Chill the hell out, Zeke!" Mercer pounded his fist on the trunk of a cruiser.

After a while, a few of the other officers were eventually able to stop Zeke's strange behavior, but it was clear that something was still troubling him. With sweat pouring down his face and his chest heaving, the bothered officer frequently shifted his eyes back and forth between Officer Walker and Officer Mercer.

Then it happened. Zeke cocked his pistol and aimed it at Officer Walker's forehead.

"Die!" he shouted.

Chapter Thirty-Nine

Massacre, Massacre

Present day...

Sean tugged at his hair. "What are they doin' out there?!"

I peeked through the hole. "Nothin' right now."

"We have the area surrounded!" One of the cop's voices boomed from a loud speaker. "If anyone is inside come out!"

Sean ran up and shook my shoulder. "We can still find another way out!"

"Alright, go check upstairs!" I glanced back at Leon's body. "I wanna get him outta here somehow, too!"

"We'll see if we can." Sean bolted up the staircase.

A few minutes later, he stomped his way back down. "Ain't no way out! I checked everywhere!"

"Well, damn! That ain't..." I focused my eyes on one of the cops. "Hold up! That's Zeke out there!"

"What?! Are ya sure?!" Sean walked toward me.

"Yeah, I'm..." The wooden board fell when I pressed my face against it.

Every cop outside saw me.

"What the fuck are ya doin'?!" Sean ducked.

"It was an accident!" I quickly put the board back up.

"We have the area surrounded!" The same cop yelled. "Give up and come out peacefully!"

"What did ya do?!" Sean pounded his fist against the ground "They know we're here now!"

"I told ya it was an accident!" I dropped below the window.

"We gotta think of somethin' fast!" Sean crawled over to the other side of the room and peered through a large crack in the board covering another window. "We ain't got much time left!"

"Well, I guess we just gotta play..." While I crawled over to Sean, I gripped the side of my head to try and stop Xavier's voice. "Play the waitin' game for now."

As the minutes went by, Sean and I took turns looking through the window, and as time went by, we noticed Zeke was acting strange. Unfortunately, my mind was unwinding like a ball of twine too fast for me to stay focused for long.

"*Can't we go home yet?*" Xavier's voice echoed in my head.

I looked around the room. "Xavier? Where are ya, buddy?"

"Get a grip!" Sean yelled.

"I'm..." I put my hand to my face.

"You ain't losin' it are ya?!" Sean slapped my arm.

I took in a deep breath. "No!"

"I think you are!" He shook his head.

After he looked outside again, his jaw dropped. He told me how Zeke turned on his squad and that he was aiming his pistol at another cop. I didn't believe him. At least until I took a look for myself.

As soon as I peered outside, I heard it.

"Die!" Zeke yelled.

A shot fired. Sean and I ducked. Not even a second later, it sounded like a damn battlefield outside. Shot after shot rang in the streets, just barely muffling the cops shouting.

And just like that, it was over. The gunshots stopped. As I shook, I raised my head to glance outside.

There were dead bodies all over the ground.

"Everybody's d-dead!" I shouted.

"You shittin' me?!" Sean asked. "We gotta get outta here before more—"

"Wait!" Sweat ran down my face as I took a closer look outside. "Someone's moving!"

In between the fallen cops, spilled blood, and flashing emergency lights, someone rose to their feet.

I turned back to Sean. "I think its Zeke!"

Sean snatched a crowbar off the ground. "He's gonna kill us!"

I grabbed a monkey wrench beside him then glanced through the cracked wood. The cop was heading toward us. Sean and I braced ourselves, ready to fight to our last breaths.

A few seconds went by. Boots tapped against the concrete steps. Keys jingled. The door unlocked, making my bones rattle. As the door opened, chills shot down my spine. Then a blood splattered face peered into the room—the face of an old man.

"Remember me?" he asked.

"Who the fuck—" Sean started.

The man pulled at his own face, ripping the skin apart. A much younger face appeared from under it. I knew who it was.

"Who am I? Don't tell me ya haven't heard of me." Thane pulled off his realistic silicone mask and threw it at me. "Don't tell me ya haven't heard of Bloody, Bloody Bijou?"

Chapter Forty

Body Parts

Fourteen years earlier...

Leon struggled to hang onto his sanity while he watched Zeke drag the blood drenched carcass of their father into the garage.

"Oh God!" Zeke pulled the body along the concrete and dropped it onto the tarp. "I can't do this!" he cried, placing his hand over the bruise under his eye. "I can't do this!"

"Daddy!" Leon trembled when he saw the trail of blood Zeke had left behind.

Just then Thane walked in the room, using a handkerchief to clean the blood off his leather gloves. "What do ya think ya doing?!"

"I was just..." Zeke shuttered.

Leon was speechless.

"Don't fuck around with me!" Thane walked across the room before sending a jab flying into Zeke's eye.

"Shit!" Zeke fell on his buttocks.

"Don't make me say it again!" Thane pulled out a knife and pressed it against Zeke's neck. "Just try to run," he seethed, "and you'll end up just like him!"

"Y-yeah." Zeke nodded. "I a-ain't gonna tell n-nobody."

"Good." Thane tucked the knife away. "Come and help me get Ely."

The two of them disappeared into the house, leaving Leon alone with his father's butchered corpse. While he wiped the tears from his eyes, his mind convinced itself everything he was seeing was part of a terrible nightmare that he'd wake up from any second.

"Don't get blood on the carpet!" Thane yelled a few seconds later, returning to the garage carrying Ely's body.

"M-mommy." Leon wasn't able to see the severity of his mother's disfigurement in the darkness of the guest room, but in the light, he was able to fully witness her broken jaw and eye sockets. Now with all her other unspeakable mutilations, she was barely recognizable.

"Put her on the tarp with Clyde." Thane let go of Ely's body, making her skull smack against the concrete.

"Y-y-yeah." After wiping his eyes, Zeke placed his mother's body next to his fathers.

Thane pointed to a hacksaw lying near Zeke's foot. "Throw me that saw right there."

Zeke picked it up and looked at the dull teeth of its rusty blade. Then he dropped it and collapsed to the ground, yelling, "Oh God! Don't make me!"

"Oh stop." Thane grabbed a second hacksaw from a shelf. "It'll all be over soon enough."

"Oh God! Don't make me..." Zeke bawled, burying his face into his hands. "Don't make me d-do this!"

"What did I just say?!" Thane picked up a hammer and threw it at the side of Zeke's head.

Zeke fell to the ground and shook, holding his injury.

"Don't be a bitch!" Thane walked toward the two corpses before ripping off Ely's pearl necklace and Clyde's wrist watch. He then walked over to the counter and placed both items inside a wooden box. "Trust me it won't be pretty."

"What are ya gonna d-do now?!" Zeke whimpered.

Ignoring Zeke, Thane walked to Ely, put the saw to her shoulder, and gave the tool a nice, hard thrust. The dull teeth slipped through her flesh one by one, making blood slowly drip onto the tarp. Another good thrust and the flesh separated. By now the blood was pouring out.

"Stop!" Zeke pounded the ground with his fist. "Stop it!"

"Mommy!" Leon had to use every last ounce of strength he had to avoid vomiting. "M-mommy!"

"I thought I told ya..." Thane continued with the saw, cutting through muscle tissue and chunks of human meat. Bone was now visible. Blood splattered with every thrust. "To shut the fuck up!"

"W-what is Leon gonna think?!" Zeke's lip quivered. "When h-he gets back?!"

"Well, what did *you* think..." Thane's deviant smile revealed the tobacco stains on his pointy teeth. "After I tied ya up and made you watch?"

Zeke trembled, picking up the saw and staggering to the body of his dead father. The instant he tried sawing through one of the corpse's legs, vomit poured from his mouth. "I can't do it!"

"Stop whinin' and toss the body parts in these!" Thane pulled on Ely's arm until it separated from her body. Then he grabbed a box of large, black, trash bags and tossed it—he gave no mind to all the blood—into one of them. An emotionless scowl remained on his face while he sawed through her other arm.

"I can't do this!" Zeke yelled. "I can't do this!"

Eventually, Zeke complied with Thanes demands. Over the course of the next few hours, they both reduced Ely and Clyde to nothing but a pile of mutilated body parts. Leon sat in his little hiding spot, bawling his eyes out and convincing himself that what he was witnessing wasn't real. There was nothing he could do except watch the decapitation of his parents by two people he loved and trusted.

Leon pinched his arm. Once he realized there was nothing to wake up from, his heart shattered like broken pottery.

"Oh, and I almost forgot." Thane curled his lips and turned toward Leon's hiding spot. "I know you're in here, Leon." He picked up Ely's severed head and tossed it into a trash bag as if he truly viewed it as nothing more than garbage. "I could hear you crying the entire time."

"Leon?!" Zeke dropped one of Clyde's arms to the ground, making a thin line of blood splatter across the concrete. He tripped over Ely's torso and fell to the ground.

"Z-zeke!" Leon's young, squeaky voice carried across the garage. "What did ya do?!"

"It wasn't..." Zeke grabbed the sides of his skull. "It wasn't like that!"

"I didn't say anything before 'cause ya weren't hurting anyone." Thane grabbed some rope and a roll of duct tape. "But we're leaving soon." He walked over to Leon's hiding spot and pulled the young boy out into the open.

"Thane!" Leon's hands were bound behind his back. "Why are ya doin' this?! I thought ya was good?"

"Good?" Thane pointed to the two heavily beaten corpses. "If being good gave me the feeling I feel right now, if being good made me feel like God on steroids..." When he looked at the blood on his leather gloves, his frown returned with a vengeance. "I'd never do stuff like this."

"Is it 'cause Z-zeke was so mean to ya?!" Leon cried.

"Ya know, I hated Zeke," Thane chuckled. "But no."

"Then why?" asked Leon, sobbing.

"Well, sometimes the best reason to somethin'..." Thane glared at Leon, shaking his head. "Is for no reason at all."

"I..." Zeke took a deep breath and shuttered. "I ain't gonna do this!"

"Didn't I tell ya before I'd kill him?" Thane placed a piece of duct tape on Leon's mouth. Then he drew his knife, waving it in front of the young boy's face.

"Stop!" Zeke waved his arms around in the air. "Stop it!"

"Just shut up and put the rest of the body parts in the bags." While an evil glow took over Thane's eyes, his humanity was revealing itself to be nonexistent.

Zeke grabbed one of the limbless torsos. While blood poured from it like a hellish waterfall, he dragged it passed two garbage bags filled with body parts and stuffed it into a third, saying, "Leon's too young to see this! Blindfold him!"

"I don't see any reason to," Thane snarled. "Now put the tarp in one of them barrels in the corner of the room and go get the truck." He pressed the knife against Leon's neck, causing the boy to cry and squeal through the tape. "Keys are on the kitchen counter." After the nefarious man pressed a button on the wall, the garage door opened, displaying a group of moths fluttering around in the empty street. "And ya got two minutes before he breathes through a slit!"

"R-right." Zeke ran into the house, grabbed the keys, and then sped out into the street toward the truck.

"Idiot forgot about the tarp." Thane dug out a pair of handcuffs from his pocket and then used them to cuff Leon to a 65-pound barbell. Afterward, he walked over to the tarp before folding and placing it inside one of the barrels. "Here he comes."

Zeke pulled his cousins truck into the garage and hoped out. Thane then closed the garage door. His two helpless family members soon found themselves trapped with someone who just wasn't all there.

With a scowl on his face, Thane walked toward Zeke and picked up one of the garbage bags. "Now help me put these in the back of the truck."

Zeke nearly collapsed to the pavement. "How could ya do this to us?!"

"Well, remember how when we were little, and grandma and grandpa helped us look for monsters before bedtime?" Thane placed one hand on the side of the truck and lowered his head. "Monsters are real. We just never found any 'cause they don't hide in the closet—they hide in plain sight." He licked his lips. "Monsters don't have horns, fangs, or claws. They look just like you. But the thing is they're soulless creatures, and the worst ones don't come with knives or guns." A smirk appeared on his face. "They come with hugs and smiles."

"Why are ya tellin' me—" Zeke started.

"Monsters are people in this world who aren't what they appear to be." The smirk on Thane's face grew wider until it resembled a disturbing version of a crescent moon. "Monsters are people in this world who wanna hurt ya just because they can." The evil of a hellish blaze flickered inside his pupils. "You can't tell I'm one of them?! C'mon, mother fucker, just look at me!" He slapped the side of the pickup truck. "I've got blood all over my clothes, and I'm holding a trash bag filled with human body parts!"

Zeke picked up the remaining bags and placed them into the truck bed. "What's wrong with—"

"Wrong with me? This is just who I am." Thane said. "Now get those two barrels."

While Thane and Zeke loaded everything into the back of the pickup truck, Leon continued to struggle. However, even after using every ounce of strength he had, his tiny body was too weak to break free. Along with that, as hard as he tried, he just couldn't look away from the blood pools staining the concrete.

"Hurry up!" Thane tossed the trash bag into the back of the truck. "I don't have all damn night!"

"What are ya gonna do w-with me and Leon?" Zeke picked up both barrels and their seals, putting them into the back of the truck.

"Don't worry about that." Thane made his way over to Leon and released him from the handcuffs. "Just get in the truck when you're done." He gripped Leon's collar and dragged the innocent child along the concrete to the old pickup. Then he picked up the remote to the garage door opener off the ground, placing in his pocket.

"Y-ya not gonna hurt Leon are ya?" Zeke strode to the passenger's side and slipped inside.

"That's up to him." Thane opened the garage door, started the car, and then pulled out his knife.

"Ya scarin' him!" Zeke said. "He's scared of ya!"

"Do ya think he's scared of *you*, too?" Thane rested his arm on Leon's shoulders, pressing the blade against the horror-stricken child's neck. "After what he saw?"

Zeke went silent, darting his eyes away from both Leon and Thane.

Leon's whimpering continued through the duct tape while they pulled out into the street. Whenever the boy closed his eyes, visions of his mother and father's bodies being sliced to bits flashed before him. He looked to Zeke for guidance, but the hopeless look in his older brother's eyes only made his heart sink. Once he realized there was no way out, Leon put his head down, enduring the reality of what was happening.

"Shouldn't be too far from here." Thane pressed the remote's button again, closing the garage door behind them.

Leon turned his attention on the road, hoping that a passing police car would see them and come to his rescue. He was sure that the sound of police sirens would be blaring behind them any minute. But then they reached Palm Street a few minutes later.

That shining glimmer of hope extinguished itself like the last ember of a fireplace.

"Here it is. Grandma Celica's house." Thane parked the pickup truck outside one of the houses and threw the keys to Zeke. "Grab the bags and follow me." The fiendish man then dragged Leon from the vehicle and toward the old, wooden home.

Leon looked around at the area, remembering how he always thought that the bad guys never succeeded in their corrupt plans. That's how it was in his comic books after all. The villain always lost to the hero, and good always defeated evil. If that was the way it was supposed to be why was the villain succeeding with his mischievous plot? Why was no one there to save him? Where was his hero? All the color in Leon's little world started to drain, leaving it black and white. His whole life he'd lived in a bubble of fun and childish innocence.

At that moment, his bubble popped. And when it did, hellfire rained all over him.

After walking up the wooden steps, Thane returned the knife to Leon's neck. "Unlock it, Zeke."

"Just don't…" Zeke set the bloody garbage bags down and unlocked the door, avoiding eye contact with Leon. "Just don't hurt him."

The second they entered the house, Leon and Zeke gagged. With the gut-wrenching aroma strangling the life from their senses, it was almost hard to breathe. Thane, however, didn't seem to be bothered by it. In fact, he didn't even seem to notice.

"Head for the door on the left." Thane pointed to a basement door halfway down a dark hallway. "And watch the stairs."

"Mommy!" Leon's cries were muffled by the duct tape. Once again, he tried breaking free from his handcuffs while they traveled down the basement stairs.

"Don't even try it." Thane snarled, his eyes radiating madness. He hauled Leon to the bottom and handcuffed him to a radiator. "Zeke, drop the bags and get over here."

"Ya a-ain't gonna let us go?" Zeke flinched, doing as told.

"Just shut the hell up." Thane slicked his sweat soaked hair back before digging out a second pair of handcuffs from his pocket. After binding Zeke to the same radiator, he made his way back up the stairs. "If I hear ya scream for help someone's gonna find ya ribcage in a trashcan."

When Thane was gone, Zeke ripped off the piece of duct tape from Leon's mouth with his free hand. "H-hey, buddy."

"Zeke, ya are..." With tears slithering down his cheeks, Leon lifted his head. "Ya are a monster just like him!"

"I didn't have a choice!" Zeke banged the back of his head against the radiator. "He just went crazy!"

"Liar!" Leon cried. "There's always a choice!"

"No!" Zeke shook his head violently. "He knocked me out cold when I tried to stop him!" His voice trembled. "Then when I opened my eyes he was soaked in blood and..." He sobbed, putting his hand to his face. "And mom and dad was already dead!"

"You helped!" Leon sobbed, looking to the three trash bags. "You fuckin' helped!"

"I had to!" Zeke banged his head against the radiator again. "He said if I didn't clean up the mess he'd kill ya when ya got back! We went to the store to pick up the tarp and he—"

Thane returned.

"Ya know, it's kinda strange. Some people go missing..." The moment he reached the bottom of the staircase, he strolled over to the bag of body parts. "Some people get kidnapped, some people get murdered." Blood squirted from a hole in the side of one of the bags when he picked it up.

"Mommy!" At the sight of his parent's body parts being emptied into the barrel, Leon kicked his legs and swung his head violently. "Stop it!"

"Some people just run away. Most of are found eventually, dead or alive..." Thane chuckled at the sound of the dismembered corpses clanking against the drums metal interior. To him, it seemed to be more divine than a symphony sung by the most harmonious of angels. "The rest of the world can look under every rock, between every blade of grass. They can search the highest mountains, trench the deepest oceans, but some people are just never found." He repeated the process with the second and third bags. "And I'm going to make sure of it."

After dumping the last of the trash bags into the barrels, Thane roamed over to the corner of the room and picked up a 20-pound container of lye. Upon returning to the drums, the sick man untwisted the cap and poured half of its contents into each barrel. Soon the bloody, mutilated bodies of Ely and Clyde were covered by tiny, white rocks.

"I'd love to hide the bodies in my stomach," Thane said with the utmost seriousness. "But I just don't have the time for that."

"Please stop! Please stop it!" Leon trashed about. "I want daddy! I want my mommy!"

"You'll see them soon," Thane smirked.

"What..." Zeke gulped, sweating like a pig on a hot summer day in Texas. "What 'bout Grandma Cecilia? When she c-comes back?"

"When she comes back?" Thane's smirk grew. He cocked his head back and laughed hysterically. "When she comes back?!" With his eyebrows raised, he signaled to the metal drum sitting in the far side of the room. "She never left. She's still here with us…" A wicked grimace appeared on his face, and his eyes grew wide as he whispered, "Here with us *forever*."

The very words made Leon's heart sink. He whimpered, sinking his head, mumbling, "But her postcards…"

Thane walked over to a handbag sitting on a desk, pulling out a stack of postcards. "The ones I forced her to write?" After throwing the postcards at Leon, he then lumbered back up the steps and exited the house.

"He's gonna kill us!" Reality struck Leon in the face like the fist of an infuriated God. "He's gonna kill us!"

Zeke shook. "Oh shit! What did I do?!"

"Mom!" Leon cried. "Dad!"

Thane lowered a long garden hose through one of the basement windows. A few seconds later, water sprayed from the nozzle and flooded the concrete.

Hatred blazed inside Leon's eyes when they met Zeke's. "Only cowards do what they've been told when they know it ain't right!"

"That's right!" Thane boomed from the top of the staircase, his boots loudly thumping against each step. As soon as his foot hit the basement floor, he headed straight for the spewing water hose. "He didn't even try to run or escape!"

"I..." Zeke's mouth bobbed up and down.

"He followed everything I said down to the tee!" Thane picked up the hose and placed it in one of the barrels. Water sprayed on the butchered carcasses, shifting them around.

For the next two hours, Leon and Zeke watched Thane fill up both barrels to the brim. By the time he was finished, blood and bits of flesh gently floated around the murky waters of his little concoction. The collection of body parts just below the surface dissolved ever so slowly, patiently waiting to be erased from existence.

"Alright, let's go." Thane placed a seal on top of each barrel before wiping the sweat off his forehead. "Let's go to Iron River."

Chapter Forty-One

Puppets

Present day...

Sean took a step back. "Thane?!

"Drop the weapons!" Bloody, Bloody Bijou aimed his pistol at Sean.

Sean and I tossed our tools to the floor. They fell into puddles of gasoline, splashing it everywhere.

I put my hands in the air. "I thought it w-was—"

"Zeke?" Bijou snickered. "Zeke tried to save you! Why do ya think he tried takin' ya away from that orphanage?! It's because he knew I'd found you!"

"What the fuck did ya do with Tabitha?!" Sean put his hands in the air.

"Ya mean that filthy whore?" Bijou aimed the pistol at Sean's chest.

"Shut the fuck up, asshole!" Sean lunged forward.

"Stop!" I placed my hand in front of Sean.

"Don't worry. I'm sure she's doing just fine..." Bloody Bijou cocked back his gun. "Burning in hell!"

"Don't!" I could feel the blood drain from my face when I saw Bijou's wicked grin.

"Bang!" He pulled the trigger. No bullets fired—he just laughed and tossed the gun to the side. Then he pulled Tabitha's gold necklace from his pocket. "Does this look familiar?"

Sean's nostrils flared. He rushed forward and swung. Bijou dodged it and pulled out a knife, slashing at Sean. A long, diagonal gash was left on Sean's face.

"Oh fuck!" Sean fell to the ground.

Bijou hacked away at Sean, splattering blood on the floor. Soon enough, my teeth were grinding together, and I was running toward Bijou at full speed, swinging my fists like crazy.

The madman ended up dodging every blow. On top of that, when I looked up he was ready to strike. He stepped forward, raising his blade. I threw a jab to his nose. Blood dripped from his nostril. Another jab. His nose broke. But that lunatic just popped it back into place. Then he looked me in the eyes. And slashed through my chest. I screamed in pain.

He raised his knife again. I tossed two more jabs to his mouth. His lip split. For a second there, I thought I had him. But then he grinned. Each tooth was stained in blood. As hard as I'd punched him, the maniac wasn't bothered by it. His homicidal gaze was still locked with mine. He slashed again—this time leaving a gash on my shoulder.

"God dammit!" I grabbed Sean and ran across the room.

"The fuckin' wrench!" Sean shouted.

"Forget it!" I slipped in a puddle of gasoline and fell to the ground.

"Gotcha!" Bijou thrust the blade through my leg.

I rolled around in agony. My blood poured into the pools of petrol. Bijou took his chance. He aimed for my chest. Sean jumped to his feet. Just in time, he swung a left hook to the madman's jaw. It was just enough to send the deranged murderer stumbling back.

"Sean, go get the wrench!" I crawled on top of Bijou.

Bijou sent three jabs to my nose. His knife flew through the air, slashing through my side. There was no time to recover. I grabbed his wrist, pinning his arm down. He bashed the sides of my skull.

"Get the fuck off me!" Bijou's punch split my eyelid.

Sean rushed up and swung the monkey wrench. Bijou took it right to the mouth, spitting out a tooth. He kicked me in the shin. I staggered back. Then before we could do anything, Bijou headed for Sean. Sean froze. Bijou slashed. The blade sliced through Sean's forearm. Sean winced in pain.

Sean was still too scared to move. So I snatched the wrench. And then swung at the knife-wielding psycho. Blood flew through the air. Bijou hit the ground. And once again, I thought it was over. But then the maniac jumped up and tossed a powerful uppercut at Sean.

Sean stumbled back and tripped over a tool box. He fell, slamming his head against the concrete. I yelled for him.

No response.

A smile spread across Bijou's face. He turned around with his sights dead set on me. "Your turn!"

Seeing Sean did like that had my blood boiling. I threw the monkey wrench at Bijou. He dodged. Then he came after me.

"Fuck, Sean! Wake the fuck up!" I scrambled to get out of the way of Bijous mad rampage. "Sean!"

Sean lifted his body but fell back down. "Y-yeah."

Bijou hunted me like a lion after its dinner. Anytime I tried to defend myself, he sliced me open. The only option was to run. But it seemed like this guy trained for situations like that. Not only that, but it was obvious The Devil's Haven had only one, true devil. And the worst part was he was inches behind me. Unfortunately for me, that devil lived up to his name, and he made it clear he loved leaving a bloody, bloody mess.

Soon that deadly game of cat and mouse ended when I got hold of a metal rod near Leon. After I got the chance, I swung it at Bijou's face. It was a direct hit. But that didn't stop the madman from slashing open my forehead.

Blood dripped in my eyes, clouding my vision. I couldn't hit him a single time.

"Take it!" Bijou sliced again and cut open my cheek.

I swung one last time, cracking the serial killer in the face. He fell back into the metal cabinet which toppled on top of Leon's body. Bijou himself tripped over a small grill. When he fell to the floor, his knife slid through his thigh. He screamed. I cleared my eyes and rushed at him. He plucked out the knife. But it didn't matter. I was already bashing in his cranium with the rod.

"Hey!" Sean rose to his feet but fell to his knees.

I took my eyes off Bijou. A second later, his blade slid through my ankle. An agonizing scream exited my mouth. Then my body hit the ground. Blood poured. My hands trembled. He stood up and stumbled toward Sean with his knife out.

"Stop!" I rose and hobbled close behind him. "Sean, move!"

"I can't!" Sean tripped when he tried to run. "The room's spinnin'!"

I grabbed Bijou's shoulder. He shoved me into a pile of cardboard. The maniac staggered closer to Sean. But there was no way I was losing another friend. I darted between them, ignoring the pain.

Finally, he was close enough. I swung. He sliced. Again and again—both of us. The harder my punches were, the deeper his cuts went. The deeper his cuts went, the harder my punches were. The more I moved, the quicker my blood poured out. And the quicker my blood poured out, the closer I was to death.

And he loved every minute of it.

I gave Bijou a hard crack in the jaw. His eyes rolled back. The knife dropped. He fell to the ground. Soon he was taking more powerful blows to the face.

"Go to fuckin' hell!" I yelled.

"Come with me!" Bijou pulled out a lighter. He lit it and tossed it into a puddle of gasoline.

Fire spread through the building instantly. The flames took over everything in sight. Even then I was too concerned with Bijou to care. I turned back to the bastard and repeatedly trashed my fist into his eye. His face pummeled up. Memories of my parent's bloody bodies flashed before me. My lips curled. Our blood boiled in the flames. He tried to break loose.

But I kept swinging.

The flames grew as fast as the hate in my chest. I struck his face one last time. His jaw popped outta socket. His teeth were stained in blood. He grinned, whispering, "I liked cutting people open. Didn't matter who."

"Shut the fuck up..." I slammed his head into the concrete until his eyes shut. "And die!"

By then his face was so swollen, he didn't even look human. Bloody, Bloody, Bijou's body resembled his love for blood, guts, torn flesh, and death.

But it didn't make me feel better.

I hobbled through the flames to Sean and helped him to his feet. As soon as he saw the fire, he grabbed my arm and pulled toward the stairs, yelling, "Let's go!"

"Leon!" I turned back to our friend and noticed the flames creeping toward him. "We can't leave—"

"He's gone!" Sean jerked my arm. "Ain't nothin'—"

Suddenly, Mike appeared at the top of the stairs. "I thought y'all needed some—"

"Mike!" A smile spread across my face.

"Fuck! More cops!" Sean picked up a screwdriver and rushed at Mike.

"Sean, stop!" I grabbed the back of his shirt. "He's cool!"

After a few seconds, Sean turned to me and nodded his head.

"My name is..." Mike extended his hand.

"We don't have time!" I rushed them both up the staircase. "We gotta get the fuck outta here!"

While the flames grew high, we ran up the staircase and to the window. Sean and Mike crawled through first. For a second, it seemed like it'd be a clean getaway.

But then...

"Help!" Leon screamed. "I'm still fuckin' here!"

I cupped my hand over my ear. "Hear that?!"

"Hear what?!" Sean tried to pull me out the building. "Let's go! I don't hear—"

"Fuck!" Leon's screams continued. "Fuckin' help me!"

"Leon's still alive!" I pulled away from Sean. "I'm goin' back!"

Chapter Forty-Two

Enter the Ghetto Kingdom

Fourteen years earlier...

Leon cries filled the room. He feared for his life, wondering if he'd make it through the night. Before long his demented cousin had unlocked his handcuffs, and he was being dragged up the stairs.

"Let me go!" Leon sniveled. He didn't realize it, but the events he had witnessed were splitting his mind in half like a guillotine blade to a fresh neck.

"Where are ya goin'?!" Zeke hollered.

"Here." After tossing Zeke the handcuff keys, Thane put his knife to Leon's throat again. "Guess what happens if ya try something stupid?"

Zeke unlocked the handcuffs and followed Leon and his psychotic cousin up the staircase. Then Thane stopped and turned toward Zeke, demanding the handcuff keys back.

"Ya ain't gonna get away with this!" Leon shifted his body to the side, trying to free himself.

"Oh really?" Thane dragged Leon out of the house and back to the truck. "We'll see 'bout that."

When Thane reached the vehicle, he opened the passenger door and shoved Zeke inside. He then walked to the other side, forced Leon to the middle seat, and then got in himself.

"S-someone's gonna find us!" Zeke shouted. "How are ya g-gonna explain that?!"

"Explain what?" Thane took off down the street. "Explain how my cousin, Zeke, went crazy and killed everyone?"

"I..." Zeke's jaw dropped. "W-what?!"

"Yup!" Thane pressed the pedal to the floor. "It was you! Don't remember?! I sure as hell do!"

"Ya can't do that!" Leon cried. "I'll tell the truth!"

"Tell the truth when you're dead?" Thane smirked.

Leon's face turned ghost white. "Ya wouldn't do that!"

"But I would." Thane sped through a red light, nearly colliding with a taxi. With a villainous look in his eyes, he swerved across the lane, saying, "And I am."

Leon clung on for dear life. The young boy desperately tried to separate himself from the situation by focusing on the rearview mirror. The thick, black clouds of smog trailing behind him brought him some consolation. However, it wasn't much. After all, at his age the last thing that crossed his mind was death.

But now it was here. It was in the very air he breathed. And soon his life would disappear just like the smog.

He darted his eyes in every direction, searching for a way out. A paperclip stuck in between the seat caught his attention. After shifting his eyes from it to the handcuffs and then back again, he picked it up and placed it inside his pocket.

"Never thought it'd be this easy." Thane pulled into Iron River Park, drove down a dirt slope overlooking the river, and then parked behind a tall oak tree near the water. "I really didn't."

"Ya really are a monster!" Zeke pounded his fist against the dashboard.

"Yeah, I am," Thane grinned. "But so are you."

"I..." Zeke glanced at the cold, rapid tides of the river.

"Exactly." Thane hopped out of the vehicle and onto the rocks of the river bank. After scoping the area for anyone who could be watching, he made his way over to Zeke's side.

"W-what are ya g-gonna do?" Zeke trembled.

"Don't really know." Thane pinched the tip of his knife and held in front of Zeke's face.

Zeke swiped away the steel blade. After wrapping his hand around its blood-soaked handle, he aimed it out the window at Thane. But Thane swung his fist at Zeke's jaw, knocking him out cold. The knife fell to the rocks below. Thane carefully picked it up, making sure not to smudge Zeke's fingerprints.

"Wanna predict tomorrow's headlines?" Thane removed a clear, plastic bag from his back pocket and placed the knife inside. "Junior Deputy murders own family, commits suicide in Iron River."

"Please stop!" Leon banged his head against the driver's seat. He soon realized that his heartbroken cries did nothing but cause joy to grow inside of Thane's cold, black heart. "I thought ya loved us?!"

"When you kill a rat, or a roach do you feel anything?" Thane walked over to Leon.

"We ain't cockroaches or rats!" Leon pressed his face against the steering wheel and took a long, deep breath. "We're family..."

"Well, it's like this." Thane reached through the window and put the vehicle in drive. "They always say that love is blind." The madness in his eyes returned. As he waved goodbye to Leon, a sadistic smile grew on his mug. "Well, so is evil."

Leon trashed around. It was useless. Soon the vehicle hit the freezing cold river water. It seeped in the ride. He continued to struggle. In one last attempt, he removed the paperclip and jammed it in the keyhole of his handcuffs. However, the river water was swallowing up the truck too fast.

"Zeke, wake up!" Leon yelled. "Wake up!"

Zeke opened his eyes and turned to Leon. "Leon!

"Zeke, I can't get out!" Leon placed the paperclip in Zeke's palm.

"Help me! Don't leave me!"

"Alright, alright!" Zeke's hands trembled while he inserted the paperclip inside the keyhole. But by then the water was up to his chest, freezing his veins.

"Zeke, hurry! I can't..." The unforgiving water swallowed Leon whole before he took a breath, leaving him gasping for air below its icy surface.

"Leon!" Just when the trunk sank beneath the frigid river water, Zeke unlocked the handcuffs.

They swam out the window and reached the surface of the river. But they met its powerful current. All their thrashing, all their attempts to swim back to shore were useless. Their exhausted bodies couldn't handle it.

Leon fought to keep himself from going under. Not being able to swim, he gasped for breath and then grabbed Zeke's shoulder. Then he waited until Zeke paddled over to a large, floating tree branch and grabbed hold of it. Leon shivered and clamped his arms and legs onto it like he were some type of parasite, not daring to let go.

"Head toward the shore!" Zeke yelled, being carried farther and farther away by the river.

Eventually, he was sucked below the surface.

"Zeke, come back!" Leon followed Zeke's instructions, but his tiny body was barely a match for the vigorous current. "Don't leave me here!"

"Go get help!" Zeke's head appeared above the water before promptly disappearing again.

Leon held his breath, terrified the water would slip inside his lungs if he inhaled. Under the surface, debris brushed against his body. Algae slipped between his fingers. Harmless they were, however, to the child's imagination, it was demons trying to kill him. He screamed his heart out. Water filled his mouth, causing him to break out in a coughing fit. By the time the water was shallow enough for him to stand in, his limbs nearly gave out.

"Zeke?!" Without a soul in sight, Leon stood by himself in a chilling breeze that made his very bones shiver. What was worse was the river carried him so far he couldn't pinpoint where he was. "Anyone?!"

Water dripped from his clothes. He headed toward a forest ahead, hoping he could find a house or a group of hikers.

Leon continued on, his sneakers squeaking long after he entered the woods. While he walked through its moss covered trees, he couldn't shake the feeling of being scared and alone. What he didn't know was it was something he would soon grow accustomed to.

The traumatized child walked through the forest, persistently searching for anyone who could help him. Unfortunately, the farther he walked, the more he realized there wasn't a single life form around besides the crows in the branches above.

He stopped for a moment, longing to wake up in his bed and go about his day as usual since even his tedious chores and copious amounts of homework seemed like heaven. After walking a bit farther, he rested against a nearby tree and pictured himself in the arms of his mother and father.

"Cockroaches are hard to kill." Thane bellowed from behind. "I thought ya said you weren't one."

Leon shuddered. When he turned his head, his eyes met the sick, sadomasochistic gaze of his cousin.

"Run," Thane whispered, a homicidal stare blazing in his eyes. He bent down on one knee and put his lips next to Leon's ear, whispering, "Run like ya just saw the devil."

Leon flew through the forest like a bullet, jumping over logs and fallen trees. Thane ran after him, dodging a low hanging tree branch. Leon slipped in a pile of leaves. He fell to the forest floor. Thane pinned the young boy down. Then he grabbed a large stone and raised it in the air.

"Don't!" Leon put his hands in front of his face.

Suddenly, someone body slammed Thane to the ground. "No!"

"Fuck!" The stone fell from Thane's hands. When he spotted the perpetrator, anger flared inside his bloodthirsty eyes. "Who the fuck are—"

The figure picked up the stone and swung savagely. Thane yelped, falling and cracking his head against a boulder.

"Mike?" Leon rose. "How'd ya find me?"

"I saw ya...screamin' in the water." Mike pointed to the river. "I couldn't get there..." He looked to the ground for a few seconds. "Fast enough."

Leon noticed the knife sticking out from the back of Thane's pants. After hesitating for a few moments, he made his way over and took it out the plastic bag.

"What are ya—" Mike started.

"Fuckin' bitch!" With a cloudy and yet murderous haze taking over his mind, the only thing he wanted to do was to slice open his cousin's neck and let the blood spill out onto the leaves and tree roots below.

"Stop!" Mike placed his hand on Leon's shoulder.

"He killed my..." Leon's eyes filled with tears.

"It ain't gonna..." The look in Mike's eyes made it seem like he understood everything Leon was going through. "Make ya feel any better."

Leon lowered the knife, stuffing it into his pants. Without uttering a word, both he and Mike walked through the forest. The entire time, Leon was unsuccessful in stopping the tears from dripping down his face.

"Where we gonna go now?" Leon watched a group of crows scatter from the branches above his head, wishing he was one of them, wishing he could fly away from all the grief and anguish. "I ain't got nowhere else to go."

"Ya don't got..." Mike looked down to Leon and cracked a half smile. "No home no more?"

"I..." Leon paused and thought about waiting for his Aunt Agatha to return, but the thought of her secretly being another monster crossed his mind, and he just couldn't bear to face that possibility. "No. I ain't got nowhere to go."

While the two of them trailed off, Leon wondered how he'd adjust to his newly found homelessness. In a single 24 hours, his life came crashing down like a rockslide. And like the towers of a corrupted paradise, his purity crumbled, gradually turning him into the same monster he so very despised.

About half an hour later, Zeke's voice echoed from the riverbank. "Leon!"

"Zeke?" Leon spun around to see his older brother walking out of the river. A smile appeared on his face.

"Do ya…" Mike took a good long look at Zeke. "Know 'em?"

Suddenly, something changed deep inside Leon. His smile turned grim. His nostrils flared. After clenching his fists, he turned his back to Zeke and endured the lingering heartbreak within his chest. "I ain't never seen him before."

"Are ya sure? I can't see his face…" Mike's eyebrows rose. "But he looks like he's lookin' for ya."

"Leon?!" Zeke continued to yell. "Where are ya, buddy?! I'm here for ya!" He dropped to his knees. "I'm sorry!"

"I'm sure." Leon took one last look over his shoulder. "I got no family."

"Well, then let's…" Leaves and twigs crunched below Mike's feet when he walked forward. "Go."

"Yeah." Leon gritted his teeth and vanished with Mike into the unknown.

Eventually, they found themselves back in the city, aimlessly searching for a new home. They heard a familiar voice.

"So it's the pussy again?!" Devin ran out of a burger joint, munching a double cheeseburger.

Leon clenched his fist, saying nothing.

Devin walked toward Leon. "What's wrong, homo?

Leon cocked his fist back, not hesitating to let one fly into Devin's mouth. Devin dropped the burger. Leon sent another blow straight into the bully's windpipe. Devin clenched his throat, dropped to his knees, and gasped for breath as he choked on bread, cheese, and meat.

Leon turned to Mike. "Let's go."

Mike raised his eyebrows. They continued on, leaving Devin to bleed and cry by himself on the pavement. They disappeared together, eventually coming across a long, lonely road on the outer reaches of the city. The two of them trailed along that road toward a junkyard but stopped when they saw an old, wooden Violet Haven city sign.

Leon's facial expression turned sour. When he spotted a red spray paint on the ground, he grabbed and shook it. Then he spit on the sign before changing its wording to 'The Devil's Haven.'

"Now when people come to this hellhole, they all know to run like they just seen the devil," he snarled, tossing the can to the side. "Not just me."

"I don't think..." Mike walked along the road. "That's right."

Leon didn't respond. Instead, he walked toward the junkyard. Upon reaching it a few minutes later, he pulled open the rusty chain link fence, revealing stacks of crushed cars and other scrap metal. The two of them entered, walking along its path of pebbles and glancing at the trash and debris that surrounded them.

"Doesn't look..." Mike picked up a plastic bag. "Like anyone comes...here."

"Nope," Leon gritted.

Mike pulled a tattered Spiderman comic book out from the bag and handed it off to Leon. "Didn't ya...say ya love comic books?"

"Love?!" Leon yelled, ripping the comic book to shreds, tears pouring down his face. "I don't love anything! I don't love nobody!" He stomped it into the mud. "Nothing! Ever!"

"Ya know..." Mike shook his head. "Ya don't look the same from yesterday. It's like..." He sat down on an old couch. "Ya a different person now. And not in...a good...way." He ran his hand through his nappy hair. "You alright?"

"Yeah, I feel fine." Leon turned to the cracked side-mirror of a nearby car and looked at the lunacy in his wide, bloodshot eyes which now resembled Thane's. Never in his life had he seen so much anger on one person's face before. But he didn't care at that point. "I feel just fine..."

Before either of them knew it, four years had gone by, and one day Leon—who was now fifteen years old—was searching the city for food to bring back home, dirt covering his face and tattered, ripped clothes. After finding a few discarded apples, two old slices of pizza, and a half-filled water bottle, he made his way back to the junkyard, but upon arriving, he saw something that made him drop his meal.

It was a police cruiser.

Not wanting to alert the officer, he crept around to the back until he found a spot where he was sure he wouldn't be seen entering. He then carefully climbed the chain link fence and hopped over to the other side on the hood of a tarnished ice-cream truck.

After jumping down and creeping around rows of cars, he spotted the officer talking to Mike. He ducked down and pulled out his knife.

"How long have you been living here?" The officer asked Mike. "This place isn't for kids."

Mike shook his head and twirled his foot in the gravel.

"Can't speak, son?" The officer looked around the area. "You can talk to me. I'm a good guy."

Again, Mike said nothing.

Leon crept closer, concealing himself behind vehicles and scrap metal.

"We can't have you living here, son. You might hurt yourself." The officer led Mike toward the front of the junkyard. "Don't worry; we're gonna find you a home."

When Leon was close enough, he hid behind a Toyota Celica and placed the knife in front of him, gritting his teeth while waiting for the perfect moment to strike. However, he caught eyes with Mike. Upon noticing the blade, Mike shook his head.

After exiting the junkyard, the officer placed Mike in the back of the cruiser. "Just come with me. You'll be alright."

Soon the officer was taking off down the lonely stretch of road toward the city. Leon desperately ran after them at full speed, trying to catch up to the speeding cruiser, but before long it was out of sight, and he had no idea where they were going. All he could do was stop in the middle of that road, feel the leaves, dirt, and freezing cold wind brush against him, and watch the vehicle become smaller and smaller until it was nothing but a pinpoint.

With his head down, he trailed back to the junkyard, and when he was far enough inside, he headed toward a nearby car before bashing the window until the glass shattered. Then with blood dripping from his boney, busted knuckles, he did the same with the window of another car. Then another. And another. And another. And another.

He let out a scream that reached the heavens. A vicious snarl formed on his face. He gritted his teeth and contemplated finding and then murdering the officer who took his only friend away. But then he realized that, like a rat trapped in a cage, there was only one thing in the entire world he had the power to change.

That one thing was nothing.

Leon had the power to change nothing in his miserable joke of a life. Along with that, the city was far too large for him to track down either Mike or the officer. And so, unable to handle the loss of the last thing he cared about, he dropped to his knees and repeatedly pounded his fist into the gravel, giving no mind to the fact that his bloody, swollen hand was already broken in several places or even that a heavy rain was starting to pour down on him.

And then, there in that abandoned junkyard, that ghetto kingdom of garbage, rat corpses, crushed cars, and broken glass, the troubled lost-boy was left to rot. From simple things which he enjoyed, such as comic books, to things which were deeply seeded in his heart, such as the relationship he had with his family, Leon had lost anything and everything, anyone and everyone he had ever came to love.

Now while his own blistering hatred of the outside world molded him into a shell of his former self, there was nothing left for him to do except patiently wait for someone to take his hand and lead him to a land void of misery and anger, a land where he wouldn't starve to death if he didn't dig through dumpsters and garbage cans.

Little did he know, no one would lead him there for no one would be the only person who would ever care.

Chapter Forty-Three

The Storm before the Calm

Present day...

L eon screamed, "Fuck! Help me!"

"He's still alive!" I looked at Sean and Mike. "I ain't leavin' him!"

"You ain't gonna make it back!" Sean tried pulling me out the window.

"No!" I pulled away. "I'm goin'!"

"Shit, man!" Sean gestured to the pipe bombs on the wall. "Them things ain't just there for decoration!"

I ignored Sean and dashed to the burning staircase. And that's when I saw him—Xavier. In the middle of the flames, chaos, and Leon's cries for help, he stood at the bottom of the staircase and waited for me to save him.

"Help!" he cried. "Don't leave me alone again!"

The room spun. I hobbled down the staircase toward my brother. Halfway down the ringing sound returned. This time it was so loud I puked over the railing.

"Fuck!" Leon's voice traveled through the flames. "I don't wanna die!"

"Xavier!" I stopped when I reached my brother. "I'm here, buddy! I'll get ya outta here this time!"

Leon squirmed on the ground. "Wadda ya doin'?! Get me outta here!"

"Shit! Leon!" My eyes darted between Leon and Xavier. I squeezed my shoulder wound and stepped into the fire. "I'm comin'!"

"No!" Xavier cried from behind. "I thought ya was gonna save me!"

"I am..." I waved away the clouds of smoke. "But—"

"Hurry!" Leon's thrashed harder. "Fuck!"

"Xavier, just stay here!" I hurried to Leon, using my arms to shield my face.

"Fuckin' help me!" Leon was entirely encased in flames. "Help me! I'm dying god dammit!"

When I reached him, I grabbed the cabinet. But the hot metal burned my fingertips, and I jumped back.

"What are ya doin'?!" Leon's screams almost drowned out the sound of the blaze. "Fuckin' help me!"

"The smoke!" Xavier yelled. "I can't breathe!"

"Xavier! I'mma be there in a minute! Just stay there!" I ignored the pain and tried again. Even then that damn cabinet wouldn't budge. "Leon, this shit's too heavy!"

"Oh God!" Leon's sobbed. "Oh God!"

I gripped Leon's hand and pulled. It was no use. That cabinet was stuck on him like a mousetrap on a rat. "I can't get this shit off!"

"*It hurts!*" Xavier continued.

"God dammit!" Leon shouted. "Help me!"

That's when I noticed a long, metal pole on the ground. I picked it up, put one end under the cabinet, and then pressed down. The cabinet moved. But my injury wouldn't let me lift it more than a few inches. It fell back down. Leon squealed.

"*Where are ya*?!" Xavier's voice shot into my ears.

My mind raced. I gripped the sides of my head and looked toward Xavier. Then at the flames. For a second, I wondered if it was pointless trying to help Leon.

"Stop!" Leon thrashed his body. "Don't leave me here like this!"

The second he said that, my mind snapped back. I gripped the cabinet with one hand and pulled up. Leon grabbed my other hand. I tugged. Blood poured from my ankle. He slowly slid out. I tugged harder. The blood poured faster. He kicked his legs until he was free.

Even then it wasn't over. The flame still blazed on his body, scorching his flesh. He frantically brushed off the fire while I used a nearby fire extinguisher to put out the flames.

Over the next few minutes, we smothered the fire until there was nothing but smoke drifting off his body. Then I got a good look at the hot, red blisters on his skin. He didn't even look like Leon. He just looked like some deformed alien.

"Fuck man! Thought ya was just gonna leave me here." Leon ran his fingers through his hair that'd been burned down to patchy buzz cut. "Thought ya wasn't gonna come back."

"Shit, man! So did I!" After I put Leon's arm around my shoulders, we both scurried through the sea of fire and over to the staircase. "We gotta get to a fuckin' hospital!"

"So ya some kinda superhero then?" Leon smirked as we ran up the steps. "Savin' everybody and whatnot."

"I guess so." I reached the top and helped Leon over a fallen radiator. "Anyway, back in the junkyard. Sorry I..." I led him to the window. "Ya know."

"Don't worry 'bout it." Leon exited the building.

"*Wait!*" Xavier cried.

For a second there, I ignored my minds games and tricks. But they were too powerful.

I turned toward the staircase. "Xavier!"

"What are ya doin'?" Sean reached through the window and grabbed the back of my shirt.

"We gotta..." Mike said. "Get outta here."

"No!" I pulled away from Sean.

"Kid," Leon yelled, "he ain't there!"

A loud cracking sound filled my ears. When I looked up, this large wooden beam was falling straight for me. I jumped back. The beam crashed to the ground, sending smoke, dust, and embers in the air.

I stood to my feet and looked at the beam. Besides a small hole, the exit was sealed.

"Shit!" Leon looked through the hole. "What the fuck?!"

Sean slipped his hand through and tried pushing the beam. "It won't move! Ya gotta try from the other side!"

"Hold up!" I dashed to the edge of the staircase. "I gotta get Xavier first!"

"No! You'll die!" Leon screamed. "He ain't there! He ain't there!

"The pipebombs!" Sean shouted. "The god damn pipe bombs!"

I ignored them and ran down the scolding staircase. Then I looked to the spot where I'd last seen Xavier. He wasn't there.

"Xavier! Where are ya?! We gotta go now!" I dashed into the ocean of fire and looked around the room, my heart pounding. Blood dripped from

371

my ankle. "I don't see ya, man! Say somethin'! Say anything!"

"*Over here!*" Xavier's figure flickered in the corner of the room.

"Where are…" I coughed. "Where are ya?! We gotta hurry! We gotta leave!"

He hid behind a stack of crates. "Help!"

I ran through the blaze. But then I reached the crates. Xavier was gone again.

All that smoke was getting me. I covered my mouth and nose and darted to a corner. Then I saw a boarded window. Maybe I could escape. I ran toward it at full speed and pounded on it. The board cracked and fell. My heart sunk.

Steel bars were on the window.

"Shit, man!" Sean appeared on the other side. "Hold up! We're gonna get ya out!"

"I can't find Xavier!" I covered my eyes and sobbed. "I'm fuckin' scared!"

"He's not in there!" Leon's voice was so hoarse I could barely hear him. "Ya gotta find another way to—"

"No! I ain't leavin' him!" I grabbed the steel bars and shook as hard as my body would let me. "I can't leave him!"

Sean reached through the bars and pulled me toward him. "You killed Xavier! It was you! He's dead! Gone forever!" He looked me in the eyes. "You will die here for no reason at all!"

His words cut deep—even deeper than Bijou's blade. It was the third time I'd come face to face with what I did. And it was just as heartbreaking as the night it happened. I stood there in tears in the middle of those the flames feeling like an idiot.

"I'm gonna..." Mike dashed around the building. "Try the front door!"

The flames grew more and more intense by the second. After Mike returned, he told us he couldn't break down the door. And that was it.

There was no way out.

"I called the..." Mike gripped the window bars and shook. "Fire department from my cruiser. Should be...here soon."

"Ya hear that?! Just hang on, man!" Sean sobbed.

"This shit ain't fuckin' real." Leon rattled the steel bars. "This shit ain't fuckin'—"

One of the pipe bombs exploded. Fire ripped through the air. Rubble flew in my face. I took a deep breath. Smoke flowed into my mouth and down to my lungs. Tears dropped from my eyes, hitting the flames below.

"Holy fuckin' shit!" Sean ducked.

"Shit! I can't see!" I covered my eyes.

"Watch out!" Mike shouted.

The twisted staircase was falling straight for me. I ran for cover and hid between a brick wall and a refrigerator.

The staircase hit the ground, slamming against Bijou's carcass. Thousands of embers fluttered through the air like snowflakes. Smoke and dust rose to the ceiling.

"Kid!" Leon reached his arm through the steel bars. "Where are ya?!"

Whimpers broke through my quick, short breaths. "I'm still here!"

The flames were closing in on me. Death was so close I could almost hear its demented laughter.

A mammoth sized, wooden beam fell in the middle of the room. A wave of smoke flew toward me.

"They're outside!" Leon shouted. "Get to—"

A second pipe bomb exploded. Fire swallowed the entire building. Black smoke and embers flickered in front of me. In the middle of the flames, I dashed to the front door.

I pounded on the door. "I'm here!"

Not before long, the firemen broke down the door. They pulled me out and placed a blanket around me, putting out the flames.

"Anyone else inside?!" one asked.

I turned back toward the fire.

Xavier's figure still flickered behind all the smoke and embers.

"No." I shook my head. "Nobody's inside."

"There's no one else!" He hollered back to his squad.

They walked me down the concrete steps and toward a line of ambulances, fire trucks, police cars, and fireman who were spraying the building with their firehoses. Leon was on a stretcher, being lifted into an ambulance, while paramedics were tending to Mike and Sean.

Up ahead, were the bloody bodies of the fallen cops Bloody, Bloody Bijou had slaughtered. A paramedic lifted his head when he came across Officer Mercer, yelling, "This one's still with us! Get another ambulance over here! He's bleeding out bad!"

While the firemen walked me down the concrete path, Xavier's voice trailed after me one last time.

"Wait for me..." he said. "I'm still here."

"But ya *ain't* here, Xavier..." I whispered, looking over my shoulder into the fiery blaze. "And that's my fault."

Chapter Forty-Four

Repentance

In the future...

During the next few weeks, Sean, Leon and me found ourselves in the hospital. Even though Sean's and my wounds healed in about a month or two, Leon suffered from burns which left most of his body scarred and discolored. His face was the worst of it, looking like it'd gone through a blender. But even then he was still his same old self.

As soon as we got better, the cops investigated everything from the junkyard to Bloody, Bloody Bijou and his victims, and after being taken in again and again for questioning, the case was handed off to the FBI. They investigated Tabitha's death. Luckily for me, her blood was found on Thane's clothing.

However, Sean, Leon, and me eventually found ourselves in front of a judge for the men we'd dumped in Iron River. Fortunately, Tonya and Clemecia were able to hire a lawyer for us, but it still looked like the prosecution had us pinned against a wall.

"All arise!" said the bailiff. "Court is now in session!"

I rose from my seat along with everybody else and glanced around the courtroom. It was so jam packed that lines of people went out the room and into the hallways. After word got out that not only had Bloody, Bloody Bijou's identity had been discovered but he'd also been killed by me, everyone and their mom wanted to know who I was.

Ironically, I was undergoing a murder trial of my own.

"Judge Thao presiding," the bailiff continued.

"Please be seated," said the judge.

Judge Thao shuffled through a stack of papers, and after announcing what we were all gathered in the courtroom for, he told the district attorney and our lawyer to give their opening statements.

The DA stood up and walked over to the jury on the far side of the room. "Your honor, ladies and gentlemen of the jury," he said, "the defendants in question have been charged with the murders of Chad Williams, Tom Gilmore, and Thane Jenkins. The evidence will show that the defendants murdered the first two men in cold blood, put the bodies in the back of the victim's own car, and then drove the vehicle into Iron River. Further evidence will show that one of the victims had water in his lungs after death, indicating that he was still alive while he was in the trunk of the car." He turned and pointed at Sean, Leon, and me. "With the evidence I will I present to you, I will prove that these three men are guilty as charged. Thank you." He returned to his seat.

Our lawyer made his way to the jury. "Ladies and gentlemen of the jury," he said, "my clients are being charged with murder, but by law they are presumed innocent until proven guilty. During this trial, you will hear the events leading up to the deaths of these men, and you will find out that, in all three cases, my clients were in fear for their lives. Therefore my clients are not guilty."

After both sides were finished giving their opening statements, Judge Thao turned to the DA. "The prosecution may call its first witness."

"We call Marty Moore to the stand," said the DA.

Just then the bus driver I recognized stood up from one of the pews. The bailiff led him to the witness stand, and after Marty swore in front of the court, he was questioned.

"Marty Moore, what do you do for a living?" asked the DA.

Marty stared back with a hazy look in his eyes. "I'm a bus driver."

"And exactly how long have you been a bus driver?" The DA put his hand to his chin.

Marty let out a loud, obnoxious sigh. "'Bout 27 years now."

"Good, good." The DA glanced at me. "On the night of Monday, August 21, 1995, were you working, Marty?"

"I believe so, yes," Marty responded.

"You believe so or yes?" The DA raised his eyebrows.

Marty let out a louder sigh. "Yeah, I was workin'! Jesus H. Christ, man!"

"Thank you." The DA pointed to Sean, Leon, and me. "On that night, did you happen to see any of those young men?"

"I definitely saw the one with the cornrows..." Marty pointed to me. "But, I don't remember seein' the other two."

"So, for the record, you definitely saw him that night?" The DA eyed me carefully.

"Oh God..." Marty whispered, pinching the skin between his eyebrows. "I just said yes for Christ's sake! Anything else ya need?! I had to drag my ass here all the way from—"

"Order!" Judge Thao slammed his gavel against the sounding block. "Order in the court!"

"Okay, thank you. That'll be all." The DA gestured Marty to return to his seat. "No further questions."

After Marty shook his head, he left the stand. Then the DA walked back to his seat, returning to the front of the court with a TV, VHS, VCR, and a brown, paper bag.

"Your honor, ladies and gentlemen of the jury..." He popped the VHS into the VCR. "I would like to show you Exhibit A. This is a video taken from the security footage of Bus number 23."

The video played. On it, I could see Leon, Sean, and me interacting with the bus driver and then taking our seats.

Right after it showed us getting off the bus, the DA turned off the TV and dragged it back to where he found it.

"As you can clearly see, those three young men were on the bus that night. Further inspection reveals blood on their clothing." He pulled out a plastic evidence bag that had my old wife beater in it. "The same article of clothing I have here, so, at this time, I would like to call the FBI forensics expert, Jin Gang, to the witness stand."

A tall, Korean man made his way across the courtroom to the stand, and after reciting the oath, he took his seat.

"Mr. Gang, how long have you been a forensics expert for the FBI?"

"Let's see..." Mr. Gang rubbed his chin. "I started my career when I was 24, so that would be about 17 years now."

"And are you confident in your..." The DA paused. "Abilities?"

"Very confident, sir," Mr. Gang responded.

"Good then..." The DA held up the evidence bag filled with my old wife beater. "Are you the one who analyzed this shirt?"

"Yes, I am." Mr. Gang folded his hands.

"And what were your findings?" The DA shot our lawyer a dirty look.

"Mostly dirt, but..." Mr. Gang adjusted his glasses. "There were traces of human hair and blood."

"Who did the hair and blood belong to?" asked the DA.

"The results from the hair were inclusive." Mr. Gang ran his hand through his hair. "However, we found that the blood belonged to Mr. Williams and Mr. Gilmore."

"Chad Williams and Tom Gilmore?" The DA asked.

"Yes, that is correct," answered Mr. Gang.

"Thank you. No further questions," responded the DA.

I sat there, watching the DA bring in witness after witness to the stand and present more and more evidence to the courtroom. He went through everything from our fingerprints being found at Thane Jenkin's house to the footage of my interview with Officer Mercer.

Eventually, Leon was brought up. He refused to answer any questions. However, after the DA asked him about his relationship with Thane Jenkins, he went cussed out the DA, raised his middle finger to the entire courtroom, and then was found in contempt of court.

Next Sean was brought to the stand who tried to answer the questions honestly, telling the courtroom we were defending our lives.

Finally, I was on the witness stand, repeating most of the things Sean already said.

"Do you have any family?" The DA asked.

"Nah, I ain't got none," I looked to the cameras in the back of the court.

"What about a home?" His eyes met mine.

"Just that abandoned junkyard outside the city." I glanced at Clemecia and Tonya.

"And how long were you living there?" he smiled.

"I'd say 'bout five or so years." I wiped the sweat off my forehead with my shirt sleeve.

"You did realize that was private property, right?" His grin grew.

"Yeah, but---" I started.

"So, ladies and gentlemen," he said, "we have a *criminal* who has absolutely no regard for the law whether it's trespassing, theft, grand theft auto, or even murder! Is this really the type of person we want living in our community? There are enough—"

Our lawyer stood up. "Excuse me, your honor, he's out of line!"

Judge Thao stroked his chin. "I will allow it."

"As I was saying, there are enough crooks living in Violet Haven! We don't need anymore!" He turned to me. "Why don't you tell the courtroom what happened on that night of August 21, 1995?"

"Well," I started, looking around at the courtroom. "We were in the junkyard that night, and this car drove inside it. We hid so they wouldn't see us and then all of a sudden both of them started fightin'."

"Then what happened?" he asked.

"One of them shot the other one dead." The ringing sound returned to my ears. "And..." I wiped the sweat of my forehead again and tried to focus. "And he tried hiding the body where Sean and Tabitha were."

"So that's when you grabbed the gun and shot him?" He slicked his hair back.

"Yeah." I massaged my temples.

He turned to the jury. "Five times?!"

"That's right." More sweat poured from my face.

"What was going through your mind during that time?"

"I just wanted…" I glanced at Sean. "To save my friends."

"Did it ever occur to you that maybe that man wouldn't have killed either of them?" asked the DA.

"No, but—" I began.

"So tell us what happened after that?" He gestured at the jury. "How did you dispose of the bodies?"

"Well…" I tugged at my ears, trying to stop Xavier's whispers. "We put them in the back…of the trunk." The whispers wouldn't stop. "And then we drove them to Iron River."

"And that's where—" he started.

"I killed…" I couldn't take the guilt anymore. While tears streamed down my face, I dug my fingernails into my forehead, and yelled, "I killed my brother! It was when I was a kid! It was an accident!"

Twenty or so minutes went by. After sharing my story of that night, the only sound to be heard in the courtroom was my sniveling. When I looked at the people in the crowd, I saw some of them showing pity and some of them disgusted by me.

Either way, none of them knew what to say.

Judge Thao slumped back into his chair. However, Clemecia and

Tonya—both of them had their hands glued to their mouths and noses—had nothing but tears dripping from their eyes. On the other hand, Mike and Sean stared at me like they were glad I was finally facing what I did but sad to hear the actual story of what had happened. Even Leon looked like he felt bad.

"Your honor, he..." The prosecutor stumbled over his words. "He..."

After a few more minutes of silence, Judge Thao cleared his throat before asking both the DA and my lawyer if either of them knew anything about what I had just said. Neither of them did.

The trial continued. In the end, Sean, Leon, and me were found guilty of killing Chad Williams and Tom Gilmore, but innocent of killing Thane.

After the trial, I led the police into the forest and to Xavier's grave where they dug up his body. When they removed him from the ground, my mouth fell open, and I turned away. Xavier was nothing but a skeleton. Staring into his soulless, sunken-in eyes and his bones that were stained with the earth made me sick to my stomach.

Xavier was sent to the local coroner, and weeks later, we were back in the courtroom for a second trial regarding his death.

My lawyer told the jury of how the death of Xavier was a tragic accident, twisting the story to make it look like I was some sort of victim. He went on to say he knew me as a kind hearted spirited person in the time he'd come to know me.

It made me sick.

Eventually, the jury was asked to consider the evidence and information that was presented to them.

"Has the jury reached a verdict?" asked Judge Thao.

A short, stubby man stood up from the jury stand and fumbled with a scrap of paper. "Y-yes."

The court clerk walked over to the man, grabbing the verdict form. He made his way over to the front of the court, handing it to Judge Thao.

When the jury was asked to announce the verdict, I almost puked.

While the same short, stubby man read off the case details, I couldn't help bounce my knee up and down until he got to the actual verdict.

"We find the defendant," the short, stubby juror read, "innocent."

Chapter Forty-Five

Freedom

Three weeks later...

Afew days later, Sean, Leon, and Mike—he had his own separate trial for helping me escape from the hospital—and me found ourselves in orange jumpsuits in a long line of prisoners who were all waiting to board a grey prison bus.

When the four of us boarded it, I stepped into the dirty vehicle which was filled with graffiti, gang writings, and scratches. Just near the door, a guard carried a loaded shotgun, kept a scowl on his face, and glared at everyone who walked past him like he was daring them to try something.

Once we walked by him, Sean sat down next to a large, bald man who was covered in tattoos, Mike took a seat next to a quiet Mexican dude, and I sat near a skinny, black dude who didn't look too much older than me.

Leon took his seat. A tall man in front of me snickered.

"What's wrong?" he asked, looking at Leon's disfigured face. "Get face fucked by Rosie O'Donnell?"

Leon gritted his teeth, rose from his seat, and sat down next to the man, shouting, "Don't make me put ya body in a tub of acid, fucker!"

"Alright, shit." The man shook his head and looked out the window.

While Leon settled down and everyone else found their seats, the bus driver started the vehicle and drove out of the parking lot toward the outer reaches of Violet Haven, passing shops, and houses that were familiar to me. Halfway out the city, I rested my forehead against the seat in front of my and twirled my thumbs.

A short time later, the man next to me pointed out the window. "Yo, Johnny! That shits still there?!"

When I lifted my head and looked to where he was pointing, I spotted the junkyard still standing tall like we never left.

"Yeah, I know," the man behind us said. "Look at that nasty shithole. Think anyone lives there?"

"Nah, nigga." The skinny dude shook his head. "Just look at it. Looks like the entrance to hell. Ain't no way anyone lives there."

After letting out a chuckle, I put my head down and nodded off.

Chapter Forty-Six

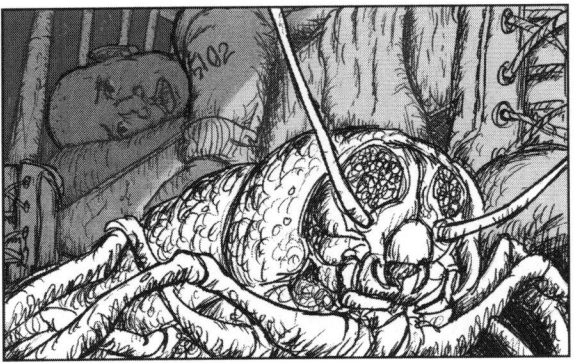

Who I Am

Afew hours later, we stopped outside a series of large connected buildings, all surrounded by chain-link fences and razor wire.

Almost as soon as we drove through the gate, by the armed guards, and passed the towers filled with more guards gripping sniper rifles, we were pulled off the bus one by one and led into the prison.

As my breath quickened, the staff searched me, gave me prison clothes, assigned me a number, handcuffed me, and then shaved off my hair.

Eventually, I was brought to my cell. As the door slammed shut, I glanced at my dirty cot, the bricks that surrounded me, and the center drain hole on the floor. Then I walked to the cell window, gripped the bars, and stared at the clouds overhead and the buildings in the distance.

While fresh air flowed into my face, I was starting to realize something. But it didn't hit me until I looked back at the bars keeping me in my cell.

It was real.

Later that night, I woke up in a pool of sweat, my heart pounding. After sitting up from my cot, I walked to the sink, turned on the faucet, and then splashed my face with water.

It was only then that I started to remember part of the dream I'd just had.

In the dream, I'd found myself in the middle of a forest filled with fog. On the ground white feathers and pools of blood lead to four beaten angels huddling together, their heavenly bodies covered with deep cut wounds.

When I stepped toward them to help, they screeched and flew away.

While their feathers fell, I saw it—the monster they were running from. It's glowing, yellow eyes locked onto me through the thick fog.

At the same time I screamed, it roared, sending nearby animals scattering in all directions. Two seconds later I was dashing after the angels, knowing if I stopped I'd be torn to shreds.

As the flashback faded, I wiped the water from my face and stepped to the front of my cell, pressing my head against the cold, steel bars as the memories slipped into my thoughts.

While I chased the angels, I looked to the sky to see one of the angels suddenly burst into flames. She tried staying in the air, but it was useless. She was falling too fast.

It's strange, but when I saw her crash to the ground like a speeding meteorite, my heart sank. It was like seeing a close family member being taken off life support. Even then I held my breath, praying she was still alive.

With every bit of speed I had, I darted through those trees toward her. However, by the time I reached her, there was nothing left but a pile of bones, bloody feathers, and mounds of smoldering flesh.

Once again, the dream faded. While I stood there trying to remember it, I looked at the dirt caked beneath my fingernails.

I flopped back down on my cot and stared at a cockroach crawling over a crack on the floor, letting the rest of the dream come back to me.

Visions of my muscles tightening and my fists shaking filled my head. The fact that I couldn't save the angel boiled my blood to the point where there were only two things on my mind; saving the rest of the angels and murdering the monster that hurt them.

I continued running, but it wasn't long before two more of the angels met the same fate as the first. Once again I held my breath, but there was nothing but bones, feathers, and flesh.

Soon my thoughts about murdering the monster overpowered my thoughts about saving the last angel.

The cockroach on my cell floor skittered across the room and into the corner, finding a crumb of some sort and eating it.

I thought about the dream, wondering who could kill something so peaceful, something that was incapable of hurting another living being.

A partial memory of me running to the edge of the forest and seeing the angel collapsed on a cliff entered my head. Except that was it. The rest wouldn't come to me.

For the next hour or so, I went from sitting on my cot to pacing back and forth in my cell trying to remember it.

No luck. Well, at least not until I sliced my finger on a jagged piece of metal on my mattress frame. The blood dripping from my cut reminded me of an ocean of it—an endless sea of blood and severed body parts over the cliff where the angel was.

Then I remembered how when she saw me, she cried and looked to an enormous crack in the sky which had thousands of angels flying in and out of it.

The moment I looked into the crack tears fell from my eyes—the kind of tears that would come from someone the first time they looked into their newborn child's eyes, the kind of tears that would come when two people got married, the kind of tears that would come when someone got cured of cancer.

Even with the wind blowing the rotten stench from the bloody ocean into my nose, that crack made me feel safer than I did when I was a kid and my mom and sang me and Xavier to sleep at night.

I looked back to the angel, taking another step toward her.

"No!" she cried. "Stay back! Please don't hurt me!"

"I just wanna help!" I put my arms out.

"No!" She looked toward the crack again. "Just let me go home!"

I checked over my shoulder for the monster. "H-how do I get there?"

"T-to where?" she asked, shaking.

I pointed to the crack. "There."

Her eyes narrowed. "H-h-heaven?"

"Yeah."

"W-we have to t-take you there, b-but the m-monster..." She stared at me for a few seconds. "Every time w-we come here to s-save people he s-slaughters us."

"If I kill the monster could ya come back and take me to Heaven?"

"I-if the m-monster wasn't here, we could s-save everyone," she said.

"Then I'll do it." I looked her in the eyes. "I'll kill the monster."

"C-can I go h-home?" she pleaded.

I nodded.

She spread her wings and flew through the air, however, just like her sisters, her body burst into flames.

She fell straight into that ungodly ocean. Soon I headed back into the forest, ready to spill the monster's blood.

While treading through the forest, I glanced around and gazed at butchered corpses I hadn't seen before. With all the bite marks and slashes throughout their decayed bodies, there was no doubt in my mind they were more victims of that horrific killing machine.

After following the trails of bodies, I found myself where I originally was—the feathers and pools of blood were still there. Everything was exactly where it was when I left...including that devilish monster.

He stared me down with those damned evil, glowing eyes of his. When I took a step forward, so did he. It was clear he was just as ready to kill me as I was to kill him.

"Stop!" I yelled, feeling beads of sweat drip off my chin.

The creature roared at the same time I spoke.

I picked up a nearby rock and continued toward him through the fog. He, also, continued toward me.

Soon we were face to face. Now I could see him much clearer; his deformed face and body, his razor sharp claws, and his soulless eyes. There was nothing human about that thing.

It had to die.

But then I saw something that made my stomach turn. The rock fell from my hand and I stumbled back, falling into the pools of blood.

Yet again, my memory of the dream cut off. As snores from other prisoners down the corridor filled the air, I dug my dirty fingernails into my knee and tried to remember the last bits and pieces of the dream. What happened to the monster?

It was dawn when I remembered the cockroach, but by then it had disappeared, and parts of the dream were coming back to me.

I remembered standing up from the pools of blood and making my way back to the monster. While leaves and twigs crunched beneath my feet, it slowly came into focus.

But there was no monster. When I was close enough to see through the fog, I pressed my hand against the mirror resting against the oak tree in front of me.

Then I stared at the horns on my head, the sunken eyes on my face, and the feathers and blood caked between my razor sharp teeth.

As the final flashbacks faded, a shiver slid down my spine. Was I evil for what I'd done? All the hair on my body stood on end. Was I a bad person for leading Tabitha to her death? Memories of her dying filled my head. The walls of my cell seemed to close in on me, making my breaths short and quick.

Was I a monster for killing my younger brother?

As I shook in the corner, visions of the axe sliding through his neck flashed before me.

An hour went by before the prisoner in the next cell over said something.

"Hey, buddy, how was your first night?"

I made my way to the front of the cell and then told him about the dream.

"So you were the monster, huh?"

"Yeah, I was." I picked at the dirt under my finger nails.

"And why do you think that is?"

I stood and the front of the cell with my hands gripping the cold, steel bars and told him everything, just like I did in the courtroom. Then when I was finished, he said something that surprised me.

"You remind me of myself."

"How's that?"

"I used to be a therapist," he began. "One day I came across a patient who'd done unspeakable things to children. For the next few years, I tried to help him fight his urges. But the more time I spent with him, the more I realized he felt nothing for what'd he done. There was no helping him."

"So what happened?"

"Well, by the things he told me, I could tell that his urges were beginning to overtake him. One day, I was walking him from my office. A little girl with pigtails was sitting in a chair at the end of the hall. That twisted smile on his face—he wouldn't stop staring at her. At that exact moment, it came to me; there was only one cure for him."

"And that was?"

"Death."

"Death? What did—"

"What did I do? I did what I had to. I did what was necessary to ensure that children would be safe from him."

"Shit, man..."

"There's no doubt in my mind he would've destroyed another life if I hadn't taken his. And my time in this prison cell is worth the possibly countless kids he would've hurt." He coughed. "Here's the difference between a bastard like him and someone like you: he lived for self-gratification at the expense of others, you don't."

"I never thought about it like that." I continued picking out the dirt from my fingernails.

"With all that guilt, with all those negative emotions you told me about, are you happy with the life you have led?"

The word 'no' slipped out my mouth before I had time to think about his question.

"Then find something that makes you happy."

"That's much easier said than done. Sometimes I feel like it's easier just to give up," I said, eyeing the cockroach skittering across the floor.

"It is. But as humans, that's what we do; make something from nothing, fly after our wings have been clipped, revive our dreams from the nightmares this life's created. Even if we fail all our suffering, all our pain, all our unhappiness will end. We are not eternal. This life is not forever. And neither is our misery."

"True," I said, chuckling. "Funny how we forget that."

"Right," he said, "one day no one on this earth will remember us, we'll be non-existent and not even memories of our children, our children's children, or even our children's children's children will contain us."

I ran my fingernail along the steel bars and listened to what he had to say.

"Speaking of children, we don't think about any of that when we're kids. We're too busy exploring life to see people becoming drug addicts or committing suicide just to hide from it. Life is cruel, it's depressing, horrific, and if we let it, it will beat us down until the only peace we will ever know is death."

"Most of our caregivers," he continued, "try their hardest to protect us from those horrors, but alas—"

"We find it ourselves," I said.

"And then we, in turn, try to protect our children from it to no avail," he said.

"Damn. None of that's very motivating." I put my hand to my chin.

"Really?"

"I mean, yeah, why would it?"

"If you were shown two different paths that lead to two entirely different places, with one place bringing you nothing but joy, wouldn't be more motivated to go there if you found out the second place will bring you nothing but pain?"

"Well, yeah, of course."

"In this world, there are levels of darkness that extend beyond normal human comprehension. If you want me to lie to you, I can say that there is always a way out, but the truth is sometimes there is no way out. Sometimes we suffer until our last breath."

"So what do we do then?" I turned my ear toward him and tried to absorb every word that came from his mouth.

"In all honesty, there is nothing we can do except deal with it until we die. However, the only question is have we reached that point," he said. "Do you think you've reached it?"

This time I thought about his question before answering. Xavier and Tabitha were gone, but I still had Sean, Leon, and Mike. Even Tonya and Clemecia seemed like they cared about me. There were people who'd be there for me, people who I knew I could trust. Not only that but my prison sentence wasn't life long—I'd be out one day. One day I'd have a second chance at.

I felt a smile relax my face as I said, "No I haven't."

"Most of us haven't. With that being said, there is an equal amount of light as there is darkness and no one is responsible for finding that light for you except you."

Soon after he said that, he ended the conversation and told me we'd talk again.

With all his talk of being human, I wondered what Mike, Sean, and Leon thought of me. Did they think I was a monster for what I'd done? For all the people I'd killed, for leading Tabitha and the officers to their deaths?

I had to find out.

The next day I rounded up Sean, Mike, and Leon, had them sit with me on the bleachers in the yard and then told them about the dream I'd had.

"A monster?!" Leon cackled. "Kid, I don't know what ya talkin'—"

"Wadda ya mean you don't know what I'm talkin' about?" I pounded my fist on my knee. "I killed four people! If I wasn't here, Xavier would be!" I pounded my fist on my knee. "And so would Tabitha. The two guys from the junkyard..." I shook my head. "Look how many deaths I've caused. I'm not a hero, just another murderer."

"You're right," Leon said. "You are a murderer."

I started to turn away. "So you—"

Leon put his hand on my shoulder. "But did ya ever enjoy killin' anyone?"

"No."

"Look, Xavier was an accident," Leon said. "And them two guys from the junkyard...I mean, ya were tryin' to protect Sean and Tabitha. You weren't killin' 'em 'cause ya—"

"I think," Sean interrupted, "what he's tryin' to say is that all ya wanted was for us to be safe."

"Exactly!" Leon said.

"And Tabitha?" I asked, staring out into the distance. "I led her to her death. If I hadn't brought you guys back to Palm Street, she'd still be here."

Sean stared at me dead in the eyes. "None of us knew that was gonna happen." He pointed his finger at me. "If it wasn't for you, we probably would've died a long ass time ago. Me and her didn't know what the hell we were doin' out in those streets. All you ever cared about was our well-bein', all of us."

"Look, kid, a good person can commit an atrocity, but a genuine monster never commits a true act of kindness." Leon spit to the side.

"Act of kindness? What are you talkin' about?" I asked.

"Ya saved my fuckin' life," Leon said.

"Yeah, but—" I began.

"You stood...up for me when no one else...would," Mike interrupted.

"You helped me track down Tabitha's killer," Sean said.

"Ain't no monster this side of the galaxy that would've done any of that shit," Leon piped in. "Trust me. I know."

"If I'm not a monster, who or what am I?" I looked at Leon, then Sean, and finally Mike.

"Damn, kid." Leon spat and then looked directly in my eyes. "Ya just don't get it, do ya?

And then I noticed something in his eyes I'd never seen there before.

Hope.

In the midst of all the chaos in his eyes, all the defeat, the fury, the madness, the pain, the heartbreaking losses, the infinite stretches of soullessness, there was a look of hope. That hope was like a sailor clinging onto a life raft in the middle of a hurricane, but it was still there.

Was I the one who put that there? Was I the one who reignited the will to live inside another human being? Me? A crazy, worthless homeless guy?

The rain that was stating to pour down wasn't cold enough to put out the blazing fire burning in my chest.

They—my brothers, my pack of street rats who were still searching the maze for the cheese that wasn't there—looked at me like the way Xavier used to look up to me as an older brother.

My purpose wasn't to escape my suffering; my suffering was guiding me to help others escape theirs. All my struggling, all my grief was supposed to be there, not to make me stronger. It was there so I could help my pack of street rats find their way out the cheeseless maze.

While those thoughts went through my head, the fire in my chest grew into an inferno. Something inside me changed. It was like I went from being angry at myself and the world to accepting myself for who I was and the world for how it was.

I realized I'd done horrible things, but I wasn't a horrible person. And even with all my guilt, pain, and anger on the surface, there was still someone on the other side of the darkness who had some sense of what was right and wrong, someone who fought for his friends, not just for himself.

But most importantly, there was someone down there who was still human. And in the midst of violence, misery, and anguish, that person never stopped fighting the horrors life threw at him, that person continued to help others even though he could barely help himself.

And that person was me.

Printed in Great Britain
by Amazon